Path of
Least
Resistance

Ω

C. Marcus Parr

C. Marcus Parr

C. Marcus Parr

et

Published by Et Cetera Press International
Sandy, OR 97055
Copyright © 2009 by C. Marcus Parr
Designed by C. Marcus Parr
Set in Times New Roman

ORIGINAL COVER ART BY LESLIE CHENEY-PARR
[www.cheneyparr.com]

Author's Note
An article "Chance Killer Virus Find Sparks Safeguard Calls" written by Paul Tait and published by Reuters on Thursday January 11, 2001, 12:21 AM ET, was the inspiration for the fictitious Reuters news release that appears in the text, "Possible Killer Virus May Strengthen International Treaty." In utmost respect for Mr. Tait's work, I want to acknowledge his originality in reporting an actual event, which has been fundamentally modified here for dramatic effect. The data analysis and language contained in the article in the text of this novel are purely fictitious or used for dramatic purpose.

The W.B. Yeats' reference is quoted, of course, from "The Second Coming."

ISBN: 978-0-578-03194-1
1. Fiction—Hollywood—Movie Business—Screenplays. 2. Virus plague—Biological warfare, Fiction. 3. Mind reading— Soothsaying, Fiction. 4. Drug & alcohol abuse. 5. Title

Path of Least Resistance

This is a work of fiction. Names, characters, places and incidents are either the product of the author's imagination or are used fictitiously. Any resemblance to actual events or locales or persons, living or dead, is entirely coincidental.

et

Published by Et Cetera Press International
Sandy, OR 97055
Copyright © 2009 by C. Marcus Parr
Designed by C. Marcus Parr
Set in Times New Roman

ORIGINAL COVER ART BY LESLIE CHENEY-PARR
[www.cheneyparr.com]

Author's Note
An article "Chance Killer Virus Find Sparks Safeguard Calls" written by Paul Tait and published by Reuters on Thursday January 11, 2001, 12:21 AM ET, was the inspiration for the fictitious Reuters news release that appears in the text, "Possible Killer Virus May Strengthen International Treaty." In utmost respect for Mr. Tait's work, I want to acknowledge his originality in reporting an actual event, which has been fundamentally modified here for dramatic effect. The data analysis and language contained in the article in the text of this novel are purely fictitious or used for dramatic purpose.

The W.B. Yeats' reference is quoted, of course,
from "The Second Coming."

ISBN: 978-0-578-03194-1
1. *Fiction—Hollywood—Movie Business—Screenplays. 2. Virus plague—Biological warfare, Fiction. 3. Mind reading—Soothsaying, Fiction. 4. Drug & alcohol abuse. 5. Title*

For Joe Pindell—you left too soon

C. Marcus Parr

Path of Least Resistance

Ω

C. Marcus Parr

et
Et Cetera Press International
2009

The ultimate predator kills itself.
Bob Smith

Chapter 1

The party was over.

My gold-plated Sig Sauer tasted warm and expensive, and I willed my finger to pull the trigger.

The night was hot enough to cook smog. Most of the windows were opened, and all the lights were off in my California bungalow. A ghostly television glow from next door haunted the living room, and laugh tracks from a rerun of *Happy Days* scored the scene with irony. I reminded myself, we all die of irony.

The TV voices took shape before me in the form of my accusers. All my ex-wives were there. All the deceived starlets that had consented to my casting couch were there, laughing at my expense. My suicidal parents hovered in the corner. The shade of my old man said that I was a worthless piece of garbage, a plagiarist and a hack. I was all show, no boat. The Old Man must have told me that a hundred times. Even my self-pity was hackneyed.

The living room was like a prison cell with zebra shadows across the floor from bars on the windows. I lived on The Hill, a gunshot from downtown Los Angeles, where home security was a way of life. I stared at the wall clock as the secondhand swept the dial, eclipsing the luminous minute and then the hour hand. At the three o'clock position, the mechanism caught on a defect and faltered.

For as long as I lived in Echo Park, I had to reset the time every day. Tedium enslaved me. Not that it mattered, not anymore, not now at the beginning of the new millennium when my life was unraveling. This time I was going to do the deed. I would never have to compensate for anything again, or ever have to set the clock.

With the gun in my mouth, my mind began to wander. I realized that the bungalow would be there long after I was gone. People would empty the place of furniture, and the house would be sold. Nothing would change much. Buildings and landmarks endure, but individuals die. Houses go on; occupants don't.

Then the desperation passed, as it always did.

Who was I kidding?

I pulled the gun out of my mouth. The residue of oil tasted like Diesel exhaust, and I spat on the carpet. I balanced the weight of the Sig in my palm and tried to remember how I had acquired it, in a divorce settlement or from a former girlfriend in her rush out the door? I had always considered it a suitable instrument to a lady's suicide but not my own.

My resolve weakened. To fortify it I rummaged the coffee table for the bottle of Wild Turkey. I gripped the neck and brought it to my mouth, draining the last of the liquor.

I had no friends, no visitors to my modest house in Echo Park. Had I killed myself, my body would in all likelihood rot on the sofa. Weeks would pass before a neighbor called the cops and complained about the stench. But even then, after the remains were bagged and tagged, there would be little fanfare. I doubted my death would merit a two-sentence obit in *Variety*. My epitaph should read: *He came uninvited and left before we knew he was here.*

I rolled the empty bottle of Wild Turkey across the carpet. It clinked against the leg of a chair. The notion to do away with myself returned.

"Time to run the credits," I mumbled. "Such as they are."

Once again I lifted the handgun. I had difficulty fitting my index finger around the trigger. I was not drunk enough. There was not enough booze in the world for what I was about to do. I looked for anything around the living room that might help draw the curtain on this final act. A cocktail glass on the coffee table held an ounce of cold comfort and glowed in the flicker of the neighbor's television. I leaned forward for one last swallow before replacing it on the phosphorescent water ring.

I opened my mouth. The gunmetal rattled against my teeth, and once again I willed myself to pull the trigger only to be disabled by a poverty of guts.

Then, from out of the night, I heard the croaking of frogs at the bottom of my dead swimming pool.

"Mr. Austin?"

"Jeez!"

I removed the gun. I jerked forward, kicking the coffee table and breaking the cocktail glass. My heart galloped up my throat.

Someone in silhouette stood on the threshold of the sliding glass door leading to the backyard where the frogs sang *a capella*.

I fumbled sideways for the table lamp. A surge of embarrassment flushed my cheeks—here was another shameless moment in a life of shameless moments—just as I found the switch for the light.

A man much older than I, thin as a pencil in a wrinkled two-piece gray suit, stood in the doorway. A small beige suitcase dangled from his left hand.

Oddly, as I sat exposed on the couch in a pair of boxers and a tank top, gun in hand, my thoughts ranged from how uncomfortable the stranger looked in a wool suit to how ridiculous I must have appeared. For a split second I wanted to believe that I had imagined him standing there, that this figure was nothing more than the invention of a wrecked mind. Surely, reality was playing a dirty trick on me. Yet, the vision lingered a while longer.

I raised the Sig and aimed it.

"Mr. Austin," the stranger said, stepping into the room and ignoring the gun.

Hyperventilating now, I noticed on the coffee table the broken cocktail glass between an empty Chinese food container and the *TV Guide*. Spilled Wild Turkey dampened the carpet.

"You're Charles Austin, the movie director?" he asked.

I said nothing.

"I've seen all of your movies, Mr. Austin. I'm a huge fan."

The stranger lifted the beige suitcase and balanced it on his hip. The brass latches clacked open, and he removed a manila envelope.

I lowered the gun. I wiped my face with my free hand and gave the intruder the once over, head to toe.

He was clueless. In the frayed business suit and a pair of flip-flops, he gave a pretty good impersonation of the late Howard Hughes with the beard and straggly hair. Grubby toes and yellow toenails stuck out from under the folded cuffs. He looked harmless enough, in a word, pathetic.

I placed the Sig, business end out, on a pile of *Hustler* magazines. While picking up shards of the cocktail glass, I cut myself. Mumbling through my fingers, I said, "Who the hell are you?"

"Mr. Austin, it's an honor to meet you, sir. Your films..."

His phony sincerity made me angry. He had no idea who he was dealing with.

The stranger shut his eyes in reverie and recited the titles of movies that my old man had directed years ago.

"*After the Gold* and *Splendid Rain*," he said. "And oh, *Autumn Light*. Just beautiful. What a masterpiece."

I laughed to blow off the ache of tension in my shoulders.

"You got me confused with the Old Man. I'm son of."

The stranger's face looked paralyzed as though shot through with Botox.

"What do you want?" I said.

He blinked and dropped the manila envelope at his side.

"My name is Bob Smith. I'm a screenwriter."

"Sure you are."

I combed the fingers of both hands through my thinning hair and touched the rubber band of my ponytail. The old dude really pissed me off. I picked up the broken glass and carried the shards to the trashcan under the kitchen sink. Bob Smith followed. With the suitcase in one hand and manila envelope in the other, he looked encumbered and off balance.

"I've brought the screenplay with me," he said.

I flipped on the fluorescent kitchen lights. They sputtered and droned like hummingbirds. I wrapped a paper napkin around my bloodied fingers and red blossomed across the tissue. The sight of my own fluids distracted me momentarily.

Bob Smith cleared his throat and pressed forward with the envelope.

"I'm not in the market right now," I said, leaning against the counter and tightening a grip around my finger.

"But I need your help, Mr. Austin."

"What's this *Mr. Austin* crap?"

"I'm trying to show my respect."

I smirked and turned in search of the Tanqueray in the cupboard.

"Look, porno's my thing, okay? I'm not into the Old Man's bullshit. Not *Autumn Light* or whatever. *Death Stopped for Me*. Jesus!" As I wiped an unclean glass, the discolored napkin fell to the floor. I noticed a blood smear down the side of the glass as I filled it with gin.

I slurped the drink. "If you got some adult treatment, I'll take a look."

Bob Smith held out the screenplay.

In a single motion I took the envelope and dropped it on the counter, irritated now and grinding my teeth.

The son-of-a-bitch, I thought, *intruding on The End.*

The rush of adrenaline had washed away what my shrink would have called "suicidal ideation." I was left trembling beneath the kitchen lights as I sucked down the gin. I glanced at the clock on the stove. The secondhand ticked, and I realized that the moment had passed. I have never been able to overcome my own inertia.

"I need your help," Bob Smith said.

I gave him a sidelong glance.

"You know what?" Setting the glass down as I came to my senses. "I think we're done here." I managed a wry smile and slicked back my hair with a hand dampened by condensation and blood.

Smith slouched in defeat.

Enlivened by the liquor, I felt a surge of generosity toward the old dude. I put my arm around his shoulders and gave an amiable pat on the back, startled by how emaciated he was. It was like embracing a cadaver.

We blinked at one another without making sense of the encounter.

I gestured at the envelope.

"Relax, I'll give it a look-see," I said, all the while grinning through the blatant lie and winking a Hollywood wink. I could feel the booze now, second-stage effects of bleariness, as I ushered my late father's last devotee toward the front door.

"I wrote my telephone number down," Smith said as an afterthought. "It's—"

The phone rang. I threw up my hands at yet another interruption and went to answer it in the kitchen.

"Yeah?" I barked into the handset.

A solicitor for an auto glass replacement company had launched into a sales pitch before I could tell her where to stick it. I pressed the off button, grumbling obscenities, and I returned to the entryway.

Bob Smith had left.

The hinges on the front door squeaked when I opened it and looked out at the velvety gloss of an empty street. Nobody there, only the crickets holding their breath. I shut the door and made my way back to the living room with the idea of watching a skin flick on cable. I planned to camp out on the couch and pour three more fingers of Tanqueray, maybe do a couple lines of cocaine. I grinned at the sweet arithmetic of inebriation.

Suddenly, Bob Smith stepped out of the guest toilet, into the darkened hall.

It stopped me dead cold.

"Damn it all!"

"Sorry. I had to go to the bathroom. You'll read it then?"

"Soon as you get the fuck outta here." Once again I opened the door, and my intruder walked out.

Bob Smith hesitated at the curb before crossing the street. He seemed distracted by something in the night sky. Constellations or celestial portals, there was no telling which.

"Good night, Mr. Austin," he called.

I issued a curse on my father's fame and watched as Bob Smith descended into the cheerless dark.

Then I, Duncan Charles Austin, Jr., ill-fated son of the world famous movie director, slammed the door shut and rambled back to the living room. My heart raced. There was no telling if the Wild Turkey or visitor were to blame. Bob Smith gave me the creeps. He played the role of vagrant, not a screenwriter; a quasi-spiritual flake from Topanga or a yogi wannabe from Venice. A freak.

I double-checked the lock on the sliding glass door.

In the kitchen I tumbled into a chair when the sour grit of nausea rose up my throat. I took slow, deliberate breaths, but the world refused to settle into place. What I needed was some pharmaceutical help to ameliorate the alcohol, and I traipsed off to the bathroom to retrieve it.

I kept the cocaine next to the Vicodan tablets, Bayer aspirin, and antihistamines, third shelf in the medicine cabinet. As a recreational doper, I have found the most conspicuous hiding places to be the safest to stash the goods. I returned to the kitchen with the bindle and laid out two lines on a ceramic plate. Without pretext of straw or rolled dollar bill, I did the powder directly off the plate.

Alcoholic waves pitched the bungalow to and fro before easing into the doldrums while I snorted two more lines. The notion of doing away with myself sank below the event horizon as the black hole of depression gave way to a supernova of mania.

I leaned back to enjoy the dance between cocaine and depressants. There, in the fierce kitchen light, Bob Smith's manila envelope stood out against the disturbingly orange ceramic tiles. Written in a trembling hand were a signature and address, the Glide Hotel on such-and-such street, Los Angeles. Above these notations was a telephone number scrawled in pencil.

Skeptically, I pulled the screenplay from the envelope. On the first page was the title *Path of Least Resistance.*

Chapter 2

I once had a close friend who suffered from schizophrenia. One night he hallucinated his wife as a spider. His story reminds me of Kafka's *Metamorphosis*, except in this case, his wife did not turn into a spider or cockroach. She died unexpectedly during the night. In the morning after surviving yet another self-destructive binge, he realized he had imagined that his wife, now dead, was a spider. That's when he got serious about taking his meds. Within weeks, the responsibility for her death weighed so heavily on his sobriety that he did away with himself at the Beverly Hills Hotel, the venue of many negligent Hollywood suicides. But who are we to judge how others check out. We all commit suicide, one way or the other.

When I told my therapist this story, he corrected me. It was Kafka's protagonist, not the wife, who changed into a cockroach. I knew this to be the case; I was simply trying to illustrate how I felt at the time. Later in the session, he went Freud on me by drawing parallels between my misogyny and fear of intimacy. After he said that, I stopped keeping my appointments.

Ω   Ω   Ω

The reflective light of late morning drew a herringbone pattern through the jalousie windows, across the ceiling. As usual, I greeted the day with nausea.

Sweat glued my hair to my face. The membranes in my nose were so swollen from a night of bingeing that I could not breathe. I was naked as the porno videos ran in the VCR. The tape was looped, a continuous montage of men with women, women with women, combinations thereof. On that morning after, the last thing I wanted to see was a guy going down on some broad, not at ten thirty, not in the fierce California sunlight.

Giving in to a half-hearted search, I cursed the remote and shut off the TV with a shoe. The electronic dot vanished in the Sony like Tinker Bell.

A cigarette usually helped when I was nauseated, and I fumbled for the pack on the nightstand. I put a match to the Marlboro. Tobacco was like aspirin, and I hungered for anesthesia.

I got up and headed for the bathroom. The light through the windows seared my eyes, and I shut the blinds. I balanced the cigarette on the edge of the sink and let the tap run until I felt some heat. I moistened my gray-blond hair and combed my hands through it with a glob of gel from an open jar. I tied my ponytail with a rubber band, managing as best I could to conceal the bald spot.

I sucked the cigarette and set my teeth in the filter while I stood before the toilet to take a piss. I was three months shy of my forty-sixth birthday, and I worried about my prostate.

"Gonna have to drink more water," I told the toilet.

My pecker was chaffed from abuse. Around two in the morning, after Bob Smith's brief visit, I had considered calling a companion service but could not locate the number in the Rolodex. I ended up beating off to video. By morning I felt sheepish and vaguely ashamed, as I usually do.

I took a drag and dropped the cigarette in the bowl. It gave an aborted hiss, and I flushed.

I went to the closet and pulled several pairs of pants and shirts from the hangers, tossing them on the mattress. I chose canary yellow slacks and a silk shirt with a repetitive print of unidentifiable sea birds. I slipped into a pair of topsiders, no socks. I looked straight out of a Coen Brothers' movie.

The phone rang in the kitchen, and I made my way down the hall to pick up.

"Hello?"

"D?"

It was Curtis LaGassa, my so-called partner. At the time, we had worked together for about six months. Ours was an unsatisfactory business relationship. I suspected him of stealing my contacts, storing them up like grain for some future famine. It was only a matter of time before I cut him off.

"You up?" LaGassa asked.

"What's it sound like, I'm fucking talking in my sleep?"

For weeks we had worked with a serious major trying to sell our product. In those days Rainy Day Films, part of an enormous multinational entertainment empire, was having a love affair with the motion picture industry. They had a string of blockbusters that year, which made the founding father of the company, Sty Raines, very powerful. However, his was a fickle power, difficult to keep should the next product bomb, and as such, Raines was cautious. He rarely committed to anything.

Curtis and I had been shopping the rights to a property about a woman who falls in love with her stepson, who in turn is accused of murdering his father. I was not married to the idea, but after a series of disappointments and compromises, it was all I had. The treatment had crossover potential in Europe, if the sex scenes showed enough skin. Maybe it could make a return on DVD and Blu-Ray. Sty

Raines and one of his associates, Max Gleason, were lukewarm to the idea until that morning.

"Hey hey, listen, I got some bad news," LaGassa said.

I carried the portable handset to the living room and estimated how much coke was left on the mirror. I must have done the whole gram.

"Gleason's not buying."

"You *talked* to him? That's not how we work, Curtis."

Under no circumstances was LaGassa to act as the front man. That had been understood from the beginning.

"No, no, he called me. You weren't picking up, so…. Look, D, they're just not buying."

I was too angry to say anything.

"Sorry, man," LaGassa said.

"*Sorry, man?* I work my ass off, and all you got to say is sorry man? Bull-fucking-shit."

I wanted to throw the phone against the wall.

"Ain't my fault."

I switched ears, bent over and ran a moistened index finger over the glass and sucked on it.

"What's with you, Curtis?" I mumbled. "Playing both ends against the middle?"

"No."

LaGassa had little idea what playing both ends against the middle meant.

"Look, D…I got another party."

"Would you listen to this?"

"I wanna run with it, okay? It's very dope. People from New York, gonna take a meeting. You fly with that?"

I sat down and picked up the razor blade, chopping what few grains were left on the glass.

"Did you hear me?"

I leaned over and snorted.

"Doin' a line this early, huh?"

"What is this, twenty-fucking questions?" I wiped my nose on my palm. "Screw you. You sank my deal."

"Your deal? Why is it, why is it *your* deal? It's my property."

"How far you gonna get without my name on it?"

"I call you up to na-negotiate," Curtis said. He stuttered when he got nervous. "What, you raw this morning, D? Been up all night, playing cha-choke the chicken with your video wives?"

"Blow it out your ass."

"Listen. Gleason shit canned us 'cuz, 'cuza you. Nobody'll work with you."

"Fuck you."

"When's the last time you made product, D? Never, that's when. Whoa, late breaking news. Fa-film at eleven."

"Eat shit."

"How in hell I get mixed up with you?"

And with that Curtis LaGassa disconnected.

I hurled the portable against the fake fireplace. The plastic exploded in a shower of electronic confetti.

For sure, LaGassa had stolen my concept and was shopping it to another major. I was out of the deal. After six weeks of meetings and conciliations, the treatment was kaput, and I had nada. Zilch.

On the coffee table, resting on a pile of skin magazines, the gold plate of the Sig Sauer caught the daylight. I stood looking down at it, contemplating its meaning in an otherwise meaningless morning.

I was small potatoes in the business. A minor player. Over the previous year I had worked but failed as a talent agent, associate producer, and script broker. Throughout my career, my projects rarely made it to screen, and it seemed lately all I did was take meetings. I was not in the movie business; I was in the meeting business.

A movie called *Boccaccio's Daughter* was my last meaningful project with a major. It had potential as a serious piece of art but got caught in a financial squeeze. When production went over budget on the fifth consecutive week, the major and distributor cited breach of contract and pulled out. At that point we had fifteen hundred feet in the can, all of it irrelevant. After the producers sold out, the new investors called for scenes of rough, gratuitous sex. What had started out as a sensitive self-discovery film of a young woman in love with a college professor was released as an NC-rated tit flick with a new title *The Girls of Magna Cum Loud Sorority.* The investors had promised one hundred grand if I finished the movie on their terms. After the accountants were done with the income statement, I ended up with expenses paid and little else, but I knew how to milk the reimbursement system. Coke and Scotch came under the "Entertainment" column.

Still eyeing the handgun, I sat on the couch to open a fresh pack of cigarettes. I put a match to the Marlboro and inhaled.

Bob Smith's screenplay lay next to me. It had been typed on an old fashioned typewriter, complete with typos. On the previous night I had ranged through parts of it but could not recall details. The last page was marked.

> *Something is happening to ~~Doe~~ Joe Dawson's brain. He hears (the audience hears) a faint, high-pitched grinding like a dentist's drill. He holds the back of his head and moves hsi hands forward to cover his ears.*

Ordinarily, I read treatments back to front, starting with the final scenes and working in reverse order. Something caught my eye on the next to the last page—the name D. Charles Austin, Sr. My old man was a screen character driving his washed-out topaz 1986 Cadillac El Dorado Coupe de Ville down the San Diego Freeway. In bumper-to-bumper traffic, the very car I had inherited broke down in the scene and stranded him in an unfamiliar part of town.

Why in hell would Bob Smith write the Old Man into the script?

I needed to get a feel for how the writer treated his subject, and so I turned back a few pages:

> *SET SHOT: <u>Interior of Vietnamese Restuarant</u>...to establish place. Lunch hour, customers fill the booths; a racket of pots and pans comes from the kitchen; a teen-aged Vietnamese girl waits the tables; two underage Asian boys fill water glasses.*
>
> *DIFFERENT ANGLE: <u>Mr. Austin</u>. Mr. Charles Austin sits alone at a booth. He is fingering a napkin, folding it into an origami shape of a small bird. He looks up.*
>
> *LONG SHOT: Two men in business suits have been waiting for a table near the front door. They are annoyed that Mr. Austin is sittting alone, in a booth, while they have to wait.*
>
> *OVER SHOULDER: <u>Mr. Austin</u>. He looks up (camera follows hsi line-of-sight) at the waitress. She is smiling.*
>
> *MEDIUM: <u>Vietnamese Waitress</u>. She holds a pencil and a pad of paper.*
>
> *WAITRESS*
> *"Have you decided?"*
>
> *MEDIUM: <u>Mr. Austin</u>. He picks up the menu for the first time to glance at it. He shakes his head and smiles back at the waitress.*

*DIFFERENT ANGLE: Mr. Austin
hands the menu to the waitress.*

Mr. AUSTIN
*"Tell you what. My guest is running late.
So, I'll just have a beer for now, okay?"*

*CLOSE UP: <u>Mr. Austin's Hands</u>. He
fiddles with a cigarette lighter by
balancing it on its edge. Then he twirls it
between his index and middle finger. His
thumb strikes it and the lighter produces
flame.
DIFFERENT ANGLE: The female
customer in the next booth leans over to
speak to Mr. Charles Austin.*

FEMALE CUSTOMER
"No smoking here."

*MEDUIM: <u>Mr. Austin</u>. He grimaces
and narrows his eyes at the woman.*

Mr. AUSTIN
*"I know that. Whole fucking state is
nonsmoking."*

I lowered the page. It was full of typos, which made the presentation very unprofessional, something destined for any agent's slush pile. What kind of scam was Smith trying to pull by throwing my father into the mix? It made no sense.

*MEDIUM. <u>Mr. Austin</u>. The waitress
places his cold beer on the Formica table
along with a glass.*

*CLOSE UP: <u>Mr. Austin's hands</u>. As he
pours the beer into the glass it foams over
the rim and spills out across the table.
    LONG SHOT: Mr. Austin leans out of
the booth to shout for the waitress.*

Mr. AUSTIN
"Can I get some help here?"

*DIFFERENT ~~NaGLE~~ ANGLE: One of
the two businessmen waiting near the
door shakes his head in disapproval,
further irritated by the delay.*

What lay before me was a poorly written screenplay,
full of outrageous errors, but it presented an opportunity. I
gathered up the pages and stuffed them in the envelope,
more or less acting on impulse. I usually acted on impulse,
not brains. In my business, balls are everything. It's what
separates the wheat from the rest of the miserable bastards.

Ω   Ω   Ω

I took another hour to get it marginally together, to steel
my courage. I ate cold pizza, the only thing in the fridge,
and did half a gram of coke while looking for the car keys.
I convinced myself that *Path of Least Resistance* was all I
needed to offset my losses with LaGassa. It was time to
take a meeting to sell the treatment. It was time to take a
meeting with Pig Boy.

Max Gleason weighed over two hundred and eighty
pounds and stood around five nine or so. He was the one to
deal with at Sty Raines' shop. As executive vice president
and associate producer, Gleason had twenty people
reporting directly to him, the count depending on how

many were fired that week. You couldn't stick anything to the man. Nothing was his fault, no matter the circumstances or his contribution to the failure. If a product went south, Gleason was the master of spin. He always managed to pin the blunder to some poor underling who had spent a career clawing his way to the top only to be sacrificed like so much mutton.

Gleason dressed impeccably. He wore hand tailored suits, none of this Hart, Shaffner & Marx for him, nothing off the rack. He had a pair of Italian shoes for each day of the week; had his shirts custom-made. He wore vulgar pinky rings with semi-precious gems and a gold bracelet, probably worth five grand.

His favorite haunt was the Wildwood Bar & Grill in West Hollywood. During the summer Gleason held court at an outside table, beneath a tricolor umbrella. On this particular day Gleason sat outside, alone, eating. He wore Nikon wrap-around sunglasses and a silvery jumpsuit. He looked like Porky the Pig fresh off the *Star Wars* set.

I drove past the Wildwood, searching for a parking space large enough for the '86 El Dorado Coupe de Ville. After parking the Caddy, I entered the restaurant. I was the last person he expected to see.

"Hello, Max."

He paused dramatically over a plate of veal *parmigiana* in porcini mushroom sauce. He wiped his hands on a napkin tucked in his collar. He had a let's-talk-business look before he recognized me, and his countenance fell. I stood with my back to the sun with Bob Smith's manila envelope in hand.

"Duncan," Gleason said with flat disinterest. He took pleasure in calling me by my given name, something he knew that I detested.

"Can I join you?"

I took a seat, and immediately the waiter attended us.

"Go away, Claude. He's not staying." Shoveling in a mouthful of pasta, Gleason waved his free hand.

"Max," I said, placing the screenplay between us. I picked up a breadstick and nibbled it. "You rejected my treatment."

"Couldn't be helped. Did what I could." Gleason slurped a Chianti Classico Reserva, chewing with the porcelain ingots of his dental work.

"Thought we had a deal," I said.

Gleason's belly rolled in a deep, stifled belch.

"You know better than that. No deal 'til the ink's dry. Even then." Gleason peered over the rim of his sunglasses. "Who knows that better'n you?"

"We had an option."

He swallowed and waggled a finger in the air. "Never had a contract."

"You and Curtis workin' this now?"

"We dialoged the opportunity."

"It's mine, Max. I own it."

"Oh, please, Duncan, spare me." Gleason chortled, stabbing a roasted red pepper with the fork. "No one owns anything, least of all in this town."

I glanced at a nearby table full of young people, taken directly from the pages of *GQ* and *Vogue*, living *la dolce vita* in the Whatever Age. They sipped lattes and Aquadeco, ate gazpacho from shallow bowls and razor clams on sixty-dollar lunch plates. One in their party, a striking blonde whose tight, peach sweater showed off her new tits, glanced at me through a pair of Christian Dior's. I knew the face, not the name. She was just another anonymous TV personality with chutzpah, that you might see on *Dancing With the Stars* or *Lost*; a wannabe pretending to be somebody else because she didn't know who she was. She dismissed me with a self-satisfied pout as she returned to her friends. I gave my attention to Pig Boy.

"Come on, Max. Don't make me beg. For old times sake."

"What old times?" Gleason scooped a forkful of calf meat and shoveled it into his mouth.

"I'm down to my last enchilada. Living on stems and seeds."

"That's no concern of mine." He chewed and stirred his fork nervously in the sauce.

"Look, I know Pop and you were close."

Gleason dropped the fork and threw down his napkin. "What're you saying, Duncan? Your father gives me a break a thousand years ago and now, what? Out of the blue, you come to collect?"

"Thought you might be reasonable."

"You want me to be reasonable? If life were reasonable, I'd be dining alone."

My temples throbbed. I thought about how nice it would be to do a spoon in the car.

"You don't hold a candle to your old man."

The insult was wasted on me. The cocaine binge and Wild Turkey had finally run their course and left me hollow like a dead vacuum tube. My mood was on a descending trajectory. I could feel myself falling on a bungee cord of emotions in a metaphysical Xtreme sport.

Gleason picked up his fork and ate again in an approximation of having sex with the food.

"I'm going to tell you something, Duncan. Give you a little piece of advice. If you don't slow down, you're gonna be dead. You're outta control, blackballed already. Exiled, ferchrisakes." He shook his head. "Nobody does drugs anymore."

"Give me a break."

"Look around. What do you see? That's right. Nothing but young people. Willing to kill their mother for a reading. Their high is a returned phone call. And they're polite, Duncan. They smell good. Say thank you. Probably floss for all I know." Gleason took a breath. "But *you*. You, on the other hand, insult the crap out of me. Take a look in the mirror. Next to them, you're garbage."

"Oh, thank you, thank you very much."

"Where were you last night? I called, no answer. You're high right now, aren't you? Holy shit. Didn't you get the memo? Cappuccino and megavitamins are in, Duncan. Low-fat vanilla lattes, health clubs and Botox. Not coke or getting high. The Eighties are over, ferchrisakes." Gleason stirred the fettuccini. "Now, if you'll excuse me."

The blonde girl at the next table was eavesdropping. She smiled behind a vacuous mask of no-one-home. I cocked my head contentiously, and she looked away.

It was anyone's guess how I had let my life get so out of control. Three miserable divorces, the kids—products of my first marriage—who never called, a career of making cheesy skin flicks for cable, what a miserable ass I was. At the top of the list, the suicide of Mom and my old man had knocked the breath out of me. I had learned of their deaths from an article in the trades, not from the coroner's phone call, not through a family friend. The tragedy of their suicide dragged me down for a year and left me with a sense that life was meaningless and death an arbitrary inevitability. I sought help through psychotherapy, but when that didn't pan out, I went back to doing what I did best—drugs. After the funeral, I spent a good part of my inheritance on cocaine. It stands as one of the most disreputable things I have ever done.

For as long as I can remember, I have run my life on two unremitting emotions, self-loathing and anger. There is no doubt where it will end.

Long ago I had given up caring what happened to me. My life had gone bad like an old banana. I had few friends and fewer prospects. When I needed them most, my friends rejected me. No one returned my calls, no one extended courtesies. After the folks died, the people I most relied on let me rot in self-pity.

I watched the blonde at the Wildwood as she joked with her "friends." Giving air kisses on proffered cheeks, she glanced my way and shook out her hair with a scowl. She had yet to learn what I had learned from such heartless corporate nerds and their consumerist zeitgeist. As soon as the friendship lost exploitation value, the phone calls came to an end, lunch dates fell into perpetual delay, and the party invitations went unanswered. The New Hollywood wasn't so much a dog-eat-dog world as it was shark-infested effluence.

"You still here?" Gleason said, snapping a breadstick in half.

I reached down to adjust myself. I mulled my options.

What difference did one miserable soul matter in a city of millions? No one cared. Certainly not the moneyed jerks at the adjoining table. Max Gleason could not have cared less what happened to me. I knew that. There was no point in lying to myself. Not anymore.

My thoughts ranged over the image of my handgun—the Sig Sauer—at home, on the coffee table. I wished Bob Smith hadn't interrupted what was supposed to be my final act.

Gleason saw the despair in my eyes. His voice softened a little when he said, "What'd you expect ol' Maxi to do, huh?"

He liked to refer to himself as Maxi, an endearing nickname that no one, other than he, ever used.

"Seriously, Duncan, you look pretty bad."

"Cut me a break, okay?"

Gleason took pity on me but no more than had I been road kill. I looked pathetic in my ridiculous clothes, gaunt from weeks of abuse. I was a balding, anachronistic sleazebag with a ponytail.

Claude the waiter removed Gleason's plate and asked if there would be anything else. Gleason declined as he belched into his napkin. Nearly every food server in L.A. was an aspiring actor. Claude was a better waiter than actor.

"Look," Gleason said at last. "If you've got something to push, I'll give a listen."

I squared my shoulders and wondered if I had heard him correctly. My mood changed in an instant.

Gleason shook his head.

"No promises. Understand? I'm not making any promises. But I'll listen to what you've got."

I picked up the screenplay and hustled it across the table.

"LaGassa's out. This new property just fell into my lap. It's bigger than dinosaurs, Max. Bigger than sinking boats."

"Don't exaggerate." Eyeing the screenplay, he read the title aloud. "Who's the writer?"

I swallowed and shook my head. "You wouldn't know him."

"He got a name?"

"Bob Smith."

Gleason rolled out a laugh. "Bob Smith?"

"That's his name, okay? Look, read it. For my old man."

Chapter 3

I had yet to get the picture.

I was on a drug run. Like everything in L.A., to go anywhere you have to drive. To go shopping, get cash at the ATM, see a movie, pick up a hooker, whatever, the automobile is a necessity. In that vast western empire, all roads lead to one meaningless distraction after another.

Back in the day, consumerism was my life, even in the depths of the Great Recession. I shared a jaded ennui with the rest of the culture, being driven to acquire things that ultimately failed to satisfy, yearning to succeed within a burst economic bubble. I am no different than anybody else, really. We all want our piece of a pie that, long ago, was carved and served up by the corporations. As far as Wall Street is concerned, in the pursuit of happiness we should work forever in abject servitude and play the game in hopes the puppet masters won't cut our strings. For far too long, we have lived beyond our means by buying what we cannot afford with money we do not have.

Oftentimes, I have wondered whether or not there is more to life than yearning for the unattainable. Back in those days, if anybody needed salvation, I did, but the religion of drive-thru prayer palaces offered little comfort to an atheist. As far as I was concerned, movie making and Jesus were part of and parcel to the same Land of Make-believe. Both required a healthy suspension of disbelief. For my own personal deliverance, I desired a tidy catechism through the holy sacrament of little white lines. These were the centerpieces of my faith.

My connection, Xavier Murphy, lived in the San Fernando Valley, where more pornographic movies are made than in any other place on earth. It was a pain in the ass to make the trip from where I lived near old downtown L.A. to Xavier's mean little street off Sepulveda. The neighborhood bordered gangland, but I was compelled to shop there because too few kingpins trafficked in powder cocaine. Crack and crystal meth were reasonably easy scores. A cruise through any intersection in South Central will prove my point. But cocaine powder is another story. As a nostalgic drug, it has become scarce and expensive.

Xavier's clapboard house squatted in a row of other seedy looking houses with iron-barred windows. There was never any place to park. The bangers left their Chevy's and Honda Civics on the dead lawns, blocking the sidewalk. I kept the El Dorado running in the middle of the street.

It was a hot afternoon in late September, and the sun burned like a pink sedative through the hydrocarbon haze of Southern California. I was glad to have worn shorts and a tank top as I stepped out of the car. I shielded my eyes from the glare off the automobile windows. My arms had a ghostly athletic look from a passing interest years ago in weight lifting. Lately, I relied on using to keep trim.

The gutter stank of spilled beer and urine. Through a house window a trash TV audience screamed, and the sound of rank discontent deepened my paranoia. On any given day, white people were not tolerated in Van Nuys. It was a good thing that I drove a loser ride. Otherwise, I ran the risk of becoming a statistic.

I watched Xavier's kid, Arturo, stroll past a crew of bangers. They stood around admiring the metallic opalescence of an Impala. Arturo glanced sideways, self-consciously cool. The boys bobbed to the beat of a sub-woofer. A gansta was rapping that he "ain't gonna be nobody's niggah." When they saw me, their arms slackened and they struck a rapt pose.

Arturo and I had been conducting the Murphy family business for a year without having exchanged so much as a how-do-you-do. I figured him for fourteen. He would have been in junior high school had he not dropped out.

His baggy chinos and flannel shirt swallowed him up. He wore a bandanna, sunglasses, the works. Other kids Arturo's age usually carried. Glocks were the thing in Van Nuys. Miles away in South Central, the bangers carried Smith & Wesson's. You defined Los Angeles neighborhoods by gun manufacturer.

From the front of the house, Xavier Murphy watched through a hole in a plywood window. After I paid the three bills, I got back in the Caddy and drove away. Arturo lit a cigarette and got down with his homies when I took a hard right onto Sepulveda for the freeway.

The onramp was jammed, the freeway bumper to bumper.

I slapped the steering wheel. I could feel a depression coming on. I fingered the envelope of powder in my pocket.

The automobile defined Los Angeles as no other city. The concrete arteries that fed Westlake to Irvine, Studio City to Long Beach, from the Valley all the way down to Orange, were clotted. Nobody in their right mind even considered getting on the freeway at four o'clock in the afternoon.

"This sucks."

I had a love-hate relationship with L.A: I loved to hate it. I hated the yellow water from the tap and the ceaseless hum of traffic in the back of your head. Living in L.A. was like living in a future that failed. I hated the fast food joints and box stores. It was Franchise City, as far as I was concerned, with fantasy architecture and strip malls. Only in L.A. could you find the first MacDonald's restaurant preserved as a historical monument. Above all, I hated the Southern California habit of devouring the weak and hopelessly infirm, because it put me at risk.

But it was home, and you cannot hate home. To do so is to curse your genetics.

The El Dorado coughed all the way up the One-Ten to the Golden State interchange. A grinding noise issued from the bowels of the thing followed by smoke out the tailpipe. The driver of an eighteen-wheeler rumbled past and flipped me off.

I took the nearest off-ramp and ended up in an unfamiliar part of town. There, empty lots behind rusty chain-link fences stood full of trash. Here, a vacated strip mall painted in graffiti. Nearby, a knot of idle teenagers weighed my vulnerability. They wore the colors of the Hoover 18th Street Crips with wrap-around shades of resolute hostility.

The car coasted for another two blocks before the power train gave out. I pulled to the curb beside a Taco Bell. I was considering my options when the cell phone beeped.

"Duncan, that you?"

It was Pig Boy.

"You sound like you're in a fish tank."

My head felt submerged in something dank and hot, in the middle of an involuntary abstinence. I scratched the imaginary bugs under my skin. Until that morning, Xavier had not returned my calls. His answering machine had stated something about vacation, but I doubted a drug dealer ever went on vacation. Relief was in sight, though, after the minor score. I ran my finger down the edge of the bindle.

"What's up?" I said.

From a year of abuse I had the attention span of an Irish setter. I half-listened while fingering the cocaine.

"Sty wants a meeting with your writer-boy."

The heat built up inside the El Dorado, and I rolled down the window. People on the street paid the old car no attention. I figured, parked outside the Taco Bell, I could do a spoon, no problem.

"Say that again, wouldya?"

I expected a punch line. Gleason was playing stand-up to my distracted audience.

"A meeting." Pig Boy was laughing. "I caught you by surprise, didn't I? I read your treatment. Now understand, no promises. We're basing this on your fragment, but it's persuasive, Duncan. Scientist with amnesia predicts the future. Why didn't you tell me it was about the end of the world? It's got undertones of good against evil. It's like a fable or something. Let me say up front, we got a good response from the focus group."

"You ran demographics already?"

"Listen, the committee wants a reading. From what we dialoged on the conference call, Sty's open. But, hey, listen, you gave me a partial. It's more log line than treatment. Where's the rest of it?"

"I got it."

"Send it overnight. You don't sound excited, Duncan. Thought you'd be excited."

"Okay I'm excited."

The vise of abstinence squeezed my head.

"We're set next Tuesday, at ten. At the office. Is your schedule clear?"

The last came with a load of sarcasm.

"Don't pull my chain, okay?"

"Listen, Duncan, this could be good for you. Make sure that, whoever this Smith is, make sure you prep him. Clean him up. Some of the losers you've dragged in…Sty hates that. Make sure Mr. Smith is presentable."

My right ear was ringing, so I switched.

My head rang from a high-pitched whine behind my ears, from that terrible place inside that craved self-destruction. It sounded like a dentist's drill.

"So, we're set. We'll see you at the meeting?"

I had forgotten something, but it took a moment to figure out what it was. The address and phone number of my new client were on the envelope that I had given Pig Boy at the Wildwood. I had neglected to copy down Smith's numbers and had no way of getting in touch with him.

"Say, Max, you got that number handy?"

"Smith's? You should carry your Palm."

"I can call him from here."

I heard Gleason toggling through a list of addresses on his Blackberry.

"Some place downtown. The Glide Hotel."

Gleason repeated the number, and I wrote it on an empty box of MacDonald's French fries.

"Okay then? You might do a feature after all, Duncan." More chortling from Pig Boy. "Ciao," he said at last and rang off.

I threw the cell phone on the passenger seat and ripped the bindle from my pocket. As I opened it on the vinyl bench, I licked my thumb and transferred the powder to my gums, grunting with labile satisfaction. Breathing more easily, I picked up the phone to call for a tow truck.

$$\Omega \qquad \Omega \qquad \Omega$$

They towed the car to a garage off Temple, near the Sycamore Hotel. From the business office in the repair shop, I called Smith, keying the number Max had given me. No one picked up. I called again. Nothing.

"Who in hell doesn't have a service in this town?" I said, staring out the window at the Sycamore Hotel.

It had a crumbly edifice, reminiscent of an aging film star in garish makeup. It looked like Gloria Swanson in Wilder's *Sunset Boulevard*. The new owners had done nothing to restore her former elegance. Instead, they coated the facade in thick yellow, green, and red paint. They were turning it into a restaurant. The complement of colors made me sick to my stomach.

The Latino mechanic with tattoos on his forearms gave me the bad news. He would keep the El Dorado overnight and call me in the morning.

"What is this, a hospital or a garage?" I asked, grinning slyly.

The mechanic did not appreciate the humor.

"You wan me call a cab or somethin?"

By the time I caught a taxi, dusk had settled, and the driver of the Yellow Cab refused to deposit me on The Hill. "The Park's a bad place, man," he said behind the safety of Plexiglas. As such, I had to walk up the steep incline, in the dark, toward home.

I lived at the end of a blind street in the L.A. version of New York's Lower East Side. Echo Park sat within the downtown radius, between Dodger Stadium and the Glendale and Hollywood freeways. Years ago it was a cohesive neighborhood, home to a diverse culture, before City Hall bulldozed it in the name of urban renewal. Its chief inhabitants were then Vietnamese who came to this country after we bombed the crap out of theirs. It reminded them of home.

I could see Dodger Stadium from the bungalow. During night games the banks of floodlights dressed up the sky. On that evening the Dodgers played in another city, and it was relatively quiet in the forgotten memory of Chavez Ravine.

Long ago a gangbanger had shot out the streetlights, casting Echo Terrace in the residue of city shine. On my front porch I was framed in monochrome, catching my breath from the climb. Below me, the boulevards were laid out in jitterbug incandescence like a circuit board.

Some people might consider Los Angeles beautiful at night, but splendor and apathy are borne of distance. Up close it is a meat grinder.

I checked the mailbox and found, to my surprise, an envelope. Smith had personally delivered—there were no stamps—another installation of *Path of Least Resistance.*

I fumbled for the house keys. Behind me the silhouette of palm and eucalyptus stood against a wash of neon from fast food joints and traffic signals. A police helicopter circled, techno-totalitarian like something out of *Blade Runner.*

The house inside was dark as a movie theater.

I was anxious to get down to business. I threw the keys and wallet on the coffee table and laid out the three one-gram bindles on the mirror. Immediately, I appraised them and found that Xavier had been a stingy bastard.

These were dry times. *The Los Angeles Times* had recently reported the biggest cocaine bust in history, on the high seas, twenty-two tons of the Inca's curse. No matter how greedy my connection was, I would have to make do.

I hit the booze, celebrating the option on my property a little prematurely. Scotch was a poor substitute for cocaine, but I wanted to preserve the stash. I stuck mainly to the single-malt. I made a mental note that here was another item to stick under the Entertainment column.

I cranked up the stereo until the bass guitar dusted paint off the stucco. I was in a nostalgic mood for REO Speedwagon, .38 Special, and Blondie, and I put the CD on shuffle. Years ago I told an ex-wife that Western civilization should be remembered for room service and nurses, but most of all, for inventing the shuffle button. Freedom is letting a machine do the work.

After downing nearly a quarter of a fifth, I decided I had been disciplined long enough.

Half the high of doing drugs is working the paraphernalia. Following a routine, I spread the wings of Xavier's bindle and tapped the powder onto a circular mirror. Then I removed two pharmaceutical grinding plates from a leather-carrying pouch. The grinders were made of glass, thick as lithography stones and green as icebergs. Using the flange of a razor blade, I scraped the coke off the mirror and onto the grinder. I mulled it over. Powdered cocaine needs grinding, to crush and evenly distribute whatever cut my connection had used. Most traffickers and petty dealers cut with Mannitol, a baby laxative.

After separating the plates, I reached across the coffee table and pushed the mute on the remote, and the living room was suddenly thrown over to a deafening quiet. My ears rang. Anticipation tightened the back of my throat.

From an ashtray I took a silver straw and leaned down and took two quick hits from the bulk on the pharmaceutical glass.

I shut my eyes and rested against the cushions of the couch. Someone told me once that cocaine stimulates brain chemicals called neurotransmitters. Every time I snorted, I flooded my brain with hormones that occur naturally in my body. I often joked that it wasn't cocaine I was addicted to but neurotransmitters. I loved who I was on coke.

For the rest of the evening, I sat on the couch in my underwear with my feet propped up on the coffee table, a glass of Scotch in one hand, Smith's latest installment in the other. I laughed to myself. Smith should have named the treatment "The Further Adventures of a World Famous Film Director."

Once again, my old man, referred to as *Mr. Austin*, was the center of the scene at a film production company called SuperMax. In a plush conference room, the Old Man pitched a concept with the same title as the screenplay. I had some difficulty keeping track of the numerous characters in the scene, each presented with nicknames.

There was "Mr. Big" the movie producer, and an actor named "Storm Mountain" of all things. Mr. Big was the stereotype of a movie producer who smoked a Churchill cigar and had a pencil-thin mustache. I noted along the margins to speak with Smith about changing the characterization. No one would believe it.

Throughout the scene Mr. Austin summarized the concept of *Path of Least Resistance* for the production execs. There were objections raised and alternatives proposed. There was an underlying current of office politics in the scene that Smith seemed to have drawn from experience. Smith had captured what it was like to have your treatment subjected to wholesale revision at the hands of the money people. And who should be in the scene but a character representing my old man, recovering from a hangover. Smith had it wrong; my old man never touched the stuff. He was as sober as a Mormon Bishop.

Around ten o'clock, I watched the last hour of a Forties flick on cable but was unable to identify the director. The hard-boiled detective referred to women as "dames," and the women sounded as though they inhaled helium. I was nearly asleep with a half-emptied bottle on the couch when Bob Smith showed up.

Smith stood behind me, in the dining room. His image reflected in the Sony.

"Mr. Austin?"

I nearly jumped out of my skin. I screamed and leaped off the couch.

"You scared the living shit out of me!"

He came around to my side to face me.

"I want my screenplay back," he said.

"What in hell're you talking about?"

I put the fifth on the coffee table. My heart refused to settle down to a regular beat.

"Today, I saw one of your movies, Mr. Austin, and no offense but I've made a terrible mistake."

I avoided looking into the blue righteousness of the man's eyes.

"You are not the man to make my movie."

I took a "cleansing" breath, something my therapist had suggested I do when unable to make sense of things.

"Look," I said. "I'm closing the deal. We got a reading next Tuesday with the big enchilada. I called you earlier but you didn't answer. You don't have an answering machine, you know that?"

"I want the screenplay back. I confused you with your father. Your movies are completely unacceptable. I can't in good conscience let you make my movie."

I squinted at the dude, trying to figure out what it was that gave me the shakes. He wore the same clothes and carried the same small beige suitcase. He looked like a homeless guy on vacation. For sure, he was on some kind of trip. Still, I knew, if I were to cash in, I had to persuade the old bugger to let me pitch his treatment.

"We're in negotiations," I said. "They love it. Probably get Harrison for the lead."

With a note of disappointment in his voice, Smith said, "You haven't even read it, have you? The character is more like me."

I smirked. "Like someone who breaks into houses?"

"I want my screenplay, Mr. Austin."

"What the hell you worried about?"

"I want it back."

"No can do. They called a meeting. Next Tuesday. Gotta be there, Bob. Give 'em the final installment."

Smith was expressionless.

"It's finished, right?" I said.

"There isn't going to be a meeting."

"Do you own a pair of dress shoes? You'll need to get cleaned up for this. You know, shave. Take a shower."

Bob Smith sighed and shook his head, frowning.

"You're drunk."

"That's right. And tomorrow I'll be sober," I said, "and you'll still be old."

"I will not deal with an alcoholic."

With the beige suitcase dangling at his side, Smith opened the sliding glass door. He stepped through and a faint breeze blew a litter of dry leaves across the carpet. He stepped into the dark, and in a moment he was gone.

I went to the door and leaned through the opening, my head pounding with Scotch and cocaine.

"You wanna see drunk?" I shouted. "I'll show you drunk."

Smith's retreat through the garden was registered by crunches across the pea-gravel walkway. I heard the latch drop on the back gate.

"Hey!" I called out. "*Hey!* We got a meeting next Tuesday. You hear me, Smith?"

Chapter 4

The Tuesday meeting went poorly.

Rainy Day Films office building was a pink granite, blue-glass copy of a Rem Koolhaas structure, perched in the Hollywood Hills. I arrived by cab a few minutes early and gave the guard at the gatehouse my name and business card. Behind his aviator glasses, he resembled G. Gordon Liddy. He called upstairs. I heard a voice through the phone line, a distant voice as though from Kafka's castle, floating in the air far away.

The guard returned the card and said, "You're not on the list."

"Have to be. Max Gleason set it up."

The guard's only humanity was reflected in the sunglasses. He was more impediment than human being.

"Sty Raines set up the meeting." I had a pissed-off edge to my voice. "He personally called the meeting."

A dozen cars had lined up behind the cab, expensive foreign jobs with vanity plates and privacy glass. The guard told my driver to pull to the side as he waved the other cars onto the lot. My cool circled the drain. By the time the security supervisor was called and they found my name on somebody's to-do list, the guard had stripped me of whatever confidence I'd managed to build over the previous week.

The Development Committee met in a conference room on the top floor with a million-dollar view of the competition, the old Warner Brothers studio, and now part of the AOL-TimeWarner-CNN Empire. Gleason entered the conference room and pumped the hands of half a dozen executives, his gold bracelet rattling. His aura changed from enthusiasm to disappointment upon seeing me enter the meeting, alone.

He sidled up, and without the pretext of a smile, he said, "Where's the writer?" Pig Boy looked volcanic, about to blow.

"Attending personal business."

I had hoped to take a back seat and let Gleason defend the concept before the committee. Bob Smith's absence probably had a lot to do with his sudden bad humor.

With a smile for everyone else, he said to me privately: "I never could trust you."

I wanted to explain the deal at the gatehouse, but by then, Pig Boy had turned to one of his colleagues, and Sty Raines entered through a private office door. We took our seats.

The room was fashioned after four stage sets, each wall representing a successful Rainy Day movie. Sty Raines' hand carved oak chair came from *Dawn a Plain Maiden*, a period piece loosely based on Queen Elizabeth I. The wall behind him was surfaced in stone. The four other executives and two lawyers sat on opposite sides of the table. At my end of the room, the table stood against an Old West backdrop. Gleason sat with me, a glaringly empty chair between us. The table was set with yellow legal pads and coffee mugs imprinted with "Looks Like Another Rainy Day™".

Wearing a charcoal gray business suit and canary yellow tie, I felt out of place. No one else wore a business suit in Hollywood that day. I battled a hangover, but the familiarity of a migraine and nausea calmed my nerves. I nervously fingered the latch on my briefcase. It was empty, just like my future.

Years ago after I dropped out of college, I had worked for Sty Raines as a glorified taxi driver and film set waiter. My dad had called in a few favors with a production exec, a relic from the old studio system, and I got the job. Two weeks into making the movie, I was fired for screwing a key grip girl on her lunch break.

The man who had fired me sat at the table, M. Chandler Tate. Time had not treated him kindly. He looked hollow to the core, worn down by ambition. He'd been fitted with dentures since our last meeting and had more teeth than seemed possible. His toupee was as I had remembered it.

This was an industry of make believe, but Sty Raines was the genuine article. He was a stout, bald man who carried around an Upmann cigar because he liked the effect; the same brand President Kennedy used to smoke. He flashed an Oyster Rolex set to New York time and Pacific Standard. With the corporate offices on Fifth Avenue, he had to keep in touch.

Movie production was a sweet business. Low overhead, healthy profit. The job of executive producer meant more than simply fronting capital. Producing was at the heart of deal making, contract negotiation, distribution, product endorsement, in addition to conception and execution, and all of it paid a percentage. Sty Raines had an estimated personal worth of over a billion. He was *the* major player, in possession of more liquidity than many in the business.

As CEO, Sty Raines ran a division within the largest multi-media organization in the world. Through creative accounting, his return on investment per product appeared small on paper despite an earnings column in the hundreds of millions. This was intentional, a kind of cotton-candy accounting practice. The office building where we sat was leased by Rainy Day Films, the production arm of the company, from Rainy Day Enterprises at an exorbitant four hundred bucks per square foot. Enterprises charged a high rental fee because, by manipulating production costs, they contrived an artificially high rolling break.

"Okay, people," Sty Raines said, opening the meeting.

"Sty," Gleason said, "we got a very cool concept."

I was speechless. Surrounded by the usual suspects in the movie biz, I sat stupefied by the parallels with Smith's screenplay and my life. Before me sat characters taken from *Path of Least Resistance*. Instead of "Mr. Big," I faced Sty Raines; or perhaps "Mr. Big" was Max Gleason? Looking at the faces around the conference table, I soon realized that no counterpart to "Storm Mountain," a character reminiscent of Rock Hudson, had joined us. Perhaps I was making too much of Smith's latest episode, but it was impossible to deny that there were uncanny similarities to this concept meeting and the one depicted in the screenplay.

As my mind wandered, I recalled similarities between a scene involving the old man's car breaking down on the San Diego freeway and my own experience of a few days earlier. Sweat collected on my neck and rolled down my back as I struggled to rectify these coincidences.

"Let's move, people," Sty Raines said, clapping his hands.

Gleason nodded at his assistant, a young man wearing a polo shirt.

Darnel Preece was just another soldier in a company of ass-lickers. He flipped open a valise to remove the screenplay, which was earmarked with yellow Post-It Notes and paper clips. He handed copies of a synopsis to a female producer who sat next to me. She caught me sneaking peeks down her unbuttoned blouse, at the fashion statement of her pink nipples. Preece referred to her as Miz Landau.

Preece leaned toward her and asked politely, "Please, would you mind helping me distribute these?"

"Mr. Preece here will give you something of the idea we have in mind," Gleason said.

"Go ahead, Mr. Priest," Sty Raines said.

Darnel Preece blinked at the mistaken identity.

I smiled at the faux pas. In our hideous world of make believe, Darnel Preece would rather change his name than correct the CEO.

"Thank you. By way of background, we've done some preliminaries. We've estimated completion cost, excluding post-production, between fifty and sixty. This would give us an ROI in the multiple of three range. This, of course, does not include distribution, publicity, and what the elements may contract for. There's no packaging at this point. We haven't run the numbers for the rolling break."

The rolling break was critical to making a profit in movie production. It was the amount and type of extra cost calculated to draw out the point of profitability from several times the cost of production to a point approaching infinity. Advertising, duplicating film prints, salaries, leasing agreements on facilities that the company owned, interest paid on bank loans, any and all bogus costs were exaggerated, thereby reducing the bottom line. Accountants used the rolling break to explain why points paid to movie stars earned next to nothing on blockbusters. Gross receipts were one thing; points paid to actors and writers on profit margins were subject to manipulation.

"From a negotiation standpoint," Preece continued, "our focus group results are positive. The demographic is strong, most of the participants ranked the concept between an eight and ten. When casting, it is Mr. Gleason's recommendation that gross profit or point participation be excluded from any contractual agreements. The focus group results were that strong. Flat rates for the talent plus low points to the headliners are our recommendation, but again the bean counters've not completed the numbers."

"What about merchandising rights?" Miz Landau asked.

"Shouldn't be a problem," Gleason said with a nearly imperceptible nod in my direction.

Preece continued. "Now that each of you has a copy, let's begin. 'Path of Least Resistance' is about an ordinary man, a microbiologist, who's visited at night by aliens. There is an establishing shot to open the movie, which gives the audience something to chew on. The aliens give our biotechnologist the ability to know the future, but he's in conflict about this. Can't bring himself to believe what he's seeing is real. Like any normal person who sees things, he's worried about his sanity. But the audience knows that what he sees *is* real. That's the hook. There's trouble ahead. The aliens tell our protagonist the world is going to end. There's going to be a plague from a bioengineered virus."

"What the hell's bioengineered mean?"

It was M. Chandler Tate. Despite being a mere associate producer, not an executive vice president, Max Gleason's official title, M. Chandler Tate tried to get the upper hand at the meeting.

"It's from biotech. They make bioengineered something or other. The writer uses the name XyberGen."

Tate nodded.

"Is that a real company?" Miz Landau asked.

One of the lawyers said, "Sounds like a cohesive development opportunity."

"People, we can change it," Sty Raines said. "Let's go. Let's go."

Preece turned to the first page.

"Let's begin with the treatment as it is written, from what we have. The protagonist works for a biotech firm."

"Excuse me, excuse me."

Tate again.

"Don't say 'protagonist.' It's annoying as hell. What's the guy's name?"

"Joe Dawson. Would it be better if I used the character's name?"

"Yes, much better. Go on," Tate said, striking a more relaxed pose.

Gleason gave a nod to Preece.

"Joe Dawson is one of the chief engineers at XyberGen. He's been assigned to a project for the Department of Defense, the Pentagon. They're looking at ways to neutralize chemical and biological weapons of mass destruction, but during their research they uncover something very dangerous, a virus that could end all life on Earth."

"I see synergy with AIDS," Miz Landau said.

"Yes, that may be something we could use," Gleason said.

Preece flipped to the first Post-It Note.

"The first act begins at night in a quiet, middle-class neighborhood. We open with a shot of Joe Dawson's house. A moonless night. His family is asleep, and Joe Dawson's snoozing on the couch. The television is on. He wakes up to shut it off. He's about to climb the stairs to go to bed, that's when the aliens visit him."

"Excuse me, but, I mean, aliens?" It was Tate again. "A bit passé aren't they?"

"What in hell kind of genre is this?" one of the attorneys asked.

"Our last alien product netted less than five on opening weekend," Tate said.

Preece looked again to Gleason for direction. Gleason was stone-faced, letting the boy hang on his own.

"Although Chandler's correct in his thinking," an older woman said, "Bix Films grossed nearly three hundred fifty last year with their *Edge Palladium*."

Everyone enumerated in terms of millions of dollars.

The older woman was lost in shoulder pads and a thick wool jacket. Audrey Whistler-Cox was Vice President of Brand Endorsement, the department that negotiated with Coca Cola, Nike, Ford, and other multinational corporations to have their products and logos appear in Rainy Day films. She was a promotion specialist, a middle-aged woman in a business obsessed with youth, a self-described survivor. Whistler-Cox had undergone numerous face-lifts and chemical peals over the years until her expression was fixed in permanent astonishment.

"And it was an alien picture," she said at last.

Sty Raines shut his eyes and rattled his loose hands. "Let's go, let's go."

Preece turned the page and continued with the pitch.

"Let me set the scene. The Dawson household. Joe Dawson has shut off the TV. He hears something outside. He thinks people are trying to break-in. Actually, aliens are visiting him. We, the audience, know this, but he doesn't. After a very tense opening scene, Joe Dawson—"

"Look," M. Chandler Tate said. "Just use his first name, okay?"

"The tension builds on screen with...*Joe*...running to the front and back of his house, terrified someone's trying to break in. He opens the door, but there's no one there. The mystery is, the audience knows three aliens are outside, trying to break in. A close encounter between Joe and the aliens takes place, but without Joe's knowledge."

"This is a paradigm shift," Whistler-Cox said.

"The following day, Joe has no memory of the attempted break-in. There is a scene of Joe in the shower. He's got a rash on his side, a red triangle of raised skin. We know the aliens have put it there, but he doesn't know. He shows it to his wife, Chloe. She's a nurse. She cautions him to keep an eye on it. He goes to his job, and at work funny things begin to happen."

"Thought this was a drama," Tate said. "Not a comedy."

"By funny," Gleason said, "Mr. Priest means...?"

He turned to Preece with raised eyebrows.

"I mean, he has a premonition. He envisions the death of a secretary. And he thinks he's losing his mind because he can read people's thoughts. Then, later, at a party, his closest friend, a guy named Norm.... Well, let me explain. This character is Joe's neighbor and colleague from work. Anyway, Norm dies of a heart attack at a backyard party. Joe has a vision of Norm's death *before* it happens. He actually foresees the event. Funeral arrangements are made, but Joe tells his wife he can't attend. He's too messed up over the loss. He sneaks into the cemetery alone and watches the service from a distance. This is where things get really magical. His wife discovers him there, in the cemetery, and he begins to cry and little flowers sprout up where tears have fallen on the grass."

"Has regulatory seen this?" one of the two attorneys asked.

"There's a sense of magic in it," Miz Landau said.

"Now the action begins to accelerate. He takes a leave of absence from his job. He tells Chloe he needs professional help. He's hallucinating. Keeps seeing Norm, his dead friend, smiling at him at work. As we shift from Act One to Act Two the story progresses, and we find our hero in a privately run mental institution. He's committed himself. He can't believe what he's seeing. Aliens have given him the ability to know about the future. He keeps having nightmares about a plague, about a sort of manufactured Black Death that kills billions of people. Anyway, at a low point in his cell, I think that's what you call the rooms in those places. He's visited again by three aliens. Only this time they tell him that he's been chosen to save the world."

Preece paused to assess the interest level in the room. Everyone wore his or her game face, an expressionless mask of studied indifference. One of the attorneys gripped a skinless tennis ball in his right hand. The veins in his temples swelled.

Preece found his place in the script and continued.

"In this psychiatric facility, the aliens explain why they're visiting Joe. The scientists at the biotech company, where he worked, have genetically manipulated a virus. It's a very deadly virus, and if it gets loose, the aliens tell him, all life on Earth will die. Not just human life, but *all* life. Everything will die."

"What a bunch a crap," Tate muttered.

People loyal to Whistler-Cox shot Tate an unsanitary look. Gleason said nothing.

"Well, after all," Tate said in his own defense, "this is turning out to be a grand cliché."

"Something like *Mr. Postman?*" Whistler-Cox said referring to Tate's huge financial blunder of the previous year.

Gleason nodded for Preece to continue.

"Now," he said, "the aliens tell Joe he has to stop the biotechnologists, colleagues at his company, from experimenting with the microbe. Unfortunately, we are missing a few pages in the treatment. So, without knowing the details, we assume Joe breaks out of the mental institution because he calls his colleagues from a pay phone on the street, late at night. He tells them that they must stop work on the virus. But the scientists have no buy in. Joe then tries to talk sense to the owners, his former employers. He visits the company and pleads with them to stop the biological warfare experiments. But they won't listen. They think he's nuts. So, what he does next is, he takes his life savings and buys time on a local television station to argue his case before the public."

"Hey, wait a minute. I heard about this," Tate said.

"Yes, wasn't something like this on the news?" Miz Landau asked.

"Please, let the boy finish," Sty Raines said.

Gleason nodded at Darnel Preece.

"Joe finally gets on TV to warn people. He makes a statement on the public access cable channel, but nobody's willing to listen. Everyone thinks he's an opportunist trying to grab publicity or maybe sell something. Even his wife, Chloe, doubts him, and she leaves finally, files for legal separation. She can no longer tolerate his ranting and ravings."

"I like it," Sty Raines said. "My gut tells me we might have something here."

The room became oppressively quiet. No one breathed. Sty Raines occasionally used sarcasm to make a point. He was notorious for it. Members of the Development Committee wondered if this was not one of those occasions.

"Who wrote this?" Sty Raines asked.

"Some fresh talent, chief," Gleason said.

"Well, I like the voice. We may need to hire a writer to expand the cohesive development thing, fill in the details, but I like it. Don't anyone interrupt Mr. Priest here. Go on, go on."

They waited for Darnel Preece to continue.

"That's..." he said anxiously. "That's it."

Tate was gleeful. *"That's it?"*

"Well," Preece said, looking to Gleason for support. "That's all we have at the moment."

"Surely it doesn't end this way," Whistler-Cox said.

Such an inconclusive ending did not meet her expectations. For the first time that day she looked at me with her frozen startled expression.

"Mr. Austin here gave me only this sample," Gleason said. "If we want to move forward, I am told, we have the freedom to do so."

"You know what?" Sty Raines began.

Everyone shifted to look at the producer.

"I like it very much. Very much. It reminds me of something. I don't know. Something. Does it remind you of something?" he asked.

"Could be an emotional vehicle," Whistler-Cox said.

"It's commercial."

"We could be talkin' box office," Miz Landau said.

"I think it has spiritual meaning," young Preece said to Gleason's chagrin.

"Yes," Sty Raines said. "I can see that. Something for the Xer's and the Fundamentalists."

Despite Sty Raines' approval, M. Chandler Tate sulked behind his coffee mug.

"Everything would be peachy," Sty Raines said with a sudden frown, "if Mr. Austin here produced the writer. But I don't see him."

I cleared my throat. "He's sorta hard to get a hold of."

"Where is he?" the CEO asked.

I shrugged.

One of the attorneys said, "I have another meeting in ten minutes."

The two attorneys looked remarkably alike in collarless jackets. They were corporate lawyers by training.

"You're wasting my time."

"He needs to do a lateral assessment."

"Mr. Austin," Sty Raines said. He shut his eyes and tugged an ear. "You don't seem to understand. We like your concept." He forced a smile. "But how can you expect us, how can we take the next step? I gotta have a finished screenplay."

Sty Raines lifted up the manila folder and dumped the screenplay on the table, pushing it toward me. "This is not a screenplay. It's an idea."

"Max, convince this guy, will you," Whistler-Cox said.

"It's out of my hands, people." Gleason grimaced. "Mr. Austin represents the property. He assured me the writer'd be here. I'm as disappointed as you are."

"Well, how does it end? That's what I wanna know," Sty Raines said. "How the hell it ends."

I sighed. "I don't know how it ends."

"For the love a..."

"But I promise, I promise, I'll get the rest of it. Believe me." I leaned forward and gathered up the screenplay and put it in my briefcase. I was glad to finally get a copy, having forfeited the original to Pig Boy.

"You need to think outside the box," Whistler-Cox said. Turning to one of the lawyers, she said, "My cell phone died. May I use yours?"

"Well, then." Sty Raines rose out of the chair. "That's it. Gentlemen, howza 'bout lunch?"

"I'm open to that."

Gleason turned to me and whispered, "I knew I couldn't trust you. You blew it."

"Look, I'll get it, Max. Really."

"You are so full of shit."

"Before the week's out."

Pig Boy shot me a look of utter disapproval.

I winced and shut the clasps of my briefcase as the development executives left the room.

"Max," Sty Raines said at the door to his private office, "make sure you get us the writer. I gotta know how this thing ends."

Chapter 5

In Hollywood the closest thing to heaven is a rerun. With fame comes the afterlife of late night and cable television. When an actor dies, or loses their appeal, they do not end up in the arms of Jesus. The dead live on in syndication.

Ω   Ω   Ω

It cost me nearly fifty bucks to take a cab from Rainy Day Films to Echo Park. On the ride home I used my cell to call Bob Smith but I got no answer. At home I called again. This time it was busy. I waited, called once more. No answer. I confirmed the number with the phone company.

"It's a pay phone, sir," the operator said.

"A friggin' pay phone?"

I continued to call on the off chance that Smith, or anyone, would pick up.

Finally, at the end of the day, Bob Smith answered the phone.

"I've been trying to reach you for hours."

"I want my screenplay returned to me, Mr. Austin."

"Look, you gotta buy a phone. We can't do business like this. Not every time I need to talk to you."

"Mr. Austin, I saw *Madame Pussy* today."

I shut my mouth. *Madame Pussy* was a skin flick I had produced some time back, to make ends meet. It was not my proudest piece of work, but I have to eat just like everybody else.

"Where's my screenplay?"

"That's why I called, Bob. Can I call you Bob? Look, we need some face time."

"I don't want to meet with you, Mr. Austin."

"Call me DC, okay? We're partners now."

"I want the manuscript."

I threw the phone down and tried to control my anger. I knew if I let emotions rule, I'd blow this last break in my pathetic movie-making career. But I had to negotiate with a guy who looked like warmed-over shit and who roomed in a resident hotel. "Just my luck," I said to myself. I picked up the phone again. "What do you want? Name it. You wanna nice car? Fine. I can get you a condo in Malibu. How's that sound?"

"I don't need anything."

"That's nuts. Everybody wants something. Look, Bob, when was the last time you had a good piece of ass? I can get you two teenagers on Spanish fly. All you gotta do is work with me, okay?"

"I want my screenplay," Smith said.

"Okay, okay, tell you what. I'll give it back if you meet with me. If you don't meet me, you don't get it back. Simple as that."

Smith thought for a moment.

"Where?"

"Kwon's. Do you know it? Chinese place. Corner of Temple."

"I'll find it. What time?"

"Lunch tomorrow."

The following day I waited at a booth in Kwon's from 11:45 AM until two o'clock, drinking one Tsing Tao after another until I was drunk. I overheard a couple of business men in the next booth talk about a two-headed cloned sheep developed by scientists at Johns Hopkins University. The television on the kitchen counter blared loudly above the cackle of the locals. It was set to CNN. I sipped beer while watching a tongue-in-cheek story about a UFO sighting by a pair of Nevada ranch hands. Smith never showed up.

In the afternoon I stumbled home. The day was wasted. I sat on the couch and watched a network news show. I learned that the real estate market was still in the toilet. A troubled teen had brought a handgun to school and murdered the principal. Flesh-eating bacteria had hospitalized two janitors in Albuquerque. CNN carried a piece about an anonymous mass grave in Kosovo. Later, some talking head, an economist with a fat television contract, explained why the "economic downturn" was more or less a permanent condition. And actor Bobby Uppity, Jr., was arrested once again on drug charges. Same old same old.

I watched a commercial for Dodge Ram trucks in which one of my ex-wives laid on the hood in a bikini. She looked great wearing a sequin thong with her red hair loose over her shoulders. On second thought, it must have been her daughter. My ex was past her prime for the role.

I ate stew out of a can and went to bed early with the intention of reading Smith's screenplay from start to finish. I had given it short shrift. At the concept meeting, not knowing details of the storyline had put me at a disadvantage. I knew that the plot involved a coming plague caused by a virus created in a science lab. Preece had stated something to the effect that the company worked on contract for the Department of Defense. It was a hackneyed concept, and had disappointed me. I had expected more from the treatment, I suppose, a theme that was more original in scope. There were scenes throughout, however, that bore an uncanny similarity to events in my life. The Caddy breaking down on the freeway and the concept meeting itself seemed taken from Smith's pages. Somehow he had created the illusion within the screenplay of foretelling the future. It was quite the parlor trick and unnerving.

I fluffed the pillow and lay back, organizing the screenplay on the bedcover according to scene. Before launching into the work, I went to the kitchen and prepared a pitcher full of martinis and tossed one back as I returned to the bedroom. There I realized that I hadn't had much water all day, and it was back to the kitchen for a glass of iced tea. By the time I settled into bed and had tossed back a second martini, I shut off the light and fell asleep before reading a word.

I dreamt about my dad who had fallen down a well on a farm. The farm looked like the stage set from *The Wizard of Oz*. Ordinarily, I dream in Technicolor, but my dream farm was right out of the Dust Bowl. My old man was drowning at the bottom of the well, and unless I threw him a rope he would die. I searched inside the barn for a length of rope to save him. The barn was full of menacing fat spiders. I found a length of nylon cording and ran outside to lower it into the well. As I pulled with all my strength, the cord slipped around my dad's neck. As I pulled him to safety, the rope strangled him.

I woke up, sweating. I wondered what my former psychotherapist would make of the dream symbolism.

In the darkened bedroom there were new shapes in addition to those familiar to me. I had an eerie feeling that a presence had joined me in the middle of the night.

I turned on the light.

Bob Smith stood at the foot of my bed.

"Holy shit!" I screamed.

"Sorry to have scared you."

I wheezed like an old bellows, hand at my chest, sitting up in bed.

"You gotta...learn to knock."

"Is this how you treat my screenplay, Mr. Austin?" He gestured at the chaos of pages strewn across the bedcover.

"We had a date, you know? You missed lunch."

"I came to apologize."

"Great timing."

Fright gave way to frustration, and I threw back the blanket. I gathered up the pages and held them like a weapon, frozen in a dramatic stance. I couldn't think of a thing to say.

Smith pulled a manila envelope from his beige suitcase and quietly slipped it onto the corner of the bed.

"You give me no choice," he said. "I have to trust you."

I was afraid to say anything for fear that he, like a wild bird or something, might fly away. I picked up the envelope and fingered the sleeve of pages. It appeared to be more of the screenplay, another fragment.

"Give it to the producer, if you like."

"Look," I said, sitting on the edge of the bed, "they're gonna make your movie."

I reached for my Marlboro's. The pack was empty.

"If you say so."

"You know, you scared the living shit out of me. Again."

I floated a laugh, but Bob Smith was as deadpan as Buster Keaton.

I thought about how good it would feel to finish the last of Xavier's coke, just a few lines to wash away the absurdity of this rude awakening.

"Drugs have never solved anything," Smith said.

"What'd you say?"

Smith folded his arms across his chest.

"You're a train wreck, Mr. Austin. How I confused you with your father..."

He shook his head wearily.

Nausea clawed at my chest. The effects of the martinis were long past the euphoria stage. Being insulted by a moralistic asshole was not at the top of my bucket list, especially in the middle of the night. I cleared my throat and gave a cursory glance at the envelope.

"I'm not doing this for you," Smith said. "I'm doing it in spite of you."

"Well, don't do me any favors."

Smith shook his head. "You need to dry out, Mr. Austin. Stop doing drugs."

"There's the door, Bob. What the hell am I saying? You know where it is. Or do you float through walls? You some kind of ghost or something?"

"You haven't a clue what I am."

I struggled off the bed. My vision drained of blood, and for the moment little pond beetles swam across the wallpaper. I rubbed my eyes.

"You know something, you know something?" I caught my balance and glowered at him. "You came to me for help, you know? I made good on my promise."

Smith gave me one of his all-knowing looks.

"You were about to kill yourself."

His allegation left me speechless.

The dude's eyes wandered, his attention drawn elsewhere. He placed the small suitcase on the floor and cocked his head like a dog listening to a high-pitched whistle.

"Earth to Bob," I whispered.

His eyelids fluttered, and he took a startled breath. His bewilderment lessened as he reached down to pick up the suitcase.

"You gotta problem?" I asked of his mooncalf expression. When I had his attention again, I continued. "This could be the biggest thing since *The Godfather*. Sequels. More money than you can imagine."

"I'm not doing it for money."

Smith stepped back and leaned against the bedroom wall.

"Lord Almighty, I hooked up with a saint. Just my luck. Man, would you stop being such an asshole for one minute?"

I eyed Smith. He looked shrunken, defeated. He blended so perfectly with the pattern of wallpaper that I thought he might disappear.

"Be reasonable. Gleason and Rainy Day, they're gonna make your movie. I think we can haggle a percentage. You get what I'm saying here? You're fly with that, right?"

"You're a poor listener."

Smith rested his head against the wall. He looked older somehow.

"You all right? You a little under the weather or something?" I grimaced. "Can I ask you a question? Most people…you know, people in the business…they're pretty well known. But you, I mean you're not exactly a household name."

"Why should I want to be famous?"

"Everybody wants that."

Smith shook his head. He was definitely older than I had guessed after our first meeting. The halogen lamp on the nightstand deepened the wrinkles around his eyes and the creases in his brow. There was no mistaking the fact that Smith was on the other side of sixty, maybe older, a candidate for plastic surgery.

"How old are you? Forty-something?"

Smith's eyes glistened in the lamplight like pitted marbles. "You think I'm much older than that, but I'm thirty-seven."

He was a bald-faced liar.

"I underestimated you, Bob. Nobody looks like you at thirty-seven. Unless they did some serious partying." I laughed.

"Or unless they've seen the face of doom."

We said nothing for the moment. I was thinking, *You made a big mistake banking on him, DC.*

"Look," I said, "look, I'm in the middle of the parlay. They want a piece of your action. But you gotta start treating me with a little more respect."

Suddenly, without explanation, Bob Smith turned to leave.

"Wait a minute."

I picked up Smith's envelope and hurried after him.

Reaching the sliding glass door, Smith turned and said, "I'm tired. I'm going home."

"Are these the final scenes, Bob?"

He stepped through the door. I followed but the broken patio concrete was brutal on my bare feet and I retreated.

"Listen, tell me how it ends."

From the darkness, Smith said, "Read what you have and maybe you won't want to know how it ends."

I stood in the doorway, listening, but no sound came from the garden gate or gravel walkway. As I was about to close the door, I looked up. Radiance from Los Angeles washed out most of the stars, leaving a few isolated remnants of the galaxy. I counted three or four points of the Big Dipper. The constellation was as familiar as the pattern of freckles on my forearm. The stars winked back, and I shut the door and went back to bed.

Ω   Ω   Ω

The next morning at ten o'clock, after a breakfast of cigarettes and coffee, I called the garage. My car was ready.

"Hadta order the parts special, man," the mechanic said. "You gotta old car, you know that?"

"Well, they don't make 'em like that anymore."

The mechanic said it was a good thing they didn't.

I considered the inconvenience. To pick up the Caddy I would have to ride the bus from The Hill to the garage off Temple, a forty-five minute ordeal. In a mobile culture, life was mobility. Without wheels I was put at a disadvantage. To make up for lost time, I decided to bring the screenplay and read it on the bus.

It seemed to me that only Third World immigrants used the Los Angeles public transportation system. So proletarian. Don't get me wrong. I don't dislike people of color. It's just that I have never enjoyed mixing with anyone whose personal hygiene is worse than mine, because for some reason, bus riders don't seem to apply deodorant on a daily basis, perhaps forgetting to bathe more than once a week. After paying the fare, I sat in the front of the bus, on a side-facing bench between two obese women. Their body heat scorched me. I arrived at the repair shop not in the best of moods, and when the gum-chewing receptionist presented the excessive bill, I went ballistic. Based on his hourly wage, the mechanic was making more than most medical doctors, and I told him so.

"Oh yeah? Well, she purrs now. Ain't no pussy magnet, forchur." He shrugged with a grin. "But it'll get you where you wanna go, amigo."

You're no friend of mine, I was thinking.

On edge and tweaked, I drove the Caddy to Forest Lawn Cemetery to visit the folks. It was around noon. I needed to figure things out, and I knew the graveyard was as quiet as a library. Death was a powerful force in the universe, and I came to pay my respects.

Parking in the shade behind the mausoleum, I massaged the ache between my eyes. I had not slept well after the old dude's break-in. He had rattled my cage, showing up like that. I lowered the driver's window to take in the air. I needed to settle my nerves, and the usual remedy was unavailable. Xavier had refused my calls. He was more disconnection than drug connection. A Jones had gotten the better of me, but the disorder of graves with lop-sided statuary put me at ease. Past the monuments and gravestones, the only sign of life was a burial taking place perhaps fifty yards away, in a grove of cypress.

Inside the mausoleum, the ashes of my parents were interred in a crypt. While my mind drifted, I thought about my father. Only once in my life could I remember when the Old Man had showed an ounce of affection.

When I was ten or twelve years old, the Old Man had an LP that featured the voice of Winston Churchill. It was a special interest recording of London air raid sirens during the Blitz. He wore the album out in the late Sixties and early Seventies when nuclear war threatened our survival. Back then, the possibility of nuclear annihilation was very real to my mind, and I had read everything I could get my hands on about atomic and hydrogen bombs. I became a student of megatonage and throw-weight, ICBMs and theater weapons. I devoured non-fiction books about Hiroshima, the destructive power of the hydrogen bomb, about Soviet delivery systems, in addition to the end-of-world novels *Alas, Babylon!* and *On The Beach.* As a kid, I had a morbid fascination with the Third World War, not unlike a cancer patient who must learn everything he can about his or her terminal malignancy.

The first time the Old Man played that record, the air raid sirens sent me ducking for cover, my heart racing from fear. I had been sitting on my bed reading, and the sirens caught me by surprise. The Old Man turned up the volume, and I ran downstairs in abject terror. I had less than ten to fifteen minutes before the bombs started to fall. I knew that my imminent death could be an agonizing one. If the blast wave and heat did not incinerate me, then the mushroom cloud would rain its slow poison. I would die incapacitated in my own runny excrement. I knew well the effects of radiation sickness, even at that tender age.

With London's sirens screaming, I ran down the entry hall not knowing which way to turn, where to spend my last seconds. I threw open the front door, and who should be standing there but a Girl Scout in pigtails.

We stood blinking at one another for a second or two. She was about my own age and she carried a basket of brightly packaged cookies.

It was then that my father came up from behind and placed his hand on my shoulder. Startled, I looked back. There was human kindness in his eyes, for a change.

When I realized that the world was not going to end, I used my lawn-mowing money to buy five boxes of Girl Scout Cookies. Then I sat in the backyard beneath a flowering plum tree and ate my way through each box. The grass was lush and damp and intensely alive. I prayed to God that I would survive to my twenties. I wanted to sit on the grass in my old age, but in that world, in the world of Cold War hostilities, I didn't think it possible. I have always had a morbid fascination with death, including my childhood fear of nuclear annihilation. I suppose that was why I loved *Path of Least Resistance*.

But on that day, back in 1969, it was the only instance in my life when the Old Man touched me.

My shrink once said that my emotional problems stemmed from an unsatisfactory relationship with my father. I have always sought father figures and mentors, the shrink told me. Nothing could be further from the truth. The Old Man never liked me. If our "relationship" was considered unsatisfactory then he was to blame, not I. Besides, the feeling was mutual.

Over the past year, after the funeral, with every word I spoke I heard the Old Man admonish me. I heard him tell me that I was stupid, or call me an asshole. Maybe Max Gleason was right. Maybe I was garbage, a low-life scumbag who would never live up to his famous father. After he committed suicide, for twelve months I suffered an unrelenting depression. My business contacts and relationships ended up a big fat zero. My résumé would not get me into the finer restaurants of Beverly Hills let alone heaven. I realized that I had become a cheap suit who produced nothing but porno; a cokehead whose sweetheart was a video whore. Something had to change, but I felt otherwise powerless to change it. Sitting in the Old Man's car and staring at the granite mausoleum, the thought struck me that I might soon join my graveyard relatives, but I knew that nobody would attend *my* funeral.

I grew up in the Seventies when L.A. was laid-back, like that Neil Diamond song says. I had an uneventful, although privileged childhood. I attended the best private schools, got all the breaks money can buy. I attended a prestigious university, for all the good it did me. Life handed me diamonds, and I crushed them in the muck. I lived my life as an endurance race to test how far I could run on the outermost brink of madness before killing myself. I pissed away millions. I abused the one woman in the world who truly loved me. I ruined my health. Even my kids hated me. If you produced a movie based on my life, it would bomb.

Surrounded at Forest Lawn Cemetery by thirty-seven million living Californians, I had never felt so alone.

I was drowning.

I opened the car door and stepped out and headed for the mausoleum. I needed some air. The temperature was cool inside, cooler than I remembered from my first visit to the place. Etched on the same marble panel was my mother's and the Old Man's likenesses along with name, date of birth and death. These were etched on a single panel although they rested in separate crypts. In death as in life, they had separate bedrooms for as long as I could remember. I ran my finger down the carved image of my mother and rested my forehead against the polished stone.

Nine months before I was born, almost to the day, my mother suffered a near-fatal car accident. Internal injuries, broken bones, concussion, the works. No one expected her to make it. She defied the doctors and fate by surviving the first thirty days in a body cast, immobilized and enduring acute pain. None of her physicians registered concern when she missed her period. The physiological processes of trauma victims often shut down, but when she was off her cycle for three consecutive months, they ran a test. It came back positive. By then my mother had routinely received morphine sulfate for pain, injected into her medial artery, and she—along with the fetus—was addicted.

When I was born, my old man hired a part-time nanny to raise me. It was no one he knew, nobody from the movie business, just a girl from a nanny service. The nanny cared for me during the first six months of my life, while my mother had surgery to repair the damage to her body. It was a time of great suffering.

When my mother came home from the hospital, my nanny was let go. From Christmastime 1958, in the midst of the Cold War, there is a photograph of my parents at the hearth, near the tree, gloomy as ghosts. I used to carry the picture in my wallet. It shows Mom sitting in a chair, the Old Man behind her standing at attention, in a starched shirt and elegant cravat. Mom holds a fat smiling baby. She looks radiant, valiant, despite her arm in a cast. The three of us are together for the first time in six months, refugees from pain, having lived in the valley of death for so long.

It is an inspirational photograph, and equally deceptive because underlying the apparent joy was a current of despair. The Old Man's life had changed. Things were different. He had become a nursemaid to his wife, no longer a world famous film director. With her purple scars and shattered limbs, Mother's renowned beauty was a thing of the past, preserved only in photographs taken before the accident. And the baby, although unaware, carried the potential for tragedy.

The three of us were a rag tag bunch of walking wounded: a mother who nearly died from injuries that made her wish she had; the Old Man who compensated for feelings of extreme inferiority by browbeating me; and a baby, returned to a "family" after many months in the care of a surrogate, who had entered into life in a perpetual state of narcotic recovery. "Home" for the Austin's had been remade. It was altered so irreparably that my parents adapted to the change each in their own way, by becoming emotionally numb and isolated from the other.

A dark secret burdened the Old Man back then. He felt guilty for the car accident and for passing me off to a stranger. In the Christmas photograph, he stands to one side as though not belonging there, as though he had been plucked down amid the holiday trappings of two acquaintances. While the years wore on, he grew into an incurably bitter man defeated by what life had dealt him. Once, he admitted to me that, because of the accident, he had missed out on making his Masterpiece, missed out on the immortality attained only through fame, missed out on winning an Oscar for Best Director. Instead, he shamed himself by working for an inferior studio. For seven days a week he avoided his wife and child by making one flop after another until the critics based his notoriety on these instead of the pre-accident work. Worn down by bad reviews, he became a man who easily took offense at the most benign criticism of his technique. Yet, he continually reproached me for my personal style and enthusiasm.

When I was a teenager, as I arrived back home from a night at the cinema, the Old Man chastised my regard for François Truffaut's *The 400 Blows* and the French Wave. We argued for over an hour, shouting at one another, until I conceded his stubbornness and retreated to my bedroom. I could *relate*—as we said back then—to Antoine in *The 400 Blows*. Here was a character with whom I identified: in his teens, typecast as a troublemaker, misunderstood, a boy who did poorly in school and yet who quoted Balzac. I, too, felt set adrift by my parents. I, too, turned up my jacket collar against the bellows of the world. I, too, had read Balzac. It was my Holden Caulfield phase, and my father should have overlooked it.

I know now, at forty-six, the Old Man found my appreciation for other directors intolerable. D. Charles Austin, Sr., could not allow another giant to supplant his own conceit of greatness. By my simply mentioning Truffaut, he must have burned with jealousy. Perhaps he even went so far as to blame me for the collapse of his esteem. I don't know.

It was during those days that my mother kept to her room, by and large, for fear someone might set eyes on her once beautiful, deeply scarred face. My father would bring home business associates, expecting dinner, but she kept herself locked up in her room. Eventually, their social life was as bleak and empty as our house. Nothing happened at home. Nothing at all. How different was the mausoleum from our house back then? If I saw her at all during the day it was like bumping into a zombie from *Night of the Living Dead.* She was lifeless and pale, a female Lon Chaney, Jr., in *Phantom of the Opera.* We avoided one another for the most part, although I dearly loved my mother.

Only one day a week could I rely on the flicker of life to enter the house, a flicker that came from a movie projector. Every Sunday afternoon, the only half day that the Old Man spent away from the studio, he locked himself up in his private study to watch his old movies and to relive past glory. Without his knowledge or approval, I often sneaked into the closet and watched along with him. At times the Old Man laughed. On one occasion he wept. But more often than not he just sat in his Barcolounger like the marble likeness that raised me.

I pushed away from the crypt and teetered a little in the middle of the floor.

I stared at his image.

I should have been more attentive. Perhaps then I might have done something to stem their downward spiral of depression. Had I been a better son to them, they might still be alive today. I thought to myself, in scenes like this the camera closes in on a tear in the hero's eye. For all the tears I had shed over the past year, they failed me at this moment.

In defiance of posted warnings, I pulled out my Marlboros and lit one up while sitting on the bench that faced my parents' crypt. No one was present to complain. And sure as hell, the dead wouldn't. In a quick survey of their ages, I learned that my silent companions had lived in the days when smoking was socially acceptable behavior. Everyone in the movies smoked back then; even moviegoers were allowed to in the theater. Bette Davis had one going in most scenes. "Fasten your seatbelts. It's going be a bumpy night," she said in *All About Eve,* punctuating the air with her cigarette. Back then smoke was a prop. I crushed the Marlboro on the floor and grimaced at the fact that it had most likely been smoking that prematurely entombed most of the corpses here. The sign on the wall read No Smoking. Just to be safe, I picked up the butt and slipped it into my jeans pocket.

The air inside the mausoleum was too full of memory, and I left it for the comfort of the Caddy.

Pushing back the front seat as far as it would go and running the AC, I thumbed through the screenplay, reading casually, and I thought about the chances of getting it to screen. Smith may have written the most spectacular treatment in cinematic history, but he was doing everything possible to screw up the deal.

I shook my head. He was not worth the trouble. No one was, no matter how brilliant the screenplay.

In the very least, a good screenplay has to speak to you. It can be a crass vehicle contrived to resuscitate an aging star's career. It can exploit sex and violence. Its plot can be as thin as Calista Flockheart. But the story must *speak* to you. On the other hand, a great screenplay has all the elements of the human heart. It should draw tears out of your minds eye.

Path of Least Resistance fell into neither category. The treatment was ripping itself apart.

I read one scene after the next trying to understand Smith's theme, but the plot seemed to shift and be replaced by something else. The treatment committed the mortal sin of inconsistency. At the concept meeting, I had learned something of the plotline, but for a story about the end of the world, it needed thematic resonance in order to be great. What was the take-away message? Were there commercial endorsement potentials with the cute little aliens? Why would anyone pay to see such a movie?

By laying down ten to twelve bucks and entering a darkened multiplex, the moviegoer willingly suspended his disbelief for ninety minutes or so. Smith could write about yellow snakes slithering out the protagonist's ass, and the audience would love it as long as they could relate to the hero or anti-hero. Suspension of disbelief within the context of a likable character, that's what movie making is all about.

I tried to concentrate on the screenplay, and after a scene or two, I considered the likelihood that the character of Dr. Joe Dawson might be Smith's alter ego. Many writers wrote from personal experience. Although the six million screenplays submitted every year were not necessarily autobiographical, the premise and storylines were often material mined from life. By the looks of Smith, the episode in the psychiatric facility could have been based on personal experience.

Yet, the persona in the screenplay was nearly a generation younger than Smith. Dr. Joe Dawson was described as a scientist, a research microbiologist. Any similarity between the two ended there. Smith was no brainiac, no Einstein. The only trait that he shared with test tube jockeys was eccentricity. Smith was the quintessential nerd, up to his elbows in middle age.

Still, the treatment read closer to autobiography than fantasy.

The overlay of fiction on a factual landscape had an intriguing quality. I was relatively certain that XyberGen, the biotech company in the screenplay, actually existed. A few years ago *The Times* ran a story about their IPO. XyberGen stock had caught my interest in the days before cocaine consumed my disposable income. Several months later a local news show did a piece on a disgruntled XyberGen employee who advocated a moratorium on biological weapons research. Around the same time, PBS reported on the government's poorly supervised biological weapons stockpiles. The news hour included footage of a protest in eastern Oregon, outside the gates of a base where the weapons were stored. One of the protesters held a sign with the name "XyberGen" scrawled across a skull and cross bones. I wondered if Smith had this image in mind when he wrote the screenplay.

The more mundane aspects to *Path Of Least Resistance* were surely autobiographical. Much of the story seemed taken from common places and events: the Dawson house in La Jolla; Smith's grasp of middle class values; and, again, the biotech company. How could a homeless man like Smith know the intimate details of the American dream, describe comfortable houses and convey the good fortune of a professional career unless, in the past, he had owned a comfortable house, earned a graduate degree, and pulled down two or three hundred grand a year? Had Smith "had it all" and lost it? Was *Path of Least Resistance* his autobiography served over an icy rancor with an apocalyptic twist?

I lit a cigarette and cracked the window. I turned back to the beginning and read the opening:

*P*ATH OF *L*EAST *R*ESISTANCE *(working
title)*

*Black screen with white lettering, no
soundtrack yet; theh only sound is the
chirping of crickets. Dissolve to Exterior
Suburban Landscape at night. Credits
appear and dissolve. All lower-case
white letters. Soundtrack:* ~~Mosart's~~
Mozart's Requiem, *first movement.*

*PAN: City lights seen from high
evelation, through a line of trees, a
backdrop of stars. The constellations
hang like ornaments in the Monterey
pine and eucalyptus, and among these
are the visible stars of Ursa Major—the
Pointers and Mizar—dominating the
northern quadrant of Southern
California sky. The Pacific Ocean surf
shimers with opalescen̶tce in the
distance.*

*DIFFERENT ANGLE: On this autumn
night the Big Dipper shines upon a
tranquil upper middle-class
neighborehood in La Jolla, California.*

*LONG SHOT to SLOW ZOOM: The
modest, middle-class home of Dr. and
Mrs. Joe Dawson.*

PAN: The house, from the garden.
*Only a few windows in the house are
illuminated.*

*HAND-HELD CAM: Move toward the
house, to one of the lighted windows.
The crickets chirping suddenly ceases,
as though someone or something has
intruded here.*

*STABILIZEd SHOT: <u>through the
window to interior</u>. A man is seen half-
asleep in a chair, watching television.*

The character Joe Dawson works for a biotech company
on contract with the Department of Defense. His work in
biotechnology leads to the discovery of what Smith refers
to as "the common Phage," a virion genetically
manipulated into a lethal pathogen. Predictably in the
screenplay, Pandora's box is spilled and the virus kills
billions of people. Smith's premise about the end of the
world was as believable as little green space aliens and Joe
Dawson's mind reading. The old dude had watched far too
many episodes of *Mystery Science Theater 3000*. None of
the nonsense we see in movies happens in real life. He
should have known better than to try and sell such
hackneyed rubbish.

In *Path of Least Resistance,* Smith failed to define
where fact ended and fiction began, but more importantly, I
had to ask what in hell my father was doing in it.

Smith was playing a perverted game of manipulation
with his holier-than-thou attitude and false sincerity. Who
in hell did he think he was, dragging my father's memory
through the mud, turning Charles Duncan, Sr., into a movie
character? And to what purpose, other than to humiliate
me? Smith had broken into the bungalow, or so he claimed,
because he had confused me with the Old Man. What a
load of bull! There wasn't a soul alive who didn't know
about the suicide of the world famous director and his

disabled wife. Smith knew what he was doing, showing up on the night I was about to blow my brains out. Smith's ulterior motive was either to ridicule my father or to humiliate me. And I wasn't about to let Smith smear my good name.

As I read more carefully, it seemed to me that the screenplay illuminated the charade that was my life. It aired my family's dirty laundry for the world to ridicule. Was this Smith's intention, to expose me as a lying degenerate? No worries there. Every player in Hollywood knew me for what I was, a shiftless loser. Perhaps Smith had another purpose, to sully my father's good name?

I decided that it was time to learn more about Smith's ulterior motives. It was time I turned the tables by finding out who he really was, who his people were, where he came from. Armed with his personal information, I could expose the skeletons in the Smith family closet as he surely intended to expose mine.

I stubbed out the Marlboro.

Across the cemetery lawn toward a low windowless building, a funeral service was taking place. The hearse pulled away after delivering its cargo to the gravesite. A gathering of mourners wore somber shades of gray and black, while a member of their party recorded the proceedings on a videocam.

"You go, guy," I said, chuckling to myself.

I had never before seen anyone take videos of a funeral. Who would want to relive such an occasion? The American way of death in Los Angeles was macabre enough with its silk-lined caskets and Este Lauder corpses without resorting to videotape.

I revved up the Caddy and drove toward the exit. Leave the dead to bury the dead. A bottle of single-malt waited for me at home.

Chapter 6

I woke up at five o'clock in the afternoon, the next day. The diffused sunlight glanced off the puddle at the bottom of the pool, and I rose from bed for a beer. Passing by the front hallway, I noticed another manila envelope shoved into the mail slot. I grumbled an obscenity as I retrieved it.

"He's got to learn to use a phone. Or stamps."

Along with Smith's latest installment was a newspaper clipping stapled to the first page. The newsprint had a faded yellow patina, and the brittle edge looked burned. In the desolate coolness of the hallway, I leaned against the stucco wall and read the clipping:

```
Tuesday May 8 10:17 AM ET

  Possible Killer Virus May Strengthen
          International Treaty
            By John Boland

San Diego (Reuters) - California
scientists announced on Monday that
they had created a killer virus from
the same germ that causes the common
cold. At a news conference these same
scientists called upon the
international community to put an end
to biological weapons research.

"At the very least, the BWC (Biological
Weapons Convention) must be given
```

greater authority to prevent such
future discoveries from falling into
the wrong hands," Dr. Saloni Gupta
said, a member of the research team.

Gupta and scientists at XyberGen, a San
Diego biotech company, applied
recombinant DNA techniques that could
be easily modified to biological
warfare. In their research of a cure
for the rhinovirus, the common cold,
XyberGen scientists genetically
modified a virion or single virus
particle that proved fatal when exposed
to laboratory animals.

Gupta, who assisted a U.N. team to
investigate biowarfare agents in Iraq
after the Gulf War, called for an
immediate update of the 1972 Biological
Weapons Convention.

"This is not a call to stop valid
scientific study around the world or
cut off legitimately sponsored
research, especially if conducted under
the code of conduct. What we want is to
make sure nobody, no rogue nation or
terrorist organization, can abuse the
results," she told Reuters.

"Today the convention forbids the
development of biological weapons,"
Gupta said. "But the international
agreement has no teeth. There is
absolutely no way of policing it. And
if you think a country like North Korea
is cheating you can't do anything about
it."

Gupta is the Executive Director of
Molecular Science Research at the San
Diego headquarters of XyberGen

Biologics, Inc., which created the virus.

A scientific paper on the genetically modified rhinovirus is scheduled to appear in Nature magazine next Wednesday. Although the common cold is no more than an inconvenience to healthy individuals, tens of thousands of elderly and asthmatics die each year of the illness. A cure for the common cold, Gupta pointed out, was the motivation behind the research. However, the modified XyberGen rhinovirus, XER-64, was shown to kill mice by wiping out part of their immune system.

A total of 162 countries have endorsed the BCW pact, which dates back to the Cold War. BCW bans the development, manufacture and stockpiling of bacteriological and toxin weapons. Negotiations to reinforce the convention have been unsuccessful in the past few years. Gupta expressed hope that member states would consent to allow a U.N.-backed body to monitor and halt dangerous biological research.

Gupta and scientists at XyberGen said the Defense Department was aware of their research before they submitted it for notification next Wednesday in Nature and for a more formal publication in the coming month in the U.S. Journal of Virology. Before publication they wanted the world as well as the scientific community to be made aware of the nature of this expertise and its implications for public safety.

"Over the years scientists have made surprising discoveries, almost by pure chance--penicillin is a good example," said Ralston Hightower, XyberGen's Chief Executive Officer.

"In this case, we found that certain changes to a rhinovirus can render it lethal and impossible to immunize against. The best defense against any abuse of this kind of advanced technique is to issue a global warning," he added.

The team created the virus by inserting a gene very similar to that which produces smallpox into a rhinovirus and resulting in the genetically modified "super virus" XER-64. Instead of producing antibodies to attack the invading virus, all experimental mice infected with XER-64 were stripped of part of their immune system and died within forty-eight hours.

Hightower acknowledged the danger of such biological research, but also hoped that the XyberGen technology would help researchers elsewhere design better, more effective vaccines against influenza and other potentially harmful infections.

The contents of the article had a greater effect than two shots of espresso.

Was this Smith's not-so-subtle way of authenticating the screenplay plot? I made a note to myself to speak with him about changing the name of the biotech company. Neglecting to protect principals from litigation and defamation might cost me an option with Rainy Day.

I returned a little shakily to the kitchen and decided to steer clear of the booze. I plugged in the Mr. Coffee to brew a strong pot. While I waited for the coffee maker, I sat on a stool to read Smith's latest installment.

The new scenes were disjointed and, once again, disappointing. A wholly new character was introduced, someone referred to as the Delivery Boy. This shadowy figure lurked behind the front action and threatened the protagonist, Dr. Joe Dawson, along with the Mr. Austin character. Introducing a new character so late in the story was unacceptable. I grabbed a pen and scribbled my objections across the page, tearing the paper in the process.

I read a revision of the scene in which Joe Dawson visits the world famous movie director to persuade him to make a movie. The action was so familiar that it raised the hair on the back of my neck. In the scene, Dr. Dawson tells Mr. Austin, "The movie will be a warning to stop biological warfare research." The dialogue was taken verbatim from my conversations the other night with Smith.

And then there was a transitioning scene where the powerful movie produce, Mr. Big, meets with Mr. Austin. The producer warns him "unless you get me finished product, I'm gonna do whatever it takes to get it, understand?" They argue. "When I tell you to finish the thing," the producer says, "you get it done or else."

"What in hell's that mean, *get it done or else?*" I asked myself. "Who does Smith think he's messing with?"

It was time to take action. Things were spinning too fast, out of control.

The will to act has never come easily to me. I have spent my life avoiding responsibility and decision-making. But Smith had thrown down the gauntlet, whatever a gauntlet was. Up until then I had invested most of my time pursuing an option with Rainy Day. *Path of Least Resistance* was all I had at the moment, and Smith was doing everything he could to screw up the deal. He was no different than LaGassa or the rest of the jokers who passed through my life. They came in, messed up, and left me to do the dirty work. It was high time I took control of the situation.

The screenplay contained many elements taken from real life, and I knew that Rainy Day Films would redline the branded names to avoid lawsuits. There were more lawyers working in Hollywood than worked for the federal government. My job that afternoon was to remove potential stumbling blocks on the way to scoring an option, in spite of Bob Smith. In the dining room I spread the screenplay on the table and immediately set out highlighting references to XyberGen and Mr. Austin. On a legal pad I wrote down a series of suggestions about name changes.

To verify my suspicions, I picked up the telephone. First, I checked out the biotech company. I called information and got the general number for XyberGen of La Jolla. I wrote down the number in the margins of the legal pad. Next, I checked the address of the Dawson house in La Jolla, to confirm it. The telephone operator refused to give a phone number associated with the address alone. "You'll have to give me a name, sir," the operator said. I disconnected and called information again, but this time I asked for the number of Chloe Dawson of La Jolla, California, and gave the name of the street, Boxhead Drive. There was no Chloe Dawson living at that address. "What about Frank Dawson?" I asked. "Sorry, sir. Not listed." "Well, they probably moved. Any forwarding numbers?" I asked. No.

I called the San Diego Property Tax Assessor's Office and requested information on the property. I repeated the Dawson address, and the bureaucrat said that the family living there was not named Dawson but Smith.

"We got Smith's coming out the woodwork," I muttered to myself.

The county bureaucrat said that the family had purchased the house late last year. I hung up and called information. Only this time, I asked for the telephone number of the Smith's on Boxwood Drive. I was connected automatically. A woman answered.

I said, "Hello, you don't know me, but I'm a friend of Joe Dawson's."

"Yes?" the woman said uncertainly.

"I was wondering if you could help me out. I've lost their number and I'm here in town today. Wanted to give them a call."

"Well, they don't live here anymore."

Bingo.

"I know. They've moved, but if you have their number, I would really appreciate it."

I looked at my reflection in the dining room mirror and made a face at the audacity.

"Okay, I think I put it here somewhere. Hold the phone." The woman put down the phone to look for the number. She returned. "Yes, it's an out of town number. In Las Vegas, I think."

I wrote the number down.

"Thank you, Mrs. Smith. Oh, by the way, you wouldn't be related to Bob Smith, would you?"

"No," she said. "There are no Robert's in our family."

I disconnected and called the number in Vegas and got an answering machine. It was a woman's voice.

"You've reached the Dawson household. Neither Frank nor I can come to the phone right now but leave your name, time of day you called, and we'll get back to you as soon as we can."

I did not leave a message.

I flipped to the first scene in the screenplay, searching for details. The movie started out so peacefully, so fatally bourgeois in the home of Joe and Chloe Dawson. Their son Frank goes to bed while Dr. Dawson makes sure the front door is locked. As Joe Dawson feels his way through the darkened house, it becomes obvious that someone or some*thing* is trying to break in. Domestic tranquility turned to nightmare.

So, the Dawson's were a real family. Persons by the name of Frank and Chloe actually existed, and they used to live on Boxwood Drive in La Jolla but now lived in Vegas. The message on the answering machine had made no reference to Joe Dawson, just to Chloe and Frank.

"What's that tell you?" I asked myself.

Joe Dawson could be dead. Or the Dawson's might be separated, as was the case in the screenplay. Joe Dawson could be living elsewhere. From the sound of it, he could be living on the moon. The character was a loony-tune who assumed more identities than Shirley Maclaine. Or maybe there really *was* a Dr. Joe Dawson who, out of the crucible of stress and from his experience in handling a deadly virus, had gone mad and assumed the identity of Bob Smith. But did this mean the screenplay was based on actual events?

No, I thought. *That's impossible.*

The most glaring inconsistency, the fly in the ointment, was Smith's age. He was too old for the Joe Dawson character in the screenplay.

What was it that Smith told me, that he was thirty-seven? He looked sixty-five going on Paleolithic. With a young son and wife, maybe Dawson was thirty-seven years old, but not Smith. I considered for the moment, perhaps the events in the screenplay had taken place ten years ago. From this perspective, Chloe could have been in her mid-thirties when the events occurred. Estimating her age now at forty-five, this reduced the difference between Chloe and Dawson to fifteen, maybe twenty years.

But the screenplay took place in the present, and it named contemporary companies. The timeframe was *now*, not a decade ago or even five years ago.

"The age difference between Smith and Chloe doesn't add up," I said, jotting down my conjecture on the legal pad.

Frank, the son, presented an even more flagrant discrepancy. The answering machine had referred to both Chloe and Frank living in the household together. In the screenplay, Frank was depicted as a seventeen-year-old boy. Adding ten years would have made him twenty-seven.

"No one lives with their mom at that age."

In the screenplay, aliens visit Joe Dawson and tell him that he is the only person alive who can save the world. And then, without explanation, the aliens enchant the Dawson character with the ability to foretell the future and heal the sick.

"Nonsense."

Smith was playing a mind game. He wanted me to think that he was Joe Dawson. He had hinted around the fact that he was the same age as the biotechnologist. What had he said, that the character was more like him, not Harrison Ford? And then he'd made some reference to seeing the "face of doom," whatever the hell that was supposed to mean. *Complete nonsense.*

But the question remained: Why would Smith write a story about a real biotech company and real people?

I couldn't figure out his angle.

I wondered if the newspaper article about XyberGen had inspired Smith. Was this the reason he had delivered it to my house, so that I might draw my own conclusions? Most cinematic projects had launching points of inspiration taken from events in life, from history, or from the labyrinth of human psychology. But Smith was selling pure humbuggery. He was a ranting lunatic who had mistaken fiction for the truth.

The clean pharmaceutical grinding glasses on the coffee table distracted me momentarily. I was suffering through another dry spell with Xavier on "vacation." I hoped the man was on a trip to Columbia. I hoped Medellín.

During coke droughts, my nervous energy hit the red zone. I had to do something, get mobile, go for a drive, or I would go nuts.

I decided to drive to Vegas and look up Chloe Dawson. In Vegas I would inquire about her husband and ask if she knew Bob Smith. I thought about the kid in the cemetery videotaping the funeral, and I decided to bring my camcorder. Get some pictures of the family and confront Smith with images of Chloe and Frank Dawson. It was a slick plan. Showing video of the Dawson's should elicit a reaction from Smith. By confronting him with the truth, I would force him to answer questions about who the Dawson's were and what his connection to them was. If I rattled his cage a little, maybe I would secure another scene or two.

And then there was the plentiful promise of Las Vegas cocaine to consider. It was the most persuasive impetus for my going there. I could probably score a gram in the honor bar at the hotel.

I checked the time on the malfunctioning clock above my fake fireplace. Seven-thirty or thereabouts. I had time to shower, change my clothes and grab a bite to eat before driving across the desert.

Ω Ω Ω

I drove the El Dorado east on U.S. 15. It was the middle of the night. I had no coke and no prospects. I was running on empty through flat, dead country.

I left Echo Park after the eleven o'clock news and, fighting freeway traffic all the way to the San Gabriel's, I arrived at the town of Arden near the Vegas city limits just before three in the morning. Somewhere west of Arden, I ate breakfast at a freeway Denny's, two eggs over easy with a side of bacon. Outside the restaurant in a public phone booth, I tore a page out of the white pages that listed three C. Dawson's, two with addresses. While sitting in the Caddy and listening to the radio, I matched the telephone numbers.

I drove through downtown Las Vegas and headed for the address listed in the phone book, hoping that the "C" was not a Chuck or Cathy, but Chloe. Using a gas station map, I found her address on LuLu Avenue among a blight of pastel tract houses lined up like birthday cakes. It was a Latino neighborhood, working class people within a population of one and a half million.

A former Mafia stronghold, the New Vegas was controlled by multinational corporations that had built colossal theme park casinos, fantasy-architecture extravaganzas. A gaming tourist could stay in miniaturized versions of New York City or Paris or Treasure Island. There was even an artificial Venice with gondolas in canals like swimming pools, gliding shoppers through a mall. Money and sex ruled the roost in Vegas, but the seat of power had shifted long ago from Romantic thugs like Meyer Lansky and "Bugsy" Siegel, the founding father of Sin City. Like everything else in this country, the power shifted to the sanitized boardrooms of oil, telecommunications, and entertainment empires. Big Business owned and operated the town.

It was a big town with a small town attitude. Redneck and proud of it. During the boom years, the locals struggled to come to terms with "foreigners" who spoke Spanish and Tagalog, the folks who mowed their lawns and did their dirty work. High real estate prices confined the resort housekeeping staff and hotel dishwashers to the northwest neighborhoods, away from the high-rises and "respectable" tracts. It was not where I expected to find the divorced wife of a biotech engineer, even if she were a figment of Bob Smith's imagination.

I was parking the Caddy across the street from the house on LuLu Avenue just as a woman in a nurse's uniform stepped onto the porch. As she locked her front door, I stared at her white uniform.

The woman in the screenplay was a nurse. I had struck pay dirt.

I stepped out of the El Dorado and called to her.

"Chloe? Chloe Dawson?"

Startled by my approach, the woman said nothing as she hurried to a blue Ford Taurus in the driveway. She got in and locked the doors, started the motor.

I walked up to the driver's side.

She mouthed the words "Go away."

"I just want to speak to you, Mrs. Dawson. That's all. Ask a few questions."

She put the car in reverse and nearly ran over my foot.

I went to my car for the camcorder and got a shot of the Taurus as she turned the corner. I gave chase but lost her in morning commute traffic near Highway 95. There I pulled to the side of the road to figure out my next move. In the distance I saw the fantasy hotels, a Roman palace and a pyramidal incongruence wavering in the heat, adult amusement parks on anabolic steroids.

As a nurse, Chloe Dawson might have worked at any number of doctor's offices or hospitals in Vegas. Locating her would be time-consuming. I could camp outside her house, but such tactics bordered on the criminal. If the Nevada state cops picked me up for loitering or stalking, all they had to do was run a urinalysis and I'd be in lock up for ninety days. Still, an option with Rainy Day was at stake, so I decided to push my luck.

There were several medical centers in town, two of them large, the third belonging to a managed care organization called Valley Health. I had no luck there. I got lucky at the University Medical Center on Charleston Avenue. I rang up the hospital's general number on my cell and was connected to Chloe Dawson in the Intensive Care Unit.

"Hello?"

"Yes, Mrs. Dawson, my name is DC Austin. I'm a film maker…"

The line went dead.

That evening when Chloe Dawson returned home from work, I was waiting for her. I had parked the Caddy down the block while I hid in the shrubbery at the side of the house, camcorder in hand. This spy gig really excited me. I was trembling, and it probably had more to do with the thrill of the chase than the ambient temperature. Thermometers broke one hundred that day.

As she drove up and opened the automatic garage door, I slipped in behind the car before the door closed. An overhead light switched on. I hoped it was bright enough to put the shot in the camera.

When she got out of the car and saw me inside the garage taking video pictures, Chloe Dawson screamed. She frantically searched for something in her purse.

"No no no," I said, shutting the camera down and raising my hands in the air. "All I want to do is ask some questions. That's all."

She pulled out a can of pepper spray and aimed it.

"Get out!"

I cringed. "You're Mrs. Dawson, right? Chloe Dawson?"

She depressed the nozzle but the sprayer malfunctioned. Nothing came out.

Straightening my posture, I asked, "You got a kid named Frank?"

"None of your business," she said, fiddling with the nozzle. Her fingers were bloodless like polished bone. "I want you out of my house right now."

"A friend a mine," I said calmly. "A friend of mine named Bob Smith, he wrote a screenplay, and you're in it. So is Frank. I just wanna talk to you about it."

"Get out. Now!"

I stood my ground. I considered shooting her again. I raised the camera, snapped it on, and watched her reaction through the viewer.

"What the fuck are you doing!" she screamed.

"I just want to ask a couple questions. That's all. Like, how's your son? How's he holding up after the alien invasion, you know?"

"Wha...what are you talking about?"

"In the screenplay. It's kind of complicated, but your husband, well, didn't he tell you about the aliens?"

She moved to the left, and I followed her with the camcorder. Chloe had her hand at her mouth. She looked near tears.

I was getting good shots.

"Talk to me, Chloe."

"How do you know my name?"

"Like I said, the screenplay. Tell me, you know a guy named Smith? Bob Smith?"

It was as though I held the most powerful weapon in the world. She shrank beneath the lens, became something forsaken folding on itself, tumbling hysterically to the garage floor, weeping, victimized.

The scene was not meeting my expectations. I had expected her to yell at me, put up a fight. I had not figured her to collapse submissively in a pathetic heap.

I shut the camera off.

"Look, Mrs. Dawson, I didn't come here to harass you. Sorry I broke into your garage, but look, maybe it'd be better if I talked to your husband, to Doc Dawson. He here?"

Chloe struggled to stand. She leaned against the wall and pushed the button that opened the garage door. The mechanism rumbled like an old dishwasher motor.

"Get out."

Again, she aimed the pepper spray.

"Okay okay."

This ain't worth it, I thought, and I backed out of the opened garage.

Just then Frank Dawson walked up the front steps carrying a shoulder bag. He was a typical teenager in faded blue jeans and a branded sweatshirt. Nike was written all over him. He crouched to look inside the garage and saw his mother and me.

"What's up with this?" he asked.

"This man broke into our house," Chloe said.

Frank, a good sized boy, bigger and in better shape than I, put down the book bag and moved aggressively toward me.

"Hey, look, Frank..."

"How you know my name?"

"That's your name, ain't it?" I said, keeping my distance. "Where's your dad, Frank?"

I decided to take a stab at the idea that had been gnawing at my brains for the past few days.

"Your pop a scientist or something?"

Frank looked to his mother.

"Honey, just come inside. We'll call the police once you get inside."

"No, call 'em now. If I go inside, he'll run."

The three of us stared at one another in an ultimate Mexican standoff. I thought about lifting the camcorder, but what was left of my conscience prevailed upon me.

Finally, I asked, "Frank, you ever seen any aliens?"

Frank had a bewildered look mixed with a measure of pissed off.

"Mrs. Dawson," I said loudly, "at your neighbor's funeral, at Norm's funeral, did your husband cry?"

"How does he know dad?" Frank asked, moving protectively beside his mother.

Chloe dropped the pepper spray. It clinked on the concrete and rolled beneath the Taurus, her hand at her mouth. At that moment I believed that she was wondering how this complete stranger knew the intimate details of their lives. You could tell from her expression, she questioned if Joe Dawson had possibly sent me to her.

"Did his tears turn into daisies or something?"

I raised the camcorder and got a shot of the two of them inside the garage.

"Mom?" Frank said.

I focused the camera on Chloe. The angle of the setting sun caught her hair just so. Ermine with highlights. She shoulda been in pictures. She had a noble quality, the way she carried herself. By upsetting her, by exposing her vulnerability, I questioned my motive for driving to Vegas in the first place. I had no right to do that.

Frank entered the viewfinder with clenched fists.

The camera weighed heavily in my hand, and I shut it off. Perhaps it would be better for all concerned if I just left them alone.

"I'll give you two seconds to leave before I pound you," the boy said.

"Okay okay." I raised an arm in surrender. "I'm out of here."

The kid rushed to block my escape.

Chloe shouted, "Let him go, Frank. Just let him go."

I turned halfway down the driveway and faced them one last time.

"A man named Smith broke into my house and asked me to sell his screenplay, *Path of Least Resistance*. The characters in it are named Chloe, Frank and Joe Dawson. Can you explain that?"

"Go call the police," Chloe told her son as she pushed the button to close the garage door.

I lifted the camcorder and got a shot of her knees and the back of Frank's legs before the door shut. I jogged down the block to the El Dorado and threw the camcorder on the passenger seat.

"That was interesting," I said, as I drove recklessly toward the Interstate. I still had a dry nose, but the camcorder was full.

Chapter 7

The day after my Vegas trip to see Chloe and Frank Dawson, I was depressed. I sat at home pondering the Sig Sauer on the coffee table while I listed my options on a yellow legal pad. It became more or less my Last Will & Testament. Depression is something I have lived with my entire life like a black mongrel dog that occasionally shows up to take a bite out of my ass.

The phone rang in the middle of my self-loathing. Who should call but my former partner, Curtis LaGassa.

"D, that you?"

I got up to adjust the living room clock and cursed my luck.

"Well, if it isn't Curtis."

He expected me to initiate the conversation, maybe take up from where we had left off. When I did neither, you could hear the sweat in his voice.

"You there, man?"

"Yeah, I'm here."

"Hey, look, D...I need your help."

I narrowed my eyes. I have studied how Clint Eastwood strikes a pose of the movie-star tough guy, and this was how I saw myself.

"Why call me?" I said.

"Listen, I...I'm in a jam."

I was thinking the dialogue fit my erasable mood.

"How's that any a my concern?" I said, again in my best Dirty Harry.

"They put a contract out on me, okay. Ten friggin' large."

I smiled.

"Finally scored a contract. All by yourself." I laughed.

"I'm sah-serious."

"And so am I, Curtis. But you know what?" I worked my jaw muscles. "I don't give a shit."

"Look…"

"You fucked me. Nobody fucks me."

"They come to, to my house, okay." His tone moved beyond pleading, into the realm of desperation. "They shot my dog."

I let the news sink in. I felt nothing. I never liked his damn dog.

"Sounds like you stepped in it big time."

"Hey, dude, I got pinched to shoot a triple X, okay? In San Fernando."

"Not interested."

"Would you listen? They want money shots, the whole nine yards. *Driving Miss Daisy Mae.*" LaGassa laughed nervously. "Porno in the limo. They paid up front, couple twenty grand. As far as I can tell, some out-of-towners hold the note. Heavies mainly, probably Russian. But ya…you know, the talent turned out to like *guys*, ferchrisakes. Couldn't get hard. You coulda pumped him full of Viagra, nothing. Like a sock full of Jell-O. Na…now they want a new stud, and they want me to front the capital. I'm tapped out, D. I ain't got it."

"What'd you spend the advance on, Curtis? Booze? Chicks?"

"Don't get sah-self-righteous, okay."

"Got something you wanna say to me?"

Curtis paused. "I need your help."

"Don't think so."

"Lemme crash at your place. Just be, be a couple a days, I swear."

"Last time we talked, Curtis, you called me a loser. Said I had shit for brains. Now you call up and beg for asylum."

"Please."

"I hope they whack your ass."

I slammed down the receiver, and the phone rang the final round.

LaGassa had pissed me off just enough to dispel any notion of doing away with myself. Instead, I called a courier service to have Smith's latest scenes delivered to Gleason at Rainy Day. I telephoned Pig Boy to alert him to its arrival, but he refused my call.

Ω   Ω   Ω

Money is at the heart of the movie business, and movie producers take their investment personally. If something goes wrong on the set or if an actor threatens to renege or the screenwriter goes on strike, the producer raises a stink. It is not all they raise. Some producers are capable of murder. If you don't believe me, ask Phil Spector.

Pig Boy set up another meeting with the Development Committee at Rainy Day. They had read Bob Smith's latest installment with confusion and disappointment. Pig Boy called to vent his spleen. He said *Path of Least Resistance* was maddeningly incomplete like a serialized Victorian novel.

"Listen," he said, "we got the heroine tied to the railroad tracks and the hero's nowhere in sight. And what's up with the change in names. Who's this Smith character?"

Having forgotten the parts I had read, I had no idea what he was talking about. At the meeting, I figured they would hoist me by my own petard.

Within the week I found myself in the same chair, in the same Rainy Day executive conference room, surrounded by the same players in the movie industry. Of course, Bob Smith, despite my repeated calls to his downtown flophouse, failed to show. Once again I arrived inappropriately dressed in a polo shirt, khaki shorts, and sandals. Everyone else wore two-piece business suits, variations of black.

Gleason opened the proceedings.

"Gentlemen, my assistant here will provide a reading of what we've got so far. But before we continue, I have to caution you, the treatment is unfinished."

Sty Raines' face reddened as he sucked his skull down into his chest. Years ago, on a television nature show, I saw a penguin do exactly the same thing. I figured that it must be an aggressive posture in humans as well.

"Max, Max, Max." Sty Raines shook his head. "What gives with this guy?"

"We can work with what we have, chief," Gleason said.

The others in the room protested. Sty Raines raised his hand in a royal manner to shut everyone up.

"How much we got?"

"Well over half. Let's begin. We all have copies?" Gleason said, floating a hopeful smile.

Sty Raines folded his claw-like hands. His flaccid elbows smudged against the mahogany table as he rested his head. His gaze shifted to Gleason's assistant.

Darnel Preece cleared his throat.

"There's a radical scene shift at this point. Do I need to summarize where we are?"

Sty Raines shook his head. When his gaze fell on me, he glowered.

"What you have before you is a virtual rewrite of the treatment. I've provided a paragraph synopsis. In these new scenes, our main character, Joe Dawson, has been mugged and he takes on a new identity. He fancies himself a street prophet named Bob Smith." Darnel Preece turned to Gleason and asked, "Would this be a bad time to bring up the rabbit?"

"Rabbit?" the producer said.

Sty Raines and I did a double take. This was news to me, too. When I read the screenplay, I had noted the change of names from Dawson to Smith, but I remembered nothing about *rabbits*. Once again, I failed to do my homework.

M. Chandler Tate was the first to speak up. "What in hell's this all about?"

"It's explained in the synopsis, sir," Preece said.

"Do me a favor," Tate said, shifting his weight in the chair. "Do me a favor. Summarize the damn thing."

"Would you call this the beat or an inciting incident?" Audrey Whistler-Cox asked.

I knew that the beat was a critical moment in the structure of a story when conflict caused a change, and I also knew that an inciting incident launched the plot into even wider conflict. She was splitting hairs.

"It's more of a plot point, I think," Preece said. "Or the arc of character development. An emotional transformation, yes, but frankly, I'm not sure how the rabbit fits into this."

Whatever. Smith's lamebrain concept did not float my boat. What role could a demented mystic play in a screenplay about a scientist who was visited by space aliens? And where in hell did this rabbit come from? It was nonsense. I knew Smith to be capable of the subtle arts of passive-aggression, but this was outright subterfuge. Changing the name of the main character would give Sty Raines good cause to shitcan the project. My chances for landing an option were becoming remote at best.

Preece took great lengths to explain how street hoodlums attack Dr. Joe Dawson, troubled family man, former mental patient, and send him to the hospital with global amnesia. Upon release, he reinvents himself as a street prophet and faith healer named Bob Smith. His head injuries are so severe that he creates an imaginary friend, a six-foot tall white rabbit. Members of the Development Committee laughed out loud at this, and one of the lawyers said something about copyright infringement of the old Jimmy Stewart movie, *Harvey*.

I marshaled the will to maintain my game face.

"Although it's not exactly spelled out in the screenplay, we can show it through flashback," Preece said. "A couple of scenes of Joe Dawson doing biological weapons research at XyberGen. He has in earlier scenes confessed to his wife Chloe that he was exposed to the virus. In a way, this explains his ability to read the future. We can flashback in that scene. Do a voice-over. He tells her that he's worried the exposure might have something to do with hearing voices, seeing things that aren't there."

"Like the rabbit?" Tate asked, using a sarcastic tone.

"Yes. And now he's aging rapidly. But in the new version, it has nothing to do with aliens."

Sty Raines raised his hands in protest. "We cannot cut the aliens."

At that point in the proceedings, I wanted to go home and blow my brains out. Any hope for an option was dashed. The Black Dog of suicide sat at my feet, flossing his canines.

"No sweat, chief," Gleason said. "They're in."

"If it's all the same to you people," Sty Raines said with crass sarcasm, "our partners in Nippon like it. So, we keep the damn aliens. Done deal."

Gleason nodded at Preece who carried on.

"After Joe leaves the psychiatric facility…do all of you remember that scene? That's when his marriage ends and his wife files for legal separation? Good. We're on the same page then. After spending his life savings to warn the world of the coming plague, people reject him for a lunatic. We watch as Joe Dawson loses his memory after a mugging on the street. After that he lives in a homeless shelter. Lets himself go. Grows long hair and stops shaving. We can do a densely constructed flash-forward to set the stage. Morph a rapid aging thing.

"Eventually, after living on the street for some time, Joe Dawson assumes a new identity, that of Bob Smith. And he spends his time on street corners prophesying. This is where he imagines a six-foot rabbit, his friend. They talk about the end of the world."

"This makes no sense at all. Halfway through the movie the name of the hero changes? Then we get rabbits. This is nuts," Tate said.

"Isn't Bob Smith the name of the writer?" Audrey Whistler-Cox asked, looking to Gleason for an answer.

"Never mind that," Sty Raines said, coughing into his hands. "Never mind. Just tell us what happens."

"Okay. Joe Dawson is now known as Bob Smith. Should I call him Bob? Would that help?"

They all agreed.

"Joe Dawson, now Bob Smith, ends up living in a homeless shelter. He suffers from a mysterious illness. Exposure to the virus, referred to in the text as the Phage. Now understand, exposure to the Phage has aged him prematurely. Do we want to change it so the aliens make him grow old faster?"

Preece directed the question to Sty Raines.

"You mean to tell me," Audrey Whistler-Cox said. "Do you mean to tell me, not only has his name changed but his appearance changes? How can we expect people to know who in hell he is?" She resembled Frankenstein's monster with the enormous shoulder pads of her suit jacket.

Preece nodded. "We can get Industrial Light to do the morph, if you like. But, yes, these are the changes in the scenes we received this week."

"I'm having a hard time with it. If the Phage or plague are one in the same," Audrey Whistler-Cox continued, "how is it that Joe Dawson doesn't die outright?"

Preece shrugged as he flipped through a few pages. "It's explained in the text. He's exposed to a radiated version of the virus. It didn't kill him, but I'm not clear on why not."

One of the lawyers raised his hand to stop Preece from speaking. He said, "Do the aliens shoot some kind of x-ray that ages him? I just don't get this."

Preece looked desperate. "Our latest version is a rewrite, sir. Bob Smith..."

"Smith-the-writer or the new character?" Miz Landau said.

"Christ, this is giving me a headache," one of the attorneys said.

"Smith, the writer," Preece said, "has changed some things, and we're trying to adjust our storyboard to these alterations in plot and character. In the current version, Smith the writer explains that Joe Dawson's exposure to the microbe has changed him at a cellular level and given him the ability to see the future. Not aliens."

"Nope, not gonna happen." Sty Raines shook his head. "That is not gonna happen. We keep the aliens. Done deal. Continue."

Preece resembled the proverbial deer in the headlights.

"People on the street call Bob Smith the Soothsayer. He spends his time preaching about the end of the world on street corners all over L.A. and in Las Vegas. He warns everybody of the dangers of a coming plague. Remember, now that he has special powers...of course, we can show that the aliens have bestowed this power. But for our purposes today, we need to know, not only can he read the future, but also this new character can read people's minds and is a faith healer. He knows who's going to die and when."

"We established that earlier, in the garden scene," Audrey Whistler-Cox stated. "When Joe Dawson knows his buddy Norm is gonna have a heart attack, right?"

"Yes, that's correct. So, now the audience knows Bob Smith can predict the future and heal the sick. There's a series of voice-overs, a narrative style with music. More Mozart than Andrew Lloyd Weber. Bob is shown curing the sick. I've put a Post-It on the scene where Bob lays on hands. He has disciples who believe he's some kind of messiah."

"This is like the Jesus thing," one of the lawyers said.

Preece gave an enthusiastic nod.

"Most of these scenes take place in Las Vegas. Our focus group indicated a high acceptance of Vegas as a backdrop. Over thirty-five million people visit there each year. Very strong demographics on place."

"How do we work the faith healing thing?" the other lawyer asked. "Those same demographics indicate we'd pull eighteen percent from fundamentalist Christians. This could capsize that margin."

Sty Raines pressed his eyes shut and shook his head. "I will discuss none of this until I hear the rest of the fucking story. Please."

Nervously, Preece continued: "Bob gathers a following. He calls for a mass demonstration of anti-war protesters from all over California to make a pilgrimage to Las Vegas. People, he says, should rise up in protest against biological warfare. 'They'll kill us all,' he warns. He walks the streets preaching about the end of the world. He becomes something of a tourist attraction." The young man glanced over to see M. Chandler Tate's response. "By then, the national media are interested in him. He's notorious, but because he's grown a beard and changed his looks, no one from his former life recognizes him as Dr. Joe Dawson, the microbiologist. As far as they're concerned, he's Bob Smith, crazy street prophet, the man who preaches a vision of apocalypse."

"This is very money," Audrey Whistler-Cox said.

"What about the rabbit?" one of the lawyers asked.

"How is it he heals people? I don't get it," Tate said. "And how in hell does it relate to the plot?"

"I've given this some thought," Gleason said. "Picture this. The aliens empower him with the ability to cure disease. Forget about this virus exposure thing. It's too complicated. People wanna see aliens. So we give 'em aliens. Right, chief? Now, it isn't emphasized in the treatment, but we work it out on the storyboard. Shoot a scene in the mothership when the aliens scan Joe Dawson with a device of some kind. Ebersbach is available for the rewrite. His people gave our people the green light."

M. Chandler Tate creased his brow and leaned over and spoke privately to Gleason.

"Look here. Rewrite negotiations? Hell, Max, that's my department. I didn't approve that."

"People, people, people!" Sty Raines shouted. "Come on."

Preece turned to the last yellow marker in the screenplay.

"There's another shift in perspective. This next act is shot in the home of Joe Dawson's wife and son. Remember, their names are Chloe and Frank? They're watching a local television news program about the street prophet Bob Smith. He's being interviewed by Jerry Brooks..."

"Not *the* Jerry Brooks?" Miz Landau said.

"We can't have that," one of the attorneys said.

"Continue," Sty Raines insisted.

"Chloe and Frank recognize him, the man being interviewed on TV, as Joe Dawson. Chloe's angry that her estranged husband has given up everything, his family and career, for some crazy idea about saving the world. It's clear that she doesn't believe the world's coming to an end. Seeing him on TV, however, she decides to seek him out, go down there and confront him. She wants to see once and for all if their marriage can be saved. Maybe get him the psychiatric help he needs. So, Chloe and her son Frank drive down to The Strip, searching for Bob Smith."

"Wait a minute. Hold it. You've lost me once again," Audrey Whistler-Cox said. "No woman would do that." She thumbed the previous pages. "I thought they were separated?"

"Again, we've got some gaps here."

"Can you get us the storyboard on this?" Miz Landau asked.

"People, people," Sty Raines said. "Work out the details later. Mr. Priestly?"

Preece cleared his throat.

"Chloe and Frank Dawson find Bob Smith preaching to a mob of homeless people and drug addicts. The scene will be shot at a corner of South Las Vegas Boulevard, surrounded by casinos. We've already contacted the MGM Grand. They're interested in a brand agreement. Anyway, on the street Chloe and Frank try to get the prophet's attention. He sees them, knows who they are, but he won't acknowledge them. The wife and son turn away in despair. As mother and son cross the street, a car runs a traffic light and hits the boy. Runs right into him. He's severely injured."

"Like *An Affair to Remember*," Audrey Whistler-Cox remarked.

"When the ambulance arrives, Bob Smith walks over and sees his son lifted onto a stretcher and into a paramedic rig. Chloe his wife speaks to him 'Look, what you've done,' she says. 'You killed my baby.' The next scene is at the hospital. Frank, their boy, is in a coma."

"Now, who's Frank again?" M. Chandler Tate asked.

"Their son. Jesus! Joe and Chloe's *son*," Sty Raines said.

"The doctors don't hold out much hope for him," Preece continued. "They tell Chloe that his chances are slim to none. In their medical opinion, nobody can survive such a severe head injury. If he survives, they say, he'll be a vegetable.

"Bob Smith enters the hospital through the emergency room. He uses his powers of clairvoyance to learn where they've taken his son. Smith sneaks into Frank's intensive care room. For the moment, no one else is in the room. Frank is attached to a respirator. There are monitors of various kinds. Intravenous tubes running into his arms. Holding back tears, Bob Smith takes his son's hand and says, 'Frank, wake up! Wake up, Frank.' And Frank's eyes begin to flutter. He takes a breath and wakes up. The boy reaches out and grabs his father's arm. It's a very big emotional scene."

"This is good," Sty Raines mumbled.

"Don't you think the resurrection thing might piss off the evangelical demographic?" Tate asked.

Sty Raines shook his head and gestured for Preece to continue.

"Chloe rushes into the room, sees what's happening. Other nurses rush in and push Bob Smith away. Remember now, he looks like a homeless man. He's become a notorious street preacher. Nobody sees him as Dr. Joe Dawson. They don't want this guy touching the sick kid. Anyway, Frank appears to be cured. Vital signs are normal. He's breathing on his own. They're debating whether to remove him from the respirator. Chloe is crying tears of joy, and the doctors are befuddled by Frank's miraculous recovery. In their midst, and we can use an invisible wipe technique in this shot, Bob Smith slips silently away into the night."

There was a deafening quiet in the room. All eyes were on Sty Raines.

"Do not tell me that that's it."

"What about the goddamned aliens?" an attorney asked.

"Forget the aliens. What about the plague?" Miz Landau said.

"I'm afraid that's all we have, sir," Preece said like a good little soldier. "At the moment—"

"Dammit all!" Sty Raines shouted. He slammed an open hand on the table. "Would somebody tell me how this thing ends, for the love of God?"

"What about the rabbit?" an attorney asked, appealing to Whistler-Cox. "I mean, you introduce a rabbit, and then, what, it disappears?"

To the meeting I'd brought my camera bag. Nestled at my feet, it contained DVD copies of my encounter with Chloe and Frank Dawson. At that moment, with the disappointment of the executive committee, I doubted very much that they would want to see home movies of my adventures in Las Vegas. Instead, I smiled bravely like a lamb on the sacrificial altar.

Gleason scowled at me. "What in hell's going on?"

"Guy's been difficult to work with," I said. "Bob Smith, the writer, I mean."

Audrey Whistler-Cox folded up her business tent and said, "I'd like to endorse it, Max, but..."

M. Chandler Tate smirked. "Three time's a charm, Max."

Gleason turned to me and said in a low voice, "Duncan, you must have a death wish."

The look in his eyes was chilling. Ordinarily, I dismissed him as Bozo in Gucci, but there was something treacherous there, something pathological, like the suicidal recruit in Stanley Kubrick's *Full Metal Jacket,* before he shoots the drill sergeant.

I shrugged and said, "Lighten up, will ya?"

Gleason leaned closer.

"You screwed me for the last time." He thumped a finger in the center of my chest. "This is the major leagues, boy. Or don't you get it?"

"I get it, Max."

He shook his substantial head. "No, you don't."

Fade to black.

Ω   Ω   Ω

In Los Angeles the automobile is more than a car; it is a telephone booth.

On my drive home, I mustered the courage to call Pig Boy on my cell.

"This is Maxi."

"Max, it's DC. Duncan."

"Biggest laughing stock in L.A."

"Listen, Max—"

"Where in hell was your writer today?"

I hesitated.

"And what kind of nonsense you pedaling here? Fucking identity changes. Christ!"

I winced.

"This is bigger'n both of us, Max," I said. "But listen. Hey, I have to tell you, I drove to Vegas. There's a gal living there, right out of the screenplay. Her kid, too. Freaked me out."

"I don't know and I don't want to know what you're talking about. What we want is finished product, Duncan, that's all."

"I know, I know, okay? But listen, I met Joe Dawson's wife."

"Who in the hell is Joe Dawson?" Gleason said contemptuously.

"The guy in the screenplay. Look, Max, I think Smith stole the treatment. Or the people in the treatment're real and he's violating some privacy laws or something. But they're real, Max. I met them."

"If your screenwriter plagiarized it, if it's stolen, I'll bring legal down so hard you'll never work in this town again, understand?"

"Max, all's I know is the Dawson family is *real*."

"I don't have time for this. Get us finished product or forget it."

Gleason hung up.

I had thoughts of leaving town.

I never wanted it to end like this. I had prospects once; all the privilege money could buy. I attended the right schools that, despite the least of my efforts, provided a pretty good education. I showed promise. My first wife and kids used to adore me. My peers respected me. Don't ask where it all went, but my advice to you is never get in a pissing match with God.

Chapter 8

Two days later the offices of Rainy Day Films called to set up a private meeting with Sty Raines. Although no insinuation was made, I figured the CEO wanted to deliver his tirade personally.

To say that I drove to the administrative site with trepidation is an understatement. The HMS Path of Least Resistance had hit an iceberg and was sinking fast. Now it was time to think up ways of murdering Bob Smith and then doing away with myself.

Sty Raines' personal assistant, Chip, ushered me into the big man's private office at Rainy Day Films. I expected a showcase of accomplishments with movie posters on the walls, Oscars and mementos on shelves. But there was nothing of the kind. The walls were stark white, the furniture minimalist chic. Aside from the ceramic desk in the shape of a Dykstraflex motion-control camera, two plain lacquer chairs occupied the room.

Pig Boy had arrived early. He ignored me while Chip made the unnecessary introductions and left the two of us to our animosity. Sty Raines was in the bathroom. We listened to the toilet flush and water run in the sink. Pig Boy said nothing as he chewed a wad of gum. Sty Raines walked out tossing a linen towel in the wastepaper basket, a copy of *Variety* under his arm.

Behind the desk a picture window faced the vast metropolis girdled by freeways. Haze limited vision to a quarter mile much like a photographic lens softens and romanticizes a subject.

"Would you look at this?" Sty Raines shook his head as he scanned the trades spread across the desk. "I'm gonna have to pay for a force majeure."

Most film production was insured to the hilt with indemnities for acts of God, epidemic, fire and flood, you name it. That morning Sty Raines read negative comments made by a California Senator to whose campaign he had refused support. By way of revenge, the Senator had called for a full investigation of Rainy Day Films. No insurance coverage in the world could protect Raines from the wrath of a corrupt politician.

He looked up from reading *Variety* and said, "Hungry? Can I get you something? Seltzer? Danish?"

I declined.

Raines turned his attention to Gleason. A month of frustration spilled out of his eyes. He jammed his index finger on the intercom.

"Chip, bring me that tray from this morning. The Danish."

He leaned back in his chair, looking the part of a big time movie producer.

"I'm gonna say something to you, Max, and I don't want you to take it personal." He paused briefly. "I never liked you and let me tell you why." He glowered at the man. "This cockamamie bullshit. You put me in an embarrassing situation. Delay after delay. How come it takes a goddamned eternity to get the final scene? Tell me that."

"Sorry, chief," Gleason said. "Done everything I can."

Sty Raines turned his attention to me.

"And you, you sorry son-of-a-bitch. Your writer adulterated the tone, completely screwed up the plot. What in hell is this thing about a goddamned rabbit! Jesus! And tell me you're gonna change the name Smith back to Joe Dawson."

I appealed my case to Pig Boy. "Nobody sent me a memo on that."

"There was no memo," Gleason said under his breath.

"It used to be sophisticated. Had mythic references, a Prometheus kind of thing. Pathogen-as-Frankenstein meets ET. But let me tell you something. I'm no longer taken with it. You can't change a plot or the hero halfway through a goddamned feature."

"I have to say, Smith's been difficult to work with," I said. "Done everything we can."

"Well, you've outdone yourself," he said.

Raines removed an Upmann from the desktop drawer, stuck it in his mouth, and compressed his lips in a muzzle of indignation.

"I took a bet with Tate you'd pull it off. He was sure you'd blow it. And the son-of-a-bitch was right."

"We may have to cut our losses," I suggested.

From Sty Raines' reaction, I could tell it was the wrong thing to say. His eyes widened as the blood pressure rose a couple hundred pounds per square inch.

At that point I wanted to retreat, go home, call up Xavier, chase down a couple white lines. Maybe my connection would have something for me.

"We'll get through this, chief," Gleason said cautiously. "I have my people working on it day and night. Not to worry."

Sty Raines' glare fell on him momentarily before it evaporated in a shit-eating grin. Some people called Raines the consummate seducer. Others said he was nuts. I'd say he's schizoid. His personality was a two-faced mask of comedy and tragedy. You never knew which one you were going to get. He would bestow praise and adoration on the undeserving only to devastate their pride by issuing mockery and blame in the same sentence. When you felt like crawling down the nearest hole, he convinced you that your project deserved an Oscar. Flattery and insult were what he did best. He was Master of the Deal.

"Not to worry, no thanks to you. Once again, Max, I pulled your ass out of the fire." He grinned past the cigar. "I sold a percentage. Our little Japanese friends bought it."

My mouth fell open.

"Congrats, chief," Gleason said, but you could hear the insincerity. Renegotiations tended to cut out the middleman, Pig Boy's official position.

"Does this mean I have an option?" I asked.

Both men ignored me.

"We got a good price, but I don't have to tell you what a pain in the neck these goddamned slopes are. Already pitching ideas at me. Since your writer boy is so damn lazy, I figured, what the hell. Let our new partners rewrite it." He clasped his hands and shook his head. "It's money in the bank." Sty Raines was smiling now but his eyes still harbored anger.

"What kind of," I began. "What kind of rewrite we talking here?"

I knew instinctively that Smith would not allow anyone to doctor the screenplay.

"They want to keep the bit about aliens, but they want 'em to attack Disneyland. Go figure. It's a Godzilla thing, I guess. You know the Japanese." He raised his eyebrows. "They want the hero to blow up the mothership with a virus bomb. Adolescent shit. Special effects'll push cost, but they're willing to front the capital." Sty Raines shrugged with a resigned, self-satisfied smile.

"If Japan's happy," Gleason said.

"Thrilled." The corners of Sty Raines' mouth were moist with drool on his cigar. "I'm not against throwing in some action. Stalone-type stuff. You know what I'm talking about. A sex scene or two."

"Goes without saying," Gleason said, shifting his weight in the chair.

Raines grimaced and tugged on an ear.

"I'm thinking, I don't know. Maybe Campaña and that new chick. What's'er name? Everybody wants to see 'em naked and doin' each other. You know who I'm talkin' about. But, hey, you gotta ask yourself, how's it gonna play in the States. Oh, yeah, I forgot to tell you. Our partners added a twist on the alien thing. In the Smith treatment, they're invisible, right? Well, Japan wants to green screen it, ET types. *Close Encounters* type of thing. Also, they want some topless bimbos in the Vegas scenes. Max, get the storyboard people working on that right away."

"I don't know. Not sure it's a good idea," I said, remembering Smith's aversion to my film, *Madame Pussy*. "If you don't mind my saying."

"Yamashita's got this thing. Any excuse to see naked, period," Sty Raines said, leaning forward. "You, get your writer working it. I don't want to get halfway through production and end up with a shitty rating. Cost us big time."

Chip, the executive assistant, walked into our meeting with a silver tray arranged with pastries. Gleason chose a chocolate Éclair and picked a napkin from the stack. My stomach was in knots, and I declined. Chip placed the tray within reach, on the desk.

"Gentlemen, a little eye-opener?" Sty Raines asked.

Gleason shook his head with a mouthful of whipped cream.

An eye-opener might be just the ticket.

"Sounds good," I said.

Sty Raines ignored me.

"Chip, give Yukitushi a call."

"Mr. Yamashita," Chip confirmed.

"Whatever." Sty Raines checked his wristwatch. "What time is it in, uhm, what the hell, wake him up. Tell him we need to conference."

After Chip walked out and shut the door, the only sound in the executive suite was Max Gleason's chewing. What would my old therapist have said about Pig Boy's appetite?

Sty Raines rose from his chair. "I need a drink."

It was twenty-three past ten in the morning.

"Whatever you're pouring," I said, ever hopeful.

Raines frowned. He poured a finger of Napoleon brandy into two crystal snifters and handed one to me. I managed to politely rise halfway out of my chair. Gleason had chocolate on his chin. Pastry crumbs were strewn on the carpet beneath him.

The man raised his glass. "Want you to be the first to know. We agreed on a title. *Virus Wars*. Great, ain't it?"

I nearly choked. Smith would hate it. I emptied the brandy snifter in one swallow.

"When can we expect a rewrite from your boy?" Raines said. "I was thinking, I don't know. Maybe focus on the aliens. But you can't pull an audience on knockers alone. Got to rethink it. Run another focus group. I'm thinking teen-age demographic here. That's who'll see it."

Sty Raines sipped the brandy while I placed the snifter on the desk.

"Tell me, what's with your writer anyway, he on something?"

I shook my head.

"I got a problem with motivation at this point. Would you explain the name change? Dawson disappears and we end up with some asshole named Smith?"

I shrugged. What I wanted was another brandy.

"Wasn't it Dawson who worried this virus thing would end up killing everybody? That's the concept, right? Now we got some prick healing people on the street. And then there's the goddamned mugging and the sudden appearance of a six-foot rabbit. This makin' any sense to you?"

"No, sir," I said.

Gleason wiped his mouth on the napkin and reached for another pastry.

"What you're saying, chief, makes sense. Let me dialog it with Committee and get back to you. I'm sure we can work something out..."

"Max," Sty Raines said in exasperation. "Max, I'm not talking to you. I'm talkin' to our friend here. Mr. Austin. Charles, am I right?"

"DC."

"Knew your dad, son. Hell of a director. Best in the business. Sorry about…. Well, you know." He took a sip of brandy. "The reason I'm still talking to you after all the shit you put us through, well, it's really because of your dad. Had it been some asshole, you would a been long gone."

Sty Raines raised his hands to stop me from interrupting.

"Get your writer boy in line. These creative types, so sensitive about their art. Won't compromise principles. Shit. I'm sure your boy'll come round. Sounds like he's new to this, but I can count on you, can't I?"

"Yes, sir."

"Tell you what we want. Change the fucking name of that biotech firm. Research tells me the name's registered. Can't have that. I got no problem with the weapons of mass destruction thing. Keep it. Tell your writer boy we're keeping the aliens, work 'em into the final scene. But then we got a bigger problem. That mind-reading shit, I can't accept it. Bring back the hero, Joe Dawson. That's what the people want. The goddamned story is based on his perspective."

Sty Raines clasped the snifter in both hands, pleased with himself.

"People ask me what we do, what producers do? Can you believe it? You know what I tell them? Very few motion pictures are made when you think of the number of stories we get. More submissions in the trash than stars in the sky. Am I right? Of course, I am."

Gleason agreed.

"Sometimes my wife's family asks me, they say, why, Mr. Raines, why does it cost so much to see a feature film. And you know what I tell them? I tell them what our average cost is. Seventy mill. And their God damned mouths drop." The old man made a face. "You know as well as I do, we got to earn two, two and a half times cost to break even. They don't get it. Don't have a clue. The movie-going public's dumb as shit."

He swallowed his brandy and addressed Gleason.

"Know what I think? I think the rolling break on this deal will turn out okay but we have to play the figures right. Hide the numbers from the sushi eaters."

"Stretch the point of profitability to several times cost," Gleason said.

Sty Raines snapped his fingers. "Won't know what hit 'em. Get Audrey to work the endorsements. Sign General Motors for the cars. Get the preliminaries contracted. I think we can sign Pepsi or Coke. Maybe spark a bidding war. Does anybody smoke in the picture?"

"Sty, who do you see for lead?" Gleason said. "We called Leo's people, but he's busy. How about Harrison?"

Sty Raines shook his head. "Too old. Besides, have you seen his scale lately? He asked for twenty on his last picture. I want to sign a nobody. Make a couple changes, and the story'll carry it. We don't need a magnet. Stars. Hell. They're spoiled what-you-call-its? What's the word?"

Gleason shrugged and reached for another pastry.

"What's the word I'm thinking of?" Sty Raines said.

I wanted to suggest *amoral narcissists* or *beautiful sociopaths*. But I said nothing.

"Whatever. You know what I mean. Used to be money wasn't everything. Back in the old days we worried about art. We *cared*. It was blood, sweat, and tears, let me tell you. Not today. Too much cynicism. Suddenly the talent came down with a killer instinct. All of 'em. Smile like goddamned hyenas."

Sty Raines paused to finish the drink.

"Mr. Raines," I said, "I have expenses that I'd like to talk with you about." I figured it was as good a time as any to ask for an advance.

Raines swallowed and waved his free hand in the air.

"Forget it." He leaned forward. "You stuck me in development hell on this. Get your boy to change the ending. Then we'll talk. Or I'll put your ass to the fire, Charles. You understand what I'm saying?"

"I'll get a rewrite. Count on it."

"It's gonna be a blockbuster," Gleason said.

I gave Gleason a sidelong glance. It seemed to me that Pig Boy was attending a different meeting.

"I want respectable product. This topless shit's got me worried."

Sty Raines got out of his chair to signal the meeting was over.

He returned to the wet bar. With his back to us, he said, "On your way out, Max, give Chip an estimate so we can clue-in Japan. Shouldn't take more'n a week, right?" He turned to me. "Or will your boy need more time?"

"No, sir, one week should be enough," I said.

"Have a nice day, Max."

Gleason made his exit but not before giving me a disapproving frown. The door shut softly behind him.

When I arose from my chair, Raines said, "Stay, Charles. I got something to say to you."

I sat down, and Sty Raines returned to his desk with a full snifter of brandy. None was offered to me, but the predatory look in his eye burned away my desire for another drink.

Through clasped hands, he said, "I want you to understand something. You got a decision to make here. Fix it or get fixed yourself."

His emphasis said it all.

"Tell me, you using right now? High on something?"

No sir, I was going to say, but he continued.

"Whadda they call it nowadays? In my day we called it Blow or Crank or something. Dope."

I was about to explain that methamphetamine and cocaine were different entities.

"I don't care if you snort poontang, okay? All I care about is making the picture. Finish the screenplay." He counted on his fingers. "Cut the mind-reading shit, cut the rabbit, cut all the crap. You got five days. I think that's generous, don't you? How you fix it is up to you. But believe me, when I tell you to get it done you get it done."

"Done deal, sir."

Raines shook his head and shut his eyes. When he opened them, I noticed how bloodshot they were, mottled like pitted glass. They reminded me of Bob Smith's eyes.

"Well, you ain't done shit yet," he said. "You used up a month of excuses. If I were you, I'd screw the writer. Finish it myself. That's what I'd do."

Okay, I was thinking. *I can do that.*

"Otherwise," he said, "you could end up on the wrong side of trouble." A grin stretched his old lips. "You see, Mister Yuckyshita committed twenty and I'm not giving it back. That's million to you. More than you can imagine."

Sty Raines did not know me. I could imagine a lot of money.

"Let me be honest with you. I don't like renegades. The Japanese got a word for it." Raines stuck the Upmann in his mouth and said between clenched teeth: "They hammer down the nails that stick up."

He removed the cigar for emphasis and sucked up the saliva in the corner of his mouth.

"You're not one of them nails that stick up, are you, Charles?" His expression collapsed to deadpan. "Now get the hell out. Screenplay. On my desk, five days."

Chapter 9

It was time to take a meeting with Smith on his home turf.

The Glide Hotel in downtown Los Angeles had been built before 1920, before the boom years, before Mulholland, Owens Valley and the water wars. Years ago the Red Cars used to stop right outside the grand entrance. There was an indentation in the sidewalk where carriages and cabs dropped their fares. I have tried to imagine what the Glide looked like back then. Noble occasions had taken place in its once spacious lobby.

In its later years, the Glide catered to battalions of street poor, and the lobby functioned as their barracks. I entered and was observed by the patrons roosting on a threadbare sofa. They had the stuffing knocked out of them, both the sofa and the occupants. A desk clerk sat behind a chicken-wire cage. At the side of the lobby, a dim staircase led upstairs. Somewhere in the labyrinth of narrow hallways was Bob Smith's dismal room.

The black man behind the chicken wire wore a soiled leather cap and a purple shirt, unbuttoned at the collar, with a gold necklace of an astrological sign. The man said nothing. His eyes surmised me as either walking wounded or drug casualty.

"Afternoon," I said. I put my hands flat on the desk to show I was not armed.

The man nodded once. "We full up."

"I'm not looking for a room."

I was edgy, and my voice sounded thin, strained. I shifted the weight of my canvas shoulder bag.

"Trying to locate an old buddy."

The man's eyes were like hard-boiled eggs shot through with blood vessels.

"An old dude named Smith. Bob Smith? He live here?"

"Got a million Smith's. And they all be named Bob."

From an ashtray he took the butt of a cigarette and put a match to it. Tails of smoke curled around his head.

"He's a lot older than me. About your height. Slim. Long gray hair. Wispy beard."

"Ain't seen 'em."

He dropped his eyes to a magazine about automatic weapons, to an article on ammo.

I was not dissuaded.

He looked up. "If I see 'em, I let 'em know you come by."

Heat rose along the back of my neck. Sleep for me had become a thing of the past, and with the trip to Vegas, with Pig Boy's insulting bullshit, and a dry nose, my patience was long gone. I unzipped the shoulder bag and removed the camcorder, aiming it at the clerk like a gun.

"What the…?" he said, turning away from the camera.

I spoke with a voice tighter than a virgin.

"You got a name, man?"

He shook his head.

"I see you like guns."

"Ain't none a your business what I like."

"Bet your parole officer'd make it his business."

I had his attention now. I pressed the record button, and he reclassified me as bad news.

"Turn that thing off."

"All I want from you is Bob Smith's room number."

"Three flights up. Room three oh two."

I lowered the camcorder. We held stares momentarily, and I smacked my lips with a smirk.

"That's a wrap."

$$\Omega \qquad \Omega \qquad \Omega$$

I knocked at room 302. No reply.

Knocked again, this time more urgently.

"Yes?" came a muffled voice

"Open up."

I heard someone shuffling across the Linoleum. Once Smith cracked open the door, I pushed my way inside.

He staggered back in shock.

I slammed the door shut, feeling blindly behind for the lock, and set it. I stood there catching my breath.

The old man said nothing. He looked like warmed-over road kill.

"Hello, Bob."

He tottered slightly only to steady himself on the arm of a chair.

"Looks like your visiting habits've rubbed off on me. Oh, nice digs," I said through a counterfeit smile. "By the way, Chloe and Frank send their regards."

That got him. Smith fell into the chair.

"Wanna see some pictures?"

I tapped my shoulder bag and strolled to the sink in the corner, acting cocky. I glanced at my image in the sullied mirror. I looked drawn and haggard. I turned to face Smith. He was the poster boy for infirmity.

"You have pictures of...?"

"The Dawson's. No Joe, of course. Wasn't home." I was awash in a kind of petty victory over him. "Got them right here." I tossed the shoulder bag on the bed. "Let's take a look."

"What is it that you want?" Smith demanded.

"What I've always wanted. The rest of the screenplay."

"It isn't finished."

I ran a palm over my hair and touched the band of my ponytail. I sat on the edge of the bed and thought about pulling out the camcorder and shooting Smith right then and there. But these things had to be done delicately. Otherwise, he might bolt. The situation required a degree of diplomatic skill and charm.

"We have no business together, Mr. Austin. I dissolve any responsibility you might feel."

"Look, friend, you can't get rid of me, like I was some piece of garbage or something."

For the first time since entering, I became aware of Smith's bad housekeeping practices. The place looked like a hamster cage. Technical magazines, library books, and newspapers were stacked on the floor. Yellow legal pads, the pages filled with outrageous scribbling, were strewn across the bed. In one corner was a cardboard box supporting an array of glass tubes, graduated cylinders, and a Bunsen burner attached to a propane tank. The room resembled a miniaturized version of the original *Frankenstein* set at Fox studios.

"What you cooking up here, Bob?"

Smith rubbed the arm of the chair.

His beige suitcase lay open next to the cardboard box. Smith pushed out of his chair and shut the suitcase. His pallid complexion reddened with anger.

"Are you pissed off I got pictures of Chloe and Frank? Tell me who they are."

Again, no response as he sat back down.

I had the upper hand, but I wasn't sure exactly how to exploit it. I was flying on automatic pilot.

"And the treatment, what'd you do, steal it? It's about real people, ain't it, Bob? Some of that shit really happened."

Smith nodded.

"You saying yes or no?"

"Yes."

"Yes what?"

"It's true."

I snorted a laugh. "Not that alien shit. But the part about the woman, the kid, right?"

"No," Smith said finally, looking at the floor. "I mean, yes."

I got down real close, in his face, nose to nose.

"You gotta work with me, Smith, all right? Tell me what the fuck you mean." He had exceeded the limits to my patience. "I didn't come here to play charades."

Smith was hyperventilating. He looked like he was about to explode. It was as though he fell into a trance with visions of Black Death crawling up his spine.

"Hold on, Bob. Now don't blow a gasket."

"*I am...!*" Smith shouted. "*I* am Joe Dawson!"

I did not believe him.

"So, you're Joe Dawson and you talk to aliens?"

"No, in the script I took poetic license. The visions come to me. I needed a literary vehicle."

"Oh, a literary vehicle. I studied that in school, Bob. Well, now we're talking," I said. "So, what, you're a character in your own goddamned screenplay? Tell me something, Bob. Why'd you write my old man in there?"

"The character is meant to be you," he said.

I huffed.

"Okay, okay. Let's pretend for a moment you're Joe Dawson." I grinned like Jack Nicholson in *Chinatown*. "What? You, Dr. Joe Dawson, were locked up in that cackle factory, right? Okay. Tell me, what kind a drugs they serve in there, you know, to hallucinate goddamned aliens?"

Smith had the look of a man facing his executioner.

"Don't play games, Bob, all right? If you're Joe Dawson, I'm the fucking Tooth Fairy."

"What is it you want?"

"What is it I want?" I said, exasperated. "I want to know how it ends."

"The screenplay?"

I snapped my fingers and pointed. "Bingo."

"I can't do that."

"Why?"

"Because I don't know how it ends."

"Then do the next best thing. Finish it."

He shook his head. "Time finishes it."

I stepped away. I needed to put some space between us or I'd clobber the dude. My shoulders ached from adrenaline, and I took a deep breath. My therapist had given me a list of things to remember when I found myself angry, but I had lost the list an hour after the appointment, which really made me mad. By confronting Bob Smith in that cramped hotel room, I scowled at the irony in my life.

"Look," I said, "let's not fight over details. We need to talk agent to client." I sat on the corner of the bed and folded my legs in a relaxed pose. "I need you to do something. You gotta change the Smith character back into Dawson. Got that? Oh, and dump the rabbit. What in hell you got a six-foot rabbit in the picture for?"

Smith looked at me as though I'd just shot his dog.

"Okay, and another thing, the aliens. You know, they kind a strike me as, I don't know, necessary to the story. Hey, I'm not married to the idea, but the production people like them."

"Seventy-five percent of Americans believe in angels. Just as many believe that aliens are real."

I snapped my fingers. "There you go. What did I say? But you gotta bring 'em back, Bob. You can't cut the aliens out of the screenplay."

I evaluated the old guy momentarily. I took a measure of his sobriety. Since our last meeting, he appeared to have aged another five years. I glanced at the makeshift chemistry set in the cardboard box. I figured that Smith might be making illicit drugs.

"I'm afraid to ask, Bob, but do you know these aliens, personally? You know, do they visit once in a while, send postcards or something?"

He nodded, and I laughed out loud.

I got up off the bed.

"You know what, you are certifiable."

I leaned on the windowsill. The glass was grimed over from a century of filth, and I rubbed a circle in it. It faced the brick wall of the building next door, five feet away.

"I don't care what you think, Mr. Austin," Smith said.

I faced Smith in the chair.

"Well, you'd better. If you want your movie made. By the looks of it, I'm your only connection. You got no choice."

"Don't threaten me, Mr. Austin."

I pursed my lips. Up until then, I had behaved and I'd tried to be reasonable, but the dude left me no choice. I picked the shoulder bag off the bed, removed the camcorder and shoved it into Smith's hands. As he looked through the viewfinder, I pushed the play button. He squinted at the images dancing within.

"Tell me, who are they?"

Smith pressed the camcorder to his right eye, his mouth gaping.

"That's Chloe and Frank, ain't it?" I said. "Where you 'spose old Joe Dawson is, Bob?"

Smith thrust the camera away. His mouth was moving but he made no sound. He dropped the camcorder on the bed, and I picked it up.

"Why, why did you do this?" he asked.

"I read the screenplay, Bob. Real interesting, you know? All those parallels with real stuff. So, I had to find out for myself, make sure you didn't steal the concept. Tell me something. That pretty lady there, you bangin' her or just pretending? You know, doin' a little bashing the Bishop?"

Smith rose out of the chair.

"You've gone too far."

Neither of us said anything for the moment. I resisted the cruel urge to giggle at the absurdity. Smith folded his arms to keep his hands from shaking. He sat back down, defeated.

"Mind if I get this on film, Bob? For posterity." I lifted the camcorder.

Smith shook his head.

"Oh, come on. This is good." I gave a staccato laugh. "So, you're Joe Dawson, a scientist. Convince me. Tell me some scientific shit."

Smith shook his head.

"Come on, Bobby Boy. Let's hear about test tubes and whatever. Get it all on tape."

Once again, he declined.

I lowered the camera.

"You're a lying son-of-a-bitch, you know that? Jesus, why in hell, why'd I even..." I was exasperated. "I'm at the end of my rope here." The very words reminded me of my dream about the Old Man garroted in a well.

"The reason I came to you, to your father," Smith said, "or who I thought was your father..."

He shut his eyes in pained humiliation.

"Yeah, you thought. I know. But he's dead."

"I wanted your father to make a movie of my story, to convince the world of the danger, that what we were doing, what we made..."

Smith bowed his head.

I raised the camcorder and hit the record button.

"Please." Smith begged.

"You were saying?" I circled him with immodest vitality. "Something about the movie, world in danger?"

"You couldn't possibly understand."

"Try me. We can shoot this documentary style."

Smith looked up, addressing the lens with compassion and despair.

"You are so much a part of what's wrong with our culture. The corruption of it all. The new millennium had so much promise." Tears fell from his blue eyes. "The worst of humanity."

"Don't mince words now, Bob. Let it all out. Tell me about, I don't know, tell me about XyberGen," I said, gleefully.

"You have no idea. Not at all. How did I ever think I could warn the likes of you?" Smith shook his head.

"Go ahead, warn me."

The tiny motors of the camcorder whirled.

"We face our extinction. A plague!"

"This is good, Bob," I said. "Tell me again about Joe Dawson. Chloe. The whole shootin' match. Come on, don't be shy."

Smith got up and stepped forward. "Please. Shut that off."

"No can do, Bobborino. No can do."

I circled around the garbage on the floor behind me.

"What is it? What is it you *want* from me?!"

The walls rang from his shouting, and the world beyond the room fell silent.

I lowered the camera. I *had* come to the end of my rope.

"Let me ask you something, let me ask you something." I paced the cramped room. "Where in hell do you get off putting my old man in your goddamned movie? What does he have to do with this?"

Smith became nervously animated. He reached under the bed covers and pulled out a sleeve of perhaps fifty pages. He nearly fell on me with it. He slammed the latest installment of *Path of Least Resistance* against my chest, and then he collapsed in the chair. Tears stained his eyes.

"That's real Oscar material, Bob."

Up to that point I had not believed his histrionics one iota. I shoved the camera into the shoulder bag. A few pages of the screenplay fluttered to the floor, and I bent to retrieve them. I could hear the rasp of Smith's lungs sucking air. He trembled uncontrollably in the squalid light of a bare light bulb. I focused on his despair like a camera lens concentrating on his pathos. For the moment, I suspended my disbelief.

"No harm done, right?" I said, almost apologetically. "We'll forget this whole episode ever happened. Tell our grandchildren about it over roasted marshmallows, about how you saved the world, right?"

I grinned.

"Don't mock me."

I swung the bag over my shoulder.

"As I remember, you came to me."

"I don't want your help," he said.

"It's a little late for that, ain't it?" I turned away.

"You have what you came for."

"That's right."

We said nothing to one another for two or three frames, letting the tension dissolve.

"We're close to an option," I said as an afterthought. "Let's not screw it up. Settle down and forget this harebrained shit. You're not some fucking character in your own screenplay, man. Cut yourself out and cut my old man. Got it?"

I reached for the door.

"Do me a favor, Mr. Austin? Please, don't call me anymore. Our business together is finished."

"We'll never be finished, Bob."

With that fond fare-thee-well, I left and slammed the door behind me.

Chapter 10

There are monsters in the world.

Five days after my meetings with Sty Raines and Bob Smith, I sat on my dining room floor in the orange light of late afternoon, staring at my retreating image in a mirror. If I sat with my back against one mirror and faced the mirror on the opposite wall, I could create the illusion of infinitely repetitive images like that famous shot in *Citizen Kane*. I counted seven frames of myself, Marlboro in hand, a bottle of Old Bushmill's on the table. Beyond that, the image was indistinguishable, converging to a single point. There are limits even to the power of infinity.

I was thinking about how I was going to finish Bob Smith's screenplay. Once again, he had given me twenty pages but the product remained unfinished.

I took a drag and crushed the cigarette in an overflowing ashtray. Spread out on the table were legal pads and Post-It Notes with scribbles and doodles, arrows and sketches. The pages of the screenplay were stained with coffee and burned by cigarette ash. Empty cartons of take-out soured the air. A fly buzzed in the bottom of a carton, stuck to chicken chow mien from Kwon's. I had been working nonstop. My craving for cocaine had waned over the past week, but the termites of fatigue ate away at my stamina.

It was around six in the evening. Coffee and nicotine no longer had an effect. I had switched to Irish whiskey mainly for relief of the ache in my shoulders and the back of my legs. During coke droughts in the past, I had relied on clonidine to ease the craving, but all I found in the medicine cabinet was an expired prescription bottle of Vicodin. Earlier in the day I had taken two tablets. Sleep was pawing at me, but more had to be done.

I had decided, since Bob Smith had dicked me around with an unfinished screenplay, I, Duncan Charles Austin, Jr., would complete it for him.

I faced imposing obstacles. The first hurtle was relatively easy, converting "Bob Smith" into "Joe Dawson." This required a pint of Whiteout and some diligence on my part. Next, I tried to rework the mind-reading element. In my opinion, clairvoyance stretched the audience's willingness to forgive paradox. What I had assumed would be a relatively harmless correction, however, altered the course of the plot. By dropping the hero's extrasensory perception, I wiped out the foreshadowing details that established the theme. Inasmuch as the denouement should feel authentic to the audience, with the essential changes made, my version proved illegitimate. I changed the name of the biotech company from XyberGen to ZyborgGene and briefly considered what I should do with the names Chloe and Frank; should I change the name "Dawson" altogether to avoid a potential lawsuit? Added to the mix, Rainy Day's partners, the Japanese, had called for an R-rated action movie. I wasn't sure what they wanted. And so, in red ink, I wrote "naked" before each reference to the space aliens.

I redlined every mention of the absurd character called Rabbit. It seemed to me a nonsensical thing that added nothing to the plot.

Cutting the character that represented my old man, however, was impractical. His role was essential to the narrative. In the end I decided to conceal his identity by changing his name to Elwood P. Suggins, taken from a

Jonathan Winters' comedy sketch. Regarding scenes that played close to my circumstances, I was powerless to modify these. For instance, if I rewrote the scene in which the Cadillac El Dorado Coupe de Ville broke down on the San Diego freeway, I had to change elements of every scene that lead up to it and those that followed. As such, the screenplay was constructed much like a house of cards, impossible to rearrange without an ultimate collapse.

Any rewrite is a formidable task, and I am neither an imaginative nor tireless screenwriter; but Sty Raines innuendo about fixing it or suffering the consequences proved sufficient motivation.

After five days of hard work, I had yet to correct the plot inconsistencies let alone to cull out the typos.

As a ghost-editor I was essentially stealing Smith's creative property. Ordinarily, I could not have cared less about moral and ethical issues, but the law protected people like Smith whether or not the screenplay held a copyright. Although there were more lawyers than actors in the business, I figured, what the hell. Smith was an unknown, unconnected in Hollywood, and as far as my reputation was concerned, I was beyond disrepute. Depending on the breaks, my intention was to give the old man a chunk of change for his trouble, to shut him up. My generosity, of course, depended on securing a substantial advance from Rainy Day.

In the middle of my musings, a knock came at the sliding glass door.

I looked up.

Bob Smith was standing there with his suitcase.

I picked up the screenplay and my notes and shoved them under a stack of magazines and old newspapers on the table. I went to the door and opened it.

"Bob, you learned to knock."

Smith walked in and sat down in the chair beside the couch.

I could not keep my eyes off the suitcase. The dude never left home without it.

"Someone is trying to kill you," Smith said.

I didn't bat an eyelash. I'd grown used to his nonsense. "What, aliens chasing you again?"

"No," Smith said, shaking his head. "Someone unknown to you is stalking you."

I closed the sliding glass door and may have locked it; I cannot recall. But I figured even paranoiacs have real enemies.

"You look tired, Bob."

He took a deep breath.

"He wants my suitcase. Wants it badly enough to kill for it."

"Who, Bob? Who you talking about?"

"A man."

"You piss somebody off or something? Steal his soap down at the hotel?"

"No. I saw him in a dream."

I rubbed the ridges in my brow. The Vicodin had me fuzzy and addlepated.

"You been smokin' some shit, Bob? Some bodacious weed?"

I switched on the floor lamp, and the light from it caught him like a half-moon, cratered and worn. He was borderline geriatric.

"So, why come here? Last time, I thought we ended this thing…whatever it is."

Imploringly, Smith looked up from his private thoughts.

I pointed to the dining room table.

"You'd be proud of me, Bob. Been working non-stop on the screenplay. I really want to make it into something, you know? Since you're not cooperating in that department." I shook my head melodramatically. "How am I supposed to deal with this crap, boogie men in your dreams?"

Smith's voice dropped half an octave.

"In less than a hour, a man will knock on your front door. You'll answer it. He will ask you your name. You will return with a wisecrack, and the man will pull out his gun and strike you on the side of your head."

"Look..."

Smith raised his hand to silence me.

"He will drag you into the hall closet and tie you up with duct tape. He has been trained to look for something. He'll rip your house apart in search for this."

Smith gestured at the beige suitcase.

"When he doesn't find it, he'll come back to you in the closet."

Smith had my full attention.

"His instructions are to take whatever means necessary to acquire it."

"Well," I said. "Since you seem to know that, Bob, why don't you just give it to him."

Smith shook his head.

"It means a great deal that you believe I'm telling the truth. Your life depends on it."

I sat on the couch and pushed aside a stack of unopened mail on the table. I picked up the Sig Sauer, checked the safety. Satisfied, I flipped it off.

"Bring 'em on."

"You don't understand. What I saw would have taken place had I not warned you. Now, I don't know what will happen if the man finds us both here."

"How in hell do you know this?"

"I *see* it."

"Like shit," I muttered. "Like what, some kind of *Sixth Sense* thing? You see dead people?"

I fit the Sig in the waistband of my jeans and went down the hall to check the front door. It was unlocked. I set the deadbolt and returned to the living room. I was feeling hyper.

Smith seemed genuinely alarmed but indecisive and entrapped by paranoid delusions. I was thinking it was going to take an act of Congress to get the man to finish a rewrite.

"Tell me, this dude, he in the neighborhood?"

"I don't know."

"You said you see things."

"When I'm nervous the visions are unclear."

"Right. A myopic visionary."

"We have to leave."

I was losing patience. Forget the screenplay and forget the option. *Nothing is worth this kind of grief.*

"No, you leave, Bob. I have work to do."

Smith shook his head. "We need to go right now. Right now, in your car. It's the only path open. The rest are blocked."

That rang a bell.

"Path, eh? Tell me something, Bob. You living your screenplay or something? It's like you're in some kind of movie, man."

Smith shut his eyes. "We have to go now."

"Picking up psychic transmissions, are we?"

Smith opened his eyes and said, "This person, he's very dangerous."

I stood there blinking at him and weighing his absurdity against my paranoia. Smith might be onto something. Maybe I should take precautions. I rummaged the coffee table for the keys to the El Dorado and, once found, held them up. They jingled like a fishing lure.

"Tell you what. Let's make a deal. I'll play along. We can go for a ride. But afterwards, you gotta help me out in return. I want you to finish the screenplay. We got a deal?"

Smith gave a single nod.

"Can we go now?" He picked up the suitcase.

I patted the Sig Sauer in my waistband and said, "Sure. After you, Bobby Boy."

Ω   Ω   Ω

The Caddy hummed smoothly, and as we toured the deserted streets of downtown, I realized I had misjudged my Latino mechanic. The man knew Cadillacs. The engine never sounded so good.

On the passenger seat, Smith was silent as stone, gripping the suitcase on his lap.

A half-empty bottle of Bushmill's lolled between us, provisions for our impromptu Diaspora.

I clicked on the radio and dialed to a talk show. I kept the volume low, static murmur in the background. Rush Limbaugh railed against the liberals. We must have meandered through Echo Park for half an hour, up and down Temple, across Virginia.

"Why are we going in circles?" Smith asked.

"Well, where else can we go?"

"We should go east. It's safer there."

"East?"

I came to a stop at a traffic light. I eyed a clique of teen-agers at a phone booth outside a strip mall.

"Las Vegas," Smith said.

The bottle of whiskey listed against my thigh.

I sensed what Smith was driving at. Chloe and Frank came to mind. The traffic light changed, and I drove through the intersection.

"Tell me something. This killer, why's he coming after me? You said he wants your suitcase."

"My appearance has changed, and he doesn't know what I look like. He went to the hotel and asked for me by name, but..." Smith's voice trailed off.

I thought about my own encounter with the desk clerk at the Glide Hotel.

"If he doesn't know what you look like," I said, "how did he follow you to my place?"

"He didn't. He has your address. And pictures of you. A dossier."

I pulled to the curb, shut off the engine, and yanked the emergency brake.

"How do you know that? Fuck!" I punched the steering wheel in frustration and honked the horn by mistake. "Your shit drives me nuts."

Smith faced forward and said flatly, "If we're going to work together, you're going to have to clean up your language."

I habitually reached for the Bushmill's but caught a glimpse of Smith's reproving stare, and I withdrew.

"I'm not cleaning up anything, you got that?" I wrenched my ponytail. "Look, Bob, tell the truth. You came looking for a place to crash. All this business about dreams of scary guys, come on. No offense but who's gonna put a hit on you?"

"It's the Delivery Boy."

That hit a nerve. It felt as though my brain was full of maggots that had made their way upwards from my stomach.

"Bob, that's a character in the screenplay. He's kind of a mystery man or something."

He shook his head.

"I got it wrong. Sometimes I don't see clearly. The visions, they're like smoke. This man works for the government."

I turned the ignition key and put the El Dorado in gear.

"That's it. That's it. I'm not listening to your crap no more."

"Our lives depend on what you do. Please."

"You know what?" I shoved my index finger in the old guy's face. "You're nuts."

"You cannot go back to your house. Not now. He's there."

"Is that right."

We drove a couple of blocks before Smith spoke again.

"Please, if we go back..."

"Oh, I'm going home, all right. And I'm gonna prove to you what a pile of shit this is. Boogie men and fucking government. Whoa. And I used to think you were a pretty good screenwriter. This is the lamest plot I ever heard. The least you could do is come up with something original. Like aliens, for instance."

"Don't mock me, Mr. Austin."

The lights in the bungalow were off, and as I punched the automatic garage door opener, I was trying to recall if I had left them on or not. I pulled the El Dorado into the garage, and the overhead light went on. I glanced at Smith. The old man was in a trance.

"Okay, out of the car. Come on."

I opened the door.

Smith sat rigidly against the passenger seat, his mouth moving silently.

I heard the fall of shoes on the pea gravel walkway, behind me. I held my breath, straining to hear, my heart climbing up my throat.

Someone was in the backyard, near the gate. The sound drew a picture in my mind. Whoever it was heard me as well and had stopped. I listened for the clink of the latch, but it never came.

"Is that?" I whispered to Smith, who was catatonic at this point.

I pulled the Sig from my waistband.

I pushed the button to close the garage door, and the apparatus engaged and rumbled shut. It reminded me of Las Vegas and the Dawson's garage. Only this time, I was the victim.

I went into the house, crouching before going through doorways, the business end of the gun aimed at the menacing dark. Blindly, I went into the kitchen. The only light came from the luminous dial on the stove clock. I went down the hall and into the living room, taking advantage of knowing the floor plan. The sliding glass door lay open, admitting a shine from my neighbor's porch light. I flipped on a lamp.

I have never been the cleanest of housekeepers. Even my rent-a-maid, Marta, who used to come once a month to scrub toilets and do the dishes, could not compensate for my indolence. That's why she quit. But on this evening, after our brief sojourn around Echo Park, the living room had never looked so trashed.

They—the Delivery Boy or whatever—had overturned the dining room table and coffee table, most of the chairs. Yellow legal pages were tossed across the floor. Both mirrors were shattered, and the lamp cast splinters of light against the walls. The couch was dissected with a kitchen knife. The packing grazed like miniature sheep on the carpet, the knife thrust into a cushion.

I crept into the bedroom, the Sig Sauer preceding me. It was in similar condition. My video collection lay in heaps of unwound serpentina. The mattress had suffered the same fate as the couch. The contents from the medicine cabinet in the bathroom lay crushed on the tiled floor, a rainbow of prescription drugs.

At that point, the surge of adrenaline had exhausted me. I sat on the toilet, the gun dangling between my legs. I picked through the pills.

When Smith walked in, I lifted the Sig. His eyes widened as he stepped back, afraid I'd shoot him by mistake.

"I warned you," he said. "You put us in great danger by coming back."

"Where's he now?"

"Gone."

"Good."

"He'll be back."

Among the pills, I found a Vicodin and popped it in my mouth.

"Can you put a name to this asshole?"

"Whitaker. His name is Whitaker Fetch."

Chapter 11

At around one o'clock in the morning outside the Conestoga Motel, I stood in a light rain waiting to use the payphone because, in all the confusion, I'd forgotten my cell. A working girl with a pierced nose and eyebrow, and hair the color of a Butterfingers wrapper, smacked chewing gum as she swore into the receiver. She made her point with lavish use of the word "fuck," sometimes substituting "shit," but more often than not relying on the old standby. I remarked to myself that "fuck" could be used as an adjective, a verb, or a noun. What other word in the English language offers more flexibility?

The working girl's voice echoed against the 7-Eleven across the street.

Close by, in the shadows of a doorway, Bob Smith waited out of the rain with his beige suitcase. The malfunctioning neon of the motel sign—"estoga tel"—reflected in the pavement.

I pulled a Marlboro from my shirt pocket and snapped the lighter. I was hungry and too tired to be angry with the inconsiderate hooker. My hair, leather jacket and jeans were damp from the drizzle. I was not a happy camper. It never rains in Southern California, proving that even the climate was against me.

I fiddled the loose change in my pocket. There was something in there that did not belong, and I took a look at it. A bullet. I rolled the warm metal between thumb and finger. The Sig Sauer made a hard impression in my waistband.

Who did I think I was, Clint Eastwood? With my luck, I would fumble around with the Sig as my enemy's automatic weapon ripped the flesh off my bones.

I twisted my neck to crack the muscle tension. Behind me, a promotional balloon of Mickey Mouse in a used car lot waved its gloved hands in the breeze.

I watched the perilous traffic along Santa Monica, drivers unused to the slick street. One block up from the hotel, a fender bender brought out two black and whites, their emergency lights playing like Christmas in the wet asphalt. I tossed the Marlboro in the gutter, and it hit the pavement like a comet.

Mine was a Theatre of the Absurd. I was running from an invention in Smith's screenplay. And I was on the run with an old man whose delusions of Apocalypse surpassed my own. All of my hard work to finish the product had been trashed along with the contents of my house. My hope for signing a contract and securing an advance from Rainy Day was pulverized. And still, *still* I had a dry nose, no coke for more than two weeks. I felt like a cockroach frying in a skillet.

I could not get the image of my trashed living room out of my head. I wished I had thought to bring a bottle of Jack Daniel's, anything to ease the pain in my lower back and legs. The Vicodin I had taken earlier was wearing off. I searched for another cigarette but the pack was empty. Metaphor of my life.

I was pretty certain that Bob Smith had it wrong about the Delivery Boy. I figured the Japanese were putting the screws to Sty Raines. Twenty million is a lot of money. That kind of loot can buy a busload of contract delivery boys. I figured, the negotiations with Yamashita had gone awry and Sty Raines resorted to outside talent to cop the rest of the screenplay. The incentive to "retrieve" the screenplay ran along the lines of extortion and threats to physical violence. Whoever Whitaker Fetch was, I'm sure he had no interest in Bob Smith's suitcase.

But a few hours earlier, the old man's paranoia had proven real. It freaked me out. I did not hang around to meet this Whitaker Fetch. I had stuffed a change of clothes into my knapsack. Instead of calling the cops, I had filled my pockets with shells from the gun box that I kept in the underwear drawer. Then, with a wallet full of credit cards and cash, we ran for our lives.

We jammed out of the garage without headlights, nearly running over two kids playing hoop down the Hill. I took the 405 north. We drove up Sunset to Santa Monica and took a left. In West Hollywood, I pulled to the curb to check the rearview mirror. No one, no cars, tailed us. Whitaker Fetch may have been too clever to show himself on a tail. After an hour or so of randomly circling West Hollywood, we ended up at the Santa Monica pier around eleven. By then I needed a place to crash.

We rented a room for one hundred and two dollars at the "estoga tel" on Wilshire, cheap and anonymous. I was relatively certain that we'd managed to lose Whitaker Fetch. After checking into our room, Smith fell into a negative stupor. He blathered on about how special government agents or space aliens were tailing us. I pointed out to Smith, the motel telephone worked.

"Why don't you give 'em a call, Bob?"

Tears rolled down his bearded jowls, and he shouted: "All is lost. All is lost!"

Hallucinations for sure, but it gave me the willies. I was thinking, *Maybe I should steal a yacht. Get the hell out of Dodge.* That's when I decided to give Pig Boy a call, to straighten out a few things.

After another five minutes of my standing in the rain, the girl with the chrome-yellow hair hung up the damn phone, and I entered the booth. As I lifted the receiver and put four quarters in the box, she asked to bum a smoke. I know a crystal freak when I see one. Her eyes had black half-moons, and she slouched like a parenthesis. She was no more than nineteen going on forty-five. I handed her the pack with a shrug.

When our fingers touched, I looked into the vacant black holes of her eyes. Her question was, You lookin' for some company, big boy?

I hesitated before shaking my head when the silhouette of Bob Smith stirred in the dark.

She crushed the pack and wobbled away on starved legs in an extreme mini.

Smith slouched toward me and entered the booth.

"She'll be dead in six months," he said solemnly.

"That's what I like about you, Bob. Always so positive."

I keyed Max Gleason's private number. It rang six times.

If the Delivery Boy were on contract with Sty Raines, Max knew about it.

It would have been more convenient to make the call from the phone in our room, but I considered the payphone more secure. Paranoia struck deep. I worried that the motel phone was traceable. The Delivery Boy was unknown to me. He could have been a master of electronic surveillance, for all I knew.

"Maxi."

"Hello, Max, It's DC."

"Duncan," he said offhandedly.

"Say, we got a problem."

Gleason muted the receiver. He was not alone.

"You listening to me?"

"I have nothing to say to you."

Bob Smith stood beside me, his breath reeking of green onions. "Use the name," he whispered, mouthing "Whitacre Fey-itch." I mimed to Smith that I had no idea what he was talking about. "Go on. Go on. Say it," he hissed, but I waved him away.

"Somebody broke in, Max. Sons-a-bitches trashed my crib."

I gave Smith the okay sign, and he stepped out of the doorway and into the rain, shaking his head.

"I don't know what you're talking about," Gleason said, and he hung up the phone.

Discouraged, I winced at the anger rising in my blood. A hard rain hit the pavement in countless diamond bursts. From fast food signs and faltering neon advertisements to traffic signals, the city lights were blurred in the glossy dark like a Jackson Pollock oil painting. Farther up the block a car alarm went off, alerting no one but annoying all.

Again, I keyed Pig Boy's telephone number.

When he answered I said quickly, "Don't hang up."

"What kind a game is this, Duncan?"

"Was it you and Sty sent that asshole to my house?"

"Honestly, I haven't a clue what you're talking about."

I explained details of the evening's events, even went so far as to enunciate the name Whitaker Fetch and ask once again what the Delivery Boy's connection might be to Rainy Day. Meanwhile, halfway through my story, Gleason spoke to someone privately off line.

"You listening to me?"

"Partners are involved now. The Japanese," Gleason said. "They may have sent someone, I don't know."

You could almost feel him smiling through the phone.

"Fuck the partners," I said.

"Duncan, you're stalling. And frankly, I'm worried about your grasp of reality. You actually think, what, Sty hired some kind of hit man? Are you out of your mind?"

"He was in my friggin' house."

Gleason sighed. "You know what we want. Why can't you just give us what we want?"

"I'll get it, okay?" I said, habitually reaching into my pocket for a pack of cigarettes before I remembered.

"You've promised that for over a month now," Gleason said.

"Smith's here. Give me a couple days. I'll get you the genuine article."

Gleason lowered his voice to a more somber tone.

"I'm only going to say this once, and then I'm going to hang up. Finish it with the elements and changes we discussed, or you will be very, very sorry."

I was replacing the receiver when Smith walked up to me.

"Max sends his regards," I said.

Without a word Smith crouched out of the rain in the direction of our room.

Ω   Ω   Ω

We were in the dark.

Light from the faulty motel sign cast a shadowed pattern on the carpet between the two single beds. I was prone in silhouette. Smith lay there breathing evenly. The room smelled of cigarettes and PineSol.

"What do we do now?" Smith asked.

"You're the one who reads the future," I said.

He mumbled something about being blocked. At first, I thought he said "knocked up" but I realized he meant blocked, as in a writer's block or something. He said the circumstances were making it difficult to "read the future."

"Why don't you give the Psychic Network a call?"

Smith turned away.

I got off the bed, stared hard at him and scratched the stubble on my chin.

"Screw you and your future."

"Why resort to profanity," Smith said to the wall. "The last refuge of the illiterate."

I reached into the pocket of my shirt that hung on the back of a chair and got a fresh pack of cigarettes and ripped off the cellophane. Smith protested. I put a match to the Marlboro and blew smoke in his direction. I sat in the chair that faced a small writing desk.

"Tell me something, Bob. I've been thinkin'. Where'd you learn to write screenplays, you know? I mean, you claim you're some scientist or something, right? Joe Dawson. Doctor of big ideas and all that."

Smith gave me the silent treatment. I took a drag.

"You ever think about finishing it?"

"You have never even read it, Mr. Austin."

"Cut me a break, okay? I'm a concept person. I don't do details."

"Prefer the big picture," Smith said sarcastically.

I nodded. "That's right."

Smith got off the bed and opened the suitcase on the floor. He handed me a thin stack of paper and lay back down. It was more of the screenplay.

I flipped on the desk light, a bare bulb on a black electric wire that hung from the ceiling.

"Is this the ending?"

Smith pretended to fall asleep.

I stubbed out the cigarette in a glass ashtray on the desk and sat down to read what Smith had given me:

Exterior. A corner of Sunset Biolevard, Hollywood.
ROLL IN: Camera rolls toward a mob of homeless people and curious onlookers, tourists hunting for movie stars. Standing among them is Bob Smith, street prophet and healer. He is ɵpreaching about the end of the world.

There it was again. Despite my insistence that he take a different approach to characterization, Smith wrote himself into the screenplay as a street prophet and faith healer.

I stared at the page, and my mood turned down a darker alley, running through the shadows. I could imagine a rabid hound giving chase. There was no amount of alcohol in the world to keep it at bay.

> BOB
> *"It will come unless we stop those people making the virus weapon. And the horror of it will make your worst nightmare pale by comparison. The scientists at XyberGen need to know how you feel. Tell them to stop making these biological weapons, these counter-terrorist devices, because they'll end up killing us all...."*

PULL IN, OVER HEADS OF ~~BOM~~
MOB: A camera crew hsa set up at the periphery of the mob. News reporter, Jerry Brooks, stands with microphone in hand and pushes his way to the center.
> *CLOSE UP: Bob Smith and Brooks. Brooks shoves microphone in Bob's direction.*

> BROOKS
> *"Mr. Smith, Mr. Smith? Jerry Brooks of Channel Seven News."*

DIFFERENT ANGLE: Over shoulder of Brooks, at Bob.
> BOB
> *"You want to speak to me."*

MEDIMM LONG: Crowd, camera crew, interview.

BROOKS
"It has been said that this thing, this extrasensory perception, of yours lets you see into other people's thoughts. Am I right?"

BOB
"That's what you believe?"
PAN: Faces of people in the mob.

BROOKS
(Grinning cyncally)
"This isn't about what I believe, Mr. Smith. If I paid you, wouldyou read my future?"

BOB
"If you like."

PAN to CLOSE UP: Brooks. He reaches into his overcoat and removes a billfold. He extracts a twenty-dollar bill.

BOB
"That won't be necessary."

BROOKS
"A freebie, huh?"
(Many of the people standing behind him begin to laugh)

CLOSE UP: BOB. He closes his eyes as the camera moves in.

FLASH: <u>Unterior of airliner</u>. The plane is ~~falling~~ crashing, adn the cabin is at a radical angle. Passengers are screaming. Theer's smoke in the cabin.

CLOSE UP: <u>Jerry Brooks.</u> The news reporter is seatedon the plane. Camera closes in on the terror in his face, open mouth, soundless scream.

EXPLOSION: <u>A flash of fire</u>.

CLISE UP: <u>Bob Smith</u>. He blinks and adjusts to the reality around him. The mob anticipates his response to the news reporter's challenge.

MEDIUM: <u>Mob scene</u>

> ### BROOKS
> *"Well, what is this? You look like you saw a ghost."*

DIFFERENT ANGLE:

> ### BOB
> *"I guess I have."*

> ### BROOKS
> *"For twenty bucks I deserve more, don't you think?"*
>   *(He directs the question to the mob)*

> ### BOB
> *"Yes, you do. But if I tell you what I see, you'll refuse to believe it."*

WIDER ANGLE:

> ### BROOKS
> *"That's ridiculous. What a cop out."*

MEDIUM CLOSE UP: <u>Bob Smith</u>. *He*
refuses to say anything more.
  NEWS CAMERA POV: The reporter
turns to face the camera.

BROOKS
"There you have it. Just another scam on
the street. This is Jerry Brooks, reporting
for Channel Seven News."

BOB
"Stay away from heights, Mr. Brooks."
FADE TO BLACK

I had read the scene before, about a week earlier, and it
was not half bad, but Smith had modified some of the
elements. He added a commercial airplane crash. It had
nothing at all to do with the movie Rainy Day wanted to
make. I had to convince Smith of his folly, get him to
change the protagonist's name back to Joe Dawson, but
mainly to get the story back on track. I clutched the pages
like a lifejacket at the sinking of the Titanic. Smith had
compounded the screenplay's acceptance by another issue:
Jerry Brooks. He was not Smith's invention. Brooks was a
real television newscaster in Los Angeles.

"Guy's a jerk," I mumbled to myself.

The Gulf War had made his career. Before then, Brooks
had been a smalltime Middle East correspondent for CNN
only to end up in the wrong place at the right time. His
news delivery during the war carried the idea of military
battle as a form of entertainment, as though the slaughter of
innocents was just another sporting event. War as Super
Bowl Sunday.

I looked up. Smith feigned sleep.

"This doesn't push the movie along. Where does it fit in the story? Is this at the beginning or the middle? I can't figure where this is going."

"It's what *will* happen," he said without opening his eyes.

"This is a new plotline here. You can't introduce new stuff, Bob, halfway through the fucking movie. What do you say we replace this scene with aliens? Japanese want more aliens."

"I've cut the aliens."

"But it's an alien picture."

"They don't have anything to do with the plot."

For nearly a quarter-hour, I listened to Smith's even breathing until I was certain he was asleep. Then, with pages in hand, I put on my jacket and skulked out of the room, through the rain, and made my way to the motel office.

At the front desk, I wondered why folks on the night shift resembled undertakers.

The kid at the Conestoga Motel desk wore a wrinkled lime green shirt and a chocolate tie that came to the second button from his belt. He was testosterone challenged; could barely cultivate a mustache. His eyes were abnormally large behind a thick pair of glasses. If Federico Fellini were still alive and making movies, he would have cast the boy on the spot.

"Do you have a fax machine?" I asked.

"Uh huh," he said.

This positive reply was not accompanied by the next logical step. The kid was insensible, goggling with those Marty Feldman's.

"May I use it?" I said, making a face.

I included a note to Gleason, something to the effect "more to follow," and I hung around the lobby for confirmation of receipt.

When I got back to our room, the light was on. Bob sat on the bed, arms crossed.

"I didn't say you could do that. Fax my screenplay to your producer friend."

"I'm your agent," I said. "It's what I do."

Smith shook his head in disgust and lay back down on the bed. His hair was messed up. He looked like hell.

"Bob, there're a couple things we need to talk about."

I told him that we needed to cut the Jerry Brooks' scene, that the news reporter could sue Rainy Day for defamation of character. Once again, I emphasized the importance of consistency of plot and character; told him that the character of my old man had to go; that we had to change the name of the company because XyberGen was a real corporation; get rid of the damn six-foot tall rabbit; and finally, I said that Joe Dawson was the hero we would stay with from beginning to end.

"We need audience buy-in."

While he stared at the ceiling, I patiently explained that the movie might not get made unless we came up with an ending in the next day or so.

He replied: "Take me to Las Vegas and see for yourself how it ends."

I stood and yanked off my jacket and sat at the desk. I pushed a dead cigarette through its ashes in a cross pattern. I weighed the old dude's motives against my self-preservation. Vegas might not be a bad place to hide out, I considered. Get away from Whitaker Fetch. I was not interested in what the Delivery Boy had to deliver.

"One condition," I said.

Smith turned away from me.

"You and me finish the screenplay," I said. "A collaboration."

He sighed.

"I know, I know. It finishes itself. But look, I'm not driving through the goddamn desert for nothing. I get something, you get something."

"*Quid pro quo.*"

"Yeah, like that. So, you fly with that or what?"

Smith rolled over and said, "Please, would you turn off the light?" And he went to sleep.

For nearly an hour, I listened to his even breathing, insomnia being part of my cocaine Jones, that and too many questions in an unsettling day. Staring at the darkness, I shuddered. An anal retentive named Whitaker Fetch, probably armed to the teeth, was stalking me.

In an adjoining room, a hooker and her trick engaged in small talk before going at it hammers and tongs. I figured, it was the same girl who had hogged the phone and asked for a smoke. In the middle of her faked orgasm, I said to myself, "Bad actor. An embarrassment to the profession."

Smith mumbled in his sleep, "And what's your most embarrassing moment, Mr. Austin?"

"Wha.... What did you say?"

He said nothing further, and after a short time, I crossed the room and laid down on the other twin bed. I leaned into the foam pillow, but sleep would not come. Smith's question had provoked a memory too embarrassing to recall.

Years ago when I was married to my first wife, I treated the entire family to a week at the Ritz-Carlton Laguna Nigel, largely because of the swimming pool built on the sea bluff. I had come into a truckload of capital after a successful project, and I wanted to show my appreciation. The truth of the matter was, my marriage was on the rocks, and the vacation was a desperate attempt to save it. At the hotel, my wife and I spent the week arguing and drinking while the kids swam in the pool. How does it happen that the worst of a marriage looks good in retrospect?

Eventually, remembering back, I fell asleep.

I dreamt of swimming pools. There was a string of them across the Los Angeles basin. I flew above them. I could see hundreds of young girls in bikini thongs. It was glorious. Somehow, as happens in dreams, I relived the most embarrassing moment of my life.

I was sitting poolside at the Laguna Nigel. My wife Gloria was indoors while I watched the kids. They swam for hours, and I sipped martinis. I was wrapped in a fluffy hotel robe with my feet sticking out like cured hams.

The poolside waiter approached, and I ordered another. "This time," I told him, "make sure it's very dry. Do nothing more than introduce the vermouth to the gin." As the waiter walked away, I added, "And no more salad." I detested olives, even in my dreams.

Two teen-aged girls, bronzed beyond reason, frolicked in the deep end of the pool. I had taken a keen liking to them. Their budding sexuality and the goose flesh of their perfect skin fascinated me. As the girls practiced diving, I observed how the water glistened on their delicious backsides. They climbed out of the pool, and I waved. Their mother, book in hand, sat on the other side of the pool. My grotesque lust went undetected. Or so I thought.

I imagined how wonderful the world could be if the girls and I made it a threesome in a room upstairs. Around this perversion I erected an intricate fantasy that brought me to full arousal.

My children were swimming nearby, and I knew that I could not act on any of my depraved ideas. So, I covered myself and beat off under the hotel bathrobe.

I shut my eyes, and by the time I looked up, it was too late.

My daughter, Chelsea Lee Austin, caught me at it.

Chelsea knew instantly what I had been doing; so did the mother of the two teen-aged girls. She wrapped her nubile charges in fluffy towels and coaxed them inside, away from the sexual pervert.

"That's disgusting," my daughter said. "I'm telling Mom."

The rest was history.

I awakened in the middle of the night to Smith's snoring. I lay there and thought about that lost weekend at the Laguna Nigel. It had really happened. I remembered when the waiter returned with my martini. He said, "The bar closes in five minutes, sir. Will there be anything else?" I had asked if he knew the name of a good divorce lawyer. He laughed at the joke; I'd been serious. It was the most embarrassing moment of my life. Lying there in the dark motel room, I thought embarrassment was God's way of saying you messed up.

When Bob Smith had showed up unannounced and uninvited the night I nearly blew my brains out, I had been mulling over the incident at the Laguna Nigel. A whole host of mistakes had visited me that night like Bob Marley's ghost, but the incident at the hotel was at the top of the list of reasons to pull the trigger.

I could still taste the metal Sig in my mouth.

I got up and put on my jacket, went outside for a smoke. The Marlboro tasted stale, and I flicked it in a high arc. It fizzled on the wet asphalt and died. So it goes. Behind me, the trick and his whore left their room separately. As it happened, it was not the same girl with orange hair who had tried to bum a smoke. I watched as the trick drove away and the girl made her way to the street, adjusting her miniskirt over her ass. I slipped back inside the room to lie down.

At 5:00 AM, Smith was taking a shower. The lights were on. I woke up and issued unrepentant curses while covering my head with the pillow. I managed to fall back to sleep only moments before Smith rushed out of the bathroom and nudged the side of the bed.

"Rise and shine, Mr. Austin."

More unrepentant cursing.

"I need to pick up some things."

"What things?" I said.

"Get up and take me to the hotel."

"The Glide? You out of your mind?"

"There are some documents and my typewriter. I can't finish the screenplay without it."

I rose from the ashes of my nightmares.

Chapter 12

Bob Smith was reluctant to take the El Dorado to Vegas. He complained of too many additional passengers.

I had parked the El Dorado in the red zone outside the Glide Hotel and told Smith to get his things while I had a smoke. "I don't want to get a ticket," I explained. "So, I'll stay here with the car." For over half an hour, I watched as the dude lugged boxes from his room to the curb.

A dozen poor Asian and Mexican kids from the neighborhood scampered for the bus stop. They wore plastic costumes of cartoon characters and politicians that their mom's bought at K-Mart. It was Halloween. When one of the local Trick-or-Treater's jumped in front of Smith, it scared the living crap out of him.

As I stowed his possessions in the car, the back seat and trunk began to look like a librarian's garage sale—cardboard boxes full of scientific periodicals, magazines, pencils in tin cans, and manila folders stuffed with newspaper clippings. There were boxes of tattered paperback books; boxes of clothes, another box full of condiments, mustard, mayonnaise and catsup, along with half a loaf of sandwich bread. There was an Underwood typewriter along with old editions of the trades, *Variety* and the like.

I squinted at Smith through my dark glasses. The last box, the largest, and the Underwood typewriter sat on the curb between us. I waited for him to put them in the car. Heavy lifting was not part of the deal.

Oddly, I was thinking that you could hide a body in the trunk of the El Dorado when Smith said aloud, "You could hide a body in here."

I have never believed in ghosts. I am not one to lend more weight to coincidence than it deserves. But Smith sang harmony to my internal voice while I was thinking the same exact words about hiding dead bodies in the trunk of the car. The hairs on the back of my neck saluted.

I wobbled my head as though to loosen the paranormal from whichever lobe it had become attached.

"Let's finish up," I said, lifting the typewriter. "And get the hell out a here."

"I want that with me."

Gratefully, I put the Underwood on the passenger seat.

With everything stowed, Smith once again refused to get in the car. He complained in his cryptic manner that the Old Man's Cadillac had something or other wrong with it.

"Come on, Bob. Get in." I hesitated over the opened trunk.

"You don't understand," Smith said.

"No, 'spose not." My squint deepened. "You know, that Delivery Boy'll show up any minute now. Be convenient for him, both of us standing here."

Smith was distracted by a three-foot goblin that ran past us screaming with delight and gripping a candy bar.

"It's just a kid, okay?"

Smith shook his head. "You don't understand. I eat food, and the taste tells me intimate details about the animal or plant."

It was nonsense.

"Get in the car."

He removed a jar of mayonnaise from one of the boxes in the trunk and held it before me.

"This is the worst."

"I'm not in the mood, Bob."

"It's the eggs. Scores of them in something like a hen gulag. Chickens in wire cages deceived by artificial light and injected with hormones."

I yanked the mayonnaise jar from his hand, replaced it in the box, and slammed the trunk shut.

"Eggs are their little babies," Smith said. "Have you ever considered that?"

I shrugged in surrender. "No, can't say that I have."

"And then there's pork. I can't eat pork. Had a liverwurst sandwich once, almost made me crazy."

I gave an exasperated shake of the head.

"I thought that I was a hog on a farm. Really. I know what you're thinking, that I imagined myself being a hog. That isn't it at all. For a few minutes I really was a hog, the very hog they made the liverwurst out of. I was in a pen."

I went to the passenger door, shaking my head.

"Or whatever you call those things where they roll in the mud. I loved my hog wives and piglets. Loved the smell of my farmer's hands in the feed trough. For a time, all seemed well with the world."

"Bob?"

"The next thing you know, I'm separated from my family and loaded onto a truck with others, pigs I don't know. An awful man drove us to a slaughterhouse. I could smell death long before we arrived. A horrible smell. A cross between the copper-taste of blood and burnt hair.

"There was a lot of squealing and jostling around me. It was stifling in the yard where they kept us. All of a sudden I was ushered up a ramp that led into the slaughterhouse. It was so slippery with blood that I almost lost my balance. At the top, on a little platform, they slit my throat. I got all this from one bite of a liverwurst sandwich."

"Can we focus here?"

"The previous owner. He did something in the back seat he was really ashamed of," Smith said.

I explained to him that it was my father's car, D. Charles Austin, Sr. I said that shame was not part of the Old Man's vocabulary.

"He had sex with a woman in the car. Not his wife. Someone he deceived. A very young girl. You have to understand. I'm ultra-sensitive to these things."

"Yeah, you're like lactose intolerant."

"If I sit there, I run the risk of absorbing the Karma."

"Would you give it a break," I said, waving my hands in the air.

Bob Smith wore a defeated look.

"Just get in the car!"

Smith reluctantly took the passenger seat and held the beige suitcase across his lap. I walked around to the driver's side, mumbling curses like little prayers to the inexplicable.

Even so, from downtown all the way to the exurbs, I could not help but think about what Smith had said, that the Old Man had tricked a girl into having sex with him, in the car. I burned with questions that I dared not ask. Not until we hit Cajon Junction did anything close to conversation take place.

"Tell me something. You think my old man really got some chick to, you know, in the back of the Caddy?"

Smith said he did not want to discuss the affair because the image provoked by "residues of their presence" had upset him.

I grinned at the thought that I was not so different from D. Charles Austin, Sr., after all. I couldn't count the number of times I had used my position as talent agent and script broker to get laid. Apparently, the Old Man had followed the same practice. The acorn had fallen pretty damn close to the tree.

Just outside of San Bernardino, my head started pounding. On the drive east through the Mojave, I swallowed three Advils, and by the time the road straightened out in the basin, the pounding stopped. The heat was tolerable, and we drove with the windows down to augment the El Dorado's defective air conditioner.

When we passed a road sign at the side of the freeway that listed the number of miles to the next exit, Smith spoke.

"I lived in a trailer for a month, in that town."

"Oro Grande?"

Smith glanced at me.

"I had a horrible time. I'd just gotten out of the mental hospital."

"Seeing aliens and stuff?" I smirked.

Smith turned away in disgust.

"Look, Bob, there's something we need to talk about"

When he made no response, I continued.

"I got to ask you. Look, how is it you make up stuff, you know, in the screenplay? Stuff that kinda happens? Now, don't get me wrong, okay? But all this street prophet nonsense, I ain't buying it. I want you to be straight with me. You know, *mano a mano* type of thing."

"There's the exit for Oro Grande," he said, ignoring me. "My wife and son are the real victims in this whole thing. Why did you go to her house? Why did you do that, Mr. Austin? You upset her."

"So, you two pretty close, huh?" I said sarcastically.

Bob Smith's eyes watered.

"Are you living in your screenplay again?" I said, checking the rearview mirror and preparing to pass a slow truck. "What do I call you now? Dr. Dawson?"

"You had no right."

The roar of the Caddy's engine drowned out our conversation until we passed a semi-tractor trailer.

"When was the last time you saw 'em?" I asked as a challenge to his obvious prevarication.

"I visit them every day."

"Astral plane type of thing, huh?"

He took a deep breath through his nose and exhaled slowly. With a voice half an octave lower, he said, "I want you to promise me something, Mr. Austin. That you won't do that again…to my wife."

I glanced at Smith and shrugged off his audacity.

"Wife, huh? Come off it. Chloe's what, thirty-two, thirty-five at most? May-December kinda romance?" I shook my head. "You're full of it, Bobby."

"Promise me, Mr. Austin, no more pictures, or our little road trip ends here."

"Sure. Yeah. No more pictures. Promise."

I crossed my heart, mocking, grinning.

All of a sudden, Smith reached across and gripped the steering wheel.

"Hey, what the…. Let go!"

Smith showed surprising strength as he pulled down on the wheel, sending the car to the right. I fought the steering wheel, but Smith resisted with remarkable force. The El Dorado left the freeway pavement, and the tires ground against the shoulder gravel and sent up a cloud that billowed behind us.

I struggled to correct our course but could not.

I hit the brakes, but instead of slowing down, the engine whined and the car accelerated. I had lost command of the El Dorado.

"Let go!"

"Promise me, Mr. Austin," Smith yelled above the roar of the old pistons.

The paroxysm of gravel was a tornado behind us.

The El Dorado fishtailed, and I managed to correct it.

"Let go, damn it!" I shouted. "Let go!"

Smith mouthed the words: "Promise me."

Fighting to keep the car from careening off the shoulder, I shouted at Smith. "What? *What!*"

"No pictures of my wife." he said.

"Okay okay! Promise. I *promise!*"

Smith released the steering wheel, and I brought the El Dorado under control as we slowed gradually on the shoulder embankment.

I heard the Doppler effect of a car horn passing us. It took close to one hundred yards to come to a stop. A cloud of dust billowed over us and settled like confectioner's sugar on the windshield.

The semi-tractor trailer roaring past with horns blaring broke the stillness inside the car.

"You could'a killed us, you know that?"

"I made my point, Mr. Austin."

"Cut out the *Mr. Austin* crap."

I was filled with indignation. Rage was something that often took control of my emotions, but I could feel this particular anger building inside like magma.

Smith said, "Now we can proceed."

I slapped the steering wheel. "Goddamned fucking asshole."

I hustled out of the car and slammed the door shut. Smith watched passively as I kicked pebbles and dirt off the shoulder like a baseball player angry at an umpire's call. I picked up a rock and hurled it at the "Emergency Parking Only" sign. I ranted and cursed the facsimile of God. Eventually, my rage tapered, and I returned and opened the driver's door.

"This is not working," I said, leaning inside.

Smith reached across and laid his hand on mine. I pulled away.

"Don't do that."

"You're quitting, aren't you?" Smith asked.

"Whatever."

I got in the car and gripped the steering wheel.

"I think it's fair to warn you," Smith began, "if we go back now, I can't say what will happen with the screenplay."

"I don't give a flying fuck about the screenplay. We're finished here. I'm going back."

I turned over the engine and nursed the accelerator to test whether or not I had regained control of the car. I wanted to make certain the brakes and gas pedal operated as intended.

"You're lucky I don't make you walk back."

Methodically, I put the El Dorado in gear and moved forward cautiously. Then I applied the brakes, and we came to a rest, the motor purring. Everything seemed to function normally.

I leaned toward Smith and stuck my finger in his face. "Don't...do *not* touch the steering wheel. Is that clear?"

Smith stared ahead in silence.

I was thinking, as soon as I got back to L.A., I planned on getting the Caddy checked out by a good mechanic, not some Latino rip-off artist with dollar signs for tattoos. The broken accelerator and faulty brakes could have cost me my life, such as it was. Impulsively, I took the next exit and crossed over the freeway. As we entered the onramp and drove west, back toward L.A, Bob Smith tightened his grip on the suitcase. It was clear to me—he hadn't expected this predicament.

Ω   Ω   Ω

Bob Smith and I sat in a booth at a coffee shop that was attached to a truck stop with service stations selling diesel and prepackaged sandwiches. The map said we were north of Victorville. It might as well have been a place called Desolation and Want. Victorville sat on the edge of the Los Angeles sprawl. Ahead of us was a metropolis of ten million or more, behind the sparsely populated borderlands of Southern California desert.

In the cafe we were taciturn behind menus raised against one another. I was fuming over the incident in the car. We had stopped for breakfast because Smith complained that he was hungry. I simply wanted to get back to Echo Park and pick up the pieces of my life. But I figured I could use a cup of coffee to settle my nerves.

The coffee shop was nearly empty. At the counter, two waitresses and a busboy watched a game show on the Toshiba. A contestant bought a vowel, and Vanna White rotated the tiles, clapping like the goddess of kitsch. Television is ubiquitous in our culture.

Our waitress wiped the table and handed us menus. Bob Smith placed his ever-present suitcase on the seat. He reminded me of the Dustin Hoffman character in *Rainman*, persnickety and mentally defective. The waitress placed two water glasses on doilies. Her nametag read, "Hello, my name is" with a blank where the name was supposed to be. She wore a button that said "Boo" with a picture of Casper the Ghost. A bra strap drooped at the shoulder of her peach uniform. She stood at the ready, tapping a pencil on the order pad.

"What'll it be, gentlemen?"

"Coffee. Black."

"That all?"

I nodded.

I saw repugnance in her eyes. The waitress was dis'ing me. Smith and I must have looked like butt-ugly white trash with his scraggly beard and frayed business suit, and my nearly baldpate with ponytail.

Getting old, being middle-aged, and having no prospects sucked. We all want to be desired. It's what Hollywood is all about, desire being the essence of movie making. My psychotherapist told me that my harmful sexual desires arose from an inadequate relationship with my mother, whatever that means. Even Delores Austin found me wanting, as a son, as a person. It has been my experience that all species of women, legions of their persuasion, including the waitress at the truck stop, have agreed that I am wholly repugnant.

I closed the menu and looked over at Smith.

"And you, sir?" the waitress asked.

He studied the menu, browsing for the least offensive item in the breakfast column. Nothing seemed to Smith's liking.

I decided that I should eat something. "I changed my mind. Bring me a Number Five. Eggs and bacon look good."

I pointed at the picture of food.

"You betcha, doll. How do you like your eggs?" She smiled.

Things were looking up.

"Over easy. Bacon crisp," I said.

"What about you, honey?"

"Bob, the nice lady's talking to you."

"I can't make up my mind."

The waitress and I exchanged knowing smiles. I said, "He's a little picky about what he eats."

"Why don't I get your coffee?"

Once the waitress left, I reached over and pulled down Smith's menu.

"You gonna make a scene or what?" I asked.

Smith struggled to raise the menu against my resistance.

"Don't make a scene, Bob."

Smith shook his head. "Okay."

I let the menu go, and he raised it between us.

"You just don't get it. My brain works differently than yours."

"I just want some breakfast, okay?" I said, rolling my eyes. "Not in the mood to listen to your problems."

The waitress returned with a cup of coffee that she set before me. She turned to Smith with her plucked eyebrows raised impatiently.

"I'll have," Smith began, "the buttermilk pancakes, please."

"Sausage or Canadian bacon?"

"Neither, thanks."

"Costs nothing extra, hon."

"Just the pancakes."

"So, we got a Number Five over easy for you and buttermilk cakes no sausage." She retrieved the menus. "Coffee for you?"

Smith declined.

"We got iced tea," she said.

"No. No stimulants, thanks."

As soon as the waitress left, Smith leaned forward and pressed his hands on the Formica table.

"May I explain something to you?"

"Nope," I said curtly.

"I owe you an explanation."

"No, you don't."

Smith blinked.

"Perhaps it would make more sense, be more convincing if I showed you."

"Do what you like," I said, getting up from the table, irritated. "I'm gonna buy a paper."

As I turned to walk away, Smith said, "There's one behind you, two booths down."

I hesitated.

"A newspaper," he clarified.

"Uh huh."

"Over there." Smith gave some encouragement. "Take a look."

Just to prove the old man wrong, I took two steps backwards toward the other booth. The busboy had yet to clear the dirty dishes, and, yes, a newspaper lay folded on the seat, hardly touched. I picked it up.

"Don't play games, Bob. You saw this when we came in." I shook the paper at him. "You waited for just the right moment to play that out."

"Believe what you like."

I studied him momentarily. The dude was spooky with his dark eyes and exaggerated gray forelock, the full beard. He reminded me of an American Rasputin, early Twenty-First Century version. I have worked around phonies all my life, and I can smell one a mile away. His clairvoyance gig was definitely a put on. There was no way I was going to let him get away with it. No way.

"Tell me something," I said, taking a seat. "The screenplay, it's from personal experience then?"

"That's right."

Smith struck a forthright manner. I worked my jaw muscles.

"And you're sticking with this bull? That you're Joe Dawson?"

"Correct."

"No way. First of all, Chloe, your wife, she's too young."

Smith blinked.

"Take a look in the mirror, Bobby Boy. You're old. And I've seen her. You're not her type." I wagged my index finger. "She's a cutie. You're definitely not her type."

The waitress brought condiments of catsup and Tabasco sauce. She replenished my coffee and left us alone again.

"You had no right to take her picture, Mr. Austin." He was sulking.

"Well, hell," I said, "you claim you left her, right? You abandoned her, according to your—"

"I had no choice," Smith interrupted. "I had to leave them."

"Is that right?"

"Yes. What would you have done?"

"What, if I heard voices, saw little green men? I would'a called the airlines and made reservations for a weekend in Cabo. Snooze on the beach."

"Drink too much tequila."

"Yeah, maybe," I said defensively.

"No, you wouldn't have. You would have closed the shades and stayed in bed until the symptoms went away. Maybe watched some pornographic material."

Although I hated to admit it, the old man was right.

"And then, when what you thought were hallucinations persisted, when the aliens in your living room turned out to be real?"

"You said you made that up."

"Then you would have called your connection."

I sipped my coffee. He was beginning to piss me off, again.

"I haven't used in weeks, thanks to you."

"Mr. Austin, don't insult my intelligence. You're clean because you haven't been able to score in the last few weeks. Am I using the correct term, *score*? Or is it called something else?"

The waitress brought our breakfast and laid the Number Five on Smith's place setting and the short stack before me. "Do I have that wrong?" she asked, looking at her order slip.

As Smith exchanged the plates, I said, "No harm done."

My Number Five looked nothing like the picture on the menu.

I watched as Smith poured syrup over the pancakes. He poked gingerly at the stack with a fork, like a hunter probing for life in a fresh kill.

"You wanna send it back?" I asked.

Smith shook his head and cut the stack in half. He proceeded to divide it into perfect quarters and then he quartered these as well, each three-layers-thick, trim and tidy. Satisfied by the symmetry, he speared a mouthful and ate.

It was disgusting.

I poured catsup generously over my eggs, bacon, and cottage fries, swirled it in a mixture no longer resembling a Number Five, and took a bite. I glanced up to find the old man watching me.

"What?" I said through a mouthful of food.

"In the distant past, mammals did exactly the same thing with dinosaur eggs." Smith stared at his pancakes. "Clearly, they did not have tomato catsup, but mammals have been eating eggs since time began."

"Mammals," I mumbled. I could not have cared less.

"That's right. You don't think the dinosaurs died out entirely because of one cataclysmic event, do you? Your ancestors stole dinosaur eggs, raided nests and nesting grounds, for hundreds of thousands of years, reducing the dinosaurs' numbers. You, Mr. Austin, are practicing a ritual of domination of one species over another. Eating chicken eggs is a celebration of the genocide that we mammals have been practicing for millions of years. It's a battle with the reptiles for domination of the globe. It's in your genes."

I shoved in another mouthful.

"Thanks for the update."

The old man cut off a corner of his perfectly stacked pancakes.

"You see," he said, "you are under the false impression that you are alone at the center of the universe."

I wrinkled my brow at the old man and lowered my line of sight to the newspaper before me. "Why don't we just eat and not talk, okay?"

"For example. Your reading the newspaper proves my point. Your behavior, listening to the radio, watching the Today Show, all of it driven by ancient genetic patterns."

"Do we have to go into this now?"

"Have you ever gone camping, in the wilderness, and been awakened by animal sounds? That's when they do most of their communicating, in the morning. The chipmunk will sit on a branch and make noises to his pals. He's telling them what's going on in his territory. What he saw during the night. Who to watch out for. Same with whales, although their circadian rhythms are not so much nocturnal as diurnal. Nonetheless, they sing to one another about the location of rich plankton or particular currents in the sea."

"Uh huh. Not interested, Bob."

I picked up the paper and pretended to read, ignoring the old man.

"How different from the rest of the animal kingdom is you're behavior? You're gathering information on how to structure your day, Mr. Austin. Simply because we mask our instinctual behaviors in what you call civilization—"

"Look," I said, "I'm tryin' to read here. Do you mind?"

"Just thought you might like some conversation."

In exasperation I glanced up at the counter. A customer and two waitresses were gathering like flightless birds around the television. Something reported in the news had drawn their attention while a network anchor provided the details.

When our waitress hurried by the table, I asked, "What's up?"

"Oh, that? Some kind of sickness or something." She shrugged. "I don't know. Sounds kinda scary."

On the television there was a set shot of a medical center. Inset was the photograph of a female reporter. She had a bemused, unsuitable expression, as comely as a movie star. In juxtaposition, the voice-over somberly issued statistics of *le tragédie du jour.*

Seemingly unaffected by the news story, Bob Smith mopped up his pancakes.

I went to the counter and asked the waitress, "Could we have more volume, please?"

She reached up and turned the dial on the old black and white import.

"—contrary in some cases, but this is what we have at this hour."

Behind the photograph of the reporter, they ran stock footage of a research laboratory in which scientists wore protective clean-room suits. They resembled astronauts preparing to step outside the Space Shuttle.

"Of the dozen or so patients admitted last night, five are being treated in isolation. A hospital spokesperson has told CNN that the quarantine is strictly a precaution. The medical care team treating these patients has not identified the cause of a runaway infection. At this hour, CNN has learned that the patients are resting comfortably but that their mysterious illness is not responding to antibiotic therapy.

"The families of the victims are…"

I turned back to Bob Smith whose attention was fastened to his meal. To describe my feeling as panic would be off the mark. Imagine a paranoiac who realizes his fears are true, that he's not paranoid after all, and that the world is tottering toward oblivion. Was I supposed to believe what my eyes and ears were telling me?

"…without knowing the course of the disease. CNN reporting at the top of the hour."

At its heart, *Path of Least Resistance* was the story of a coming plague. It had all the elements of a good plot about a washed up movie director named D. Charles Austin, Sr., into whose life walks Bob Smith, self-proclaimed screenwriter. Smith had written a treatment about a biotechnologist who is exposed to a deadly experimental virus and ends up with a bizarre set of symptoms. He can read people's minds and predict the future. Unfortunately, the future does not bode well for humanity. A deadly virus has been loosed on the world. Bob Smith explains to Mr. Austin that only a blockbuster movie will convince the world to stop biological warfare research. The director tries unsuccessfully to sell the concept to a film production agency. Mr. Big, the film producer, likes the concept, but the screenplay is unfinished, and he will not commit until he receives a completed screenplay. But no one knows how it ends, not even the screenwriter. Variations of Smith's assertion, "the future writes itself," had always raised my ire, but now I was convinced. Now I knew how it would end. The evidence was being reported on CNN.

I rushed back to our table and sat across from Smith, catching the breath that the news story had knocked out of me. He purposefully did not look up from his meal.

"Calm down, Mr. Austin."

I reached out and grasped his wrist.

"Does that news story remind you of something?"

"It's okay. Calm down. This is only the beginning."

When I let go of his wrist, Smith's ice-blue stare paralyzed me. It felt as though I had been caught in the glare of prison searchlights in a failed escape attempt. We sat in silence for the moment while I caught my breath and waited for the pounding inside my head to lessen. The paranoia in my eyes and the compassion in Smith's were like opposing magnets.

"How does the screenplay predict things?" I asked. "What now, are we gonna start dying from a plague or something? Is that what you carry in your suitcase? You got some kinda anecdote in there?"

"*Antidote*. And no, there is no cure."

Smith's facial expression hardened with stoic resolve. I had the feeling that all along he knew this would happen, knew that he and I would be seated at a truck stop cafe in the desert borderlands when we first heard reports of a "mysterious illness." The screenplay had predicted everything, and yet I, my mind a wasteland of narcotic and alcohol abuse, had renounced the inevitable. Smith reached out and patted my forearm reassuringly.

I wanted to ask why he had not warned the victims. If he knew, why had he not telephoned the authorities at the medical center? Why had he spent the time writing a mediocre screenplay when the future hung in the balance?

"There's no way I can stop this from happening, if that's what you're thinking," he said. "Knowing what's going to happen, doesn't mean you can change the outcome."

I ran a hand over my thinning hair, reaching for the security of the ponytail.

"I can't believe this."

"It doesn't matter whether you believe it or not."

Smith went back to eating his breakfast. He was taken up by whatever sensations the ingredients on his plate inspired. From what he had told me at the Glide Hotel about his apprehension of mayonnaise and pork, for all I knew, the pancakes danced with him through fields of Iowa wheat or skipped the light fandango in a sugar maple grove. I was afraid to provoke or distract him from the phantasm.

You talk about bad timing: my coke craving was made worse by the anxiety. It has been my experience that stress aggravates the craving. Skin bugs were migrating into my brain. I was reminded of *The Twilight Zone* episode where a pregnant earwig passes through the victim's skull, in one ear, out the other, giving birth in transit to hundreds of pupae.

My breakfast sat wasted on the plate, cold cottage fries drowning in a slurry of catsup and eggs. Nausea had nothing to do with either my lack of appetite or the inferiority of the food.

When the waitress cleared the table, she asked if I wanted anything else.

I wanted to laugh hysterically, to plead that she cure my sickness of soul and take away my memory of the news report. I wanted to stop thinking about a biotech company in La Jolla named XyberGen. I wanted to spend the rest of my life far removed from the consequences of my relationship with Bob Smith. I thought about the Sig Sauer in the glove compartment of the El Dorado. I thought about masturbating poolside at the Laguna Nigel. Looking up at the waitress, I thought: *Bring me something to correct the deficit of my character before I die.*

Instead, I said, "Just the check."

When I stuck a Marlboro in my mouth, Bob pointed out the No Smoking sign.

"I was gonna go outside, if it's all the same to you," I told him. "And for your information, the whole state's non-smoking, thank you very much."

I opened my wallet and threw down two tens and made my way out of the restaurant. Through the double glass doors, I looked back at Smith, who was still seated in the booth. He was drawn to the Keno numbers on the blue monitor above the bar.

After smoking two cigarettes in the parking lot, I leaned against the El Dorado and engaged in an internal argument that I would be better off without him. The two elements of my nature entered into the dispute. My angelic nature said: "The old man's trying to tell you something, DC. Listen to him. Be patient. It may save your life."

"Forget it," replied my demons, which are legion. "You'd be better off on your own. Screw the screenplay. From the sound of it, the world is coming to an end. What are you hanging out with this lunatic for? Get out of here. Go get laid!"

As usual with these inner quarrels, the demons were victorious.

I needed to get high. I wanted to get laid.

I unlocked the El Dorado and opened the glove compartment. The Sig Sauer tumbled out and clanked on the floor. It reminded me of the reason for our road trip, but the menace of Whitaker Fetch seemed trivial compared to the coming of a Black Death. I searched for a partial bindle of coke that I may have misplaced among the obsolete road maps. Nothing. I fingered the ashtray for a roach, anything to take the edge off. There was nothing. An empty bottle of Jack Daniel's rolled under the seat. I was clean by default.

I stepped away from the car just as the old man was returning from the restaurant. He held cash in one hand, his suitcase in the other, looking the part of an idiot savant.

He handed me the money and declared happily, "I paid for breakfast. There's only eighteen there. Had to borrow two bucks."

I counted the cash.

"Thought you said you were broke."

Smith nodded his head.

"So, what, you telling me you left two bucks on the table?"

He shook his head.

I got into the car and inserted the key in the ignition, thinking that any minute now the manager would dash out of the cafe, demanding at the top of his lungs that we pay our check.

"How'd you pay for breakfast, Bob?"

"I played Keno."

"You played Keno."

He gave a self-satisfied nod.

"No, you didn't," I said.

I was wondering how much he had won. Keno had the worst odds in gambling. I was thinking, was it just blind luck, or perhaps Smith was autistic? Once again, the motion picture *Rainman* came to mind, but this time I substituted Richard Farnsworth in the Dustin Hoffman role.

"Yes, I did. Twenty bucks," Smith said. "I won."

It was as though I could feel the whole world grinding to a halt. Smith sat childlike in the El Dorado. I was thinking that his lunacy had been turned up a couple of notches. Either that or I was losing the final remnants of my own sanity.

I turned the engine over and idled it, feathering the pedal, breathing evenly.

"Bob," I said, carefully. "Why do I get the feeling you coulda won a lot more than twenty bucks?"

Settling into the passenger seat, Smith placed the suitcase on his lap. I put the Caddy in gear once he shut the door.

After a week of abstinence, my body was recoiling from a wicked Jones. I gripped the steering wheel and squeezed the blood out of my hands. Thoughts of doom sprinted through my mind like Olympian extras from *Night of the Living Dead*. The screenplay was coming to life before my eyes. The CNN News report of a mysterious illness helped me connect the dots. I imagined billions dying in the major cities of the world, pyres of burning bodies tended by those who envied them; scores of bloated dead awaiting burial that never came, orphans beside their dead parents, flies pestering their eyes where no more tears could fall; fires flickering against a dark skyline of charred buildings; civilization in ruin; chaos and anarchy, the dissolution of order. I envisioned the end of history. And Ground Zero was just down the road.

Get a grip, I told myself.

The screenplay was *only* a screenplay, I reminded myself, a complete fiction. I had been living with *Path of Least Resistance* for so long that my chintzy low-life world of porno queens and drug abuse had taken a back seat to Smith's vision of Apocalypse. I needed a couple of shots of Tequila to set myself straight.

I needed to get high, and what better place in the world to do that than Las Vegas?

I pulled the Caddy out of the truck stop parking lot and followed the signs to U.S. 15. Simply to rattle Smith's cage, I hesitated before entering the on-ramp. Rather than return to L.A., which I had threatened I would do, we headed east.

I could feel Bob Smith's smile of victory when he said, "Las Vegas here we come. I knew this would happen."

"Sure you did, Bob. Sure you did."

Chapter 13

"Hang up and drive, asshole!" I shouted.

A teen-aged girl on a cell phone behind the wheel of a convertible obstructed traffic in the fast lane. She was oblivious to the line of cars trailing bumper-to-bumper. As I passed on the right, I shouted out my window, "Hope you fuck better'n you drive!"

"Take it easy, Mr. Austin."

In an automotive rage, I turned toward Smith. "What's with this *Mr. Austin* crap? Why can't you call me by my name?"

Smith considered for a moment before replying. "I have a hard time calling you DC."

"Everybody calls me DC."

"It's like an electrical current or something."

I rolled my eyes at him. The old man smirked as his fingers danced across the typewriter keys. It was the first time in our acquaintance that he had resorted to humor. It disabled my anger over the stupid chick on the cell phone.

We drove past the Manix and Midway exits, past chaparral ranches and cattle feed lots near Baker. I was afraid the stench of manure would distract him, but Smith persevered. His fingers worked the typewriter like Bach at the harmonium, playing otherworldly music. He typed on the Underwood like a madman. Mile after mile, beyond suburban commuter traffic, past the exit to San Bernardino, he completed page after page. He folded each lengthwise and placed it in his shirt pocket. He looked like a ticket scalper at a major sporting event.

For the next half an hour, for nearly forty miles, we said little. The work kept Smith occupied. As he proofread the screenplay, he struck out passages and added new ones with intense concentration. He tucked a sheet of paper into the Underwood and spun the barrel with one hand while the other launched into a flurry of typing. He copied from a corrected page taped to the dashboard. He referred to this off and on. Once, when I scanned the radio dial for a station that played anything but gospel music, Smith protested, and I shut the radio off. He seemed bent on completing the screenplay before we reached Vegas, working against an imaginary deadline that excluded my needs or the demands of Rainy Day Films. Smith's deadline was timed to a world in which he alone lived, one that I occasionally glimpsed but was unwilling to acknowledge as real.

I sucked in the fresh desert air and glanced at the old man. "You working on the script?"

He nodded.

"Why don't you buy a laptop?"

He grimaced. "I prefer analog technology."

The old boy's a Luddite, I thought.

I reached for my cigarettes in the glove compartment. I was still shaken up by the Keno incident at the coffee shop. His winning had defied all logic. I wanted to doubt what Smith had said, that he "saw" the numbers. It was in my best interest to doubt him. After all, he was working overtime to convince me the world was coming to an end. If I accepted that he'd won at Keno, I would have to accept his assertions about a coming plague.

"So," I said, "what difference could that make now, you know, to finish the screenplay…if the world's going to come to an end?" My look challenged him. "With the plague and all."

Smith blinked and turned slowly, robotically. There was a universe of hurt in his eyes, as though he had read my mind and knew that I doubted him.

"It matters a lot that you believe me."

I raised one hand off the steering wheel in a gesture of mock apology. "I'm working on it."

"Didn't you insist just last night that I finish the screenplay?"

My poor sober brain was mulling over the possibility that Bob Smith really was Joe Dawson, husband of Chloe, father to Frank, and microbiologist extraordinaire. I was feeling ambivalent about learning the truth. I looked at Smith, really looked at him. He resembled a waxen version of Marilyn Manson—without the dress, of course. Over the few weeks of our acquaintance, I had never seen Smith wear anything but soiled pinstriped pants and a stained white shirt. He was an oddball, but an oddball with the uncanny ability to write scenes that gave the appearance of coming true, of coming to life.

"Is that a rewrite?" I asked, trying to change the subject to silence the voices in my head. "Tell me something. Where'd you learn to do that? You know, write screenplays?"

"I am an autodidact."

When I gestured that I didn't have a clue what he had meant, Smith continued.

"Self-taught. I am an avid supporter of the public library," he said at last. "Entire shelves are dedicated to how to write a screenplay."

Smith removed the page from the Underwood and reached for another on the back seat.

Years ago, I knew a pretty good screenwriter who dressed up like his characters. It was a fabulous technique for really getting into your writing. But he went too far by putting on women's clothing and wearing make-up. When a particularly challenging female lead stumped him, the poor bastard ended up on the surgery table getting a Lorena Bobbitt Special after a year of receiving hormone therapy, all in an effort to finish a difficult screenplay. When he finally became a girl, she wrote the script, but by then she was very unhappy with her new gender. She confessed to her therapist that she had been confused about her sexual identity and wanted to be a man again. But it was too late. The doctors had whacked off her manhood. Bob Smith reminded me of the writer. Both had the same *modus operandi*. How was I to account for Smith's alter ego Joe Dawson? Was he just pretending to be a biotechnologist with an axe to grind? Or was he the genuine article?

The constituents of *Path of Least Resistance* were mixed up in my perception of reality. So much of what he had written had already come true: the CNN report of a mysterious illness; the parallels between the screenplay and my life; the theme of mind reading and Smith's own uncanny luck at Keno. After I had read the first scene about the Old Man's car breaking down on the freeway, the El Dorado broke down when I was driving it. What was that all about? No doubt certain characters within the play were real. Events in my regular life had taken place that were foretold in specific scenes. It was uncanny. There were the parallels with the scene from the screenplay and the concept meeting at Rainy Day Films. But the CNN report of people coming down with a mysterious illness, that had not appeared in any scenes in the story, not that I had read anyway.

What was I supposed to believe? Years ago I worried that narcotics had destroyed my grip on reality. But Bob Smith was really exacerbating my fears. Nothing will undercut your soundness of mind more profoundly than driving through the desert with a psychic screenwriter.

Once again, I began to lose my grip on what I thought was real. My former psychotherapist encouraged me to take medication for what he called bi-polar disorder or manic depression. I told him that I wanted nothing to do with a disease that had "bi" in the name. I suppose, I am my own worst enemy, and many of the decisions I make are often reversed within minutes. Perhaps sobriety was my enemy on this road trip, I don't know. It definitely skewered my perception of the world and Bob Smith.

"How much longer to Las Vegas?"

"Hour or so. Wanna stop or something, stretch your legs?"

Smith shook his head.

The vessel of his eyes held an eternity of grief. I have never seen such sadness.

Within the hour, we pulled off the freeway near Roach and ordered lunch at a MacDonald's Drive Thru. I had a Big Mac, fries and a Coke. Smith ate nothing.

"It'll be another hour or so before we eat again," I said. "Depending on traffic."

Smith didn't care. "MacDonald's cuts down rain forests to raise beef for burgers."

He was impossible.

We gassed up at a Chevron, and I bought two Snicker's bars in the MiniMart. A sugar high is a poor substitute for drugs and booze but my body craved stimulus. Flickering behind the Pakistani at the counter, a small television blathered on about an explosion in the Russian embassy in San Francisco. CNN aired a live feed from a helicopter over The City where smoke rose from the burning building. The reporter said that the initial investigation had attributed the explosion to a terrorist organization in the United States with ties to Chechnyan separatists.

"Eh bomb, can you believe it, no-ting stop deh bananaman," the Pakistani said.

Without hearing him clearly, I was certain he had meant something other than *bananaman*. It was lost in translation.

The Pakistani smiled generously and handed me my change. "God is good. Happy Halloweenie."

When I returned to the El Dorado, I found one of the rear tires flat. It took forever to get the damn thing changed. First, we had to remove all of Smith's paraphernalia to get to the spare in the trunk. Smith was no help at all. He complained about my handling the boxes, like they were full of plutonium or something. Next, we had to get the spare fixed at the service station; it was flat as well. Finally, with the spare at thirty-two PSI, I found that I couldn't loosen the lug nuts off the wheel of the flat tire. Two teen-aged boys and I pushed the Caddy into the service station bay with Smith at the wheel giving directions. They used a pneumatic wrench to remove the lug nuts. Cost me thirty bucks and three hours of road time.

When we returned to the freeway the sun was setting behind us. Smith shouldered on resolutely, writing, but the failing light limited his accuracy on the keyboard. Before long, he was admonishing himself for the typos and rummaging through the boxes for a bottle of correction fluid. Eventually, he gave up and replaced the Underwood on the back seat. He faced forward in silence while I ate a Snicker's. For several miles our interplay consisted of my smoking a Marlboro and his expressed discontent by rolling down the window.

The El Dorado's headlights projected a cone-shaped beam that dissipated across a desolate landscape. It was eight fifteen when a quarter moon rose ancient and lonely above the desert. As the sky darkened, the moon cast a faint light upon the wide concrete of the Interstate, and from inside the car with its blue instrument lights, it felt like we were flying.

As we hurtled through the evening, one thought wore down my self-imposed rule about raising the doubt of contradiction.

"Let me ask you something, all right?" I said. "I need to know more about this Delivery Boy."

"His name is Whitaker Fetch. What do you want to know?" Smith asked.

In *Path of Least Resistance,* the Delivery Boy worked for a mysterious organization. I doubted this to be the case with Whitaker Fetch. I wanted to know for whom he worked and what he wanted with me.

"As I told you," Smith said. "He wants my suitcase."

"You told me he was trying to kill me," I reminded him.

Smith smiled. "I just said that to get your attention. Actually, he has no interest in you. Mr. Fetch is chasing after me."

"So, you lied to me."

Smith shrugged.

"Tell me, did we lose him or is he still chasing us?"

He shrugged again.

"Can't you do your mind-reading thing?" I said mockingly. "Bob, how come, if you're so clairvoyant, how come you confused me with my old man?"

"I'm not clairvoyant. I see things."

"Like Keno numbers? Tell me, how you do that?"

"I won't let you exploit me." He looked out the window at the approaching lights of Las Vegas. "This is where it ends. How do you rectify a man who comes to Earth and performs miracles, who is vilified and disabused?"

"What're you talking about, Bob?" I laughed.

"And ends up here?"

I glanced sideways. His face was etched in the blue dashboard lights, ghostlike and otherworldly.

"*Miracles?* You think you're Jesus now? Some kind of prophet?"

He made me nervous. Hell, maybe he *was* the Second Coming. How was I to know? If he were Jesus, why would he choose to reveal himself to me, an inebriated pornographer down on his luck? I squinted at Smith, and the vision of him sitting there in the dashboard light convinced me the old guy might be who he said he was.

He spoke so softly and with such kindness that I found myself leaning toward him to hear.

"Listen. Think what you will, but this is *not* just about weapons of mass destruction. We are engaged in a struggle, you and I, against the destructive nature of ourselves."

I could *feel* his eyes on me as I drove.

"I want you to remember something," he said. "I want you to remember that there are no coincidences in life." He swallowed. "Life is like reading a screenplay."

I laughed nervously, but Smith shouldered on.

"Think of our road trip as a movie. This scene is the here and now. Whatever lies ahead of you in the screenplay, let's say the next page, it is unknown. You anticipate what will happen because you are familiar with the plot and general theme, but you really don't know. On the contrary, I am able to read ahead. I know what's going to happen next.

"How different are films, Mr. Austin, and divining the future? The screenwriter performs a divination. He knows what will happen before you do, but when you watch a film for the first time, the ending or a twist in the plot surprises you. Something you didn't expect. Don't get me wrong. I'm not writing the future. I'm merely reading it. It is already written. That is, in a sense, how it feels."

"But how do you see things? Like with Keno numbers. The odds against are a million to one, you know that?"

Smith shifted his weight and turned to gaze at the rising moon. The way the light played in the dead land was lyrical.

"They came to me as a metaphor."

I said, "I wasn't much in school with metaphors and the like."

He explained patiently. "Motion pictures on celluloid, as they used to be made, are a series of still photographs strung together. These are projected by passing them before an illuminated lens around thirty or more frames per second. This gives the illusion of movement, of time. This is analogous to life, is it not? Each moment is a single still photograph linked together forward into the future and backwards to the past."

I was wondering, listening to his voice and driving that straight desert road, if Smith could change fate, maybe he could alter the future by rewriting the screenplay. And as I listened, I had an epiphany of sorts. I decided that Smith could save the world not by making a motion picture but by rewriting the screenplay and giving it a happy ending. I was going to tell him my idea when he started talking again.

"Let me explain it this way. Time is a freeway, and your life is the Cadillac driving down the road. The present is what you see around you, on either side. The past is in the rearview mirror, the future ahead in the windshield. Make sense?"

Lights from the dashboard reflected in his eyes, and I nodded.

"Good. Now in life we have options. We make choices, but unfortunately most people ignore the Map, the Guide for our choices. When we come to a crossroads or freeway interchange, the best guess about which direction to take is based on past experience. There is no way to know what lies ahead in the dark because we see only as far as our headlights."

"Okay," I said, not understanding what Smith had meant by Map or Guide. Instead, I was thinking of telling Smith that he had to rewrite the screenplay.

"Take your friend Max Gleason for example."

"He's not my friend."

"He's the sort of person whose sense of self-preservation determines his behavior. When confronted by a choice, he takes the path of least resistance. The path with the highest probability of personal gain, regardless of how immoral the consequence or unethical the outcome. As much as I hate to say this, you have wasted your entire life taking the easiest route, the least resistant path."

"Bob," I said, "what's this got to do with the screenplay?"

"You asked how I see things, how I know the future. I'm trying to explain my way of knowing. But listen. No one other than God knows the future. Did you hear what I said?"

I bristled at the mention of God.

"We are God's creations, but we are a species of unlimited options. We can leverage our options for good or for evil. It depends on the individual, on which path they choose. Collectively, the outcome of history largely depends on the choices we make. The biotech company XyberGen, they have made a collective choice. A very dangerous choice. My only hope is that the screenplay will be made into a movie and that it may do some good. For each of us, it boils down to what we choose to do with our options. Most of us take the easy route. All you have to do is take a look around to see how much we've screwed up."

Smith conceded my reaction. I rarely heard him use profanity, and I reacted to it by wheeling my head around and making a face.

"Where has this senseless commitment to technology, this madness we call progress, where has it taken us? To the brink, that's where. The threat of nuclear technology in the last century pales by comparison to the threat of biotechnology today. And it isn't just the Phage."

"You mean the virus," I said, "from the screenplay?"

"That's right. We face the danger of scientific knowledge. Our understanding of the basic principles of life has increased by an order of magnitude every decade. Did you read the newspaper article that I sent to your house?"

I nodded.

"The message of that clipping is simple. Scientific irresponsibility in today's world can lead to catastrophe on a scale unprecedented in history. My purpose in writing the screenplay, in working to make a motion picture out of it, has been to raise alarm. I've tried everything. Been on radio and television. Did you know that I was interviewed by Cokie Roberts?"

I had my doubts. "Oh yeah? Must have missed that."

"Soon after I lost my job at XyberGen, I was on the nightly news. Miss Roberts asked about biowarfare research. Nothing came of it."

Here we go again, I thought, *more identity confusion.*

"My screenplay is like a mirror. I'm asking that people look into it, to see what they have become, and see the awful choices we have made. At XyberGen we made a bad choice, a deadly choice. My purpose in getting a movie made is to hold up the mirror. But no one pays attention. Our culture is so visual. Television and the movies have distorted how we see ourselves and especially how young people see themselves and the world. Their gestures, smiles, their personalities are patterned after movie stars, and in that fantasy they ultimately lose themselves. They never find out their true nature. They think the camera is ever-present, recording lives that are patterned after make-believe ideas, make-believe people."

I shook my head and tried to make sense of his convoluted illogic.

"They're not gonna make your movie unless you finish the screenplay, Bob. Even if the future's, like, written in stone, whatever's gonna happen will happen whether we make the movie or not, right?"

Smith shook his head.

"You're a poor listener. We still have time. Nothing happens by coincidence, Mr. Austin. Even the most benign thing, like the flapping of bat wings in the night, can change the course of history. In that ridiculous city, in Las

Vegas, what we do over the course of the next few weeks will determine the fate of humankind."

"That's a little over the top, isn't it?"

"By admitting our mistakes, we are halfway to altering our fate," he said. "The problem is, Americans are spoiled. They seek easy solutions and take the easy path."

"Bob," I said, trying to stay on the subject. "We need to talk about rewriting the ending, you know? I mean, I don't know how it ends, but I got a pretty good idea."

"Do you read poetry, Mr. Austin?"

He was exasperating. I shook my head.

"Surely, you've read Yeats'? 'Mere anarchy is loosed upon the world, the blood-dimmed tide is loosed, and everywhere the ceremony of innocence is drowned; the best lack all conviction, while the worst are full of passionate intensity….'"

I knew the poem, having memorized it in school. I finished the quote with an affected Irish accent.

"'And what rough beast, its hour come round at last, slouches towards Bethlehem to be born'?"

Smith smiled. "Bravo, Mr. Austin. You surprise me. Well, it doesn't matter. The beast is us, unfortunately. We will be our own undoing."

"You lost me," I said.

"Don't make me repeat myself. My screenplay is about biological and virological weapons, about the virus that was discovered in my own lab. I've shouted from the tops of these very hills that all life hangs in the balance. No one listens. So, if I've *lost* you, it is because you were already lost."

We said nothing for a while as we passed the town of Erie and approached the Bard Mining District. I wanted to ask, since he believed the world was coming to an end, when it would happen.

Smith glanced my way.

"It will happen, Mr. Austin, soon enough. Unless we persuade people to choose another path."

That took the air out of my balloon. Why did I let myself get drawn into the tangle of Smith's mind? I scratched my chin, a nervous habit, to remind myself that in Vegas, or wherever we ended up spending the night, I should buy a shaving kit.

"What you're saying is," I said, "there's some kind of beast loosed on the world."

"The Phage is a virus that ordinarily attacks bacteria. We thought it had application in biowarfare. To be used against biological weapons, that is, as a kind of counter measure. It is an insidious little beast, Mr. Austin. The Phage has a kind of curlicue that drills into cellular walls. It becomes part of the replicating machinery of the nucleus and creates billions of offspring in a single day. It can infect connective tissue in twenty-four hours, saturating the victim. In the next phase, approximately two days post exposure, the infection breaks down the vasculature, like the dengue or hemorrhagic fever. You literally dissolve."

"Okay, okay, but...?"

"I'm trying to explain to you what we face."

"Okay, but if you're Joe Dawson," I said. "If you're Joe Dawson and you were exposed to this thing, this Phage, why aren't you dead?"

I smiled at my own logic.

"I was exposed to an analog, not the Phage itself. I don't expect you to understand, Mr. Austin. I was exposed to its benign cousin, if you will. It may hold the key to saving us all. I've been working on a vaccine. It has side-effects but it may work."

I glanced at him and thought about the suitcase he always carried around, and I thought about the chemistry equipment in his room at the Glide Hotel.

"You wanna know what I think? I think the best way to save the world is to rewrite the screenplay and give it a happy ending."

"Don't be ridiculous. The Phage is real. A monster. A thousand times more virulent than anything previously known. It is so deadly that unless politicians make choices not based on financial gain or what is politically correct, but on what they know to be right for the human race…unless the directors of the CDC and World Health Organization wake up, unless we reject all this prideful nonsense, the first of billions of medical cases will be reported here, at ground zero. Right here." He took a breath. "Rewriting the ending of the screenplay won't do anything to stop it."

"Okay, let's drop it," I said. "You're freaking me out. I mean, I didn't drive out here because of some deadly cold virus. I came out here to finish the screenplay."

"Let me assure you, Mr. Austin, this isn't child's play."

"Whatever. I'm here because you said I'd see how the screenplay ends. You promised to finish it. And that's exactly what you're gonna to do."

I had had enough for one night, listening to his end-of-the-world jive, and he sensed it. I could feel Smith's mind drifting away in the dark.

Chapter 14

In motion picture idiom, my brain was in development hell. Strung out and sober, subjected to Smith's terrifying nonsense, I was losing my grip on reality. It felt as though I was approaching Glitter Gulch like the Great Gonzo himself, stoned out of my mind on a thousand micrograms of acid. Only, instead of LSD, I was under the influence of a madman.

Finally, exhausted by his peripatetic foray, Smith snoozed in the passenger seat. With Smith asleep, I took the opportunity to stop at the first liquor store I saw, at a freeway strip mall. The pint of Wild Turkey was half empty by the time I returned to the Caddy. My cheeks were flushed from the alcohol, but more importantly, it had the effect of sobering my judgment of Smith. Booze cured my heebie-jeebies. My skepticism returned in full regalia to remind me that the old dude was nothing more than a screenwriter with a few screws loose.

The El Dorado crossed the Las Vegas city limits a little before nine o'clock when I drained the last of the Wild Turkey and hid the bottle under the front seat, smacking my lips with self-satisfaction. I took the third freeway off-ramp for South Las Vegas Boulevard into town.

The fantasy casinos floated ahead on a sea of light and from a long line of cars cruising The Strip. They say The Strip and Fremont Street Experience alone burn more wattage per year than the city of San Francisco. The laser at the top of the Luxor illuminated the low clouds. The Shuttle astronauts can see the laser from space. The vista of hotels rolled past the car windows like Pinocchio's Pleasure Island. Here was Disneyland for adults.

Contributing to the general mayhem of Sin City, it was Halloween, and the tourists were dressed in costume. The town celebrated as though it were Mardi Gras, blowing party horns and wearing carnival attire. It was difficult to tell the real hookers on the street from the tourists dressed up to look like hookers in the parade of abandon.

We neared a shabby neighborhood on East Flamingo where dead pine trees announced a mobile home park. *Paradise Court* the sign read. An obese woman, sitting in an aluminum lawn chair and wearing a scant bathing suit, pointed at the Caddy as we drove by. She was laughing, and I stared at her and wondered what was so funny.

I hit a pothole and jarred Smith awake. He cried out, "Chloe!"

At the corner, we waited for the traffic light to change.

The Wild Turkey had energized me and returned my mind to a conspiratorial state. Smith's crying out his "wife's" name got me to thinking.

When the light changed and we entered the intersection, I said, "Bob, tell me. How's about we take a little drive over to Chloe's place? See how things are? You know, make a reunion of it."

Smith shook his head.

"Why not?"

Smith shut his eyes and leaned against the door, arms folded. He yawned. "I can smell the booze, Mr. Austin. Who do you think you're fooling?"

The road took a dogleg to the right, and The Strip lay ahead. I caught the timed traffic lights to New York, New York and headed toward the Mandalay.

I set my jaw and found myself pulling on the steering wheel to discharge the pain that had worked its way down my arms. I was exhausted. We had been driving since midmorning, and I had little sleep the night before. My hands ached, and my eyes felt dry, gritty like coarse sandpaper. I needed a beer or two to follow the Wild Turkey. I was in no mood to argue. I had to settle in my mind whether Smith was telling the truth or not.

"Bob, time you faced some facts, okay?"

I was thinking how great it would be to see Chloe and Frank confront the old man, burst his bubble. It would be a family reunion from hell, for Smith at least.

I took a right and headed into the neighborhoods, into the Vegas the tourists never see.

Ω   Ω   Ω

The Dawson house was a typical ranch from the early Seventies: two bedrooms, worn-out shag carpeting, and 1300 square feet of ticky-tacky. Chloe had purchased it outright on the equity from the sale of their La Jolla home, after her husband lost his mind and entered the nuthouse. A poor substitute for their previous lives, it was nonetheless a roof over their heads but a modest house that would never be home.

Vegas was nothing like La Jolla. Chloe had one or two acquaintances in town, at the post office and bank, and a couple of friends from work—nurses—but none whom she considered close. Other women her age centered their lives on husbands and children, church and soccer practice, activities that excluded Chloe from their social circle. Of the single working mothers, she had even less in common. Despite her husband's absence, she wasn't looking for a second husband or a fling, and had no interest in the cocktail bars or dating scene. As such, Chloe spent her free time alone. She had taken up baking bread because, she maintained, Las Vegas bakers did not know French bread from Wonderbread. When loneliness bore down on her, when the frustration and anger at her husband's unreasonable behavior drained her of hope, she would bake. There were times when Frank came home from Saturday cross-country practice to a kitchen piled with loaves of warm bread cooling on wire racks, filling the house with the fragrance of yeast and crust. He would find his mother in a flour-stained apron sitting on a stool and gazing outwardly at something far away, longing for the way things used to be.

From what his mother could tell, Frank was popular at school. In his senior year he excelled in track and field as a cross-country runner. He won all conference and was one of six boys chosen to represent the county at the Interstate Track Meet in Fresno, California. He was doing well academically for the first time in his life, and he talked excitedly about college, despite the fact that he knew they could not afford tuition. Frank had adjusted to the change in their lives better than Chloe. By contrast, his mother was withdrawn, pathologically reserved in what few relationships she had formed over the past year.

When the doorbell rang that night, she had been doing a load of laundry. The rinse cycle on the washing machine drowned out the doorbell. Wearing her nurse's uniform, being too tired to change, coming home late from her shift, she was drying her hands on an apron when she opened the front door. She may have figured me for a Trick or Treater.

Even in the dim evening light, she recognized me immediately.

She slammed the door shut and threw the deadbolt.

"Mrs. Dawson?" I called out.

It isn't difficult to imagine what was going through her mind. She must have wondered why I had returned.

"Chloe?"

She later told me that she believed I was stalking her. It was the only explanation she could come up with. Ever since the afternoon I broke into her garage, images of me plagued her nightmares—a middle-aged man with a ponytail, with what she called an "underlying corruption and malevolent look."

Terror overcame her. She told herself to have courage. She knew that stalkers did not voluntarily give up the chase, and the police would do nothing until a crime was committed, but by then she figured, she could be dead or worse. She had decided that I was not going to get away with it a second time, not when I was locked outside.

She reasoned that, if she threatened to call 911, I would escape before the police arrived. The city police would have many emergency calls on Halloween. They might not arrive in time. And so, she played me along.

Chloe set the chain and opened the door.

"What do you want?"

"Mrs. Dawson," I said, smiling my Hollywood smile. "I got someone who wants to see you."

"You broke into my garage."

I shrugged. "I know, look, I'm sorry about that."

"What do you *want?*"

I shifted my weight and peered through the partially opened door to see if the kid was standing behind his mother, maybe holding a baseball bat. Gratefully, I realized, he must have attended a costume party.

"Mrs. Dawson," I began. "Someone in my car wants to see you."

I pointed in the general direction of the Caddy.

"Who is it?" Chloe said.

"Don't get upset, okay? But I think it might be your husband."

She said nothing.

"Remember that man I told you about? Bob Smith?"

"No."

She was lying, she did remember. I could tell by her tone of voice.

"He says he's a guy named Joe Dawson. Dr. Joe Dawson. That's the name of your husband, right?"

I could almost imagine the weight of her brain grinding the grist of what I had said. Her posture changed at the mere mention of her husband's name.

"If you're making this up…" she said.

"No, ma'am, I'm not. Look, I don't know if this guy really is your husband, but he tells me he is. It's kind of spooky."

She took a moment to reflect on this, and then she spoke abruptly. "Wait. Give me a minute to put on some shoes. Give me a few minutes."

Immediately, my bullshit detector went off as the door shut softly and I heard Chloe set the deadbolt. When she took longer than it would take a centipede to slip on hiking boots, I fought the urge to run for the El Dorado. It idled at curbside.

The porch light came on, and Chloe Dawson stood in the open door with her arms crossed. She floated an anxious, theatrical smile, thin and wavering. In the glaring overhead light, her cheeks trembled. She peered through the screen at the dark street. I had parked the El Dorado beneath the streetlight. Exhaust billowed from its tailpipe.

"I'm waiting," she said. "Where is he?"

"He's in the car," I said, backing down the porch steps.

Something was up. She was play-acting. I've been around actors my whole life, and I know a stage performance when I see one. Something in Chloe's voice and mannerisms betrayed her underlying intent. She had undoubtedly called the cops. Why else would she act so accommodating?

"I don't see anything."

She was reluctant to step over the threshold.

"He's written a screenplay, Mrs. Dawson. The last time…I know, it was wrong of me to break into your garage, but look, this guy Smith, he says he's your

husband. That he's Joe Dawson. Now, I don't believe him
necessarily, but I was hoping you could at least see for
yourself, you know?"

"Ask him to come here. I can't see him."

Her hand clutched something in the pocket of her
nurse's uniform, what I imagined was a can of pepper
spray. One that functioned.

I decided to call her bluff by walking halfway to the
car. I turned and challenged her to follow.

"He's shy, ma'am. He won't get out of the car."

She stepped tentatively onto the porch, and it looked as
though she listened for something in the distance. Cop
sirens perhaps.

A group of children and their mothers worked the
houses across the street, Trick or Treaters going door-to-
door. Chloe, I figured, could just as easily have called out
to them for help. But she did not. I knew that she was
curious about Smith. Maybe it was true what I had said
about him. Maybe he was her husband.

Quickly, I jogged to the passenger side of the El
Dorado and grasped the door handle. Standing there, I
turned and waited for Chloe. She drew back up the porch
steps.

"I can see from here."

"Okay," I said. "Well, here he is."

I wrenched open the passenger side door. The inside of
the car had been so completely dark that I had failed to
notice it was empty.

Chloe leaned forward to see who was inside the car.

"There's no one there," she said.

I looked.

Bob Smith was gone. For a fraction of a second, I
wondered if I had imagined the whole thing, if my
imagination had invented the old man. Perhaps I had
hallucinated the screenplay and Joe Dawson and the Phage
while recovering from cocaine addiction.

"Holy shit."

I opened the back door, and a box of Smith's garbage—his possessions—tumbled to the sidewalk. The breeze caught a few pages of the screenplay and tossed them across Chloe Dawson's lawn. A page came to rest against a carved pumpkin near the porch.

"Here's his stuff, lady. Really."

She withdrew to the door, rose up on her toes to look down the street. She was hoping for a swift arrival of the police.

The hairs on the back of my neck bristled as they often do when a cop was nearby or when I thought I smelled one. It was time for a quick exit.

I circled round the car and hopped in. Before the door shut, I had it in gear and floored it.

The back tires squealed and extruded a stink of synthetic rubber on asphalt. In the rearview, I saw Chloe Dawson running down the sidewalk, aiming at the fleeing El Dorado, with something rectangular in her fist. I saw the flash.

"Cops eat one less donut," I said, "and I'm toast."

I took the corner too fast. The right rear wheel clipped the curb and bounced the car, all two tons, sideways. It screeched and began to fishtail. I straightened it out and let off the gas.

"Slow down, man. Look cool, like you belong here."

I held my speed at under twenty-five. The last thing in the world I wanted was to run over some little kid.

But there were no little kids on the street. It was quiet. Dusk had settled in the rural neighborhood. Television light glowed lazily inside the clapboard houses, and shadows deepened along the road. Some Halloween decorations fluttered in the breeze, but other than these distractions, the night looked like any other night in suburban Generica.

I took the corner and went down another avenue in the tract, each house looking pretty much like the other. A dog halfheartedly ran after me before giving up at an intersection where I brought the Caddy to a stop. I checked the rearview mirror. No cops. No one on the street, nothing, other than the irritating dog.

For the moment I was safe, but I knew that I had to get out of town and fast. Chloe would have, for sure, jotted down the description of my car and California license number. Then I realized what she had held in her hand, a snap camera. She had photographed the car as I sped away. When the cops showed up at the Dawson's, they would issue an APB. That was how I saw it. The cops might station cruisers at the freeway on-ramps, looking for a late model car, a loser ride.

"No. My headlights weren't on," I told myself.

Even if Chloe Dawson had managed to set up her shot in time, the flash from the camera would not have carried far enough to illuminate the retreating Caddy. Without taillights, my California plates would have been in shadow, unreadable.

"You're safe, man. Relax."

How was I going to find my way out of this labyrinth and get back to the Interstate and drive back to Los Angeles? This was the challenge, but I had no maps and was unfamiliar with that part of Las Vegas. There were no visible landmarks, and none of the resort casinos and hotels shone above the little dark houses. At a stop sign, I took a right toward the flush of diffused light that I assumed to be The Strip.

At this point, I cared little for Smith or the fact that he had jumped ship. He had chickened out in the face of a reunion with his so-called wife. His claim was obviously unfounded, and his sneaking off only confirmed my suspicions that Smith was full of it.

"Good riddance."

I noticed that the beige suitcase was missing. He'd taken it with him. "One less bag to carry, one less thing to worry about," I told myself. Besides, I had his screenplay among his possessions in the backseat.

I came to a stop at yet another stop sign and squinted through the dusk as I tried to figure out which direction to take for the freeway. I saw a knot of people, kids dressed in Halloween costumes with their parents, walking along the sidewalk about half a block away. When I pulled out and took a left, I accelerated quickly and nearly hit somebody walking down the middle of the street.

"Jesus!"

I slammed on the breaks, turned the wheel and killed the engine. I rolled to a stop facing the curb.

The person I'd nearly run over was none other than Bob Smith.

He limped to the passenger side and opened the door.

"Where'n hell you go?" I said.

He slid into the car and shut the door. "If you continue on your present course," he said, pointing down the street, "we'll run into the police. They are coming this way." He put his suitcase on his lap.

I turned the ignition over. The engine rattled and made a sick, grinding noise.

"Mr. Austin, if you want to escape the clutches of the law...."

The ignition caught. Above the roar of the engine, I said, "Shut up. Which way?"

Smith pointed to the right.

I put the car in gear and drove down the street. I took a right and pushed the speed limit.

"Slow down," Smith said. "You don't want to attract attention."

I feathered back on the accelerator.

"Where? Which way?"

"Two blocks. Then take a left. We're two, maybe three miles from the motel. Don't worry," Smith said. "They won't catch us there. Not now."

"Which motel?"

Smith said nothing.

"You chickened out, man." I said. "You're a liar, you know that?"

We came to a stop at a traffic signal. I set my jaw and found myself pulling on the steering wheel to discharge the anger that had worked its way down my arms.

"If you let me drive, we will be safer. If you drive, the cops will catch us."

The light changed, and I rolled through the intersection.

"No way. In fact, I'm gonna drop you off. This ends now."

Smith clicked his tongue.

"They're closing in. Please, Mr. Austin."

"Do you have a driver's license?" I said. "No, you don't. So, how you expect to drive?"

"It'll take you over an hour to locate the Desert Rose Motel," Smith said through eyes shut tight. "Let me drive. I know where the motel is."

I scratched the stubble on my chin and swore to myself that, as soon as we got to the motel, I would cut the bastard loose.

We came to a strip mall on the edge of the housing tract where Chloe lived. Not knowing the location of the Desert Rose Motel, I pulled into a gas station to get directions. The attendant in the kiosk was dressed up like Dracula. He said he couldn't hear me through the chicken-wire glass. I shouted the name of the motel, and he cocked his head in detached contempt.

Back in the car, I said, "What's the address, Bob?"

"Unless you let me drive, you will spend the night in jail, Mr. Austin."

He did not inspire confidence. I wanted to see the old man fail. I hungered to laugh at his phony self-assurance. His end-of-the-world shtick was all show, his mind-reading a put on, and it was time for his comeuppance.

"Okay, okay, you wanna drive? Sure, you drive. I've had it!"

Smith touched his beard, and we exchanged places.

With Smith in the driver's seat and his suitcase between us, I tightened the seat belt.

"When was the last time you were behind the wheel?"

"I can't remember," he said.

"So much for your telepathic crap," I said.

Smith turned over the engine and cautiously put the car in gear, gesturing with his arm as well as the turn signal as we merged with traffic. A carload of celebrating teen-aged boys roared past, and Smith overcompensated by swerving to the right and nearly hitting a pickup truck.

"Hey! Watch it," I yelled.

Smith said, "I'll get the hang of it in a few blocks."

We could be dead by then.

As we passed through an intersection, he slowed to read the street sign, mumbling to himself. At Paradise Road, he took a left and received an irritated trumpet from some jerk in an SUV. Our crawl had not suited the importance of his urgency.

Water from a lawn irrigation system splashed on the windshield in silvery droplets, and Smith fumbled with a couple of switches, alternatively engaging the air conditioner and shutting off the headlights.

He asked, "Which one operates the wipers?"

"Your left. Next to the lights. No, your *left*."

Glowing pictures of the backsides of naked chicks momentarily distracted me as we passed the Crazy Horse Two Totally Nude Dance Club. How I longed to get laid instead of playing nursemaid to the old man.

The wiper blades swept the windshield, but not before the El Dorado drifted into the on-coming lane, across the double yellow as Smith overcompensated and corrected our trajectory. This maneuver earned us a flock of honked horns and the finger from a pedestrian in a clown costume.

I heard the siren on the police cruiser before I saw the lights.

"Shit. I've had it."

One unit, two cops. Through the bullhorn mounted on the top of the car, they ordered the El Dorado to pull over. Their reciting my license plate number seemed superfluous. I saw no other 1986 Cadillac El Dorado Coupe de Ville in the neighborhood.

There was an amusing expression on Smith's face that flashed in the whirling blue emergency lights. We pulled over, and he set the brake. When he shut off the engine I worried about the Sig Sauer in the glove compartment.

"Smooth move, Bob."

"The way I see it," he said, "they're going to issue us a traffic violation. Nothing more."

"If you knew that, why'd you let this happen?"

As we waited at the curb for the cops to check us out on their computers, we got the customary reproach from passersby in costume—happy it was us and not them. Eventually, one of the cops tapped on the window, and Smith obliged by rolling it down. It was a female cop, tight as a bull in her bulletproof vest and cop gear dangling from her belt. She wore no make-up. Dark hair spiked at the rim of her cop hat. She carried an imposing black flashlight with which she searched the car, shining it in my face. Then she directed the beam at Smith. Her tag read "Officer Kelly."

"May I see your license, sir?"

"I don't have a license," Smith confessed with a smile.

She asked Smith to repeat himself, and he did. I interjected that I had my license, and the cop told me to keep quiet.

"Sir," the cop said, "you're in violation of the law. You know that, don't you?"

Smith gave an apologetic nod.

The cop took one step back from the door with her hand on her holster. She gestured to her partner, and in the side mirror I watched as the other cop got out of the cruiser.

"Step out of the car, sir," she said.

Smith unbuckled himself and gladly got out of the El Dorado.

The cop leaned into the driver's side window and said, "You, stay in the car."

Through the back window, I watched the cops ask Smith a number of questions. The encounter seemed amiable enough. It was like old-home week, a reunion of strangers.

"Would you look at this?" I said to myself.

The female cop replaced her flashlight and assumed an almost motherly posture toward the old man. The stout male cop patted Smith on the shoulder and seemed to sympathize with him. It reminded me of that scene in *Star Wars* where Obiwan Kenobi dazzles the inferior minds of the Storm Troopers by assuring them it was okay to let Luke's landspeeder pass. The female cop pulled her citation pad from her utility belt. To my chagrin, she came around to my side of the car and tapped on the passenger window. I rolled it down.

"May I see your license and registration, sir?" she said.

"Sure."

I handed the documents to her. She checked the registration and returned it to me. She clipped my license to her citation pad and clicked a ballpoint pen.

"Don't tell me you're giving me a ticket?" I said.

With a perfect poker face, Officer Kelly said, "This vehicle is registered to you, D. Charles Austin. Is that correct?"

I nodded and worried about not having changed the registration after inheriting the Caddy from the Old Man. I also worried about the unregistered handgun in the glove compartment.

"You're in violation of code," she said. "Unlicensed personnel operating a vehicle. You're the licensed driver, the car is registered in your name. You win the prize."

As she filled out the paperwork, I said, "Cut me a break here. He was driving under my supervision."

She ripped off my copy and handed it to me, along with my license, and she scowled.

"Don't push your luck."

After further pats on Smith's back and more handshakes, the cops returned to their cruiser. Smith circled around and spoke happily through the window of the El Dorado.

"They said you'd have to drive from now on."

"No shit."

I scooted across the seat as Smith opened the passenger-side door and got in.

Buckling in, I said, "Did I just get a hundred dollar ticket here?"

"The Desert Rose Motel is over that way."

I started the car and wheeled into traffic. "You should'a warned me, Bob. Used your special powers."

"Take the next right here. The motel's two blocks down."

I saw the motel sign about one block away, enormously cheap pink neon, half of the letters malfunctioning.

Smith said nothing when I rolled my eyes with a disgruntled sigh.

"Looks worse than the Glide."

Smith shook his head.

I pulled into the parking space behind an unmarked delivery van and shut off the Caddy.

A few lights burned in the Desert Inn Motel windows. It was a hooker motel, rooms rented by the hour. The streetlights were brighter than the pink neon sign that proclaimed Desert Rose over MOTEL in vertical white letters on a rusted sign.

Smith carried his suitcase, I grabbed my knapsack.

Next to the motel entrance at a bus stop, two homeless men watched the world go by. They wore pants and jackets the color of dirt, and they shared a paper bag. One of them drank from it. The other pointed at us and laughed. He clambered off the bench and shuffled towards Smith. I was in no mood for this rubbish.

The man stumbled against Smith and asked for five bucks, and Smith turned to me.

"This man needs five dollars, Mr. Austin."

The drunk smiled an intoxicated grin and tears began to flow.

"What's your name, sir?" Smith said.

"Elmore," the drunk said.

Smith and Elmore looked to me.

I shook my head. "I'm not giving him five bucks."

Smith sighed. "Elmore Jones is the grandson of slaves, Mr. Austin."

"Wash thish," Elmore Jones said. The drunk bent over to touch his toes.

"I don't care if he's the King of Prussia. I'm not giving him five bucks."

With my declaration, Elmore Jones hobbled back to the bus stop, wiping his face in a rag and panhandling other people on the street.

"He's suffering a kind of generational pain," Smith said, squaring his shoulders. "When he was ten years old, Elmore watched his mother waste away from hepatitis. By the time he was eleven, his sister lay bleeding to death in Watts, stabbed a few blocks from their home. About a month later some men mugged him. Heroin addicts. They were not satisfied with just his wallet, Mr. Austin. They raped him."

I glanced at the two bums on the bench.

The story, I must admit, caught on the Velcro of my conscience. Elmore Jones was a rumpled, brazenfaced man with hollow eyes and swollen lips, crazed from prolonged exposure to the street. He looked as though he subsisted on fortified wine and narcotics. He slept on the asphalt of Vegas; ate scraps out of dumpsters near the big hotels and he panhandled for dope. But as sympathetic as I would like to be, in the army of the homeless he was just another conscript. Protected by my social class, I disregarded his bad luck as the life he deserved. Anonymity fosters indifference.

"He told you that?" I asked.

Smith shook his head. "I touched him. I read his story."

"That's it," I said, lifting my arms in frustration. "You wanna stand out here and play mind games, fine. I'm gonna check in, get some sleep. It's been a long day."

Chapter 15

Motion-picture directors hold the audience's attention by investing millions in special effects. Directors prefer this technique to a screenplay of substance and quality acting because they measure audiences in box-office take, not aptitude. Moviegoers cheer when the Death Star explodes, as a thousand Bedouin attack at Wadi Rhum, or when the crime boss's lieutenants exact revenge. In this reel of *Path of Least Resistance*, at Ground Zero, I learn the lessons of betrayal. No applause is requested.

Ω   Ω   Ω

Living together in an eight by twelve four-bit room, you get to know a person.

When Smith and I checked into the Desert Rose Motel, several boys, ranging in age from fifteen to twenty, pushed past us. They wore Halloween regalia. They were either dressed up to resemble skinheads or actually *were* skinheads. They had swastika tattoos on their arms and bicycle chains hanging from their belts. They looked like trailer park boys in Doc Martens and T-shirts who were either harmlessly play-acting or members of a real gang. Each drank beer from plastic containers, and their eyes stared with a glassy aplomb.

The clerk at the front desk was a foreign national, Persian or Egyptian. He asked politely if the boys were guests. No, they said, laughing belligerently and quarreling among themselves.

One boy unsheathed a six-inch knife. I recognized immediately his reckless look from having lived in Echo Park. Smith stood his ground. One of the boys turned on me. I stepped back, and he grinned a grin of victory. They had come to test the limits to their intimidation, and once satisfied, they left voluntarily with a swagger. In my life I have been in far greater danger, but the incident reminded me that the nature and timing of violence is always arbitrary.

Bob Smith mumbled, "The ultimate predator kills itself."

He referred to the skinheads, but on reflection, I took his inference to mean the human race. Bob Smith was right, of course. Homo Sapiens are the ultimate predator, the scourge of nature. After many false starts, we may have finally invented the means to self-destruction: a genetically engineered virus from the laboratories of XyberGen that was capable of killing all life on the planet. At least, this was what Smith wanted me to believe.

Amid the sudden uneasiness, the clerk said, "Welcome to the Desert Rose Motel." He handed me our room key. "Enjoy your stay."

Our lodgings at the Desert Rose had stained Venetian blinds over aluminum windows that looked out on street traffic. Our television received three channels, two of which came with sound. Our toilet and shower were installed in a closet. The pipes rattled and the water from the spigot was green. The motel clerk assured me that a plumber would be called to fix it in the morning. We would have to clean up in the sink in the corner of the room. That was the extent of our decor. That and an old-fashioned dial telephone attached to an impossibly twisted cord. The Gideon's had stayed there. They left their Bible.

The air conditioner in the room had a personality. It made all manner of noises, some of which sounded like names or phrases. "Gotta go, gotta go, gotta go" or "Vonnegut, Vonnegut, Vonnegut...." Air conditioning in Vegas is a necessity. The conditioner at the Desert Rose Motel was inadequate at best.

That night I had a dream. I dreamt that Smith's small beige suitcase was full of vials of the deadly virus. In the dream I opened the suitcase and the glass vials tumbled out and broke open on the floor. The contents spread like those black fingers of smoke in Cecil B. DeMille's *The Ten Commandments* during the first Passover in Egypt. My carelessness had condemned to death the whole world.

I awakened around three o'clock in a puddle of sweat and fell back to sleep only because of sheer exhaustion.

That morning Smith rose early, and believing me still asleep, took his turn at the sink. Bent over in boxers, his back shone frail and knuckled at daybreak. He turned round to retrieve the soap, and the light captured the extent of his decay. His nipples were nested in tufts of white hair and his stomach sagged over the elastic waistband of his underwear.

Under an armpit he ran a bar of motel soap wrapped in a washcloth. He twisted sideways and exposed a triangular rash seated on his "love handles."

Like a traitor, my brain recalled the following lines from the screenplay:

> *An equilateral triangle of reddened skin*
> *just above the iliac crest of Joe Dawson's hip.*
> *He presses his wet fingers against it and*
> *winces. Inside the triangle are three red lumps.*

Smith may have been aware of my insight, for he hid the rash with the washcloth.

I feigned sleep and spied through half-shut eyes.

By then, the details of the screenplay were familiar to me. Each character had made my acquaintance. I could recount scenes verbatim. While pretending to sleep, I recalled that the character Joe Dawson had first noticed the rash in the shower. His wife Chloe had joked that it was "love-handle disease." In later scenes, the rash blistered when the space aliens revealed their purpose in coming to our little blue planet.

Bob Smith's markings were identical to Joe Dawson's.

The evidence was irrefutable.

Smith slipped one arm into his shirt, then the other. Like a man with a heavy burden, he sat on the edge of the bed to pull on his wrinkled pants. He wheezed with a shake of the head as though conceding defeat.

"Morning," I said.

I swung my legs off my bed and yawned. I have never been a morning person until I met Bob Smith. I used to sleep past noon.

"You okay?" I asked.

Smith gave an unpersuasive nod.

Fitting into my jeans, I buttoned the fly. My thoughts surfaced in a smile. I have always smiled through my lies.

"You can't deceive me, Mr. Austin."

Smith had a way of peeling away conceit like the layers of an onion. There was no sense in trying to hide from him.

I asked, "Is it infectious?"

He shook his head.

"But you were exposed, weren't you? The virus, I mean." I laughed nervously. "Because, don't tell me aliens did that to you?"

His eyes were transparent blue and his aspect cut like an acetylene torch.

"The Phage," he said, drawing out the word and shaking his head again. "As I told you, I was exposed to an irradiated form. It's non-infectious. The only adverse effect is, well…" He huffed. "I'm aging rapidly."

Smith sat on the edge of his bed and clasped his hands, looking at the floor.

"My lab worked on a vaccine. After we discovered the Phage and reported our findings, the military expressed concern." He looked up briefly before he tied his shoes. "If our data got in the hands of terrorists, that kind of thing, it could be used against the United States. My lab irradiated live virions and then inoculated animals with it to test resistance to the Phage. The animals survived, but there were complications."

"So you guys made a vaccine for this thing?"

Smith shook his head deliberately. He stood to touch the rash through the fabric of his shirt.

"It mutates every time it replicates, Mr. Austin. Inoculating against a mutating virus is impossible."

I asked, "Does it itch?"

"At times. When you forced me to look at the videotape of my wife and Frank. As painful as it was, it was good to know they're okay." He buttoned his shirt with arthritic fingers.

"Then what do I call you now?" I said. "I mean, I don't know you as Joe Dawson."

"Why can't we just keep it the same?"

Smith stooped to retrieve his suitcase from under the bed.

"You might as well have this."

He unfastened the latches and removed a manuscript that was held together by rubber bands. It was the screenplay that he had completed on our drive through the desert. He carefully handed it to me.

"All I can say is, this is how I see the end."

Smith gestured at the screenplay while supporting himself against the sink. The simple effort of standing had drained him of energy.

"I couldn't finish it for months. Every time I sat down, I came face to face with the moment where the future vanishes. I could not see beyond, well, beyond Frank's accident."

I had not been listening to what he said. Instead, I gazed at the screenplay. My ship had come in.

"So, you finished it."

"I'm done with it. I'm no screenwriter, Mr. Austin. You have my permission to send that to your producer friend."

Smith's expression was the epitome of compassion. After my vile behavior, after my drug abuse and pigheaded manners, and the lies, he was perfectly willing to forgive.

"If I accept you as a character in this, I mean," I said, tapping the first page of the screenplay. "You're asking me to believe the rest of it. The stuff about XyberGen and the virus, you know? Your end-of-the-world jive."

Smith shrugged. "Read the screenplay. Then we'll talk."

He put on his old suit coat, and as he made his way to the door, he gently touched me on the wrist. "Listen. Don't unpack. We can't stay here. Mr. Fetch will soon figure out that we're here. We'll find another motel for tonight."

"The Delivery Boy?"

Smith shook his head. "Not just him. There are others now."

"*Others!* You mean, like aliens?"

"Don't be ridiculous, Mr. Austin. I see foreign nationals. Terrorists of one stripe or another. You will recognize them by their eccentric clothes. They've come for this."

He picked up his suitcase and opened the door, admitting diesel exhaust and the rush of traffic. And then he was gone.

I lay down on the bed in my clothes and went back to sleep.

Ω   Ω   Ω

Later that morning I awakened in a puddle of drool on the vinyl-covered pillow. The air was hot, and I threw off the threadbare blanket. Daylight poured through the window to admit the cacophony of the street.

I could feel a depression coming on. The imaginary dog of abstinence panted in the corner.

I urinated in the sink. Hours earlier Bob Smith had washed himself and put on his tattered clothes beside the sink, and I remembered seeing the triangular rash. The blanket on Smith's bed was pulled taut and crimped with military corners. You could bounce a quarter off it. My bed looked like the target of a suicide bomber. The comparison illustrated the differences in our personalities.

In the mirror above the sink, my cheeks looked flushed. I rubbed a towel in the filmy mirror and leaned closer. My eyes were clear. Vitality is the only advantage to abstinence but it's profoundly boring. Given the choice, I would have preferred starting the day with a line of coke and a cup of adulterated coffee. Still, I was robust for the first time in years. I was no longer *garbage*, despite Max Gleason's avowal.

I made my way downstairs to the lobby. Halfway down, a bolt that secured the metal banister broke, and I lost my balance three steps above the landing. I stumbled without injury. It reminded me that nothing is reliable and that we are most vulnerable within the promise of day.

In the lobby, I pushed past a family whose naked brat wailed at his mother's breast above the shouting of his father who played a slot machine. I needed fresh smokes. From the desk clerk I got change for the vending machine. The father of the child declared something to me in Spanish, which was wasted on my indifference.

The outside air stank of fried food and car fumes. At the curb, a group of elderly Latinos smoked cigarettes while jabbering indecipherably. Las Vegas was like the smoking section for the entire country. I asked for a light, and they eyed me with weary suspicion. The gutter was full of litter. Searching my pockets, I found a matchbook and put a flame to my cigarette.

Against the heat I pushed down the street of strip malls and check cashing stores, making for the Mickey D's on the opposite corner. I took in the neighborhood. There was a Mexican take-out next to a vacant pharmacy with irrelevant window ads. Next to this was an Asian-run grocery store where I bought a Bic lighter. The sidewalk was crowded with cheap hustlers and the obsolescent poor. The neighborhood seemed a dumping ground for discharged mental patients and the walking wounded whose tongues lolled and who swore contrarily. I saw a young mother with a three-year-old on a leash, begging. A policeman prodded an unconscious man who may have been dead. None of my new neighbors seemed to notice or care about anything.

Bob Smith was not among them.

At the McDonald's counter, I mistakenly ordered an "Egg McChicken" sandwich to which the skinny black teenager snarled. "Lookie here, man, we got a Egg McMuffin and a McChicken sandwich, but we ain't got no Egg McChicken." Feeling humiliated, I sipped my coffee and chewed my McMuffin at a plastic table not far from the Play Station where working mothers yelled at their kids, scolding that unless they stopped playing this instant they'd be late for work. My wristwatch read nine fifteen when I made my way back to the motel.

I wanted to call Pig Boy and tell him the good news about the screenplay. Maybe I could get him to admit that Rainy Day had contracted with the Delivery Boy. I wanted to convince Gleason to call the bastard off. There was no reason to call in outsiders—I had secured the screenplay.

In the lobby of the Desert Rose, I dropped a couple of bucks in quarters into the pay phone. With the advent of cell phones, most of the antiquated equipment in our society was left to those without means. Again, I wished that I'd remembered to bring my cell phone with me when we'd run away from Echo Park. The motel public phone was an older model that bore the tags of graffiti artists. The receiver was fetid from periodontal disease.

"Max? It's DC."

"Duncan, can I call you back? I'm in the middle of something."

"The screenplay's finished, Max."

Gleason took a breath.

"How you want me to send it?"

"You don't understand, Duncan. We're already in production."

"Production?"

"I left a message on your machine."

I switched ears.

"What?"

Gleason exhaled like a leviathan.

"We got Ebersbach to complete your partial. The committee gave its stamp of approval, and the Japanese signed off. The storyboard's coming along great. You should see it. We've made some changes. And guess who we got to direct? Stephen! I can't tell you how exciting this has been. Unbelievable. The screen tests are absolute genius. And the poster! Just a crude mock-up right now, but it's incredible. I have it here in the office."

When business went well, it was typical of Gleason to ignore you or to bury you in sheer verbiage. Over the years I have witnessed the internment of many associate producers who conflicted with Max Gleason's interest.

"Max, would you listen to me."

"Hold off, Duncan. I know you have something to say, but I'm so excited. Let me describe the poster, all right? Did I tell you we got Rolly Campaña for lead? Anyway, at the center there's Rolly in a white lab coat. He's running in mortal terror. Spaceships and aliens are in the background, and a voluptuous woman is at his side. We got Grace Taylor. I wish you could see this. Her knockers are poppin' right out of her blouse. It's three-dimensional. The title is in big red letters *Virus Wars*, slanted, superimposed. Where are you? I'll have my people send a mock-up from promo. You're gonna love it."

"Max, would you listen to me."

"Duncan. Duncan. Duncan, *you* listen for a change. Audrey signed Motorola, Philip Morris, General Motors for spots, pulled in eighteen on her work alone, not too shabby."

Gleason engaged in conversation much like he waylaid a meal: all gesticulation, no digestion.

"Max, would you shut up and listen to me? I got the screenplay."

"You have what?"

"The *screenplay*. It's finished."

"I'm sorry, Duncan, but you're out. Look, you were never good at high-concept delivery. You only have yourself to blame. Get yourself back into therapy. That's my advice."

I cursed a boatload of obscenities. I wanted to rattle his cage as mine had been rattled in the drive through the desert. I screamed into the phone that none of it mattered now that the screenplay and Bob Smith's foreboding, all of it was true; that we were doomed; that something like the Black Plague had already infected a dozen people as reported on CNN; that the end was near. My screaming into the telephone at Pig Boy got the attention of an old lady who was feeding quarters to a slot machine. She scowled before resuming her narrative with a gambling addiction.

I covered the mouthpiece and said to the old lady, "Sorry, ma'am."

Max said, "Get hold of yourself, Duncan."

"Max, *Max!* Please, the screenplay is coming true. You've got to believe me. Smith's the genuine article. I mean, everything he writes somehow comes true, okay?"

"How am I supposed to respond to that? We all know that you invented or imagined this Bob Smith. Admit it, Duncan," Gleason said. "You made the screenwriter up in your head. He's a fiction. I know that, I know that now. But look, you need help. Serious help. Take my advice and get back into therapy as soon as you can."

"Max?"

"Sty washes his hands of you, and so do I. Besides, we signed no contract, not on your partial. You don't have a leg to stand on. It wasn't even a good concept until we rewrote it."

"Max! Would you listen to me? The world is coming to an end."

Gleason did not respond.

"Did you hear what I said?"

"You need to get some serious help, Duncan."

Rather than further aggravate my sense of panic, I disconnected. It felt good hanging up on Pig Boy. But as I did so, an incoming tide of hopelessness swept over me. I could sense the future hanging in the balance.

I returned to our room. The screenplay rested on my bed, and I picked it up and thumbed the pages. The world outside intruded with brassy automobile horns and the rumbling of tourists on The Strip. The thinnest shaft of sunlight cast an oval at my feet.

I trembled uncontrollably despite the heat. I wrapped myself in a blanket and smoothed out my hair. The security of my ponytail felt immaterial. Smith's screenplay had enormous implications. It spoke of dire consequences for the human race. This was no longer about percentages or a rolling break. *Path of Least Resistance* was about how human ingenuity would bring about The End. But why had Bob Smith chosen me to get his treatment on screen? Why me, why a coke-snorting loser on the frayed end of a series of bad breaks? If his idea was to make a movie to persuade people to stop biological weapons research, then he'd picked the wrong man to get it done. Why *me?*

Any hope that I had for an option with Rainy Day Productions was kaput. My biggest worry now should have been the pathogen, but part of me still resisted believing Bob Smith. I don't know if it was his advanced age or his lunatic looks, or the dire consequences that he foretold. I simply did not want to accept his version of reality. Besides, what was I supposed to do, call the local police, the FBI or the president? And what would I say to them? How should I warn the authorities of the danger? In the screenplay, Joe Dawson rang a warning without effect, only to earn a reputation as a madman. With my abysmal wardrobe and sleaze-ball hairstyle, I would prove even less presentable than Dawson had supposedly been.

It was of no use. I had an incurable aversion to meaningful action. I sat stupefied on the bed for over an hour while the two contradictory elements of my nature debated what to do. Neither side gained a consensus.

Finally, out of the recesses of my addled brains, I remembered my idea from the previous night. It burbled up, a kind of solution to all my trouble, and shined in the circle of light at my feet like the greatest idea in the history of the world.

"What if Bob Smith changed the future by rewriting the screenplay?" I said to myself.

Was it possible to alter history with a rewrite and change what Smith saw as inevitable? Maybe Smith could shift the outcome through a happy ending. Maybe the world didn't have to come to an end after all. The most successful predator on the planet did not have to kill itself through the miracle of science.

My mood improved almost immediately when I realized what the correct course of action was. I had to get

Smith to agree to a rewrite. He had to write a happy ending. *Besides*, I thought, *Americans love happy endings.*

For the first time in my life, I was excited about something other than an option or heartless scam or a line of white powder.

I quickly made my way downstairs. I reached for a pack of smokes in the pocket of my leather jacket and pushed through the front door of the motel lobby.

I headed down The Strip in shadowless daylight toward the grand resort casinos. The sky was a zinc plate of high featureless overcast. The temperatures threatened the red zone. I passed by a street crew that was employing a backhoe to dig a hole. A transvestite in pink gloves, make-up, and hair a color not found in nature watched as the workers tore up the desert floor. Two Chinese women wearing quilted black satin jackets pushed around me, carrying paper cups full of quarters.

I looked up and saw him. Smith stood on the opposite corner amid a circle of people.

My intention was to confront him and demand a complete rewrite on my terms. If he refused, maybe I would force him to do it, perhaps confine him to the motel room and threaten him with violence like that poor miserable character in the Stephen King story *Misery*. I had to convince Smith to rewrite the ending of the screenplay and change the course of history.

As I approached from behind, he cinched his shoulders in a kind of intuitive insight. My presence always set Smith off. He was preaching about the end of the world but he ceased in his harangue about biological weapons when he "saw" me.

He grimly turned around.

"Mr. Austin."

"What'n hell you doing?"

"This is none of your concern."

He stood on a concrete planter box full of dead marigolds. He stepped down. The knot of homeless men who had been listening to him dispersed as their short attention spans lost interest.

I got right up in Smith's face.

"Smith, you've got to do a rewrite. I figured it out," I told him. "Rewrite history. *Path of Least Resistance* doesn't have to end the way you say it does. You can change history."

I could scarcely believe what I was saying to him. The words sounded about as worthless as a tinker's dam.

"There isn't time," he said. "Besides, it is the way it is."

"Would you, please, just listen to reason?"

Something in my tone pissed him off. Smith gripped my shirt lapels and leaned toward me. He shoved his finger against my chest just like my father used to do when he was mad. A tidal wave of memory and emotions overtook me.

"You have never listened to anyone, Mr. Austin. *Never!* Now you come here and make demands? I know your agenda. You can't fool me. You're a deceptive, horrible excuse for a human being."

"Bob, don't get angry with me. I'm telling you, I believe you."

"I want nothing more to do with you, Mr. Austin. Please, leave me alone."

"Bob, how difficult is it to rewrite the ending?"

"You're delusional, Mr. Austin. Do you really believe I have the power to change *history*?"

He laughed at me, and it affected my mood like the shutting of a prison gate.

That was it. I had given it my best shot. In the end, Smith turned out to be the same loser that I had taken him for from the beginning. I realized in a flash, the time had come to cut my losses. Forget the screenplay, forget about history, and forget about Smith's bullshit. All I wanted to do was go home and do a few lines off the mirror. I figured, maybe Xavier Murphy was back from Peru.

I pulled away from Smith and huffed. He was such a pathetic-looking pile of baloney.

"Listen up," I said. "I called Gleason. You know what he told me? They're gonna make your movie. That's right. But it ain't the movie you want. And because you dicked around for so fucking long, I'm out and you're out. No option, no contract. Nothing. I worked this product for weeks and this is what I end up with. I ask you for a rewrite, and you tell me to go away."

His blue eyes grew cold. He had never looked at me like that before.

"How do you know, Mr. Austin, that this isn't what I've wanted all along?"

I began to shake from anger and frustration.

"Look," I said, gripping my ponytail. "I just came by to say *adios*. I'm heading back to L.A."

Smith shook his head.

"You can't leave now, Mr. Austin. You're in the next scene."

As soon as he said *you're in the next scene*, a television news van rounded the corner. Coming to a stop in the red zone near a Gold's Gym, the driver lowered the window on the passenger side and someone in the van waved at two teen-aged girls. They squealed. It was the celebrated news reporter and raconteur, Jerry Brooks.

I looked at Smith and set my jaw.

The television crew scrambled out of the van with all manner of equipment. An overweight guy in a red flannel shirt and tight Levi's shouldered a remote cam about the size of a ghetto blaster. The other person, a women wearing a backwards baseball cap, wielded a microphone at the end of a six foot boom. She fit on a pair of headphones.

Smith leaned forward and whispered, "Say nothing to them, Mr. Austin. Not a word. You have no lines here. You are a bystander."

Seeing the camera and television station logo on the van, the homeless people stirred from their perches at the curb. They milled around the van like movie extras. Curious and distracted tourists took digital snapshots. Others pressed forward for their fifteen seconds of fame. Two teen-aged punks at the edges gave one another a high five and laughed like hyenas.

As the scene from *Path of Least Resistance* came to life before my eyes, I found myself hyperventilating. *Calm down, calm down*, I told myself. I wanted someone to convince me, this was just another coincidence.

Jerry Brooks crossed the street like a shepherd to his flock. He walked directly up to Bob Smith, full of confidence, grinning his signature grin. The sound woman positioned her microphone, and Brooks turned to the cameraman.

The cameraman said, "We're rolling."

"Good evening." Brooks spoke directly to the lens as though it and he were engaged in sexual flirtation. "Newsbreak here on the streets of Las Vegas, to interview someone we haven't heard from in a while. You may remember the man who reads the future. A few months ago, on this station, you heard about the germ that's going to bring all life on earth to an end. Well," Brooks said with a wink, "that hasn't happened *yet*, so we're here to see what the Streetsayer has to say for himself. Of course, we're talking about Bob Smith."

With an acerbic smile, Brooks glanced at the homeless onlookers and they clapped their hands. Amid this feeble applause, Brooks faced Smith and the sound woman lowered the boom.

"The last time we talked, we learned that people call you the Streetsayer. A kind of cross between—"

"Soothesayer and street person, yes," Smith said.

"Anything you'd like to predict for us today, Mr. Smith?"

"You're back to interview me."

Brooks gave a wry nod. "You claim to have this *thing*, this extrasensory perception. People say, you can read the thoughts of others. They say you know what's going to happen in the future, am I right?"

I opened my mouth to ask what in hell this was all about. Was this life imitating art or art imitating life? Who did Smith think he was, reenacting a scene from the screenplay? His acerbic eyes caught mine, and he shook his head. I shut my mouth because I had no lines in this scene.

Smith said to Jerry Brooks, "People believe what they want to believe."

Elmore Jones, the homeless beggar that I'd met the previous night in front of the Desert Rose Motel, stood among the onlookers. He shouted it was true, Smith could tell the future.

Brooks aped for the camera, grinning like a game show host, milking the irony as though nothing in life could possibly be what it seems; everything was ironic. And therefore Brooks had to treat the television audience like infants.

"If I paid you, would you read my future?"

"If you like."

Brooks reached into his overcoat to remove a twenty-dollar bill.

"That's not necessary," Smith said.

"A freebie, huh?"

The two teenagers, pierced and tattooed beyond reason, laughed at Smith's expense and punched one another in the arm.

Bob Smith seemed to go into a trance. The cameraman moved in for the close-up, and color drained from Smith's face. I knew the scene, I had read it before. The character,

Bob Smith, envisions a fiery plane crash in which the character, Jerry Brooks, will die.

When Smith awakened, his baby blue eyes bore down on Jerry Brooks. He said nothing.

"Well, what's up with this?" Brooks asked. "You look like you've seen a ghost."

"In a word, yes."

Brooks turned to the street crowd that had gathered like an obedient backdrop to his tongue-in-cheek interview. He appealed to them. "Hey, don't you people think we deserve more than this?"

The mob was fickle. They sided with Brooks.

"If I tell you what I see, you won't believe it," Bob Smith said, and the people fell silent.

"So, you're saying you won't tell me my fortune, even though I was willing to pay you twenty dollars?" Brooks feigned theatrically, his expression gaping. He cocked his head with that smile again.

Turning to the camera with perfect timing, Brooks said, "Well, there you have it. Just another scam on the street. This is Jerry Brooks, reporting for Newsbreak, Channel Seven."

Almost as quickly as they had arrived, the crew began to dismantle their equipment and prepare for departure.

"Stay away from heights, Mr. Brooks," Bob Smith called as the crew picked its way across the street.

Jerry Brooks hesitated at the curb and looked back. The cameras were off, and so the eager-to-please look was gone from his face. There was enough premonition in Smith's tone to unnerve Brooks. Bob Smith and he fixed stares for a moment. Then, he joked with his colleagues when he climbed into the van. By then Brooks had lost his signature grin.

The mob dispersed, and we were left alone, Bob and I.

I said quietly, holding back my sense of panic, "What did I just see here, Bob?"

Smith was not listening. He gazed skyward. "The culture has debased interests. I'm out of time. This will never work."

"Jerry Brooks. That's the same guy in the screenplay. What's up with that, buddy, huh?"

"They mistake sensation for substance."

Smith was saying one thing while I meant another. Communication had never been our forte.

I could not shake the sense of déjà vu. When the television crew had rounded the corner, it felt as though I'd been plucked down in the middle of the screenplay. I could have directed the shot. I knew the character's lines to the letter. I could have choreographed it.

"Tell me what the hell just happened here."

"You saw what happened," Smith said.

I was the only actor not scripted in the scene.

"Tell me something. Tell me something. Where am I in this thing of yours? Am I supposed to be my old man in this *picture* of yours?"

His mouth rose with the faintest smile.

"I mean," I said, pacing in a circle around Smith. "You got Jerry fucking Brooks in it. There are people I've met. Scenes like what just happened here. And things that haven't happened yet. So, where in the hell am I in this thing of yours? And what happens next? Do I die? Do we *all* die?"

"That's none of your concern, Mr. Austin. You told me, you're leaving town."

I yelled that he destroyed any chance I had at earning an option. He stood there as he usually did, like a stone guest. I ranted about fact versus fiction, about Jerry Brooks, about the mysterious illness popping up all across the country. I even brought up something about a two-headed cow raised in a lab by the NIH. I demanded that he rewrite the screenplay. "It's a matter of life and death," I said.

"By your own admission, Mr. Austin, you're out of the deal. Your producer friend is going to make my movie. Your job here is finished. I see that now. You can go."

"*No way!*" I shouted. I waved my hands to erase the facts of the matter. "No, you and me are *not* done, you son of a bitch. You have to agree to a rewrite, dammit."

"Time for your final scene, Mr. Austin. You need to exit stage right while you still have some dignity left."

I began to walk in a tight circle around Smith, closing the circle as I raised my fists and was about to strike him when a teenaged girl from a family of tourists screamed. I shoved the old dude to the ground and stabbed an index finger at his chest. "Fuck you big time!" I shouted. You should thank me, he said. I saved your life, he said. I trembled from a storm of emotions. I swore at the heavens and cursed the name of God.

Smith said, "Watch out for my suitcase." He clutched it to his chest.

None of my antics helped sooth the feeling that I had just witnessed a paranormal event. Smith had guided me to the very edge of reality only to forsake me. At this point, I was unsure who was cutting whom loose. It seemed the cracked sidewalk would give way to quicksand. It felt as though I was sinking.

"Mummy," one of the tourist children bawled. "That man scares me."

The days had been cruel to me. I do not work well under such conditions. Abstinence is not my friend. The residues of endless debaucheries have crushed the ruins of my brain into the Acropolis. Something of past importance is evident, but only vestiges remain. But even a ruined mind can see the truth once in a while. Within this Come-To-Jesus moment, I saw Bob Smith for who he clearly was. He was nothing more than another obstacle in my pursuit of self-medication. It was time to cut my losses. I had tied my wagon to a dead horse.

I turned away, intending to make it back to the Desert Rose Motel, fishing my jacket for the car keys, fuming with anger. I had left the car parked in the lot, and I hoped to find it unmolested. The solid reality of the El Dorado, I knew, would reassure me. I went to it quickly and slipped behind the wheel. I started the engine. She was a fat whore that car, soft and convenient, her motor humming like a blowjob. Before putting it in gear, I caught my breath. Through the aquarium glass of the windshield, I watched the parade of bleary-eyed hopelessness walk past the car, the homeless and drug addicted, the flotsam and jetsam of our culture, the chronic gamblers and alcoholics playing their end game. I was all fired up on six weeks of repressed frustration and anger, half-expecting the world to open up and swallow me whole.

A manic depression began to sink inside me like a twenty-pound weight tied to my balls. It was time to go home to Echo Park and feed the hound of my personal addictions.

Chapter 16

In Walt Disney's *The Sorcerer's Apprentice,* Mickey Mouse empowers a broom to do his dirty work. The broom becomes a mule for discipline and is virtually unstoppable. This was how I imagined Whitaker Fetch. There was no stopping him.

Ω   Ω   Ω

It felt good to sit in the El Dorado and turn on the air conditioner. I rolled up the windows and put the thing on maximum, feeling protected from the rest of the world. Strands of hair irritated my face, and I combed the sweat off my brow to stick it down.

On the back seat were Smith's typewriter and boxes of junk. The screenplay was in the motel room along with my knapsack, but I couldn't have cared less. I was outta there.

I pulled out of the motel parking lot and into traffic. I headed for The Strip. For more than an hour, I must have driven in circles, semiconsciously. I waited at intersections for the signal to change, lost in thought and unable to overcome a sense of dread. I kept turning over the facts and projecting the images in my head of mass extinction. The screenplay, XyberGen, biological weapons, Jerry Brooks' interview on the street, all of it was madness. I wanted my old life back. I wished I had never met Bob Smith, or Joe Dawson, *whatever*.

I needed a drink.

Alcohol is a form of music. I used to play Jack Daniel's when I got tired of listening to the voices in my head, voices that blamed me for my folks' suicide. To quiet the self-hatred, I have flooded enough booze into me to drown a chorus line in an off-key *Oklahoma*.

My only long-term relationship has been with ethyl alcohol. She and I go way back. Ethyl's let me down a time or two, but you can hardly blame her. She is what she is, but she has come in mighty handy in a pinch.

I found myself in the northwest section of town as I eased into a parking space in front of a seedy cocktail lounge. The name *Lou's* was scrawled in blue neon above the front door. The sign crackled with electricity as I stepped inside, into the air-conditioned obscurity of the lounge. There wasn't a window in the place. It was as anonymous as you can get. The well-worn bar was empty, and I welcomed its stale drabness. As I sat on a stool, the bartender in a white shirt, a bear of a man, wiped the counter and asked: "What'll ya have?"

I ordered The Glenlivet, neat, but the best he could do was Chevas Regal. My hands trembled, and I sensed the bartender's scrutiny as he set the cocktail glass on a napkin. "You all right, buddy?" he asked. I gave a quick nod and went to the rest room. I stood at the sink and opened the faucet. The cold water smelled of rust. I yanked the rubber band from my ponytail and combed my dampened hands through it. I felt closer to prayer and more desperate at that moment than at any other time in my life. I wished for peace of mind. I prayed to God to stop Smith's voice from prattling in my memory. I cinched my hair and replaced the rubber band. I took three deep breaths and returned to the bar.

"Not from round here?" the bartender asked. "Name's Bob." He extended his paw.

I almost jumped at the introduction. The last name in my life I ever wanted to hear again was *Bob*. Nervously, I placed my cigarette pack next to the drink.

Bob the Bartender clinked an ashtray before me.

"Where you from?"

"L.A." I pulled a cigarette from the pack. "Name's DC. Glad to know ya."

I was relieved when a couple of regulars strolled in and the bartender turned his attention to them. He poured their drinks and engaged in chitchat. They were two older gentlemen. They began playing liars dice at the end of the bar and gave me short shrift. One of them asked Bob to turn on the television. It was Newsbreak, the midday show. It gratefully wasn't showing the Jerry Brooks' interview of a notorious Las Vegas "streetsayer." In San Diego the talking head reported more cases of a mysterious illness. Three more people were hospitalized, and one was not expected to make it.

With a single jerk of my head, I finished the Scotch and winced as I placed a five under the glass. I stood to walk out.

"That don't cover it," Bob the Bartender said. "Six fifty."

I leafed out two more singles, and he stood there, arms crossed, alternatively eyeing the change and me. It was a cheap tip, below my standards.

As I turned to leave, an imposing black man in a dark business suit pushed past the front door and slowly approached me. Two less-imposing men in gray business suits and sunglasses stood behind him like inadequate bookends to a large compendium of the OED.

Somehow—Bob Smith's clairvoyance must have rubbed off on me—I knew this person to be none other than Whitaker Fetch. His companions took the booth next to the front door, never taking their eyes off me. They were edgy like border collies.

I sat back down on the stool because my legs could no longer support the weight of my panic.

Years ago, I had cast a low-budget movie based on an Easy Rawlins Mystery. This was before the days when the author, Walter Mosley, was "discovered," before he made it big. In the movie there was a federal marshal as a side character, and from what I had learned about such people, I figured Whitaker Fetch worked for the Treasury Department or Homeland Security. His inexpensive cologne spoke ATF or FBI. The man was as big as a house and looked like a Rottweiler with his small ears and shaved head. He sported a trimmed goatee.

He took a seat on the stool next to me.

Bob the Bartender asked what he wanted to drink, and the man said, "Club soda. Glass of ice on the side." He gestured at the front booth. "Same for my associates."

I stared forward, my elbows on the bar, while I contemplated what in blue blazes I was going to do. If I got up casually and then ran for the backdoor, they'd probably shoot me. How was I to know what the Delivery Boy would do? At least, in the cocktail lounge, the regulars were a deterrent to his taking any violent action.

I glanced carefully to my right, at Whitaker Fetch.

He was looking directly at me.

I nodded pleasantly like a fool and confirmed the paranoia in my eyes, "How ya doin'?"

"We need to talk, Cowboy," he said.

He had a voice so deep that it seemed to rattle the clean glasses below the bar. When he'd spoken, I saw the glint of very white teeth, two incisors, behind thick lips.

I squinted at him in my best James Dean, copping a pose.

"Do I know you?"

Whitaker Fetch gave a single nod of his polished head.

Bob the Bartender placed the club soda and tall glass of ice on the bar and carried the other club sodas to Fetch's associates.

"How much do I owe you?" Fetch asked.

Bob the Bartender said, "It's on the house." The bartender had read "law enforcement" in the customer's demeanor, and he was always generous to cops as a matter of lounge policy.

Whitaker Fetch removed his wallet from an inside jacket pocket and put twenty dollars in the tip cup.

"Give this man here whatever he's drinking?"

Bob the Bartender smirked. "Yes, sir." He poured another Chevas.

I rubbed my face in my hands and tried like hell to squeeze the anxiety out of my ponytail. I sniffed. The air conditioning had my nose running.

"Get your drink, Cowboy, and follow me."

I did what I was told. My legs felt heavy like inner tubes filled with dry sand.

We sat across from one another at a booth. Someone had spilled a drink on my side, and the floor was sticky. Sitting across from Fetch reminded me of the time I was called to the principal's office in grade school for dropping a burning match in a trashcan.

He began, "You know who I am. And I know who you are—"

"How in hell did you find me?"

I surprised myself by interrupting him, feeling the effects of two drinks. His face showed zero emotion. I figured him for a killer player of five-card stud.

"Been on your tail since Santa Monica."

I gave what he said some thought. In the past day or two, I must have checked the rearview mirror a thousand times but had not once seen anyone even remotely suspicious on our tail.

"Was it you, trashed my house?"

Again, Fetch was poker-faced, and I took up my drink and drained the glass. Fetch looked contemptuously at me and at my empty cocktail glass. He kept his hands below the table where I couldn't see them. I figured he was carrying. I thought about the Sig Sauer in the Caddy, but it was as far removed from me as the Moon.

He turned slightly and said in a loud voice, "Barkeep, can we get another drink for my friend?"

"Comin' right up," Bob the Bartender said a little too cheerily.

I leaned forward and whispered, "Tell me something, okay? What in hell you want with me?"

The bartender replaced my empty with a fresh drink and walked away.

"I want nothing to do with you, Cowboy. It's your buddy."

"Okay," I said with a shrug.

Fetch reached into his coat pocket. I half expected him to draw down on me and kill me outright, but he placed a newspaper clipping on the table and tapped it with a thick black finger.

"Do you read?"

I picked up the article. It was the same newspaper report that Smith had sent to me via the screenplay, the one about the deadly microbe created in a lab at XyberGen. Without a word, I pushed the article across the table at him. Fetch made me feel like a pacific islander living on a volcanic atoll. You never knew when it was going to explode.

"Your buddy has something of ours. We want it back."

"I don't know what you're talking about," I said.

He leaned forward and spoke in a low voice. "People I work for will do whatever it takes to get what they want. Do you understand?"

I nodded.

He picked up his club soda and sipped it. "Your buddy went on television. Made some statements about bio-warfare. It piqued our interest. So, tell me. You and he belong to the same terrorist cell?"

I had to laugh. "You must be joking. Smith's like a pogo stick with hair. What's he gonna do, blow up the post office with his AARP card?"

Fetch lifted an eyebrow as a sign that I should shut up.

"This is no joke. We expect you to cooperate."

I picked up my drink and threw it back in one swallow, hoping maybe the dude would buy another. I was wrong. There was a limit to his generosity even on a government expense account. But I was beginning to feel good again. Ethyl and I were on speaking terms, and she was about to start talking trash.

"Give us what we want and you can go."

"For the life of me, I can't figure what you want." We sat in silence for the moment. "Say, are you a Federal Marshal or something? Got a Glock under that coat a yours?"

He inclined toward me solemnly and spoke in a whisper. "What I carry and who I work for is none of your business, Cowboy."

"Ah, the *government*," I said sarcastically. "As in Special Ops?"

He was stone cold sober.

"Well, this ain't got nothing to do with me, man."

"Oh, you're wrong. It's got everything to do with you."

A beer delivery guy came through the back door pushing an aluminum keg on a dolly. I watched as Bob the Bartender and the delivery guy exchanged casual banter. I was grateful for the distraction.

"Look," I said, shifting to face him. "Your name's Fetch, right?"

He was stock still like a block of granite. I swallowed the terror rising up my throat.

"This is crazy, the screenplay and all, this whole business of Smith. The dude is nuts, okay? I tell you, you got the wrong guy. He isn't capable of doing…*anything*. Believe me. He's crazy. He thinks he's a scientist or something, named Joe Dawson."

Once again, Whitaker Fetch raised an eyebrow to shut me up. "We know that."

"You know what, that Smith's Joe Dawson?"

He shook his head. "We don't know the whereabouts of Dr. Dawson. What we want to know is, why is your buddy carrying Dr. Dawson's valise? Can you tell me that?"

I shook my head and giggled. "Joe Dawson is the name of a *character* in a screenplay. He isn't real. *Dr. Dawson's valise*. You crack me up."

Fetch cocked his head to one side.

"Oh, he's real all right. And we want to talk to him, too. But right now I got to concentrate on your sorry ass."

"Hey, are you paying attention," I said, pushing my luck. "Smith wrote a screenplay. That's it."

"He's a potential bioterrorist."

I laughed nervously. "Smith, a bioterrorist? What're you gonna arrest him for, living in cheap motels?"

He shook his head.

"We want to know the contents of the suitcase. All we want is to ask a couple questions, but the man seems to anticipate my every move." The faintest hint of a smile touched his face. It was the first expression of compassion I saw in Whitaker Fetch. "I caught up with you at that truck stop café. By the time we got there, you were gone. I've been to your motel twice this morning. Every time I been by, Smith is gone. What's he do, read minds?" He shook his head. "He's a slick character."

"*Smith*, a slick character? Are we talking about the same guy here?" I grimaced. "First of all, none of what you say makes sense. I read a lot of screenplays, and, man, your story doesn't work. America doesn't make biological weapons. I thought we signed a treaty or something. Country stopped making chemical bombs and stuff back in Nixon's day, right?"

Fetch leaned forward. "You're right. America doesn't make biowarfare weapons."

"Then I don't get it. Why are you here?"

He raised his muscular index finger and pointed at me.

"We have a right to defend ourselves against weapons of mass destruction. There are labs researching defensive measures, to protect us against a biowarfare or terrorist attack. The country has a right to defend itself." He lowered his finger. "We suspect Smith has taken a substance from a lab in Southern California."

"Look, why don't you just grab his friggin' suitcase, if that's what you want? Smith's out there somewhere, preaching to the natives. Go an' get him, Sheriff."

Again, he shook his head. "If I approached and he released the contents...that'd put citizens at risk. The scenario's unacceptable."

I picked up the empty cocktail glass and swirled the ice. "You know, I washed my hands of Smith a couple hours ago. In fact, I'm leaving town."

I pushed back on the seat as though about to get up. Fetch seized my wrist. There was nothing but brutal strength in his grip.

"Sit down."

I sat down.

I felt trapped. I glanced around at the regulars in the bar. None of them looked my way. The beer delivery guy was gone, and Bob the Bartender was playing liar's dice with the customers. I looked at the two nondescript associates of Whitaker Fetch. Once again, I was alone in the world, in need of medication, my cerebral cortex demanding to get high. The Scotch had kindled the fire.

As so often happens in times of stress, rather than retreat and admit defeat, I went on the defensive.

"How do I know you're who you say you are? I haven't seen a badge. What, you don't gotta show me no stinkin' badges?" I smiled, he didn't, and I looked away. "Far as I know, you could be some nigger here with his homies."

Anyone who knows me knows that my mouth speaks faster than my brain works. I realized my mistake only after the profanity passed my lips.

Fetch cocked his head upon hearing the "N" word. The man overworked the jaw muscles. He looked like he was doing bench presses with his dental work. He took a deep breath and seemed to be counting.

"Cowboy, you don't want to mess with me, is that clear?"

Alcohol was all the courage I needed at that point.

"So, this is what the country's come to after eight years of Bush? Trash the Bill of Rights? To hell with the Constitution? Is this what we're talking about? Tell me something, tell me something. Whatever happened to the Enlightenment, man?"

"This is about national security."

"National security, my ass." I copped a sarcastic tone. "You're wasting my tax dollars chasing after an old man with a worn-out suitcase. Oh, sounds like an important case, Marshal." The sarcasm dripped from my mouth. "Why don't you jokers secure the goddamned border instead?"

Nothing I said provoked Fetch.

"We want Smith's suitcase. I get the suitcase, and if you cooperate, I leave you alone. Then you can go back to whatever filth it is you do. Still a free country."

We sat in silent animosity for the moment while I considered what the man had said.

"Tell me what's in the suitcase. What's he got in there, dope? Smith can't have enough in there to raise a stink like this. So, what, Smith's holding samples of a weapon or something? You think he stole a bomb?"

Fetch said nothing. It was like talking to a wall, a fortress wall.

"This really sucks," I said, feeling the effects of three Scotch whiskies. The alcohol drowned all common sense. "I see no badge. You could be anybody. Look at you in your cheap suit and goatee. Is that regulation, Marshal?"

Fetch looked like a fire hydrant about to explode. The only thing that stood between me and getting the beating of my life, was the agent's training.

I snorted. "Check it out. *I'm* more black than you."

"Say what?"

"Well, look at you in your business suit and tight shoes," I said. "World's upside down, far as I can tell."

Fetch cocked his head, which was about as expressive as the man got. The volcano was rumbling and the ground shook. Had this been a Tex Avery cartoon, smoke would have come out his ears.

"Only thing happening here is discrimination against me. I probably got a legal case. Look what you people did to my house. I ought to sue your ass or whatever government you work for. Maybe make my fortune."

For a few seconds, I thought the man was going to lose his cool. He leaned forward and looked at me so hard I sobered up.

"If you had a lick of sense, you'd stop obstructing justice. It would go a lot better for you in the end."

Then Fetch gave me The Look as he pushed away from the table. Standing there, he adjusted his coat and straightened his tie. The beefy arms strained the fabric of his suit. His associates stood and did the same. I hoped that whatever government leash restrained them would hold strong. Otherwise, I knew I was nothing but quick dead meat.

"If you get in my way," he said, "I don't care if they take away my badge, I'll get you outta the way. Is that understood?"

I nodded involuntarily.

Then he turned to walk slowly toward the door. His cadence was deliberate. It spoke volumes. He opened the door for his associates, and they went out. Whitaker Fetch had the last word and put a little jive ass into his step. As he stood at the door, I caught a glimpse of sunlight through the lens of his eye as he fit on his shades. I realized that I should watch my back because even a federal employee will take only so much lip. And then he was gone.

I sat there catching my proverbial breath. I picked up the empty cocktail glass and rolled it between my palms. I thought of nothing but Smith's beige suitcase, imagining the contents to be microscopic bugs in test tubes. That frail old man in a gray suit was transporting the means to do away with us all. I took a profound breath when I recalled how Smith had first entered my bungalow like a post-modern Typhoid Mary. He was carrying the suitcase even then.

I may already have been exposed to the virus.

I waited for a few minutes before leaving the cocktail lounge. Outside, the Nevada sunlight was painfully bright. When I got back in the El Dorado, the taste of Scotch had me wanting another. I drove to a liquor store on the corner. For most of the afternoon, I ended up sitting in the car, sucking at a fifth of Jack concealed in a brown paper bag.

As I mulled over the low-down, the logical conclusion drove fear into my heart: Smith's suitcase was the real issue. He carried it everywhere. Whereas the screenplay had more than mere threads of truth running through it as a facsimile of history and as a prediction for the future, the suitcase...well, it was a time bomb, the biggest bomb in history.

I had misunderstood the truth of the matter all along. I had spent weeks trying to get Smith to finish the screenplay, but what really mattered were the contents of the suitcase. Whatever he carried in there was the key to my future and maybe to the future of the whole human race. If nothing else, if I scored Smith's suitcase and handed it over to Whitaker Fetch, if nothing else, maybe, just maybe, I might get a reward or something. A couple of grand or a trip out of town; get nominated for a commendation. But did I have the guts to turn over the old guy to his pursuers? Whatever the case, if I went Benedict Arnold on Smith, I deserved The Chickenshit Citizen of the Year Award.

Halfway down the bottle of Jack Daniel's, I fell asleep in the Caddy. I do not have a clear memory of the rest of the afternoon. I ate a Mexican dinner in a dive before smoking half a pack of cigarettes and wandering The Strip. By then, I had emptied the fifth and clutched it to my bosom like a nostalgic rune. I felt sorry for myself and regretted having been born. My cocaine Jones returned with a vengeance. If it was the end of the world, I figured, what the hell—I was entitled to get high one last time.

My only companion that day was a stray dog, black of course. You might say it dogged me from one broken-down cocktail lounge to another.

As evening fell, I lapsed into a stupor at a stripper bar. When two black kids sauntered past my booth, I whispered harshly at them, "Know where I can score some coke?"

I realized too late that they were a well-dressed young couple, arm in arm, in a word, Yuppies. The man laid into me big time.

"Yeah, dat's right," he said, faking a thick patois, pretending like he was Buckwheat. "Just cuz we be black you 'sume we dealin' crack. Sho' nuff. That be right." And then using his regular voice, he rebuked me. "You think all African American's are dope dealers, you lousy honkie bigot? I ought to kick your ass."

Well, that set me straight. I grappled with the vinyl seat, nearly falling on my can. I upset half a glass of Jack. The couple left the stripper bar, muttering how disappointing it was to encounter prejudice where you least expected it. I got up and threw down twenty, standing unsteadily to take in the topless bimbos one last time.

I staggered to the El Dorado and tumbled into the driver's seat. Only then did I realize, swimming in intoxication, that I was in an unfamiliar part of town. Rather than hunt for the Desert Rose Motel, I drove the El Dorado recklessly deeper into the neighborhood, down crowded streets of anonymous strip malls and fast food joints, through White Trash Nation. I could have been in Anytown, USA. I passed a bankrupt housing tract full of crumbling foundations. I drove into the very nucleus of terror.

Welcome to Ground Zero.

When I came to a stop sign, I asked myself, "Where're you going and what're you gonna do, man?"

Tomorrow, I decided, I would confront Smith once more. Only this time, it would be over the suitcase. I figured I could easily wrestle it away from him. Then it would only be a matter of time before I met up with Whitaker Fetch for the final scene. Maybe I could persuade him to buy another round of drinks.

I parked the El Dorado in an empty lot where a rusted Cyclone fence had fallen down. Two stray dogs ran off at my approach. My headlights threw long shadows down the piles of trash, broken concrete and a dead sapling. There were no streetlights in the lot such that, when I killed the lights, complete darkness overtook me. Above, the desert stars and the Big Dipper twinkled through the illuminated haze of Las Vegas.

I remembered something about the Big Dipper from the screenplay.

"That's weird."

The air inside the El Dorado was stale. I rolled down the window and wrapped my leather jacket around my shoulders. Glancing once at Smith's typewriter on the back seat, I wondered at its meaning. It seemed to speak of an overlooked obligation. My burp filled the car with the sweet scent of rotting fruit. Then I leaned against the door with my arms folded and I fell asleep.

Chapter 17

"Don't, Bob. Give me a minute," I said.

The sun had been up for an hour but you wouldn't know it from the desert night chill inside the car. I opened my right eye to see the misty blob of light through the foggy windshield. The figure of a man stood silhouetted against the daylight. Smith nudged me again, only this time push came to shove.

"Get off it, Bob. I'm tired."

"Where is Bob?"

My heart skipped a beat. Was it Whitaker Fetch?

I nearly choked on my tongue as the man reached into the car on the driver's side. I'd left Smith, I remembered with a start, to his own devices on the street.

The man sneered with a shit-eating grin as he reached out and slapped me hard across the face.

It *wasn't* Whitaker Fetch.

"Where is product?" He spoke with a thick foreign accent, Russian or Middle Eastern.

I managed a single punch that merely grazed him as I fumbled for the car keys in the ignition.

The door opened abruptly, and I lost my support and fell out of the El Dorado onto hard gravel, and as I managed to rise up on all fours, the peace inside my body exploded within a fury of scuffed wing-tip shoes, several pair, that kicked me in the midsection and squashed me to the ground. I vomited half-digested Mexican food and Jack Daniel's. I gripped my guts, struggling for breath that would not come, afraid to look up, afraid they'd kill me if I did, and all the while they huffed and cursed in a foreign language and hit me again until there was nothing, nothing at all.

Ω   Ω   Ω

"You ain't dead."

The world had disappeared, and I, Duncan Charles Austin, Jr., was lost in it. I believed myself to be half-conscious on a beach in Maui.

A child in a lemon-colored T-shirt, which barely covered his belly button, tossed sand in my face with a red plastic shovel. Sunlight shone through the lattice of palm leaves, and somewhere in the crushed vault of my brain, I heard rock music playing through the tin of a cheap radio.

The child spoke again. "Are you dead?"

I covered my eyes with both hands and coughed the sand from my throat. I rolled onto my side.

Someone had set fire to my kidneys.

"You ain't dead," the child said, pleased that this insensate adult toy stirred with the promise of yet another hour's amusement.

I swore under my breath, loud enough for the gods to acknowledge my misery.

The child's mother called out. "Bunny? *Bunny!*"

So, the monster's got a name, I was thinking. It's the same name my mother used to call me.

I spat a bloody jewel in the sand and managed to support myself on an elbow. I contemplated the meaning of bodily fluids when a wheelchair rolled into view. I lifted my head and saw my mother as she must have looked years ago when I was four or five years old, seated before me. She wore a flattering tank top and bikini bottom. She was radiant, despite the scars that ran in purple stitches up her legs. I was wondering how my mother had ended up in the middle of my suffering.

"Come along, Bunny," my mother said. "Let the man be." And as she rolled away, she added, "Let 'em sleep it off."

I thought, *I must be drunk.* That would explain my wooziness and the throbbing migraine.

I awoke from one nightmare into another. I was where I had ended up the night before, in a vacant lot full of trash. Garbage was my life.

A tableau of an abstract brutality had been visited upon me. Pain was banked deep within muscle, joint and bone. Trying to rise up, I fell forward, my face cushioning the fall against the broken concrete. I battled a more concentrated form of gravity. A chasm strove to swallow me whole.

I leaned against an upturned cinderblock as the heat of the day bore down and the kingdom of insects buzzed in my ears, staking a claim. I lacked the strength to swat them away.

I was alive. Pain was proof of existence, *sufferre ergo sum.* I was in no immediate danger of dying, although I would have welcomed the hiatus.

I looked at my surroundings, for the car. It was gone.

Slowly, I pieced together the circumstances. I remembered polishing off a bottle of Jack Daniel's. I must have left the car somewhere else. *No,* I thought, *that's not right.* There were men with fists and standard issue brown wing tips, but when had the beating taken place? I wondered, *The night before or this morning?*

For a time—how long I had no way of knowing—I stared at the vacant lot. My scrambled brain began to take an inventory of the litter. I bent over and vomited.

I shut my eyes and fell asleep under a merciless sun. When I awoke, the desert breeze rustled the trash. A piece of plastic wrap came to rest against my cheek. Empty soda cans and banana peals attracted a swarm of yellow jackets. The garbage gratefully diverted the insects to a new target.

"Bob," I called, "Bob, are you there?"

At some point after my first beating, the same teen-aged boys, who had harassed Bob Smith when we checked into the Desert Rose Motel, paid me a visit in the vacant lot. They were not in search of booty or suitcases filled with deadly viruses but in search of reckless endangerment. Beating people up was their idea of a good time, and they knew easy prey when they saw it. They circled round me, and when I swore at them, they beat me senseless with a rusty pipe. Despite my loss of consciousness, I have a distinct recollection of the sound made when a lead pipe strikes a ripe watermelon.

Ω   Ω   Ω

They found me wandering The Strip, bloodied and dazed, the same two police officers that had stopped Smith and me when first we drove into town. It was a day full of coincidence. The police officers showed little compassion.

I was barefooted. The back pockets of my jeans were torn off. Dried blood caked my long hair and stained my T-shirt. My eyes were swollen shut from the beating. When the first officer offered assistance, I escaped his grasp only to be corralled by the other, the female. When asked what had happened, I accused the officers of dereliction of duty. I swore that a government agent had mugged me, and the female cop laughed when she said, "You sure it weren't no little green men?" When asked for identification, I yelled something about a stolen car and I spat on their polished shoes. Then, without further provocation, I fainted.

They took me to the University Medical Center for treatment of abrasions and contusions. I regained consciousness as they shaved my head to clean the scalp wounds and apply bandages. Seeing my gray ponytail in a wastebasket, I cursed the nurses bitterly. In addition to physical trauma, my secondary diagnosis included alcoholic psychosis, and to calm me down, the biggest nurse on duty forcibly administered a narcoleptic. I hollered something about aliens and deadly pathogens but was unable to repeat my name when asked. They admitted me for psychiatric observation as John Doe Seven-MIA, Medically Indigent Adult. To protect me from further injury, I was heavily medicated. "Snowed" in the parlance of the ward.

On the first night in the psychiatric ward, I fell out of bed and struck a bedpan, which aggravated my head injuries. A pair of good-looking nurses redressed the wound and replaced my bloodied paper gown with a fresh one. When they tucked me in bed, the nurses cinched my wrists and ankles with four-point restraints.

The psychiatric ward was laid out much like a military barracks with two rows of ten beds divided by draw curtains. A gloomy cavernous room, it was a warehouse for human beings in the throes of crisis. The Linoleum floor amplified the bedlam of catatonia and paranoid-schizophrenic delusions, a chorus accompanied by electronic beeps from a few monitors. It was an impossible place to rest. Despite this, I slept for three days.

When I awoke, I struggled to free myself from the restraints. Failing that, I called for help. The nurse on duty brought a plastic pitcher and a tiny paper cup to my bedside. Her nametag read *Hollis Pickles, LVN*.

Standing over me with hands on her commodious hips, she asked a most embarrassing question: "What is your name?" It was a routine question asked of all patients in the ward.

I was dumbfounded.

"Do you know where you are?" Nurse Pickles asked.

She might just as well have asked that I calculate a Universal Field Theory in physics.

"Can you speak?"

Saliva dribbled from my mouth to my hospital gown. I waited patiently for my dislocated brains to generate an idea, but my mind was empty. I could not remember who I was, where I was, or what I was. I had no personal history that I might recall. If illustrated by a cartoonist, my mind would have been a question mark.

I reminded Nurse Pickles of a frightened animal. The pair of bandages on my head was shaped like rabbit ears.

"A bunny," she said. "You look like one of those pathology bunnies."

"Blow it out your ass," I told her.

Nurse Pickles scowled and said, "Party time."

I gratefully received another injection of whatever they were serving that day.

Ω   Ω   Ω

"Mr. Austin?"

This was not the time for levity.

In my nightmares, Jimi Hendrix played the devil, who had set fire to hell-bound souls in the shape of Fender Stratocaster's. When I awoke, "Purple Haze" was in my brain, and when I saw the face of an angel hovering above me in the psychiatric ward, I gave voice to the internal music: "'Scuze me while I kiss the sky."

Ba Da Bing, Ba Da Bang.

"Is this him?" Nurse Hollis Pickles asked.

"Yes," the angel said sincerely. "Yes, it is."

"You say his last name's Austin?" Nurse Hollis Pickles asked with a ballpoint pen poised above a clipboard.

"Something like that," the angel said.

I returned to oblivion.

Ω   Ω   Ω

"Can you hear me, Mr. Austin?" the angel said.

I looked around to see who in hell she was addressing.

The angel sat in a straight-backed chair next to my hospital bed. I was still in four-point restraints, still had funny looking head bandages. I looked like a convalescing middle-aged rabbit beneath a hospital sheet.

My eyes focused on the angel but my mind made little sense of her. By the time she said, "It's Chloe Dawson. Do you remember me?" I had recognized the face, the fall of ermine hair, the nurse's uniform. I knew her from my former life.

"There are some things I need to know," the angel said.

I wanted to request that she loosen the four-point restraints. My nose had itched for three days, and I was unable to scratch it.

She worried the fold of her uniform.

"They ran your picture on TV as a missing person. I had no idea you were here, where I work. I hardly recognized you without your hair."

The angel's eyes were sympathetic.

"Do you know where he is, Mr. Austin? Where I can find my husband?"

I did not know who her husband was.

"I've seen the reports. The authorities think he's here in town. He knows your friend. That man called Bob Smith. I need you to ask your friend about my husband, Mr. Austin," she said. "Would you do that for me? He's been missing now for over a year. Please, help me. Can you hear me, Mr. Austin?"

The movie theater of my mind played images of mass extinction, of coroners driving hearses through empty suburbs, calling "throw out your dead, throw out your dead" past vacant houses, their empty windows the sockets of skulls. Pyres raging like bonfires.

"When you came by the house, some pages of your script got loose in the wind. I read it," she said. "It's my husband's story, Mr. Austin. Your friend stole my husband's story."

From somewhere in my ruined mind, I remembered something about a screenplay.

"Joe is a microbiologist. One of the best in the whole world. He worked for the Department of Defense, really. All highly classified. My husband was a good man, Mr. Austin. A good American. He didn't even tell me what kind of work it was. Only after things began to happen, after...well, after he began to lose his mind, only then did I ask questions. But it was too late. Joe heard voices, saw things that weren't there. The last time we spoke he was in a mental institution.

"It was only after I read those pages of the script that I realized it was Joe's story. It helped me put the pieces together. But I have to ask your friend. I want to meet Bob Smith, Mr. Austin. Do you understand? Remember, you came to my house that night, with Bob Smith. Do you remember?"

I had no clue.

"There's a reason you came into my life. God and my prayers brought you to us. Can you tell me where I can find Bob Smith? Did you know he was on television? He was interviewed on TV. I have to ask him about my husband. I don't know where Joe is."

She stopped speaking because she had lost control of her emotions. She regained them and spoke again. "I haven't spoken to my husband for.... He just disappeared. Can you help me? Frank misses him so much. They used to be so close."

When it became obvious that the psychiatric patient with the head injury would not be forthcoming, the angel stood to leave, her mascara running.

"Nose?" I managed to say, although it sounded as though I had cotton gauze for a tongue.

She sat down, encouraged by my response.

"Please, Mr. Austin. Please, try to remember."

I grappled with my thoughts but nothing more came to me. Eventually, I fell asleep, and when I awoke, she was gone. My inarticulation had driven her away.

Ω   Ω   Ω

Over the weeks of incarceration, my mind became like a garden spade working the fertile soil. Memory is Mother to regret, and I was pregnant with contrition. Bits and pieces of memory returned with a vengeance. I anguished over marriages that I lost due to my recidivistic philandering. Try as I might, in my few hours of consciousness during each day, I could not form a mental image of my children. What sort of man forgets what his kids look like? Worst of all among the tableau of grief and self-loathing were the haunting martyrs of my parents.

When I was growing up I had disappointed them awfully. The Old Man had expected more than I could give. He wanted the perfect son. I was as far from that expectation as Earth is from Jupiter. My teen-age drug arrests, my high school sweetheart's abortion of her folks' first grandchild, all of it had earned the Old Man's contempt. In defiance, I had pissed on Rodeo Drive, literally, and spray painted swastikas on the porch of a Jewish film producer's mansion. These abysmal acts, in a life full of scandal, were all I could remember. Atonement should be my middle name.

I remembered that I had not been necessarily a hurtful child. You might say, I sought the attention denied me through Dad's business undertakings and Mother's disabilities. I was not the kind of brute who clipped jumper cables to frogs or set kittens on fire. My incriminations were trespasses conducted with a sense of self-destruction. Unfortunately, Hollywood's finest did not recognize my cries for help, and on a regular basis, Friday and Saturday nights were taken up with telephone calls from the Beverly Hills Police to my parents' house on Castle Place.

Before my discharge from the medical center in Las Vegas, I vegetated in a hospital bed with no more cognition than a philodendron. I existed in blissful ignorance. One night, the realization that I had contributed to my folks' suicide fit its beastly hands around my throat and choked the breath out of me. Thrown like garbage onto the ash heaps of the world, I was the most outcast of orphans. I couldn't stop crying.

Bob Smith told me once that grief was part of the healing process, but grief was not sufficient to span the wound in a heart as bad as mine.

My mother, God rest her soul, was a saint to put up with a son like me. Despite my indolence and slovenly rebellion, Mother always forgave me. When I got behind in schoolwork or smashed up my Triumph sports car, she advised the making of lists as a remedy. How making a list would remedy the situation is beyond me. However, categorizing and prioritizing life's obligations had convinced her of the power of lists, and we're not talking grocery lists here.

Throughout her late adult life, confined to a wheelchair, Dolores Austin compiled volumes of lists, more than one list for each and every day; a separate list of pain medications; a list of the books she planned on reading; another of her physicians and funeral parlors. My mother combined and abbreviated lists when she neglected to complete the "Things To Remember" from the previous day. She had orchestrated her suicide by writing a list. On it she underlined in red ink the obligation to "Call Bunny." It shames me to admit; I cannot remember our last telephone conversation. I must have been stoned.

When I had regained partial memory of who and what I was, it became impossible to forgive my actions. I hated myself. Out of self-preservation, I pretended not to know who I was. "I haven't a clue," I told the doctors. I didn't know my name and Social Security number. And after a while, as happens with brain injury, I actually forgot the incidentals of my life and returned to blissful amnesia.

Being nobody was better than being Duncan Charles Austin, Jr. Remembering nothing was preferable to facing the facts of my life.

Ω   Ω   Ω

Nearly forty-five days later, the hospital gladly discharged me into the care of Bob Smith.

After I had taken up much-needed space in a hospital room, the medical center administration was delighted to get rid of me. They had no hope of obtaining full reimbursement for services rendered to a Medically Indigent Adult, and so when Smith signed papers stating that he knew the unidentified psych patient, the administration allowed him to take this obligation off their hands.

Unfortunately, the ragged clothes I'd been wearing when the paramedics brought me to the Emergency Department were lost in the interim. They discharged me in a green gown made of the thinnest possible cotton. I wore flimsy slippers, and with my rabbit ear bandages, I was a sight to behold. Next to Smith, I was the goofiest looking six-foot tall rabbit standing outside the hospital that day, waiting for a cab.

From across the street three men in black leather jackets eyed me, each lowering their wrap-around sunglasses. They looked like foreign mobsters with slicked-back hair and pocked skin.

"Who're they?" I asked Smith.

He gave me a patronizing pat on my arm.

"Don't worry. Nothing to worry about," Smith replied. "Their time has not yet come."

When a Yellow Cab pulled up to the curb, I said, "Do you expect me to pay for this?"

"God provides," Smith said.

I rolled my eyes. "Think He could provide a pair a pants?"

A smiling Sihk named Mr. Mali in a maroon turban drove the cab. He reeked of patchouli oil. He activated the fare box and said what sounded like "Hindermost solicit" to which Bob Smith responded, "Yes, thank you, sir." They seemed to know one another.

I paid no attention to the taxi ride. I could not have cared less where we were headed. Destinations are irrelevant to a meaningless life. To wherever Mr. Mali was delivering us, regardless, I would face the humiliation of my attire. What I had hoped was to circle the block and be returned to my warm hospital bed. I had trouble recalling just exactly why I was in Las Vegas. My association with Smith was also a riddle.

"Sorry about your car, Mr. Austin."

I had no idea that I even owned a car.

With my mind drifting toward forgetfulness, I said, "No sweat. Got two more at home just like it. Good thing I didn't take the Rolls, huh?"

"I can appreciate your sense of disappointment," Smith said.

I made a face and gave him a sidelong glance.

In the car next to us, I saw an elderly lady clutching a small black dog. When she saw me, her eyes wrinkled and thin lips rose in a laugh, revealing a mouthful of dentures. I wondered what she had seen that was so funny.

Smith touched my forearm. "I know, Mr. Austin. None of this has worked out to your liking."

I laughed, not knowing what it was that had not worked out.

"But I'm glad you're feeling better."

Smith patted my knee. The thugs who put me in the hospital had kicked me repeatedly in the same knee, and I cursed at the sudden needle of pain. "Fuck, fuck, fuck…"

Mr. Mali grappled with the Plexiglas divider between the front and back to shut himself off from my profanity.

"Watch your language, Mr. Austin." Smith's stare made me feel as though I'd violated international law.

For a mile or so neither of us said anything.

"How's your memory?"

"Like a jigsaw puzzle," I said. I had the memory of a goldfish. As we approached the motel, I asked Smith, "Do I live here?"

Smith sighed. "Yes."

The cab came to a stop at the intersection of La Fontaine and Nevada Boulevard, in front of La Grande Motel. It might as well have been on the moon.

Mr. Mali spoke again in jumbled syntax.

"Periscope here?" he asked, to which Smith agreed. Mr. Mali shut off the meter and smiled. "Auxiliary fine cudgel."

We stepped out of the cab without paying.

Mr. Mali said, "No no no, Yawn. Dondi. Zit dondi."

A Cadillac El Dorado, a late model, pulled to the curb across the street. The driver rolled down the window. I could tell he was looking at me and I squinted back in his general direction. I was wondering if I knew the black man.

Smith ushered me to the front door to the La Grande Motel. He said. "Relax. Nothing can hurt you now. Relax."

When I said something about my mother, Smith navigated me through the door.

"You were easy to locate," Smith said as we climbed the stairs. "They plastered your picture all over the TV. *Unidentified person*," he said, slashing quotes signs in the air. "Help requested of relatives or friends, et cetera."

My mind functioned well enough to make the logical conclusion that Smith and I were acquainted. No other relatives or friends had come to the hospital to claim me. But still, I had no idea who in the hell he was.

Smith smiled. "Don't worry. We still have the screenplay."

"What screenplay?" I asked.

Smith gave a sigh of exasperation. "I was certain that I was the one who would get mugged. I never figured it would be you. That's why, you know, I wrote it that way."

I ran a hand over my scalp, reaching for the phantom ponytail. Instead, I grasped the rabbit ear bandages. I winced from an imaginary pain.

"That should take some getting used to," Smith said with a generous smile. "I would imagine."

Chapter 18

I ain't what I used to be. But then again, I never was.

I had entered the hospital in early November and was released around mid-December, and as far as I could tell, about a month and a half of my life was missing. I felt like a gutted rabbit lying in a skillet.

While I continued to recuperate, night after night we moved from one motel to another, living on credit. My American Express, Bob Smith explained, had been mistakenly left with the clerk on the night we checked into the Desert Rose Motel. Being an honest fellow, the clerk had returned it to Smith who, in the intervening weeks, survived on my credit.

Every day, Smith and I wandered the streets of Las Vegas. Smith carried his ever-present suitcase, and I carried a plastic milk crate that I would set up so Smith could preach his "The World is Coming to an End" sermon to the homeless and dead-enders. And every night, we stayed in a different motel, in whatever one we ended up at the end of the day.

I wore clothes that Smith had saved from my knapsack. Jeans and a bowling shirt with an appliquéd winged lizard. From the Goodwill Store, Smith finagled to get a pair of high-top tennis shoes without laces and a tweed jacket with elbow patches. The costume served to worsen my pitiable state of mind, such as it was.

The street people, meth addicts and drunks laughed at my appearance. They called me the Rabbit. "Look, here come the Streetsayer and his pet rabbit," they'd say. And they'd laugh. I hated it when they laughed at me. They laughed at me every time we showed up on a corner where Bob Smith preached to the masses.

And so, on one particular morning, because of my shaved head and odd-looking bandages, I decided not to leave the motel room. I was too self-conscious to accompany Smith on his daily rounds along Las Vegas Boulevard.

"You can't stay here by yourself," Smith said. He cautioned about a dangerous man named Whitaker Fetch. Other times he warned me about something called the Delivery Boy. This unaccountable enemy of mine apparently roamed the streets of Las Vegas, gunning for me. How I had wronged him was not explained to my full satisfaction. "Better to come with me," Smith advised. "Until the assassin has lost interest or until your stamina improves and you can take care of yourself."

I refused and threw a tantrum.

"Stop acting like a child," he said.

I cried. I buried my face in the pillow and yowled. I felt Bob Smith's feeble hand on my shoulder.

"Okay, okay. Relax. Let me see if we're in danger."

Smith seemed to go into a trance. I watched from my bed as his eyes glazed over, his lips trembled. It was as though he saw things I couldn't see. When he came out of the trance, he smiled.

"It's okay," he said. "You can stay home today."

That evening he brought to our impromptu hideout an enchilada, a bowl of black beans and rice given to him by good souls. Healthy though scant rations, this food sustained us. I had spent the day lying in bed and staring at the water-stained ceiling. To pass the time I calculated the number of perforations in the insulation tiles above the sink.

I assumed that Smith passed the time on the street as he usually did, preaching about the end of the world.

That night before we went to sleep, he said, "We can stay in this room one more night, but then we have to move."

The next day I felt well enough to consider an excursion outdoors. Before Smith left that morning, I told him that I needed to get some fresh air and that I would probably go for a walk. His eyes rolled back and showed only white. After the trance broke, he cautioned me. "That's not such a good idea. Wait until I come home, and then we can go out together, at night. Stay inside today."

After he was gone, I defied his orders and left our room. The motel had been my cage for two days. I was the resident rabbit with my absurd head bandages. Outside the motel on the street my appearance caused some alarm, dressed as I was. A clutch of Japanese tourists clicked their cameras, the flashbulbs momentarily blinding me. A child among them said, "Bugs Bunny, Mommy. Bugs Bunny!" The working poor were lined up and waiting for the bus. They laughed in chorus at my expense as I shuffled past. Rather than suffer their ridicule, I jogged to the left, off the street and into a trailer park. There, I got a glimpse of what life was all about.

I was like a child seeing the world for the first time without benefit of memory. We human beings normally process new experiences through comparison with the past. Everything I saw, heard, and smelled became the foundation blocks upon which to build a *new* Duncan Charles Austin, Jr., in the ruins of the old one.

I saw a bald man in soiled tank top kissing a hag who sucked a Pall Mall. The man had a blue tattoo scrawled on his flabby arm. This was love, I decided. I watched a boy on a bicycle drag a three-legged dog on a leash through the dusty yard of the trailer park. This was accepted behavior, I decided. Two obese women, sitting in aluminum lawn chairs and drinking beer, laughed at my appearance. "Hey, Peter Cottontail," they called. A naked three-year-old girl bawled behind them in the doorway of their trailer. A bully in a four-wheel drive pick-up spat tobacco juice out of his window and he called me a freak. I took the bars-n-stars sticker in the back window below the gun rack to be the emblems of America. A girl with a bubble hairdo sitting on a bench, smacking Juicy Fruit gum, asked if I wanted to party.

Parked between two trailers was an old car. I ran my hand along the brake lights and the stylish tailfins. They had an uncanny, familiar feel, as though the car had once belonged to me.

The driver's door opened suddenly. It lodged against the wall of the alley and effectively blocked my passage. A large man stepped out of the car. He held a golden handgun that glinted in the Nevada sunlight.

"Get in the car, Cowboy." He gestured with the gun. "Didn't figure you to carry something like this," he said, referring to the gun.

I was about to excuse myself when he twisted my arm behind my back. We struggled briefly before he overpowered and shoved me into the car. I hit my head on the steering wheel on my way across the front seat. He climbed in with the gun aimed at my head.

We sat there in the heat of the car, not saying anything. I rubbed my scalp where I'd struck the steering column.

The man wore a dark blue suit. When he smiled his bright teeth dazzled against his black skin. It was not a warm smile but one that spoke of victory.

"What kind of car is this?" I asked. I should have asked what he wanted with me or why he'd pulled me into the car. Instead, I asked about the make of the automobile. I was still in recovery and clueless.

"A nineteen eighty-six Cadillac El Dorado Coupe de Ville," he said. "Do you always act this stupid?"

I shrugged, and he lowered the weapon.

"I don't know. Brain damage." It sounded as though I had said, "Drain bramage."

The black man huffed. His sunglasses shielded all expression in his eyes. He had the head of a Rottweiler, and he wore a goatee.

"Don't play games," he said. "I need you to bring me that thing we talked about."

I had no idea who he was, but it had been my practice at the hospital and thereafter to give the appearance of knowing what people were talking about until I gathered enough information to fake my way through a conversation.

I nodded. "What *thing* exactly?"

The man leaned closer and slapped my rabbit ear bandages.

"You look like a fool, you know that?"

I was beginning to dislike him very much, and I suspected that he was the enemy Bob Smith had warned me about, the so-called Delivery Boy. What didn't make sense was his demand that I deliver something to him when it should have been the other way around. He, after all, was the Delivery Boy. To my relief he pulled back a little. He leaned against the driver's door.

"If you could tell me what it is you're looking for," I said, "maybe I could ask around, you know, ask Bob if he's seen it."

"You really don't have a clue, do you?"

I shrugged.

The man squinted at me as though I was generating an intense radiation, and he shook his head.

"How'd you get so beat up?" he asked.

I shrugged again. "I can't remember."

I gazed around me at the interior of the Cadillac. There were stacks of paraphernalia on the back seat, torn pieces of paper on the floor along with broken pencils and spilled correction fluid.

"Nice car," I said, swallowing, hoping to sound polite and complimentary.

"Your friend's got something of mine. A little tan valise."

I tried to sort out this particular clue among the jumbled memories of my immediate past, and I began to get the idea of what he was talking about.

"You mean Bob's suitcase?"

The man shook his head. "It isn't his. He stole it," he said. "Belongs to a man named Dawson. That name mean anything to you?"

He evaluated me momentarily as though I were a perplexing algebraic equation. Then when I somehow factored correctly in his universe, his voice lost its hostile edge, and he sounded like he was talking to a child.

"Look, you want to save yourself a lot of heartache? Go get the suitcase and bring it here. I'll get what I need out of it, and you can take it back to your friend. How's that sound?"

I told him that Bob didn't like me touching it and that I was not even supposed to be here. "I sneaked out less than an hour ago," I said.

The man leaned forward. "We can play this anyway you like. You get me the suitcase, and we forget the whole thing."

I thought about what he had proposed. Our communication up to this point was not done so much in words as it was through physical language and his nonverbal cues in opposition to my impaired mental abilities. But my instincts told me that I was in terrific danger should I defy his wishes or underestimate the gravity of his threat.

"Describe what it is you want," I said, "and I'll bring it to you."

I was clearly wearing out his patience. He reached across and gripped my shirt.

"Don't mess with me, slime bag," he said. "I ain't buying your stupid act. You got that?"

I winced in anticipation of another beating. Beatings were what I had come to expect from my association with human beings.

"I want the suitcase." He let go of my shirt but sat close enough for me to smell his breath, a combination of a cheeseburger and cigarettes. "Listen very carefully." He shifted his weight, and I heard the car's shock absorbers crackle like arthritic joints. "Your buddy's carrying stolen goods. You know what that means?"

"What kind of stolen goods?" I asked.

He lowered his voice. "A kind of bomb. A deadly weapon." Once again he sounded as though he was talking to a child. "Some very bad men are looking for Bob's suitcase. They will hurt your friend...and they'll hurt you, too, just to get their hands on it. It's my job to make sure these bad men don't get the suitcase. Do you understand?"

"I don't know anything about a bomb," I told him.

He looked frustrated.

"Oh, you don't, huh?" He had an angry tone. "You hang out with a guy a couple months and don't know what he's carrying in his suitcase? You're either the dumbest asshole I ever met. Or dumb like a fox."

He twisted sideways and glanced out the window. His expression softened as he fought to regain his cool. He wiped his face with his hand.

"Look," he said. "These guys, the bad guys, they won't stop to ask you questions. They'll just get it done. Three in the back of the head—"

"Three what?"

"Shut up and listen. I have something of yours, okay, that I'm willing to trade. Now, I'll give it to you if you do something for me. Do you understand *that?*"

I nodded although once again I had no clue what the man was talking about or what he had of mine that he was willing to trade.

He pulled the keys out of the ignition and held them before me. I stretched forward, and he dropped the keys into my palm.

"This is your car, Cowboy. I'm returning it to you. Government policy. Don't ask how it's being returned. And don't call the cops. It'll only complicate your life. In fact, don't say anything to nobody."

I stared at the keys in astonishment.

"So, now you owe me big time, don't you? We're friends now. So, this is what I want you to do. I want you to go and get the suitcase and bring it here. By tomorrow, by the end of the day. Steal it from your friend or knock him out to get it, I don't care. Just bring it to me. You can go now."

I hesitated.

"Go on. Get going."

I placed the car keys on the seat and stepped cautiously out of the Cadillac. I stood there beside the opened door at attention like a six-foot tall rabbit, uncertain what to do.

The man got out of the car. Seeing him get out of the car was like watching the unfolding of something impossibly big emerging from a metal egg. He pressed the wrinkles out of his dark suit and shut the door. The trailer park dog barked twice and strained against the rope tied to a hitch. Then the dog sat down in the dust, panting in the heat of the day.

"Are you playing some kind a game?" he said.

I shook my head. I was about to cry like a baby.

He waggled car keys at me and said, "Here."

He tossed the keys. They somersaulted through the air and clattered at my feet. I picked them up, my facial expression full of question marks.

"You know what to do," he said.

I walked backwards out of the trailer park, keeping my eye on him. At the street corner I ran for my life.

Ω   Ω   Ω

Smith found me at the bus stop holding my knees to my chest, rocking to and fro.

"You okay?" he asked.

I wondered who I was. How was I to articulate my feelings when their source was a mystery? The car keys ached in the pocket of my jeans. Should I tell him about the man in the trailer park?

"Who the hell am I?" I asked.

Smith smiled benignly. "You're my friend. Your name's Mr. Austin."

"Am I dying? Why does it feel like I'm dying?"

He shook his head. "Come on. Let's go home."

He took me to a new motel on Carlos Avenue. I stayed in our room for the rest of the day, napping mostly, tormented by the man's demand that I bring him Smith's suitcase. Exhausted by my adventures outside, I soon fell into a deep sleep.

I dreamed that I laid on my deathbed. I lay isolated in a sterile-looking white room. At the moment before oblivion, I realized that my life was over and that I had wasted time and that no one loved me or would weep at my passing. My life had been a series of bad choices. What I had thought was the "truth" turned out to be a lie. What had led to my demise had been a propensity for anger, depression, alcoholism and drug abuse. And as happens in dreams, scenes shift in the blink of an eye. My deathbed became the sacrificial altar at the Aztec pyramid El Castillo de Chichén

Itzá. When the priest plunged the sacred knife into my heart, my animus became my bodily fluids flowing down the channels, down the steps of the pyramid at El Castillo de Chichén Itzá. I was the fluid in the rock. Once my run was over and I pooled on the low shallow ground, there I began to evaporate and change again into something transformed of identity. I transmuted into something non-self. There was no longer the "I," only the mute indifference and cold precision, the elemental beauty of sub-atomic particles. The particles were not "I." I had disappeared. The ones and zeroes in the software of my brain were deleted, erased forever, forward and backward in time, until there was no such thing as here and now and never would be again.

In my life I have run in a series of tight circles, assuming that I knew what was important. I fooled myself into thinking that I knew who I was, what I wanted. I realized upon waking from my dream that the most obvious and easily ignored of all my bad habits, the selfishness of my behavior, was what would get me killed. As I lay in bed at the motel, the lens of truth exposed the lies that had been my life. I realized that I would die of irony. As the Nevada night fell, I refused to eat, and as I lay down again on my bed, I wept bitterly into the pillow.

In the morning I sat on the side of the bed with my shaved head in my hands. Bob Smith told me he was going out for the day and that he would not be back until much later.

"Are you going to be okay?"

I looked at Bob Smith as he stood in the doorway, his beige suitcase dangling from his hand. He left before my scrambled brains could form a response.

In the shower I let the hot water wash away the lingering dread of my dreams. As I toweled off, I noticed a thin stack of papers on Bob Smith's bed. It was something he had written. It appeared to be scenes from a screenplay.

Sitting on the edge of my bed and thumbing the pages, something unidentifiable stirred deep within my memory.

Printed in long-hand in capital letters was *"THE FINAL SCENE: Path of Least Resistance."* I could not comprehend its significance. Casually scanning a few of the pages, I came across my name in the text only once. Thereafter, my character in the screenplay was referred to as the Rabbit. I flipped back a few pages to get my bearings:

> *Exterior City Landscape. Day. Traffic sounds. Crowds of tourists and homeless intermingled. Soundtrack: Mozart's Requiem.*
>
> *PAN: Las Vegas streets seen from above, over the rooftops of casinos, below the hubbub of congestion, a world full of caustic indifference and tourist congestion. The corner of Las Vegas Boulevard. A casino resort hotel is in the background.*
>
> *STREET LEVEL: On this winter day of December 21, Bob Smith preaches to a small gathering. Some tourists in the crowd take pictures of the street preacher. A few homeless men rail at Bob Smith with anger.*
>
> *LONG SHOT to SLOW ZOOM: Bob Smith standing on an upturned crate. His head is above the crowd.*
>
> *CLSOE UP: Bob Smith's eyes. He is crying.*
>
> *MEDIUM: Bob Smith delivers his message amid generalized indifference and defiance.*

>   *BOB*
>   *"Unless we work together to put a stop to*
>   *biological weapons research, we're*
>   *doomed. Unless we stop now, we have*
>   *condemned not only our species but every*
>   *living thing on the planet...."*
>
>   *PAN: <u>The corner of the street</u>. Mister*
> *Austin approaches the crowd at the fringes.*
>   *HAND-HELD CAM: Mister Austin's*
> *(the Rabbit) POV as Bob Smith preaches to*
> *the crowd.*
>   *CLOSE UP: <u>The Rabbit's eyes</u>. He is*
> *crying.*

I looked up from reading to ask the empty motel room, "What *is* this?"

Memory does not return to the sufferer of head trauma in a sudden flash of insight. Memory returned to me piecemeal.

As I read the passage, I recalled having read another similar scene in a screenplay of the same name. It could have been years ago or yesterday when I'd read it; I had no way of judging time. I knew that in my immediate past I had played a significant role in gaining a contract—I remembered it was called an *option*—with a major motion picture production company. I recalled the rather inflated image of a man that I used to work with by the name Gleason, first name Pig Boy. I thought about this and decided that I must have the name wrong. My recall was spotty. The faces of people bubbled through my cerebral cortex, faces without names. Among them I may have glimpsed the images of my mother and father.

I tapped the page of the screenplay.

"I know this. This is my life. I've been living this."

I ran my finger down the text. I remembered that the character Joe Dawson had a wife and son, Chloe and Frank. But the main character's name had been changed halfway through the treatment. Joe Dawson became Bob Smith. Or had I confused this fact as well? No, I thought, it was true. Slowly, my mind began to fill in the blanks. Perhaps the screen character *Bob Smith* was the same person as my roommate? But if that were the case, who was Joe Dawson? More pieces of memory began to fall into place. I recalled driving my car—the Old Man's Cadillac, I reminded myself—to Chloe Dawson's house in Las Vegas. There, I had confronted her and caused considerable embarrassment and stress, although details of the encounter were lost to me. What had it been about? And why did I have this tremendous sense of impending doom? What was it about the screenplay and Bob Smith that made me feel so lost, so uneasy?

I returned to the screenplay for clues to my own memory. In the final scene, Chloe and Frank have come to see for themselves if Bob Smith is indeed the man, Dr. Joe Dawson, who had abandoned them years ago. They are eager to confront Bob Smith on the streets of Las Vegas and confirm his true identity, despite his change in appearance. In the scene, a car strikes Frank when he rushes across the street to his "father." Frank ends up in an intensive care unit with fatal head injuries. There, Bob Smith raises the boy like Lazarus from the dead. I remembered, it was a powerful scene that had earned an option with a major. I may have made a lot of money from a contract, but I could not recall the exact amount.

"I might be rich," I told myself.

I finished reading the final scene. With my finger tapping the names of Chloe and Frank, my injured brains dug up another memory. Something was telling me that the final scene had not yet happened but that it *would* happen. As illogical as it seemed, I knew that events outside the motel room were beginning to shape themselves, events that I knew intuitively could mean the end to all life on earth. How I knew this and the nature of the threat were a complete mystery to me.

At that moment my heart sank.

I turned back one page to confirm the date referenced in the text of the play.

December twenty-first.

"What is today's date?"

I picked up the telephone and called the front desk.

"Yes?" the clerk asked.

"Tell me, what day is this?"

"The nineteenth."

"The nineteenth of...?"

"December."

I detected a lilt of mockery in his voice.

I hung up the receiver.

This time I read the last remaining pages. I knew it to be a rewrite.

As the scene unfolds, the character Bob Smith preaches to a crowd on the corner of The Strip in Las Vegas. There is a six-foot tall rabbit, or a man dressed up like a rabbit, among the on-lookers. There is a slow zoom as the Rabbit notices the approach of the wife and son from Bob Smith's previous life, when he was known as Dr. Joe Dawson. Among a throng of gamblers and tourists, mother and son cross the street to confront Bob Smith.

Chloe begs Smith to tell her the truth, that he is Joe Dawson, her long-lost husband. Above protests from the crowd, she asks what happened to him at the psychiatric facility and why he has aged so rapidly. What has happened to him, she wants to know. Bob Smith rejects her pleas. He returns to preaching to the people, warning them that the end of the world is at hand. Chloe weeps on the arm of her son Frank who raises a fist against the street prophet. Bob Smith is unmoved. He knows what is about to unfold.

Written into the scene are flashbacks between what the future holds and what action he must take to protect his son.

There is a close-up of the long-suffering wife and boy as they turn to walk away. At this point in the film it is pure Sergei Eisenstein. Frank Dawson angrily rushes across the street juxtaposed with a truck running a red light. Bob Smith has "seen" this incident in his mind many times. The Delivery Boy is at the wheel of the truck, and the shot calls for "morph folding" of two images, that of the Delivery Boy's face bracketed by that of a human skull as the symbol of Death. As the delivery truck bears down on Frank Dawson, Smith knows what he must do to save the boy. It is a path that he longs to avoid, but Bob Smith will sacrifice his life to save another. He pushes past the Rabbit and rushes into the street. He shoves Frank to safety, only to be crushed beneath the wheels of the truck.

In the concluding dialogue, the Rabbit comforts a dying Bob Smith:

> *MEDIUM: <u>The Rabbit holding Bob Smith</u>.*
> CLOSE-UP: Smith looks up at the Rabbit.

> *BOB*
> *"It's finished. You must continue my work. Do you understand...?"*
> *MEDOUM: <u>Chloe Dawson and Frank</u> weeping.*

> *RABBIT*
> *"Bob, you're gonna pull through. Don't worry. I'll see to that. (In a shout) Hey, somebody, call nine one one. Get an ambulance."*

CLOSE-UP: *The Rabbit looking down at Bob Smith as he lay dying.*

RABBIT
"Bob, there's something I gotta know. I gotta ask you."

BOB
"What is it...?"

RABBIT
"You're not Jesus, are you?"

BOB
"Of course not. Haven't you heard a thing...I've told you? No, not me, not here, not now."

RABBIT
"What about the virus? What should I do, Bob. Tell me what I have to do."

BOB
(He shakes his head)
"I see it clearly now. The future is no longer blocked. XyberGen will stop the research. Don't worry. There's nothing to worry about...."
LONG SHOT: *Bob Smith dies.*

LONG SHOT to SLOW ZOOM: *The Delivery Boy running. The man who killed Bob Smith is running toward a suitcase that has been discarded at the scene of the accident.*

*CLSOE UP: <u>The Rabbit's eyes</u>. He sees
the Delivery Boy running toward the
suitcase.*

*MEDIUM: The Rabbit runs to intercept
the Delivery Boy from stealing the suitcase.
Delivers his message amid generalized
indifference and defiance.*

RABBIT
*"Someone stop that man! Stop him. He
killed the soothsayer. Someone, please."*

*PAN: <u>The corner of the street</u>. The
Rabbit approaches the suitcase just as the
Delivery Boy has his hand on the grip of the
handle.*

*HAND-HELD CAM: The Rabbits' POV
as he struggles with the Delivery Boy for
possession of the suitcase.*

CLOSE UP: <u>The Delivery Boy</u>.
DELIVERY BOY
*"Let go. You have no idea what your
dealing with here."*

*MEDIUM: The Rabbit and the Delivery
Boy struggle with the suitcase between them.*
*CLOSE-UP: <u>Latch of suitcase</u>. The
latch breaks on the suitcase. The suitcase
opens like Pandora's box.*
*CLOSE-UP (Different angle in Slow
Motion): The contents of the suitcase pour
out onto the street. They are glass
pharmaceutical vials containing the deadly
virus. The vials shatter when they hit the
asphalt.*

A knock came at the door. Smith always knocked before entering.

I hastily replaced the pages on Smith's bed and returned to mine. He entered the room balancing two Styrofoam containers on top of his suitcase. I must have looked painfully distracted because he asked, "You all right?" I assured him that I was fine as he shut the door. He'd brought dinner with him.

Bob Smith served the food on paper plates.

We ate in silence. From our room I could hear sirens in the distance like fighting cats. It was like living in London during the Blitz.

I lay on my bed watching television. There was something in my pants pocket that irritated my leg. By feeling around down there, I came up with a set of car keys. I replaced them in my pocket. I realized that they belonged to me. A rather large black man in the trailer park had returned them the previous day. They were the keys to a Cadillac El Dorado Coupe de Ville that the man had assured me was my property. How was it that I believed the car had belonged to my father?

I debated with myself whether or not to tell Smith about the car keys and the man in the trailer park. In the end, I kept the incident to myself.

Smith switched on the television. An hour-long news program focused on a disease reported in the CDC epidemiology publication called the Weekly Morbidity & Mortality Report. Fifteen cases of a "mysterious illness" were being treated in New York City hospitals, more than any other city in the United States. Public health experts said that the symptoms of the illness resembled cholera. The office of the Surgeon General released a statement calling for calm in the wake of panic stirred by the reports. "No connection or common cause has been found to link these random and extraneous cases." In the interest of public safety, the Attorney's General office issued the statement that any television network news organization making false statements about the CDC report would be open to federal prosecution under the Helms Act.

The program was interrupted by a commercial for a Caribbean island resort where nothing but young beautiful people frolicked. The advertisement persuaded me to think about calling a travel agent. I began to see the world as free of disease, a place where no one aged, where no one was ugly, poor or crippled. Everyone in the commercial was gorgeous and interesting. The actors paused over a glass of Chardonnay at the end of a day of playful leisure. The world outside our motel room, of course, did not reflect the world depicted in the commercial. I wondered which I was to choose as my primary experience?

The television commercials were made so well that it was hard to distinguish between the program and the advertisements.

At that moment Bob Smith said, "The world will break your heart, Mr. Austin."

Before the show concluded, I fell asleep and forgot about the screenplay, ignored the advertisements that promised to improve my lot in life, and I disregarded the news reports of an impending plague. The pattern of recovery from brain injury is not unlike the child's game of Shoots & Ladders. As the mind heals, it makes realizations through Herculean effort like climbing steep ladders only to forget in a catastrophic tumble down a slide. Shoots & Ladders. Forgetfulness was the nature of my injury.

On the morning of the following day, we adhered to an unrelenting routine, Smith and I. Awake at daybreak, a breakfast of whatever food we had not finished the previous night, followed by relocating to another motel. Then Smith went off to do whatever he did during the day.

On that long day, I spent a good deal of time staring out the window, worrying about vague threats that echoed in the back of my mind, something about stealing Bob's suitcase, about delivering it to the Delivery Boy.

I could not overcome a mental paralysis. I felt attached to nothing. It was beyond existential, my life. I had descended below the horizon, past equatorial sanity of the regular world, past the values of commitment and trust, and into a dark malaise. In anticipation of The End, I embraced nothing, loved no other. I stared with eyes already dead. Even the urge to self-destruct succumbed to unmerciful entropy.

Ω   Ω   Ω

By the following morning, Bob Smith looked eighty years old. I sat on my bed trying to recall if Smith had always, during our limited acquaintance, looked so bedraggled.

"I have something we need to talk about, Mr. Austin," he said.

"Okay."

"There's a storm brewing out there."

Through the motel window I squinted upward and saw some evidence of rain. Magnificent desert storm clouds brewed over the horizon of purple mountains.

"You're right."

"No, I don't mean *this* sky, Mr. Austin. I'm speaking metaphorically."

I should have known.

"Your mother and father," Smith said. "You believe that they killed themselves because of you, over something you did."

I blinked at him, the Rabbit on downers.

Smith's eyes looked like the eyes of the Sphinx, dim and ancient. "Did you know that your father had terminal prostate cancer?"

I said nothing.

"He chose not to tell you. Then, when the pain was too much, he ended it," Smith said. "He wants you to know, his suicide had nothing at all to do with you. He loves you."

My life was a mess, abounding in blunder. Why should I remember a past steeped in pain? Why not let sleeping dogs lie?

"When your mother found him, well, she was just so devastated. Couldn't go on, really. Your pop was everything she had, you know," Smith said.

"Look, Bob...I appreciate what you're saying..."

He silenced me with a raised his hand.

A chill ran up my neck and the tiny hairs on my scalp stood on end.

"Stop blaming yourself. The guilt's killing you," he said.

In the motel room I came to realize that to know the correct future path is to reconcile the past.

As soon as this thought passed through my dim mind, Bob Smith said, "Knowledge of how things will turn out does not guarantee that you can change the outcome." Like the spring of a deep aquifer, his was the voice of a man at peace with the world. "Ours is a world of multiple choice. Which path should we choose today? Little do we know that what we choose determines the rest of the journey."

"It worries me a lot," I said.

Hanging out with Smith made me sensitive to my intuitive side. I have never been a superstitious man. Yet, I could not overcome a feeling that Smith's time was coming to an end.

"It should worry you, Mr. Austin," he said quietly. "You are a man of double and triple identities. Nothing for you is what it seems."

I winced.

"Had our paths not crossed..." He clicked his tongue. "And if you hadn't pulled the trigger that night, you would have died before your fiftieth birthday of alcohol poisoning."

He reached out and touched my wrist. I saw an image of myself dying alone in an intensive care unit, yellow jaundiced eyes blotched by burst blood vessels, thin as a skeleton, bald with tufts of hair growing in patches, an inauspicious end to a meaningless life.

For an hour or more, my emotions were abraded, raw.

Beethoven's Seventh played over a radio in an adjoining room, the perfect score to the scene.

"At least through me," Smith said at last, "you've found yourself."

With that, the old man kissed my cheek. And then to lighten the moment, he gripped my shoulders for an impromptu monologue on my appearance.

"You know what," he said with a shake of his head. "You ought to get rid of those ridiculous head bandages. You'd look better without them. You're a man, not a rabbit."

He offered to remove them and wash my scalp, but I declined. I was afraid, should he remove the bandages, my brains would fall out of my skull.

Chapter 19

On the night before the screenplay came to an end, I had a nightmare.

Bob Smith and I stood on a dark outcropping of rock. He was dressed as he always was dressed, in a tattered business suit. I, on the other hand, wore a bunny costume, head to toe. I looked like an animal character out of *Alice in Wonderland*.

In my dream, Bob Smith pierced time and pointed to the heavens. The stars shone in new constellations. Among them was the Big Dipper. And there, amidst the gallery of heaven, stood two columns of light framing the entrance to a Greek portal. Beyond it was nothingness. As Bob Smith and I approached the portal, two fierce warriors bore down upon me. Terror burned away my rabbit costume. The closer these monsters got, the more I became the essence of Duncan Charles Austin, Jr. The sensation was like standing in front of a Bessemer furnace. My skin incinerated, internal organs dissolved until nothing but bones remained, and then they too liquefied in the heat.

Exhausted, I gave in to the monsters. As I closed the distance, they transformed into kindly escorts to the portal. I knew intuitively that beyond it all questions would be answered. Through it the meaning of existence would be offered like wine in a cup. Should I pass through the portal I could never return. Beyond it lay the sacred mysteries, exquisite joy and the epiphanies forbidden to flesh and blood. I was not ready to go, not yet, and I woke up.

I was alone in the room at the motel. Smith had risen earlier, following his usual routine, while I'd slept. He was gone to preach the end of the world.

I drank a complimentary cup of coffee in the lobby and watched a rerun of *Oprah* that probed the tragedy of Living with an Irritable Colon. I giggled whenever Oprah's female guest mentioned "flatulence" or "anaerobic digestion."

Outside the motel, the weather had turned ugly. The day was windy and cold. The anvil of heaven itself seemed poised over Las Vegas. My memory largely consisted of scenes from motion pictures, and the weather that day in Las Vegas reminded me of the final scene in *Raiders of the Lost Ark* where the sky boiled with evil. It was a winter solstice of doom.

I walked briskly toward The Strip, having to weave in and around a steady spawn of tourists. I had become used to people pointing out the fact that I wore rabbit ear head bandages. The sidewalks were mobbed with Christmas revelers and gamblers. Among them were the other facets to Las Vegas, the panhandlers and homeless kids with dogs on ropes, drunkards asleep on cardboard boxes. A man dressed up like a Salvation Army Santa rang a bell over a donation bucket. Our eyes met. He seemed to think that we had met in the immediate past, and I rushed away to avoid his demand for charity. Outside the Caesar's Palace Hotel, I saw an elderly couple, arm in arm, wearing identical yellow satin outfits.

I stopped at the Latino bodega at the corner. Through the grimy window I watched television along with half a dozen teen-aged hustlers. It was a re-run of *American Idol* on a portable black and white. I munched a Valencia orange that I had stolen from one of the sidewalk bins when "Newsbreak" interrupted the program with a special announcement.

The talking head, a doll-faced boy, spoke in a suitably sorrowful tone.

"We interrupt this program for a special bulletin."

On the television there was a background shot of the chaotic scene at Los Angeles International, LAX. Inset was the photograph of a female reporter. She had a calculated, stern expression suitable to the gravity of what she was reporting. The voice-over somberly issued statistics of an air tragedy.

"...first, but this is what we have at this hour."

Behind the talking head, they ran stock footage of a Boeing 737.

"Universal Airlines Shuttle Flight Three-Oh-Five out of San Francisco has crashed several miles short of the runway at LAX this morning, at approximately eight fifty. We are being told that the ill-fated plane went down over the Pacific as it made its approach."

In the crowd outside the grocery, two Latinos spoke in low tones, shaking their heads. They tried to make sense of the news bulletin.

"This tragedy hits us very hard at Channel Seven Newsbreak because one of our own, Jerry Brooks, known to those of you who watch our program, Jerry was on that Universal Airlines flight. We have received word just moments ago that wreckage of the crash has been located, and that there are no survivors."

Here was a fraction of memory come to life for me. Something in my past related to the news story but I was having trouble rectifying it. Smith would know; this I knew.

I turned and ran. Every conceivable obstacle stood in my way. I felt like a salmon swimming against the current of tourists, truant kids, and unemployed men on a malt liquor high.

As I charged up the street looking for Smith, I remembered the scene from the screenplay with Jerry

Brooks. It played like a silent movie in the empty theater of my head.

I randomly grasped the shoulders of a tourist, a complete stranger. My expression was dreadfully wild.

"Stay away from heights, Mr. Brooks. That's what Smith said," I said. "Stay away from heights. It's in the screenplay. And now it's on the news!"

The tourist wriggled free and appealed for sympathy from the indifferent strangers on the street.

I ran.

The multicolored lights, swirling and flashing, that made up the resorts along Las Vegas Boulevard brightened an otherwise dreary day. Above, the clouds seemed to thicken and darken and bear down on the city. The noise from the crowded sidewalks and traffic in the street disregarded my thoughts of terror. Hustlers and gamblers, losers and high rollers, hurried past, abrasive in their language, shouting for me to get out of their way. Among them were foreign tourists with digital cameras, Asians and Europeans speaking as though fresh off the boat on their visit to the Tower of Babel. There were conventioneers and enlisted men from the Air Force base, all of them distracted by the colored lights and noise. I stopped to catch my breath, and a drunken elderly woman sauntered up and requested I light her cigarette. I waved away the odor of alcohol and pushed through the mob.

"You in some kind a show or something?" she asked.

I grimaced at her, panting.

"What's with the rabbit get-up?'

I rushed away from her and dashed down the boulevard. I heard distant thunder. The skies roiled with storm clouds.

As I made my way up The Strip, I had an overwhelming sense of déjà vu. What I experienced in real time I had experienced before. As I examined the feeling, I realized it was not déjà vu but my memory of Bob Smith's screenplay. The final scene was about to come true.

I had to find Smith. I had to warn him.

I fought my way through the multitude, and I realized that Smith had wasted the opportunity to rewrite the screenplay. I remembered arguing with him about it in the days before my head injury. I remembered our drive through the desert. I remembered his insistence that he was a man named Joe Dawson. The scene of Jerry Brooks came back in Technicolor. The screenplay had foretold his fated plane crash. *Stay away from heights, Mr. Brooks.* Had Smith rewritten that scene, the aircraft would not have crashed. This is what Smith and I had argued about before I was hospitalized. Smith himself had said that the future was not necessarily written in stone but open to an alternative course. But those consequences were now upon us. It was pride and our defective nature that brought about tragedy. I resolved then and there to compel Smith to rewrite the screenplay and give it a happy ending.

History could be changed, he once told me, by the least among us. Well, it was my determination to change history that day.

At the corner of The Strip and Hoover, I came upon Bob Smith preaching to an assembly of hangers-on. He stood on an upturned plastic dairy crate, his ever-present beige suitcase at his side. The subject of the day was XyberGen and biological warfare. Among those who listened were two belligerent, well-dressed young men. They laughed derisively. A heckler told Smith to "stuff it up your ass."

I called out to Smith.

He saw but did not acknowledge me.

I pushed through the clutch of the crowd and yelled, "We have to talk."

He ignored me and continued to warn of the dangers to biowarfare research.

"Bob!" I shouted. "I know what happens. Bob! I remember the last scene."

Still, he refused to step down from the crate. With a wave of his hand he denied my presence and proceeded to preach to the assembly. Among the crowd I recognized the homeless man named Elmore Jones. He stood with another man who may have had Tourette's syndrome. His cursing echoed in the granite valley between the casinos.

I felt a drop of rain hit my bare hand.

"Nothing comes for free," Bob Smith said. "There are consequences to every action. Biological weapons research has taken us to the brink. There is no such thing as a free lunch."

The heckler shouted, "How about a free brunch?" The heckler got a laugh.

Smith smiled but was not dissuaded.

Someone within the crowd upset the suitcase, and Smith leaned down to right it.

"Ever since the advent of mass production," he said, "we Americans have had a love affair with the automobile. We're a culture of convenience, speed, and efficiency. Look at all these cars!"

The boulevard was congested that day.

"Listen, freedom comes with a price. We extract tons of raw materials from the environment to make a car. And what about the waste it produces during its lifetime? No free ride.

"With respect to that free *brunch*," Smith said graciously.

The heckler giggled.

"Feeding the hungry in cultures that do not practice birth control, or where religious dogma extols couples to be fruitful and multiply, this is where modern medicine and religion compound our overpopulation problem."

"Thought you had a beef with biotech," a bag lady hollered.

"In the Philippines, for example, once self-sustaining rural villages have fished out reefs and rivers, they've exhausted topsoil to keep up with the explosion of children born because the Pope espouses no method for birth control. In addition, medical science has conquered diseases that in the past stabilized village populations through high mortality rates."

"Why not do away with 'em," the heckler said, "with those weapons you're talking about?"

Off to the side, standing among the homeless and drunken teenagers and curious tourists, were three men who did not appear to belong. They wore baggy business suits of another era, conspicuous for a lack of fashion, in a word, eccentric. They looked as though they'd stepped forward in time by a decade. Each had on the same kind of aviator sunglasses, and each had his hands in his coat pockets. I looked down at their scuffed wing-tip shoes.

I knew these men, knew their shoes. Their heels and my skull had, in the immediate past, made a violent acquaintance.

I turned to Bob Smith. "Bob, we need to talk."

A thunderclap muted my voice, and he ignored me.

A homeless Tourette's sufferer cursed a garbage can nearby, and one of the three, oddly attired men took a step forward, hesitated, and then stepped back among the throng of on-lookers.

"Over-population used to be the single most critical issue we face. But no longer." Smith took a breath. "Biological weapons research has done away with that, believe me."

A woman in the crowd called out. "How can you trash the Pope? Shame on you!"

Bob Smith shut his eyes and shook his head.

"Fundamentalism's the danger. Consider the San Francisco cult that worshipped a pile of traffic barriers. In Golden Gate Park up there, authorities removed several concrete abutments and piled the rubble behind a museum. When it was decided to crush the concrete to make material for park walkways, the cult protested. They said it was an infringement of their religious freedom. You see, they worshipped the phallic symbols as lingams. The authorities were forced to allow the practice to continue. They cordoned off an area around the debris to oblige the cult's religious practice. If people can worship concrete traffic barriers, anything is possible in this country."

The woman shouted, "You're an anarchist, you know that?!"

"Yeah, like the Unabomber's brother," the heckler said.

"This is not to say we should role back time to the days when cholera killed entire families in an afternoon. We should temper our dogma by understanding the consequences of our actions. The Pope is in denial. The biggest mistake we make is adhering to outmoded and dangerous religious dogma on birth control in an already over-populated world."

The old drunkard Elmore Jones tipped his baseball cap to Bob Smith and sucked at a bottle in a brown paper bag.

A driver honked his horn, and I turned around.

At the intersection I saw a man whose face electrified a memory within the damaged part of my brain. We stared at one another momentarily. He was an African American, broad-shouldered. He wore a Hawaiian shirt and yellow shorts, running shoes. The muscle definition of his black legs shone in the light of the casino marquee.

A moment later my mind coughed up a name: Whitaker Fetch.

I had no idea how I came up with the name Whitaker Fetch, but I associated it with something threatening, something evil, without knowing the nature of the threat.

And just as inexplicably, I associated him with my Cadillac. An odd and curious mental connection. Shoots & Ladders.

As we stood staring at one another the man waved to someone behind me. I turned to see who he was waving at, and when I looked back, the man had vanished in the steady stream of tourists.

When I returned my attention to Bob Smith, I noticed that the three men in shapeless business suits were being hustled away against their will. Other men in business suits—more finely tailored—were manhandling them. Their removal left a gap among the people listening to Bob Smith, a gap swiftly filled by others who were curious to see what all the hoopla was about.

Across the congested street, among other pedestrians, Chloe and Frank Dawson waited at the curb for the signal to change. I watched them. They appeared uncomfortable, out of their element. Waiting for the traffic light to change, they stared at the chaos of hookers, tourists, and hustlers. The guileless had come to Sin City. Added to the mix was the kitsch of Christmas decorations and loud speakers blaring "White Christmas" by Bing Crosby.

Watching Chloe and Frank, I became distracted by my growing apprehension. The final scenes of the screenplay came to mind. *This* was the Final Scene, the one in which the boy, Frank, was fatally injured. Or was this where Bob Smith was killed? I had read two versions of the final scene. Which path would it be?

I shouldered through the spectators around Bob Smith and made my way to the corner.

Two well-dressed ladies brushed past me, heavily laden by buckets of small change. They nearly knocked me down for which I expected an apology. The lady with dyed red hair did not excuse herself. The brunette curled her lips around a curse.

"Merry Christmas to you, too," I said, catching my balance.

Bob Smith's eyes were on me, observing my rude behavior. I knew what he would say before he said it. He would admonish how quickly I was to anger, that my temper had got the best of me. I felt ashamed. Inside, a bank of emotion became dislodged in a powerful avalanche, and I suffocated beneath memory. I sniffed the automobile exhaust that tasted of cocaine.

If my life were a motion picture, the scene would have been set by a series of overlays, dissolves, and flashbacks. I saw a much different Duncan Charles Austin, Jr; a slightly balding man with a ponytail who snorted cocaine. I saw a gleaming golden handgun and could almost feel the impression of cold steel on my lips. I heard lies and endless profanity. I saw a man divided against himself, a little boy whose prolonged adolescence had delayed his maturity.

These mental images tightened the back of my throat, and a sudden rush of emotions overwhelmed me.

But this was not the time for self-pity. I had to focus.

The traffic light changed, and Chloe and Frank Dawson crossed the street. A flash of lightning illuminated the faces of people around me, followed by a crushing thunderclap.

In the screenplay, as I recalled, the wife and son of Joe Dawson have come to hear Bob Smith because they need some answers. Chloe Dawson came to speak to Bob Smith, to appeal to him. She wanted to know where her husband was. It was Chloe Dawson's last-ditch appeal to find Joe Dawson.

As I watched the action unfold, it felt as though I sat in a darkened multiplex. The flickering images danced on screen like children of light. The images were dazzling. I was hypnotized by their magic.

It was Frank who called out first.

"Mr. Smith?" he shouted.

Bob Smith saw the boy. His complexion drained of blood. He knew the hour had come, and he turned his back on Frank to shield himself from the reproving stare.

Next on the set, Chloe Dawson addressed Smith.

"Sir?" she shouted. "Will you at least talk to us?"

Her tears ran with the melodrama of mascara.

Frank turned to his mother and said something that I could not hear above the traffic. He shook his head in resignation. It was obvious that he had given up on this bad idea of coming downtown to speak with this lunatic who might have known his father. It was of no use.

Chloe pushed past those receiving Bob Smith's message, and she found herself face to face with the bearded old man.

At that moment, I saw a wave of recognition wash over her face. Her mouth fell open as she looked at him. Who was this man before her? Her expression seemed to ask. There was something about him, something in the eyes, despite the advanced age, that reminded her.... But, of course, it was not possible. He was much too old, and Joe Dawson was a much younger man. But still, something in the eyes...

She cried out, and Bob Smith turned to meet her stare. Their eyes were caught in memories of who they were and what they had meant to one another. It was as though the very axis of the world spun on their silent communion.

"Joe?" she said quietly.

Bob Smith had a look of absolute compassion.

"Is it you?" she asked in a whisper.

I saw tears in Bob Smith's eyes. Wherever they fell, I expected little flowers to spring up through the concrete. Along with his tears the rain began to fall, pattering at first followed by a steady stream.

Staring at Smith, I was thinking that he had so changed me, so transformed my existence that if I died at that moment, within that hour, all of my squandered promises would be forgiven. My life was fulfilled in that singular glance.

"Joe, please," Chloe said. "Talk to your son, please."

Then Bob Smith turned away from Chloe Dawson. The rejection broke like the sound of shattering glass. Souls were shattering, lives lost; eternal love seemed demolished in that instant.

Frank Dawson stood beside his mother, bearing her up on his muscular arms, their clothes dampened by the downpour.

"What're you saying, Mom?" he said above the applause of steady rain hitting the pavement. "That isn't Dad."

"Take a look, Frank," Chloe said. "That's your father's briefcase."

Frank faced Smith with a look of resentment and fury. All the emotional loss that boy had suffered for so long welled up in him. Whether or not this man who stood before him was his real father, it didn't matter. Not now. To that boy, only his mother mattered. She had become the solitary star around which his life orbited. His father, like mine, had become nothing more than a bad memory.

"You stole that from my dad," he cried out. "Son of a bitch."

Frank turned and sheltered his mother in his arms as they moved through the crowd, working their way past greater numbers of tourists who pushed and shoved one another, some unfurling umbrellas to protect their department store bags full of gaily wrapped Christmas presents. It was as though a cadre of consumers had risen from Hades to obstruct the Dawsons at this pivotal moment in history.

Chloe and Frank walked away in one another's arms.

Bob Smith watched the woman and boy. A world of hurt ate him up inside.

It was at that moment that my trance, the suspension of disbelief, was broken. I wiped the rain from my face with my hands to remove a lingering apathy. I knew what came next.

At times in my dreams I cannot run. It was as though my legs were no longer powered by sinew, but filled with sand. They were heavy useless things fixed to the spot. I stood paralyzed as I watched Chloe and Frank Dawson cross Las Vegas Boulevard against the traffic in a desert downpour.

Bob Smith stepped off the dairy crate. He glanced at me, and we exchanged a shared insight of the immediate future. We both realized that something was about to happen that was inevitable.

In the far distance, I heard a clock chime the hour.

Frank Dawson hurried headlong into traffic, and Bob Smith rushed to his aid, to save him from certain death.

There is nothing in life more important than friendship, nothing worth dying for more worthy than love. Self-sacrifice is a divine act. It dwells within the highest plane of all existence. The sound it makes in the carillon of heaven is like the purest silver bell.

I ran.

Within the camera lens of my sight, I saw Bob Smith moving toward his son. He rushed forward with all the strength his old legs could muster. For the first time, I saw fear in his eyes. It clouded the virtue of his confidence. He realized too late that he could not close the distance between Frank and his onrushing fate.

Chloe Dawson was the first among us to see it. A pale laundry truck ran a red light.

Chloe screamed Frank's name.

Frank turned just as the laundry truck bore down on him, just as the driver hit the brakes and the tires lost control on the slick asphalt.

My stride carried me over the curb in slow motion, the camera of reality ticking off the seconds. I threw my body outward and shoved Frank out of harms way. The path of inevitability was sidestepped for him. That which had been "written" had been changed. I knew in my heart that, through this sacrificial act, I had changed. All was forgiven as I awaited death. The images of my mother and father, and my children, flashed through my mind.

Through the dirty windshield of the laundry truck, I saw the horrified face of a young man. He had run the light to make up for lost time. There was no way he could stop the runaway truck.

At that moment I felt the impact of someone pushing me out of the way.

The side of the laundry truck only grazed my hip, but it slammed full bore into Bob Smith.

The world stopped. All became motionless. Sound drained away like the morning calm that settles on a high mountain lake. Cold and raw.

A pigeon pecked at the trash in a gutter full of rainwater.

I lay on the ground, insensate, within the bonds of stillness. A dull ache pounded in my right leg to remind me of life. I struggled to look up, to see what had happened.

The laundry truck came to a stop halfway through the intersection. The name of the company on the side panel read "Area 51 Laundry. Cleaning That is Out of This World." The letters were painted over a red isosceles triangle along with a poor rendition of an extraterrestrial holding a clothes hanger. When the young driver tried to bolt from the scene of the accident, bystanders knocked him to the ground and sat on him in a citizens' arrest.

Rain was falling, harder now, hitting the pavement like silver coins. Some of the people, who had stopped, the gawkers and rubberneckers, retreated from the scene, to get out of the rain.

Chloe Dawson knelt beside the crumpled body of Bob Smith. He lay dying, his soiled white shirt soaked to the skin. A few bystanders gathered round us and some offered umbrellas or their coats. Our shoulders were dampened by the rain, and then the skies opened up with lightning.

Frank Dawson stood with shoulders bent like sorrow itself, the rain running down his cheeks.

The anguish in Frank's face has stayed with me forever. When I am susceptible and tired, I see his expression. It is the epitome of sorrow.

Individuals among the bystanders began yelling at one another. The homeless Tourette's sufferer prayed to God and peppered his prayers with curses. I thought it appropriate.

I managed to crawl to where Smith lay across the asphalt now slick from the rain.

He was conscious, lying on his back. Blood streamed in wide ribbons out both ears into a widening puddle beneath him, rain and blood commingled. He was shaking violently, his lungs rasping from the liquid air.

I took up his hand in mine. Chloe cradled his head.

He said to her. "Please, forgive me."

"Joe...?" she whispered.

I shouted at someone, anyone, to get help. And once again lightning struck in the near distance and shattered the world in thunder.

Bob Smith said something in a rasped voice but I did not hear it.

I leaned down. My tears fell to his face. No little flowers grew there.

He smiled faintly, and with our hands clasped in a weakening grip, he gestured at his heart.

He said, "It's okay. Was meant to be."

"You're gonna be fine, Bob," I said.

"Listen...I knew from the beginning it was you. All this, because of you. Take care of Chloe. Take care of Frank."

The flesh of his hand grew cold.

I remembered the coldness of my father's hands, and I was thinking that we were surrogates to one another.

"Don't do this, Bob," I said. "Don't go."

His eyes were full of forgiveness.

"It's okay. This is the easy part."

I heard the sirens of emergency vehicles echoing between the fantasy casinos.

And then, finally, with his eyes wide open, he said nothing more.

His grip loosened and his eyes became fixed in the purest blue I have ever seen. I let him go. And then I stood over his broken body and wailed indignantly at the very ramparts of God, at the storm clouds that seemed to hold no hope, no future, no love.

Chapter 20

Welcome to Ground Zero.

The horror of seeing a friend die suddenly cannot be digested all at once by the human heart. Our hearts shield themselves and acknowledge the horror piecemeal, in digestible portions, as a matter of self-defense. Should the weight of mortality be felt whole, it would crush us. The heart knows best and so it merely hints at the beast of truth, allowing the mourner to process parts of the whole. As time passes the horror diminishes, and in our grief, we come to accept what has been lost.

In the moment of Bob Smith's death, the rain stopped and the world felt soundless. Traffic along South Las Vegas Boulevard came to a standstill, and the Christmas shoppers and tourist gamblers, hustlers and college kids stood like statues beneath umbrellas, leaning out of doorways. One man among them took a drag off a cigarette and lazily fanned the smoke to see the body in the street. Two Catholic nuns, an incongruent pair in that place, clutched one another and crossed themselves in their black and white habits.

The sun in the west made efforts to break through a congestion of clouds, and shafts of golden light struck the windows of the casino across the street, flooding the world with rainbows. One of them touched the brow of Bob Smith. Almost as quickly as they came into being, the rainbows faded when the angle of sunlight changed and a cloud obscured the sky, and this peaceful second among an eternity of hours of motion and clamor and disorder and fury, this pause for the memory of splendor, was drowned once more in car horns and feet shuffling the sidewalk and shouting and sirens as the world resumed its frantic pace.

Ω   Ω   Ω

I stood over the body, and as Chloe Dawson knelt and tried to make sense of what had just happened, the vulture among us picked at the remains of a life.

Whitaker Fetch, in yellow shorts and Hawaiian shirt, worked his way through the clotting mass of onlookers and rubberneckers at the accident. By his size and by his movement through the crowd, he betrayed himself. I knew intuitively where he was so urgently headed.

The beige suitcase lay where Bob Smith had left it, beside the upturned milk crate. In their hurry to see the body of the dead street prophet, tourists and Christmas shoppers jostled past the unattended suitcase, unaware what it may contain.

I knelt alongside Chloe, keeping my eye on Whitaker Fetch as he pushed through the mob.

"Please, stay with Bob."

She could not speak.

I limped through the throng of bystanders. In the instant he saw me Whitaker Fetch recoiled. He knew instinctively, I'm sure, what my objective was. We both guessed how long it would take the other to pick his way through the crowd to get to the suitcase.

My purpose in getting there first was to protect the memory of my friend, to secure his possessions from the adulteration of Fetch and those for whom he worked. I suspected the suitcase contained a biological agent, but at that moment, only minutes in the hour of my friend's death, the deadly nature of its contents was not my concern.

Whitaker Fetch had his own suspicions and purposes.

In the screenplay, the Rabbit character struggles with the Delivery Boy for possession of the suitcase, and in that struggle the latch breaks and the contents of the suitcase tumble out, shattering on the ground and releasing the deadly virus.

Of all the scenes in the screenplay that reflected events in my life, this I knew to be the finale. No matter how determined Whitaker Fetch was, I knew that I had to convince him to leave the suitcase untouched. He and I should not struggle for it for fear of breaking the latch. It was a matter of life and death.

As I shoved and pushed between the sea of onlookers in the opposite direction, and as Fetch met the same obstacles, the lights of a paramedic rig reflected in the glassy casinos and in the rain slicked street, its siren ululating.

Halfway to my objective I cut a break. The sea of tourists and Christmas shoppers parted as though I was Moses himself, and I ran for it.

I had my hand on the grip when an automatic weapon was shoved under my chin.

The gold-plated metal was warm from my opponent's body heat, and as Whitaker Fetch pressed it deeper into my flesh, memories of sitting in my darkened living room with a handgun in my mouth flooded my mind. It was my Sig Sauer.

"Let go, Cowboy," the resonating voice said.

I was outmatched.

There we were dancing around the pivot of history, the Delivery Boy and a six-foot tall rabbit. Our eyes met. We each expressed victory and defeat within that fraction of a second. I was smiling at the absurdity that we held the means for universal doom of the past, the present, and the future of human beings. Fetch had the determined look of a man who would do what was necessary, even kill, to successfully complete his mission.

I held tightly to the suitcase, but Fetch demonstrated superior strength and physical training by swinging me around like a rag doll as I clung to our mutual objective.

I fell and ripped open my cheap trousers and bloodied my knees.

Fetch brought his thick hand in a violent roundhouse slap that rang like a cathedral bell and knocked the bandages clean off my head.

I was on all fours, the world spinning beneath me. I stared at the rainwater gushing down the gutter and wondered why my brains hadn't tumbled out. The water carried loads of trash, McDonald's wrappers and torn lottery tickets, Styrofoam cups and beer cans. Among the rubbish were my rabbit ear bandages, floating away. I watched as they circled the storm drain on the corner and vanished forever.

I had lost my bandages, but my memory returned in a sudden insight, glowing like a motion picture inside my mind, the previous life and experiences of Duncan Charles Austin, Jr., all the depravity and repugnance projected in an instant recollection. I was back. Me, the despicable bastard, the profane and vainglorious prick, the coke-snorting pornographer, the liar and cheat. Hell, I have never been proud of who I am, but I was glad to have me back nonetheless. And I was back in an instant, in a flash of pain, in a Zen moment. Zen Master Whitaker Fetch himself delivered the slap across my face. It unraveled the kōan, "What is the sound of one hand slapping?" It felt gloriously good to be in command of my memory once again.

I shouted, "That hurt, you fucking asshole!"

Whitaker Fetch leaned down with the Sig tucked under my chin. He gripped the suitcase handle.

"Don't make me pull the trigger," he said harshly. "There's been enough death for one day."

My bruised body trembled uncontrollably within the overwhelming crush of the big man. It was as though I were a child again, terrified, knowing within minutes, perhaps seconds, my life would end when the bombs began to fall. I heard air raid sirens. The end of the world was nigh.

I had no choice. I gave up the suitcase.

Whitaker Fetch towered in victory, but his brown eyes softened a little to reveal the humanity between us. He would not have taken pleasure in killing me, and he seemed relieved that I had not forced him to do so.

It was at that moment, the latch on the suitcase broke.

I reached up to close it.

Whitaker Fetch looked on helplessly, holding the Sig in one hand and gripping the suitcase in the other.

The suitcase opened like Pandora's box.

Instead of glass vials full of a deadly biological substance, mere newspaper clippings, yellow from age, fluttered out like a hundred canaries set free on the wind.

Fetch and I watched as the clippings were taken up in a whirlwind that swirled over the heads of people in the crowd in a delightful funnel of streamers. I saw among the crowd a little boy clutching his mother's hand, joyful for this brief touch of magic in the air.

I managed to snag a piece of paper as it floated past, something taken from *The Los Angeles Times,* a story about a biotechnologist at XyberGen who had gone missing, but the wind snatched the article from my fingers. It floated and danced and became lost in the surge of people bearing down on me.

When I looked up again, Whitaker Fetch no longer stood beside me. He was gone. His job was done. The contents of the suitcase were benign, and he had slipped back among the anonymous faces of passersby and made himself invisible in plain sight. I was left with Bob Smith's empty suitcase and the tragedy unfolding in the street. I kneeled on the wet asphalt and watched the confetti of history float harmlessly away.

Ω   Ω   Ω

I decided to return to Los Angeles to pick up the pieces of my former life, such as it was. To avoid traffic congestion and the maddening glare from the sun, I would drive the El Dorado west down the Interstate in the middle of the night. I figured, the desert would concentrate my fatalism as I followed the Big Dipper in its course around Polaris. The constellations have an icy majestic quality, and I needed to get lost in their permanence. They had shone in that desert sky for all eternity, and they would be there long after we humans went the way of the dinosaur. I hoped the headlights of the El Dorado might reveal the future, one in which I would survive.

I would carry a single passenger, the cremated remains of Bob Smith.

After the paramedics worked on him for forty-five minutes, he was declared dead at the scene, and his remains were removed to the morgue. Chloe, Frank, and I followed the coroner's rig in the Dawson's blue Ford Taurus. We said nothing to one another. As Frank drove, Chloe wept quietly in the passenger seat. The county coroner questioned us individually about Bob's identity, but none of us knew the answer. None of us could confirm who he was. They ran a DNA test to match Bob's tissues with those on a toothbrush having belonged to Dr. Joe Dawson, but the results were inconclusive. Chloe and Frank were returned to the empire of grief all over again, and it fell to me to take care of Bob's remains. It was the least I could do.

On the day after Bob's cremation, I took the arduous road to Chloe Dawson's Las Vegas neighborhood to close the circle.

For over an hour I sat in the Caddy outside *Lou's* and engaged in an internal argument over what I should say to her. When I went inside and sat in the air-conditioned coolness, Bob the Bartender failed to recognize me, and I was grateful for that. I asked for change for a dollar.

In the phone booth I retracted the accordion door and thumbed the White Pages. I traced my finger down the "D's" until I found C. Dawson. I penciled the number on a cocktail napkin.

I fed the black phone several quarters before dialing.

After the third ring, I worried that the machine would pick up.

"Hello?"

It was a man's voice. Something I had not expected.

"Hello, may I speak with Mrs. Chloe Dawson, please?"

After a pause, the man said, "Who should I say is calling?"

I sighed.

I doubted that she would come to the phone if I identified myself.

"An old friend," I said.

"Hold on."

I strained to listen through the receiver. I heard muted voices, a woman's voice among others. I heard footsteps on a hardwood floor. Then the voices clarified, and I overheard the man who had answered the phone say, "Just said an old friend."

"Hello?"

"Hello, Mrs. Dawson."

"Who is this?"

"It's DC. DC Austin."

I held my breath and squeezed my eyes shut. I expected an immediate and final rejection from her.

"What is it?"

She might as well have said, I hate you.

"I called to say good-bye."

I waited. Nothing.

"I'm listening," she said.

"If you'd like, I can mail a copy of the Smith treatment, the screenplay about your husband. I think you should have it."

"Why?"

"Because it...well, there are some beautiful scenes in it. You and Frank, you should have it."

"Fine," Chloe Dawson said at last. "Drop it in the mail."

"Would it be all right, would it be all right if I dropped it off? I'm leaving town, and it wouldn't be any trouble."

"I don't know. I have guests."

She covered the receiver to speak to someone else, the man presumably.

"You can bring it by on one condition," she said.

A deep sense of relief shuddered through me.

"Leave it on the front porch. But I should warn you, my brother's here with me. He's a cop."

"I can assure you, Mrs. Dawson, I'll just drop it off and be on my way. Thank you very much."

I retraced my way back to her little ranch-style house and parked the El Dorado down the block. There were a lot of parked cars in the neighborhood; someone was throwing a party. The Dawson driveway was blocked by a Volkswagen bus and a police cruiser.

The name *The Dawson's* was painted in white letters on a mailbox at the curb. The dead lawn and misshapen shrubbery lent a working class air to the place. A neighbor two doors down, washing his car in the driveway, contemplated me. I was glad to have dressed appropriately in khaki slacks and a Hawaiian shirt. I waved, but the neighbor gave no reply.

The opening measures of that old Stones' tune "Let It Bleed" drifted out a second-story window. Some kid testing the limits of his stereo.

I went up the walkway to the front door. A glance into the garage had me wincing. I knocked twice and waited.

The door opened.

"Mrs. Dawson?"

A large prosaic man stood in the dark behind the screen door. He leaned forward. I saw the no-nonsense look to him.

"You the guy on the phone?" he asked.

I nodded.

"Leave it on the porch."

I put *Path of Least Resistance* on an empty flowerpot.

"May I speak with Chloe?"

The man shook his head and folded his arms.

I tried to look around him, inside the house.

"Mrs. Dawson?" I called out. "Chloe?"

The man pushed open the screen door. His expression changed from vigilance to aggression. He was clearly on the offensive.

"Get off the porch."

"Bill?" came a woman's voice. "Bill. That won't be necessary."

Chloe Dawson stood behind her brother. Through the dusty screen door, I could see that she was wearing a black dress. It had not occurred to me that her brother, and what remained of the Dawson clan, were there to support Chloe emotionally.

I picked up the screenplay and held it out like a peace offering.

"It's okay, Bill." Chloe touched her brother's sleeve. "Let me talk to him."

The man glared before turning aside.

"How's your head injury?" she said, stepping onto the porch.

I ran a hand over my buzz cut and attempted to smile. I was still self-conscious without my ponytail. I tried to say that forgetting one's identity, or global amnesia, was the ultimate consolation because I was oblivious of all that had been lost. It was only after a partial recovery that I recognized the memory of the man I had been.

I wanted to express my regret for having done the things to her and Frank. I wished to explain to her that the man I had become considered the jerk I used to be as wholly repugnant, but before I could complete my apologies, she interrupted me.

"A full recovery then?"

By a full recovery Chloe had sarcastically meant that I was back to my old deceptive ways, and frankly, I was too tired to defend myself. I had spent weeks battling Bob Smith until complete exhaustion forced me to accept his Apocalyptic vision as Gospel. Over the past few months, I had rejected the screenplay's message. I had believed Smith nothing more than a conjurer who performed a cheap parlor trick until, in the end, most of the screenplay came true. Still, even now, I could not decide if the old dude was either Jesus Christ Himself or Joe Dawson. I was too worn out to argue her point.

Chloe accepted the screenplay when I handed it to her.

"You must be the most insensitive man in America." She glanced down rather than look me in the eye. "Do you know what the title of this means?"

I had no idea what the title meant.

"My husband used the term." She looked up at me. "He used it all the time. It refers to pathogens and pathways in kind of a double entendre."

"I'm afraid..." I shook my head.

"Pathogens, viruses and bacteria, they enter the body through the least resistant route. Joe said that human behavior was kind of, I don't know, analogous to the lower life forms, I guess. We all behave the same way. Selfishly. In our own self-interest, looking for the easy way out."

I remembered.

"Bob said the same thing. When we crossed the desert, and came here to Las Vegas. Same exact words," I told her. "Do you think...Mrs. Dawson, do you think it's possible that Bob was, you know...?"

"My husband?"

I was asking her to confirm a false faith, to affirm the impossible.

"Joe disappeared at thirty-six, a little over a year ago. Mr. Smith was a much older man. The coroner said he had the body of a ninety-year-old." She shook her head and reached into a pocket for a handkerchief. She carefully wiped under her mascara. "I don't know."

"Well, I should go."

I squared my shoulders, not expecting anything more from her but hoping she would find it in her heart to reach out and shake my hand.

"Thank you, for bringing this by," she said in a final dismissal.

I turned and took two steps off the porch.

"And thank you...thank you, Mr. Austin, for saving my son's life."

It stopped me dead. I raised my face skyward to halt the surge of emotion that coursed through me. Floodgates. I turned slowly around.

"Frank's okay then?" I asked, but she made no reply.

No other words needed to be spoken. We stood a few feet apart. I thought about the meaning of coincidence in our lives. I thought about Bob Smith and the mystery of the man. From the look in her eyes, I could tell that Chloe thought about these same things. Our thoughts danced a mental *pas de deux*. I imagined in my mind's eye, Chloe and Joe Dawson holding hands, years ago when they were a young couple, how they must have appeared during a happier time, watching their son play on the beach near their La Jolla home; the scientist engaged in important government work to discover a Phage to protect the country from biological weapons of mass destruction; the devoted wife who nursed the sick, and the promising son; a world full of upward mobility, human potential, and the assurance of peace. This was what they had come to expect from the American way of life. Sometimes expectations are not realized. Sometimes the ending is an unhappy one.

How we remember the past, Bob Smith once told me, *determines the future*. And in this manner, perhaps, by choosing to remember differently, we rearrange our expectations. Instead of being careful of what we wish for, we should be cautious about what we expect.

Rather than hang around weeping all over myself, I made the decision to leave. I turned to walk away.

"Mr. Austin?"

Delayed once more in my exit, I looked into the clear suburban blue rather than face her and make a spectacle of my tears. The sky itself seemed to go on forever like the eyes of Bob Smith.

"Take care of yourself," she said at last.

On the drive back to Los Angeles through the desert night, I remembered her words and kindnesses. The memory of her voice sustained me for all those lonely miles. And in that space of time along that dark highway, I conjured up a prayer of sorts in hopes that God was listening. I asked that human beings be protected from themselves, from their devious minds. I prayed that the evil in the world, which may be our own creation, be taken from us like deadly toys in the hands of careless children. I thought of Bob Smith's suitcase and the newspaper clippings it held. I wondered—was the Phage real or was it something from Bob Smith's imagination? Was the Phage stored on a shelf in a bioengineering lab, neglected for the time, waiting for someone to come along and mistakenly drop a vial on the floor?

The cardboard box full of Bob Smith's ashes was strapped to the passenger seat while I reversed our steps of two months earlier. I filled up the Caddy at the mini-mart where we had once stopped. The red, white, and blue sign brightened the Astro turf like an oasis seen from miles away, wavering in the mirage of desert night heat. For sentimental reasons, I bought a Snicker's bar at the mini-mart. Halfway to Oro Grande, I passed a lounge that had a neon sign of a twelve-foot martini glass. It reminded me of *Lou's*. I pulled into the parking lot of the seedy-looking lounge and entered to test my resolve. The shelves of liquor did nothing for me. Neither did the skanky bartender in the push-up bra. The cocktail lounge and she were part and parcel to a life that I was leaving behind. I asked for a glass of water. I downed it in a single swig, thanked the bartender, and dropped fifty cents in her tip jar before I left.

The sun had yet to make its curtain call by the time I reached the city limits. For all the weeks of my absence, I had the feeling Southern California no longer existed, that it was nothing more than a fantasy. But when I reached the top of the grade, I could see for miles. Through the chiaroscuro of unrealized morning, L.A. lay before me like a galaxy of starlight. The Santa Ana's had swept the smog from the basin where civilization came up against the last of the Western frontier. It is a city built in the desert on dreams. A haven for dreamers, a refuge of lost hope. Alas, Babylon!

I was home.

Ω   Ω   Ω

At the house on Echo Terrace, I occupied my time by cleaning up after Whitaker Fetch. I emptied the liquor cabinet and struck out Xavier Murphy's name in my address book. Among the overturned furniture and bookcases, I found a book on meditation and sat reading with my feet dangling into the empty, dank swimming pool. Mimicking the pictures of people in the book, I crossed my legs and fell into a meditative silence. When I opened my eyes, I made a promise to fix that pool. It became a project of sorts, and I spent the last of my inheritance to repair it. One late afternoon in early January, after a full restoration, its turquoise water a sparkling gemstone, lounging beside the pool was where my neighbor caught me. I was reading the book on meditation. I introduced myself, and my neighbor remarked after the book with a pun.

"Meditation instead of medication, eh?"

I deserved his jibe. It had the effect of tempering my willpower to stay sober; if for nothing else than to show the world that I could succeed at something.

Sobriety clarifies the average mind. My mind not being average, sobriety muddled me. A few weeks after my return from Vegas, a CNN newscaster stated that the previously reported "mysterious illness" had been identified as "flesh-eating bacteria." It was a deadly disease but not the Black Death. I realized that I had not been living through a post-modern version of 1348. The screenplay did not come true, after all. CNN had me doubting Bob Smith all over again. I questioned the wisdom of abstinence and the accuracy of my insight. I even thought about calling up Xavier for a bindle of coke. Luckily, I'd tossed out his number, which maintained my sobriety for another twenty-four hours.

On the following day, to combat my cravings, I wandered the streets of downtown like Diogenes in running shoes. I searched for signs of the apocalypse but saw nothing more than the usual selfish disregard that human beings occasionally have for one another. The world would not come to an end, I realized, at least not anytime soon.

I went back to seeing my psychotherapist on a more or less regular basis, but I did not talk about my adventures with Bob Smith. The doctor said that I suffered from Post-Traumatic Stress Disorder over my parents' suicide, whatever that means. In this world every facet of human behavior has been identified and named so that it can be assigned a medical insurance number. My therapist makes big bucks treating the disorder. Los Angeles has tens of thousands of PTSD patients who have made my psychotherapist a very rich man.

After a difficult six months of recovery and therapy, and after daily power walks throughout downtown Los Angeles, a chronic blister on my right heel goaded me one afternoon into a Multiplex. There I laid down twelve bucks to get off my feet. They were showing *Virus Wars,* a Rainy Day production that bore scant resemblance to Smith's concept. In my life I have craved all forms of distraction, but I had qualms about seeing this particular movie for obvious reasons.

Theater 19 was packed, and I settled into a middle row to watch the show. When I removed my shoes, the woman in the seat next to me objected—"What do you think you're doing?" I resisted the temptation to tell her to piss up a rope but remembered what Bob Smith had said about profanity. During the previews, I munched popcorn and slurped the ersatz Coke in passive aggression.

The movie opened to strains of Mozart's *Requiem.* I cringed when I saw Maxwell Gleason's name in the credits under Executive Producer, and a kernel of popcorn caught in my throat when I read, "Based on an idea by Bob Smith." Pig Boy had cut me out of the credits altogether.

The action was not half bad in a "suspension of disbelief" kind of way. Rainy Day Films had made a reasonable facsimile of *Path of Least Resistance* as Smith envisioned it. It followed the story of a biotech company that discovers a Phage with applications in biological warfare. As the tension mounts, Rolly Campaña in the Joe Dawson role declares that the Phage will bring about an end to all life on earth. The world ignores his protestations, and eventually he is rejected by everyone, including his wife and family. Joe Dawson suffers Dissociative Identity Disorder and becomes Bob Smith, a street prophet who gathers a following through an uncanny ability to foretell the future. The plot line diverged from Smith's original when Grace Taylor, in the Chloe Dawson role, had a compulsory nude shower scene. In an arc shift, the lethal Phage is stolen by international terrorists but not before Rolly Campaña comes to his senses and opposes them. After gratuitous violence with automatic weapons and loads of irrelevant nudity, the good guys win. In the end, the President of the United States, as played by Harrison Ford, bows to negative public opinion. He calls for a unilateral ban on biological weapons research in hopes the world will follow America's lead.

I stayed in my seat to watch the credits, the habit of a professional. The joint production company logo was the Big Dipper, and I sat in the theater thinking about this coincidence long after everybody else had gone home.

The movie-going public loved the film. It became a blockbuster, and it had the effect of unifying the political will of the United States against biowarfare research for defensive or offensive purposes. *Virus Wars* proved not just another addition to the continuous stream of entertainment-as-distraction to be consumed and soon forgotten. Despite Sty Raine's bastardization of Bob Smith's brilliant vision, the film created a groundswell of anti-war protests in America, Asia, and Europe against weapons of mass destruction. University students and biotechnologists joined forces and eventually helped lead the burgeoning world peace movement, and behind these stood the people *en masse*. The Average Joe—not political leaders or the rich and famous—was the potential victim of thermonuclear and biological weapons. The vulnerable populations of cities were the targets of terrorists and ICBMs, not the military men, the four-star generals in their bunkers behind the lines, or politicians in their "undisclosed locations."

Virus Wars became the wake-up call of the masses, and the average movie fan became an unexpected proponent of world peace.

Rainy Day Films grossed ninety-two million on opening weekend, but by the time *Virus Wars* hit the video chains, Sty Raines found himself in some legal hot water. He was called before a Senate Subcommittee on Financial Corruption and Racketeering within the Entertainment Industry. Sty Raines eventually went to court to defend the accusation of fraud. He was exonerated but disgraced. It made the front page of *Variety*. In the same edition a small paragraph indicated that Max Gleason had retired from show business. In spite of his boss's legal woes, you could not stick anything to Pig Boy.

After the film's release, when an anti-war protest ensued at their corporate headquarters in La Jolla, XyberGen administrative officers tried to distance themselves from the negative publicity of *Virus Wars*. Protesters outside the corporate headquarters carried signs demanding an end to biological weapons research.

Biotechnologists at XyberGen published a "white paper" stating their intent to cease and desist in all Defense Department contracts. Despite their protests, this being reality and not a movie, XyberGen fired the scientists and continued to honor the Defense Department contract by furthering research in biowarfare defense. But by then, political pressure was brought to bear through international treaties that put an end to their risky enterprise.

In my worst nightmares I heard the equivalent of London air raid sirens during the Blitz. Instead of bombs falling from the bellies of Nazi bombers, I feared that microscopic organisms would wheedle their way into my corrupt flesh, following the path of least resistance. But the Beast, the Phage, had, at least for the time being, been shelved.

Ω   Ω   Ω

"Hello, Mr. Austin?"

It was a woman's voice, and I took a moment to recognize her.

"It's Chloe. Chloe Dawson."

I answered the phone in the dining room. Surrounding me were the archives of my father's creative work, his films, screenplays, and memorabilia. I had decided to dedicate the remainder of my life to restoring his motion pictures, and politicking for an honorary Oscar to be awarded posthumously.

Chloe and I talked openly for half an hour. From her tone of voice, I could tell she had forgiven me. Perhaps my penchant for less profane language convinced her that I had cleaned up my act.

"The reason I called, I wanted to let you know, they never found my husband. Joe is still missing."

She admitted that she and Frank, on that fateful night on the Strip, had come to prove to themselves once and for all that Bob Smith was not her husband and his father. When I asked what she believed, she said, "Frank disagrees, but the age difference was too great. Your Bob Smith couldn't have been Joe."

I wanted to mention the triangular birthmark on Bob Smith's "love handles" as confirmation of his identity, but temperance had turned me into a philosopher. Rather, I said, "I take it one day at a time, Mrs. Dawson."

We were given over to our own thoughts when she asked if I was working on anything, and I explained the details of my latest project.

"You know, he...Bob Smith made me feel so ashamed of some of the garbage I made. Well, I figured, why not restore my father's movies. It's something that should have been done when he was still alive." I grimaced to myself. "I'm not surprised really how many people have come forward with help and support. He was a good man, my father."

I asked after her son Frank, and Chloe said, "Fine. He entered college this fall. Mr. Austin, I don't know how I can thank you enough."

"Please, call me Bunny." I smiled to myself. "It's what my mother called me."

We made empty promises about getting together should I find myself in Las Vegas, plans that I thought impossible. And then we said good-bye.

Around Christmas time, Chloe called again to close the circle. She invited me to their house for a holiday supper. I accepted and asked if there was anything I could bring. "Nothing," she said. "I just hope you can make it, Bunny." For over a year, the cremated remains of Bob Smith had stood in a place of honor on the mantel of my defunct fireplace. I decided it was time to spread Bob's ashes somewhere between L.A. and Las Vegas.

In late December, the Mojave Desert seemed the likely place. However, I knew very little about Bob Smith's preferences, about his past, where he was born. It just seemed to me that he would have preferred his ashes spread somewhere between these two metropolises of the Great Western Desert. I figured, Bob Smith would have requested that his remains be scattered in a place where civilization had yet to stamp its feet. The remote austerity of the desert proved the perfect location.

There is a small state park where the Mojave River—an underground river by and large—surfaces in the sandy wastes. This was where, near a railroad trestle, I decided to spread Bob Smith's ashes. This was where the slow underground current would carry him to a vast dark aquifer amid caverns hundreds of feet below me. Dust to dust, ashes to ashes, this is what had become of the greatest screenwriter of all time. How he had managed to write a screenplay that came true will remain a mystery. I will never fully understand it. He was a man worthy of biography not unlike my father, but I am no Boswell to his Dr. Johnson. I thought of all these things as I opened the box containing his ashes.

When I spread the remains near the train trestle, some of the ash caught in the wind down an arroyo, and I inhaled it. My hands and clothing became powdered, and rather than brush it off, I honored his dust by keeping it with me. In the end, I put a match to the cardboard box that had housed him for a year and burned it in a barbeque pit. While I stood there watching the flames, a jackrabbit hopped up along the arroyo and paused to satisfy his curiosity about who and what I was. I had to laugh to myself at the implacability of the rabbit's meaning and at the irony of his coincidental appearance.

Bob Smith once said that there are no accidents, that everything has meaning. Each of our gestures, as well as the mode of our daily behavior, has enormous consequences to the outcome of world history. This was Bob's way of expressing how our daily lives were trapped by the whims of chaos theory. Bob Smith told me that the important men of the world, the presidents and senators, prime ministers and potentates, conduct their affairs under the delusion that it is *they* who shape the future, that it is they who make history. To the contrary, they are simply mired in the delusion of power over others. Bob said, "These so-called 'power brokers' are cosmically insignificant." *The meek, the least among us, the legions of poor and the sick, it is they who shape the future*, he said. All of us, nevertheless, deny this truth because we fear absolutes. We are afraid to admit that everything we do, every word we speak, each and every breath we draw has meaning and holds significance. We are afraid because it suggests that there is a God and that we have a purpose. Every unkind act, no matter how "insignificant" at the time of its commission, reverberates across history. *Everything has meaning*, Bob Smith said. We are, he told me, not evolutionary mistakes that got lucky, but possibilities made flesh. Even the seeming randomness of chance and the chaotic commingling of DNA have a meaning that is defined by the eventual outcome of history through a Darwinian dance. "How else," he said, "are we to explain the universe? How else can you explain Jupiter and a crème brûlée?"

The sun was setting, and it reminded me of a John Ford Western with scattered clouds backlit by the meridian redness of the west. The only thing missing was the hero riding off in the distance, victorious.

It took a year of clear-headed thinking to understand why Bob Smith had come to me, Duncan Charles Austin, Jr., for help in his crusade. I believe that he realized, after envisioning the end on the streets of Las Vegas, his old legs would fail him. Our partnership may have had nothing to do with making a movie or finishing the screenplay. Perhaps Smith had sought out a younger man to run like a rabbit and push Frank Dawson out of harm's way to save his life. For this, Bob Smith had put his trust in me. But how was this possible? "How is anything possible?" I asked myself. I shook my head at the sheer absurdity of the idea and returned to the Caddy.

From the Mojave, as I drove to Las Vegas, I longed for my traveling companion. I missed Bob Smith. There were so many questions I wanted to ask.

That evening, on Christmas Eve, I ate dinner at Chloe Dawson's house. As a hostess gift, I'd brought a DVD collection of my father's movies, pre-accident, his finest work. Chloe thanked me so generously you'd think I'd brought frankincense and myrrh. "I've nothing for you, though," she said, apologetically. The dinner invitation was more than enough, I told her. Her brother Bill and his wife were there. Bill eyed me suspiciously throughout the night as he drank too much brandy-flavored eggnog. I abstained out of respect for my past. Frank was home from college, and he and I sat next to one another at the supper table. We talked sports. I learned about the family. Frank talked about the classes he was taking, his professors. Chloe talked about how she was weaning herself off an obsession with baking bread. "I've taken up yoga and square dancing," she said, laughing at herself, at the incongruity of things. After dinner, while the ladies cleared the table and the cop washed dishes, I had a chance to look more carefully at the framed photographs of Joe Dawson in the living room. He may have resembled Bob Smith, but I was in no position to judge. When Frank caught me examining a family picture of the three of them taken years ago, he said, "That's sort of your livelihood, isn't it, Mr. Austin."

What he said puzzled me, and from my expression Frank correctly surmised it.

"Pictures. Facsimiles of life. Images on screen," he explained.

I had never given Frank Dawson credit for having brains, the brains of his father, but he was a lot smarter than his age would suggest.

I agreed. "You know, Frank, this picture reminds me so much of one I have at home." I looked more closely at the family photo. "I'm about six months old in it. I just realized that it's the only picture I have of the three of us, my father, mother and I, together. I treasure it."

As he collected his thoughts, Frank readjusted the picture among the memorabilia on an occasional table.

"Mr. Austin?"

"Call me Bunny. Everyone does."

Frank smiled and shook his head.

"Okay, DC then."

"My dad had a top secret job, you know? He was into some serious stuff. Working on things that made a difference."

I waited for him to complete his thoughts but he said no more.

"You're right, Frank. Your dad was a good man."

The boy wiped his face with his hands and looked me square in the eye.

"You know, my mom doesn't like talking about it, but I think, well, I think your friend was my dad. Is that possible?"

"Frank, I don't know. Nobody does."

"Before he disappeared, Dad told her that he was exposed to something in his lab. He said he thought it was aging him, or something, really fast." He picked up the family portrait again. "I think it was him because of his eyes."

Looking at the boy, as though for the first time—really looking at him—I realized that it was true. Frank Dawson had the same blue eyes of Bob Smith. And standing there in that living room, facing him, I could not help but wonder at the similarities. *Everything has meaning.*

Before I could say what was on my mind, we were called back to the dining room for apple pie and coffee.

Later that night, we sat together in the dark in the living room around the television, to watch *It's a Wonderful Life.* At nine-thirty, I thanked everyone and said that I probably would not have to eat again for several days, patting my well-fed stomach. As I put on my jacket and fished for the keys to the El Dorado, Frank accompanied me to the porch and his mother joined us, pushing past the screen door. We three stood there together, admiring the fine evening, and I thanked them once again for their hospitality. Chloe gave me a warm embrace, and Frank shook my hand.

"Merry Christmas," she said. "Now, don't be a stranger."

And as I walked away, Frank called out, "I'm glad to have met you, DC."

I bid them both a Merry Christmas and made my way through the dark toward my car. The season had subsumed the neighborhood. The little houses were dressed up in strings of red and green lights. There were plastic crèches on a few lawns; others had blow-up figures of Rudolf the Red Nosed Reindeer and Santa Claus. When I slipped behind the wheel of my car, I paused for the moment, admiring these representations of family, tradition, and stability. As I drove to the motel on that, the longest of nights, the Big Dipper shone on its run around Polaris. It chased me all the way back to the motel like a figment of eternity and with the promise that life would get better.

Also by the author

The Identity of Max Sledge
Whose Curious Stars
The Inheritance of Memory (a short story collection)
The Devil Visits Confidence (three novellas)

Author photograph by Kemmeo Parr

About The Author

C. Marcus Parr lives in Oregon. His short fiction, poems, and cartoons have appeared in literary magazines and independent press in the United States and Canada. He has published three novels and collections of short stories and novellas.

www.ingramcontent.com/pod-product-compliance
Lightning Source LLC
Chambersburg PA
CBHW030929260626
47169CB00002B/413